SAVING DRAGONFLIES

ALSO BY VICKI STEVENS

Abby Eaton Mystery Series

Shaking Trees

Other Fiction

Flames to a Moth

SAVING DRAGONFLIES

AN ABBY EATON MYSTERY

VICKI STEVENS

BLOODWOOD
PRESS

Published in Australia by Bloodwood Press in 2021

ISBN 978-0-6483831-5-4 (paperback)

ISBN 978-0-6483831-4-7 (ebook)

Cover design by Predrag Marković: predra6art

NATIONAL LIBRARY OF AUSTRALIA

A catalogue record for this work is available from the National Library of Australia

For Dad

THE DRAGON-FLY

Today I saw the dragon-fly
Come from the wells where he did lie.
An inner impulse rent the veil
Of his old husk: from head to tail
Came out clear plates of sapphire mail.
He dried his wings: like gauze they grew;
Thro' crofts and pastures wet with dew
A living flash of light he flew.

~ *Alfred, Lord Tennyson*

PROLOGUE

Chances Crossing 1979

Fleeing through the rain-soaked forest that edged the farm property was a mistake. Faced with negotiating slippery mud, fallen branches, and with wild bracken jabbing him with sharp stick fingers, he wishes he'd risked being seen, running across the open paddock to reach the road.

His feet skid on wet leaf litter. He falls to his knees in sludge, upsetting the bundle inside his backpack and causing it to kick up a fuss. The squalling grates on him like nails on a chalkboard, and he staggers to his feet.

What to do?

Eyes darting, he spies a giant Bunya pine rising out of the scrub, its football-sized cones—big enough to kill a man—visible among the sharp pointed foliage. An idea pops into his head and he rushes over to discover the rusted vehicle beneath the tree is cloaked by a rampant cat's claw creeper. The aged passenger door screeches in annoyance as he wrenches it open and leans in.

A miasma of decay assaults his nostrils: mould, mildew, rotting leather ... and something else. *Death?* He shakes off a dark memory and slips the backpack from his shoulders, placing it on the weathered seat. Unfastening the clips, he peels away the flap of worn canvas and the crying stops. Teary eyes blink up at him from a tiny, red-blotched face. He brushes his hand against a cheek as soft as a rose petal and flinches when the miniature mouth finds the tip of his finger and sucks.

Emotions stir. A moment of clarity surfaces.

Don't be stupid. Take her back to the house.

A face springs to mind, teeth bared in a fit of rage. He slams a fist into the seat's brittle upholstery and the baby lets out another howl, compelling him to speak soothing words and make a promise.

Forcing the car door shut, and stifling the noise within, he runs back the way he came.

Time is of the essence.

1

Shadow Creek 2019

A desperate whirring. Over by the bookshop window.

The stack of novels teetered in my grasp like a high-rise in an earthquake as I side-stepped around cartons of new paperbacks. Offloading the pile to a chair, I crouched and found the dragonfly, its wings a shimmering blur as it butted against the window glass. Compelled to save the tiny prisoner from dying in its search to re-enter the sunny world outside, I encased it in a cage of fingers. A tickle of wings against my palms. Grateful butterfly kisses? No, to it, I was a hungry giant, eager to end its life to sustain my own. Yet, I wasn't a threatening predator, I was its saviour.

Moving through the doorway and onto the pavement, I raised my arms skyward and recalled a quote by Khalil Gibran, something about a butterfly reminding us that just living isn't enough, that we also need freedom, sunshine, and a little flower.

'Go find that flower, beautiful one,' I urged, opening my hands, and freeing the gossamer-winged creature into the morning air.

A black-and-white flash and the insect became a magpie's breakfast.

'Oh, crap!'

'Abby, is that you?' yelled a voice from above. 'Have a look at this.'

I went to the road's edge and peered up at the sign being erected on the store roof. Painted in watermelon pink on a background of gumnut green, was the word *Ringtales*. Two lifelike ringtail possums hanging by their tails from the letters R and S grasped golden rings in their paws. My heart danced. My very own bookstore. People had asked if it was a dream come true but, to be honest, it wasn't something I'd seriously imagined. I'd fallen into it by default.

Four months earlier, my position with a city bookstore had suddenly become redundant—or so I was led to believe. Before I'd even formulated an employment plan, my husband suggested I open a store of my own here in Shadow Creek. Indeed, the small rural town, half an hour's drive from the outskirts of Brisbane, could do with a more literary fix among the cafes, restaurants, and gift shops. I had the experience, the knowledge, and desperation for an income, so I agreed to give it a go. A shop became available for rent, and here we were, putting our own stamp on the century-old store.

'It's superb,' I called to my tool-wielding spouse. 'You're so talented.'

'Hey! He's not the clever one,' came another rooftop voice. 'I designed and painted the sign. Dad just screwed it on.'

When our son strained to hold the sign in position, I understood why he had a stream of female friends. This broad-shouldered youth, with muscles flexing below the rolled-up

4

sleeves of his T-shirt, seemed to have transformed from a lanky teenager overnight.

'Sorry, Elliott, you're amazing,' I gushed. 'I am in awe of your artistic ability.'

He gave a nod of appreciation. 'Want to come join us on the roof?'

I pulled a face. 'You know full well I wouldn't dare climb that high. I'll leave it to you two brave souls.'

'Chicken. It's only three metres.'

'Don't worry, mate,' Shane said, giving him a nudge. 'The drama in getting your mum up here isn't worth it, believe me.'

He was correct. Shane and I had recently returned from a holiday in Tasmania visiting long-lost relatives which, to my horror, included several tourist attractions that tested my fear factor. My husband learned never to book a shared adventure without first passing it by his acrophobic wife.

Back inside, I surveyed the disarray. With just over a week until the shop's grand opening, there was still a lot to do. To allay the fresh ball of panic forming inside my chest, I studied the empty shelves and considered how best to arrange the stockpile of books. Should I group them in genres, by titles or authors, or aesthetically in waves of colour? Such an important decision.

I whipped around as the shop door burst open and a redheaded woman rushed towards me in a fit of tears.

'Ab-by!' she sobbed, knocking into a tower of cardboard boxes.

This startled me, not because a box crashed to the floor and vomited out James Patterson books, but in our several years of friendship I'd never seen Donna so upset. She was the one who bolstered me during bouts of melancholia with her bubbly, life-is-filled-with-roses-and-chocolate exuberance.

'What's wrong?' I cried.

She gripped my arm, her fingers tugging at my sleeve. 'I'm leaving Shadow Creek.'

I jolted back. 'No, you're not!'

'Yes, I am.' She sniffed and let go of my shirt to wipe her eyes, smearing mascara across her cheeks. 'I'm out of here. My flight to Melbourne leaves at midday.'

'Melbourne? But why?'

'Well, as you know, I turn the dreaded forty in eight days, four hours and ...' she checked her watch, 'twelve minutes, and I've realised I'm rather disenchanted with my life.'

'Disenchanted?' I planted my backside on a box of children's picture books in front of her. 'I thought you were thrilled with everything right now. After leaving your footprints all over the world, aren't you settled here in cozy little Shadow Creek?'

'Yeah.'

'And aren't you living your dream running an antique store, surrounded by curios and making money from the past?'

'Very much so.'

'Then what's the problem? Don't tell me you and Ross are having marriage troubles.'

Donna collapsed onto a paint-spattered stool. 'We are. He's let me down big time.'

'Ever-dependable Ross? What has he done ... or hasn't done?'

'Well ... it's not actually him. It's his sperm.'

I blinked hard. 'Pardon?'

'They're too bloody lethargic. We've been together fifteen years with not a whiff of a pregnancy.'

'Hang on, you weren't even interested in starting a family until ... what ... five years ago?'

She waved my comment away. 'Whatever. I consider my life to be incomplete without a mini-me or mini-Ross running around.'

'There's still time. You just need to be patient.'

'Damn patience. My good eggs are shrivelling up as we speak. I want a baby and I want it now.' A pout added weight to her frustration.

'You've both had tests?'

'Yep, I'm good to go. It's just Ross who's dragging the chain.'

'What about IVF?'

'Expensive. Fine 'n Dandy hasn't long been out of the red, and you know what Ross-the-money-Nazi is like.'

'Adoption?'

'Too many hoops to jump through. Anyway, I reckon we've missed the boat on that one. Too old.'

As she removed her left shoe to massage a foot that often troubled her, I struggled to come up with other options. 'There's more to life than kids, Donna.'

An eye roll. 'Huh, says she who so effortlessly popped out two of her own.'

'Well, you can have them if you like. I could do you a good deal.'

'Yeah, right. What are they, sixteen and eighteen?'

'Eighteen and twenty.'

'God, they'll be having their own babies soon.'

If it wasn't for her shoulders sagging, I may have slapped her for inferring I was old enough to have grandkids.

'Not being a mother is my biggest disappointment,' she moaned.

'What about not knowing who your father is? That'd be up there.'

Donna shot me an icy glare. 'Thanks for bringing that up, Abby. I'm reminded of it every frigging birthday. Unless Mum has a miraculous change of heart and lets that secret out of the bag, I'll never know.'

I felt her annoyance. When Donna turned thirty-five her

mother, Faith—during an evening together downing gin cocktails —dropped a bombshell stating that the paternal name cited on Donna's birth certificate was incorrect. The aftershock was that Faith refused to divulge the identity of an alternate father. Though Donna's attempt to extricate vital clues bordered on an intense police interrogation, her mother remained tight-lipped on the subject.

'Maybe she'll splutter out a name on her death bed,' I encouraged.

'Well, I'll be waiting a long time for that. She is crazy fit for a sixty-six-year-old woman who is planning to walk the Kokoda Track after she gets back from her New Zealand adventure. Whereas I'm stuffed from just walking up the street from my shop to yours.' With a grimace, she fed her foot back into its shoe and peeled away a remnant of packaging tape from the heel of the other. 'Anyway, Ross has talked me into going to Melbourne for a week's R & R. He's booked me a hotel room with a spectacular view of the city.'

'Not for good, then. Sounds like a great idea.'

'I'll shop till I drop, eat whatever I like, and possibly take in a few theatre shows.'

'Good on you,' I said as she stood and brushed flecks of polystyrene from her black jeans. 'You'll be back for your birthday, won't you?'

A scowl puckered her face. 'Why?'

'I dunno ... someone might want to take you out to celebrate, or whatever.'

'It's okay, Abby. I'm aware Ross is up to something. I promise to return in time to get it over and done with.'

I walked with her to the door. 'Forty isn't that bad. I've been forty for a few years now and it hasn't affected me much.'

'I guess you don't look too bad for an old girl. C'mon, give me a hug and pray the good-time fairies sprinkle happy dust over me while I'm away.'

Enfolding her in an embrace, I whispered, 'I'll pray for a truckload of happy dust, my friend.'

'Great,' she grunted. 'I can see the headlines: *Middle-aged woman drowns in a downpour of sparkles.*'

As we walked outside, I offered some parting advice. 'Keep believing in miracles.'

A hint of a smile tweaked the corners of her mouth. 'I'll try.'

I watched Donna hurry away. What should I get her for her birthday? It would have to be exceptional. Something that would lift her spirits and fend off that black dog nipping at her heels.

2

Alexandra Headland 2019

Leo squinted against the glare. The sun was a scorcher—no surprise for a summer afternoon on a Sunshine Coast beach. Its warm breath in the sea breeze whipped his long grey hair across his face and into his eyes. He should get a decent haircut. Maybe next week ... or next month. Stuff it, maybe next year. At sixty-seven, he could do as he damn well pleased.

He kicked off his rubber thongs and hurried from burning hot sand to where it was wet and cool. A wave slapped his ankles, its foam bubbling against his skin. As it receded, his feet disappeared, sucked under the yielding sand like two fat clams, and he wriggled his toes to make certain they were still there. It'd be a shame not to have feet. He shook away a dreadful scene from his past before it played fully in his mind and inhaled a deep breath of salt air.

It was quieter here—more peaceful, less hectic—unlike the patrolled area further up, swarming with rowdy kids and sunworshippers, the surf littered with human flotsam splashing and squealing. He watched a lone angler throw his line out from the rocks into the water, while at a distance, board riders waiting for their next wave bobbed up and down like bathtub toys.

A sound pricked Leo's ears, a purring coming from the north.

He shielded his eyes and spied a dot below the clouds increasing in size as it followed the shoreline. A helicopter. His arm hairs stood to attention as the thud of rotor blades escalated and time shifted.

South Vietnam 1972

The soldiers crouch in the high humidity, their jungle greens soaked with sweat, fingers cramping against gun metal. Under cover of tall grass, Corporal Leo Sweetman waits along with the rest of the platoon while the two forward scouts survey the track up ahead.

'Hurry up, fellas,' Leo mouths, hoping the tickle inside his left boot is not another wretched centipede—the buggers are everywhere. He won't miss them, that's for sure.

Only two weeks remain until he catches the freedom bird back to Australia in time to celebrate his twenty-first birthday on familiar soil. No doubt there'll be the traditional booze-up and barbecue at the farm, but who will char the steak and sausages now the old man has gone? Carl will probably step in as the head of the household and make a grand show of it, drawing all the limelight as usual. A lump lodges in his throat. Had Leonard senior, in his final moments pinned beneath the overturned tractor, given a thought to his younger son slogging it out in Vietnam? He chose to believe so.

A dragonfly appears from nowhere to hover nearby, its brilliant red colouring stark against a backdrop of green. Leo's muscles tense and a chill crawls up his spine. A grave portent? He swats the insect away and checks his wristwatch. Minutes lag like hours when you're waiting on a razor's edge.

A thousand cicadas kick into action, their steady hum building to a deafening crescendo. In this battle zone they seem shriller, coarser, angrier, and just when he can't bear the ruckus any longer, it ceases as suddenly as it had begun.

Leo sighs and flexes his fingers, wriggles his numbing toes. He could murder a beer right now.

A blast shatters the hush.

Soil rains down through air permeated with the stench of explosives. For a moment, all is strangely quiet. Then comes the screaming.

Leo defies orders and springs up and runs, his rifle held tight and close as he follows the ghastly sound to his mates.

His stomach heaves at the sight of a motionless figure on the track. Skidding to a halt, he drops to his knees and presses his fingers against the bloody throat, unsurprised to find no pulse, for the youthful face has been replaced with a messy pulp of flesh and bone. Blond tufts of hair sprouting through the gore tell him it is Ian 'Ned' Kelly.

A moan directs Leo around a crater of earth to locate Gary Dodgson, whose body is now truncated by the loss of both legs. Bloody mine!

Leo crawls close and grips the flailing arm. 'Dodge, I'm here.'

A garbled cry. 'Sweetie ... is that you?'

'Yeah mate, it's me.' He quickly assesses the damage and sees Dodge's life gushing out in pulsating spurts of crimson.

Wild eyes plead. 'Will I make it?'

'Sure,' Leo answers with more conviction than he feels. He glances up as two engineers arrive armed with mine detectors.

'Dumb crazy bastard,' one hisses. 'You know the drill, Sweetman, we go in first.'

Leo unthreads his own bootlace and ties off the jet of blood squirting from Dodge's shredded right thigh.

The medic slides alongside and unpacks his bag of tricks, tourniquets the stump of the other leg. 'We've called in a Dust Off.'

'Hang in there, Dodge,' Leo says, 'the chopper's on its way. You'll be

as good as new in no time.' As blood trickles from Dodge's mouth, and both eyes grow dark and distant, Leo urges, 'Stay with me.'

Gunfire from the dense scrub sends Leo's bush hat flying off at a near miss. He seizes his SLR and aims, but a machine gun burst from behind takes over and the enemy's shooting ceases.

Moments later, a stick grenade lobbed from a different section of bush hits the ground and rolls close. Leo lurches forward, intending to kick it elsewhere, when there is a blinding flash and a thunderous roar. Blown off his feet and slammed into the earth, a hellish pain courses through him. A fire rages through his gut.

Words whizz around him like bullets. Pressure on his stomach. A stab in his arm.

A noise above—the beating of wings, swift and powerful. Trees arch backward and the monstrous thing comes into view.

'No!' He thrashes his arms. 'Get away.'

Strong hands pin him down. 'Stop struggling, Sweetman. We're trying to help.'

Help? Leo tries to focus on the hovering beast and laughs. They've sent a giant dragonfly to save him.

The world goes soft. Pain ebbs like waves on a beach, the tide going out. He surrenders to the pull of the ocean and drifts away.

'You all right there, mate?'

Leo blinked against the brightness and discovered he was cowering on all fours at the water's edge. A surfer dripping with the sea stood in front of him, a board tucked under his arm. Young, scarcely out of his teens, he was lean, nut-brown, and broad-shouldered. Flicking dark curls away from his ocean-blue eyes, he offered Leo a hand peeking out of a sleeve of tribal tattoos.

Leo cringed. The surfer looked so much like Dodge it wasn't funny. He took the hand and was lifted to his feet.

'Want me to get help?' the young man asked, thumbing over his shoulder. 'The lifesavers up there have a buggy.'

Leo brushed shell grit from his damp skin and clothes. 'No. I'm good.'

'Yeah?' The freckled nose scrunched. 'You look like shit. Did you have a fall?'

'Nope, just had a turn.'

'Bummer. A dodgy ticker?'

He straightened his back and forced a smile. 'Nope. Just stuffed in the head. I'll be okay.'

The surfer looked in the direction of the dunes and the boardwalk leading up to the park. 'Need a hand to your car, or a lift home?'

'Geez, I'm not that messed up. I only live across the road.' Leo pointed to a rising block of units. From here he could identify his balcony by the potted phoenix palm waving to him like an eager lover. 'Thanks all the same. Good of you to check on an old fella like me.'

The surfer grinned, his white teeth vivid against his deep tan. 'No probs. Better get back before the swell dies. Seeya 'round, hey?'

Leo nodded. 'Yeah, probably.'

And the man raced into the surge—young, healthy, every limb intact.

Leo found his thongs and slipped them on to protect his feet from blistering. Aiming for the boardwalk steps, he slid his hand under his shirt and fingered the puckered scar trailing over his belly. He knew it was just a roll of the dice that decided his fate that day in the jungle. Still, anger and rage had dominated the years since, and he'd only recently found any genuine sense of peace. But not consistently. Not today, the anniversary of the ambush.

3

I heard my name called as I returned from the bakery with a cappuccino and a cream-filled apple turnover. Glancing around, I saw Donna's husband, Ross, beckoning from the doorway of their antique store.

'I need to see you,' he said, and then slipped back inside.

With a grumble, I guzzled the coffee and tossed the empty cup into a roadside bin before feeding the nibbled pastry into its packet and into my bag.

Musty scents of aged furniture and bric-a-brac greeted me as I stepped inside Fine 'n Dandy. Glinting crystal, sparkling silverware, and pretty china settings enticed me from glass cabinets, yet I fended off their beguiling charms and zigzagged around clutter to join Ross at the shop counter.

'Thanks, Abby.' His lips froze mid-smile. 'Er ... you have something under your nose.'

'Really?' I viewed my reflection in a large bevelled-edged wall mirror and discovered a chocolate Hitler-esque moustache above my top lip. I licked my fingers and swiped it away. 'Golly, how'd that happen?'

I turned and found Ross had vanished. Velvet drapes swaying behind the counter hinted at where he'd gone, so I parted the curtaining and stepped into a storeroom crammed with odd furniture pieces and cardboard boxes.

Ross's head poked out of a room to the side. 'Quick, in here. Now that Donna's out of the way, we won't get caught.'

I balked. *Get caught doing what?* Unnerving scenarios scrolled through my mind, and I glanced back at the velvet curtains and considered a swift retreat.

'Hurry,' he growled. 'I can't wait all day.' Then he disappeared again.

I pressed my bag against my chest like a shield and entered what turned out to be a modest office. Before I could even ask what he wanted from me, Ross shoved me into a swivel office chair, and I gasped as it rolled backwards on its castors and collided with a wooden desk.

He gripped the chair's armrests and thrust his face close to mine. 'It's for Donna's birthday.'

I tilted away from his salty, malt-tainted breath. 'What is?'

He rotated the chair, so I now faced a computer laptop. One tap of Ross's varnish-stained finger on the keyboard and the screen came to life in a collage of images of my absent friend.

'I'm trying to put together a presentation for her party,' he added. 'I've scanned heaps of pics but I'm not sure there's enough.' He pointed to a stack of photos on the desk next to a plate bearing a partially eaten piece of toast smeared thickly with Vegemite. 'Look, I haven't even gone through them yet.'

'So, what do you want me to do?'

He reached over to retrieve his snack and spoke while eating.

'Flick through the pile and pick out some good ones. Then check out what I've done so far and see what needs including ... what Donna would want shown.'

I lifted a couple of photos from the heap and stared at a silly shot from Donna's past: ugly knitted beanie, cross-eyed, tongue out. 'Are we allowed to embarrass her?'

'Of course, but don't get too carried away. No naked shots unless she's a baby, okay?'

How many nudie pics were there among this lot? Hopefully, I wouldn't be the one cringing. 'I'm expecting a delivery at the shop so I can only give you half an hour.'

'I'll leave you to it, then. Do you require another coffee?'

'What? Not at all.'

His eyebrows arched. 'Are you sure you don't need to feed your addiction?'

'What gives you that idea?' I snapped.

'Well, pretty much every time I look out my shop window, I catch you dashing past, sucking on a takeaway cup.'

'That doesn't mean I'm addicted. I'm under a little pressure, that's all.'

He puckered his lips. 'If you say so.' Then he strode out, leaving me to play the PowerPoint and watch my friend's life flash before my eyes.

Donna's transformation from a cute toddler into a scrawny, freckled child, and then a cheerful, adventurous young woman fascinated me. As the photos flicked by, I noted the many countries Donna had visited over the passing years. While she travelled the world without a care, I'd become a wife and mother, worked an assortment of jobs, and settled into our first home in the suburbs. Different strokes, I suppose.

I sorted through the photo stack until a shot of a small group standing on the stairs of a timber church seized my attention. In its centre stood a young, dark-haired woman cradling a baby dressed in a lace christening gown.

'Ross!' I called. 'Come here, will you?'

Approaching footsteps and he appeared in the doorway. 'Have you finished already?'

'Not quite.' I waved the photo. 'What do you know about this?'

He dropped his glasses down from the top of his head to rest on his nose. 'That was taken at Donna's christening.'

'I'm aware of that. What else can you tell me?'

'Let's see ... Faith was a real hottie back then. Still is in my books.' His grin quickly slid from his face. 'Hey, I'm not into my mother-in-law. I'm just saying she's kept her great looks. Anyway, the bloke on Faith's right is Carl Sweetman, Donna's father.'

'The man she believed was her father,' I corrected.

Ross nodded already aware Donna had told me about her mother's part confession. 'The man on Faith's left is his brother, Leo.'

I squinted. Though both men were easy on the eye, they looked unrelated. Carl had clipped dark hair, a wiry build, and conservative attire of shirt and tie. While his brother had a sturdy physique, light wavy hair edging the collar of an open-necked shirt, and a shaggy beard.

'The man behind Faith must be the minister,' I said.

'Yep, the dog collar is a giveaway.' Ross took the photo from me. 'I'd forgotten about this snap. I reckon Donna's not keen on it.'

'Possibly because it looks like a perfect family. Had Carl guessed he wasn't her dad?'

Ross shrugged. 'No idea. If he'd been suspicious, he hadn't much of a chance to find out. He was dead hours after this picture was taken.'

I snatched the photo. While Faith's face bore a beatific smile, her husband looked to be suffering from gut ache. 'How did he die?'

'Drowned on the family property during a flash flood. His death must have really shaken Faith because she later changed her name back to Crosby.' Ross leaned over my shoulder. 'Check out the guy at the rear with the horseshoe moustache.'

I studied the man's image and lurched back. 'Oh my God! I know him.'

'You do?'

'It's Gladstone Maloney. I've seen another photograph of him when he was younger, and that's definitely him.'

Stoney Maloney and I had recently become acquainted when researching my family tree, a hobby I shared with my dad. Living in Shadow Creek most of his life, and being familiar with the area and its people, Stoney had proven to be a fount of knowledge regarding local history. He was now a welcome friend.

'He's a funny old coot,' Ross said. 'A frequent shopper here. Bought a bowler hat the other day to *impress the ladies*, so he said.'

'That'd be right. He may be in his eighties, and smitten with lovely Doris, but he's still a flirt.' I shook my head. 'Fancy him knowing Donna's mum.'

'You should show him this photo. He might remember the others. Like that cute chick with the pixie cut snuggled next to him.'

My insides fizzed like a firework. I spun the chair around to face Ross. 'I've got a wild idea.'

He held up both hands in protest. 'Uh-oh, this means trouble.'

'We don't know who actually fathered Donna, right?'

'Yeah, right.'

'And Faith isn't letting on anything.'

'Correct.'

'Then if the photo was taken shortly after Donna's birth,

maybe someone in this group had inside knowledge. One of them must have had a hunch what was going on, don't you reckon?'

'Hang on, Abby. Where are you going with this?'

'Well ... what if we were able to give Donna a special gift for her birthday?'

'Such as?'

'The true name of her father.'

Ross's eyes bulged. 'And how would we do that?'

'By quizzing these people. Stoney's easy enough to contact. Maybe he knows where the others are.'

'What if they've moved on ... or shuffled off this mortal coil? Anyway, what about Faith? How would digging up the past affect her? It mightn't show her in a respectable light.'

'I hear she's not coming back from New Zealand for the birthday celebrations.'

'Well, she hasn't responded to my invitation. Probably having too good a time across the ditch.'

'So, it would be easy to keep it a secret from her ... at least for a while.'

'I dunno, Abby.' He lifted his glasses to pinch the bridge of his nose. 'My gut is telling me it could be a bad move.'

I thought he'd be more eager. I moved to the edge of the chair. 'Just think how over the moon Donna will be if it comes off, and we do find her father.'

'Unless he turns out to be a real loser, then we'd have made things worse.'

'Pl-e-e-ase, Ross,' I urged.

'And you want to do this in time for her birthday? We've only got eight days, you know. How's that going to happen?'

'Well, let's get the ball rolling and see what turns up. If we hit a snag or a dead end, at least we can say we've tried.'

He rubbed his scalp as he considered my words. 'Geez ... I can't believe I'm saying this. Okay, Abby ... let's give it a shot.'

I raised my hand for a high five and Ross responded with such force that the chair shrieked and twirled a complete circle, sending my bag flying from my lap. Attempting a forward one-and-a-half somersault with a twist, it belly-flopped, spewing its contents over the floor.

We knelt together to recover the sundry articles until Ross let out an unmanly squeal. By the eerie light of the computer screen, I saw the apple turnover lying in front of him, now squashed and savagely speared through the heart by a Libra Fleur tampon.

Ross jumped up. 'Gotta wash my hand,' he winced, and skidded on a tube of Sexy Plum lipstick as he raced from the room.

I photographed the group snap before gathering my belongings.

Reality hit like a blast of cold air as I stepped outside. How would I fit in some investigating when I had a bookstore to ready for its opening on the same weekend as Donna's birthday? *What was I thinking?*

The delivery arrived at Ringtales just as I did. My choice of furniture for the shop had been intentional—a chaise lounge, a Chesterfield sofa, a colourful beanbag—bought to encourage customers of all ages to browse and sample-read books before purchasing. Now, thanks to a local blacksmith, I had a *Game of Thrones* inspired ceremonial chair. Farming implements, gardening tools, and even cutlery had been used to embellish the ironwork, resulting in a unique piece of craftsmanship. Impressed by his ingenuity, I paid accordingly and helped position the chair in the middle of the store.

Like a queen eager to hear the pleas of her people, I took a seat, happy to stay there for the rest of the afternoon, when the sudden appearance of two young stickybeaks disrupted my serenity. With noses pressed flat against the shop window, they attempted to glimpse the proceedings inside until I leapt from the throne, grabbed a copy of Stephen King's *It,* and slapped the cover image of Pennywise against the glass. Sharp yelps and the sneaky little devils were gone, leaving smears of snot and dribble on the window for me to clean off.

Stan Gruen was later to visit. With his wiry grey mullet, ruddy complexion, and camera bag slung over his shoulder, he looked every part the editor/photographer of the village rag. Perching his bony backside on the top rung of a folding stepladder, he advised that if I wanted the shop to open with a real *bang,* a piece placed in The Talk of the Town would be helpful. Aware the next edition was due out on Wednesday, I'd assumed I'd left it too late. However, Stan informed me a quarter page spot was still available and he happened to have half an hour spare in which to take several potential pics.

'Great,' I said, before dashing off to the toilet/washroom out back to primp myself into a semblance of a chic bookshop owner.

Instructed to turn this way, tilt my chin that way, smile—not too much—I kept my eyes on a huntsman spider crawling up the wall towards the ceiling. Having heard somewhere that Stan was an arachnophobe, and fearing a frenzied interruption to my photo shoot, I elected not to alert him. Thankfully the spider behaved and Stan, unaware of its existence, maintained his composure.

I studied the images in his digital camera and raved over Stan's use of good lighting and positioning. He grunted and mentioned that after thirty-two years as a professional photographer, it would be remiss of him not to know how best to hide wrinkles, blemishes, and bags under eyes. Troubled by this comment, I chose an apt shot of me posing on the throne chair clutching a recent edition of Miles Franklin's *My Brilliant Career* to be used. After a cursory glance at an article I'd written in advance, Stan gave a nod of acceptance and rushed away to his next job: an interview with Daphne Birtwistle, who'd recently suffered a near-death experience after choking on a pickled cucumber.

An hour later, I too was out the door.

4

A petite young woman rushed out of the parking lot of the veterinary surgery as I drove through town. With her blonde ponytail swishing behind her, she sprinted along the footpath.

'Otto! Get back here!' she yelled, moments before a fox terrier jumped the curb and bolted out in front of my yellow VW beetle.

Tyres screeched on bitumen as I braked, yet there was no bump or sight of a dog racing away. Unclipping my seatbelt and stepping out of the car to survey the scene, I spotted the smarmy absconder intact and wagging his tail in front of the bumper.

'Why you little—'

'Mum!' Gemma grabbed my arm. 'Did you hit him?'

'No. Though I reckon he came pretty close to entering doggy heaven.'

The foxy cocked his shaggy head and blinked at us, innocent-like, as if wondering what all the fuss was about.

Gemma scooped him up. 'Otto, you naughty boy! What would your mother say if she learned you'd escaped?'

'Put him in chains?' I said, hopefully.

Gemma's blue eyes squinted back at me. 'Hardly. He's one spoilt pooch, you know.'

Of course I knew. He and his owner lived across the road from us at Rosella Ridge. Though I got on with my elderly neighbour, there was no love lost between Otto and me. He was a pretentious creature, and our relationship was frosty.

Gemma tickled under the fugitive's chin. 'Jean dropped him in to have his annual vaccinations and a pamper package.'

'Pamper package?'

'Yes. A wash, a groom, and a manicure. All for just sixty-five buckaroos.'

I gasped at the idea of wasting any amount of money on this mutt. 'That's actually a pretty good price.'

'It is, and then we take a glamour shot for our photo board.'

'Sounds fabulous. When can I book myself in?'

She arched her defined eyebrows. 'And would you like a bonus flea treatment?'

'Hey, why not? I'll get a discount, won't I, with you being on staff and all?'

'Depends on how co-operative you are. This one sure wasn't. He took off before he had his nails clipped.' She scratched behind Otto's ears and his eyes turned into slits, enjoying the attention. 'I should return him before Jean shows up. With any luck, we'll be able to keep this little adventure a secret.'

I was about to say, *Why, he could do with some punishing,* when a blast of a car horn had me twisting around to discover an idling SUV hitched to a horse float, the driver shaking his head. At least the man wasn't giving rude hand signals. I slipped back into my VW and drove away.

. . .

As always, I took care driving the winding mountain road up to Rosella Ridge, though I was surprised to see a peacock had lost its life among the standard roadkill of toads, possums, and snakes. Turning into our street, I aimed for the timber pole house surrounded by a scattering of native trees and blossoming shrubs. Built on the edge of an escarpment overlooking Shadow Creek township, it had become our family's sanctuary for several years since fleeing suburbia on the outskirts of Brisbane.

Elliott's aged Hyundai was parked roadside, while Shane's white ute emblazoned with *Eaton Landscaping* in red lettering stood in the driveway, still stacked with equipment used to erect the shop sign. As I slipped out of my car, my ears tweaked to the whir of a power tool coming from the backyard. What was he up to now?

I found Shane in the large shed out back that he used as a workshop. Donned in protective goggles and earmuffs, he was engrossed in sanding the surface of a large slab of timber. I stepped in front of him and madly waved my arms like an inflatable air dancer.

He glanced up, turned off the orbital sander, and pulled off his earmuffs. Flecks of sawdust littered his grey-streaked goatee like snowflakes. 'Want something?' he frowned, obviously annoyed at the interruption.

'Just letting you know I'm home. How's it going?'

He lifted his goggles and rested them on the top of his head. 'Getting there.' He dusted the timber with a remnant of an old T-shirt. 'What do you think so far?'

I slid my hand over the beautiful grain of forest redgum, and visualised the slab polished and mounted on the previously built shelving. 'It'll be a stunning shop counter,' I gushed. 'Thanks, hon.' I leaned forward and kissed a cheek powdered with wood dust.

'Should be ready to attach by Wednesday.'

'Wonderful. Are you wanting dinner yet, or do you want to keep working?'

He gave the slab a quick appraisal. 'Give me half an hour. What's on the menu?'

'Moroccan lamb with couscous.'

His eyes narrowed. 'Didn't we have that last night?'

'Yep, leftovers. I could add some more veggies.'

'As long as there's enough. Elliott is here for dinner too, remember.'

'Hmm ... in that case, I'll defrost some lasagne as well, and maybe the apple pie Mum made for us last week.'

'Don't spoil him too much or he may want to move back. We've only just got rid of him.'

After almost twenty-one years, it was nice having the house to ourselves. Gemma had recently moved out to house-share in town, while Elliott was bunking in with student friends closer to the university they attended. I decided to skip the apple pie.

'Here, take these with you.' Shane passed over a handful of mail.

I shook the envelopes free of sawdust. 'When did these arrive?'

'Yesterday. Forgot to take them inside.'

I flicked through the assortment, my gaze resting on an envelope stamped with a government logo. The buzz of the sander as Shane returned to his task drowned out my happy cry. I left him to it.

Elliott, glued to the TV—feet up on the coffee table, a packet of potato chips in his lap—watched a noisy car chase. I gave him a wave before heading upstairs to my loft study. Dropping the mail on my desk, I tore open the government envelope and removed my new business licence. Finding the document frame I'd purchased in readiness, I slid the licence inside and held it at arm's length.

'Business Name: Ringtales,' I read aloud. 'Business Owner: Aberdeen Eaton.'

Bugger! They'd used my birth name—the one my father had drunkenly chosen from a map of Scotland when celebrating the arrival of a third daughter. At least my new business cards had me correctly printed with 'Abby', my preferred moniker. Anyway, what customer would bother to read the document's fine print?

Downstairs, I went into the kitchen and took the pre-made lasagne from the freezer.

'I guess you don't need much for dinner after eating those chips,' I shouted to Elliott in the lounge room.

'I'm still hungry. What's on offer?' he yelled.

'Lasagne with salad and leftover Moroccan lamb.'

'Nope, I don't think so.'

I went into the lounge. 'What do you mean, nope? Aren't they up to your standard now you're living the high life away from home?'

He shook his dark tousled mane. 'No, I mean there's no lamb. I ate it before.'

'You ate all our leftovers?'

'Yep, it was yum.' He changed the TV channel and Ricky Gervais appeared on the screen. 'I'll just have lasagne, Mum, no salad.'

'You can have two-minute noodles, buddy. The lasagne is mine and Dad's.'

'What?' Elliott twisted his head around to face me. 'I'm sick of noodles,' he snarled. 'Where's your compassion? I'm a poor uni student forced to live with a bunch of smelly guys and a mangy old cat in a hand-me-down house with shit plumbing. You're supposed to look after me when I visit.'

'Well, you're the one who moved out to experience the real world. So, if you want more for dinner, make yourself a sandwich or, better yet, get some takeaway on your way home.' I stamped my foot to stress my point.

He offered a wry grin. 'Got ya! It's okay, I'll swing by Maccas for a meal deal.'

My hackles settled back down as I returned to the kitchen.

Elliott finally left when Shane and I started watching an episode of a trending British crime series he considered as lame. During an ad break, I mentioned my intention of discovering Donna's true parentage and shouldn't have been surprised by my husband's reaction.

'Bloody hell, Abby. Why can't you just leave things alone? Haven't you got enough on your plate at present?'

I squirmed in my seat. However, the window of opportunity that had opened up could not be ignored.

'People keep secrets for all sorts of reasons,' he continued. 'Sometimes it's to protect their nearest and dearest. Is your memory that short?'

His words hit a nerve. We'd been through a rough patch a few months back when information not shared had been kept secret for this very reason.

Shane thrust his hand into the snack bowl resting on his lap. 'Stop sticking your nose in to where it doesn't belong. Concentrate on your own problems, for God's sake.' Then he shoved a fistful of popcorn into his mouth and turned up the TV's volume.

This wasn't the first time he'd cautioned me about interfering in people's personal affairs, and he was right, I should back off. What was my rush? I could bring the idea up with Donna at a later stage and let her do the investigating. Maybe she'd even allow me to help.

Peeved that I'd been chastised like an errant child, I retreated to my loft study and slouched on the sofa with my phone, flicking through social media. I was about to add a pic to Instagram when Donna's christening photo jumped out at me. With a glance towards the stairs, I quickly emailed it to myself and then moved over to the desk to fire up my computer. A check of my emails, and I saved the photo to a folder on my desktop. Opening an internet website of archived Australian newspapers, I entered *Carl Sweetman Shadow Creek* into the search bar, and within seconds, found what I'd hoped for: a newspaper article from February 1979 reporting a tragic death.

According to the report, the flash flood in Shadow Creek after three days of torrential rain resulted in the drowning of a local man. Carl Sweetman's body was discovered kilometres away from the family property, in the creek close to town. Sadly, he'd left behind a wife, a baby daughter, and a ten-year-old son.

My spine stiffened. *A son?* Donna had never spoken of a brother.

I made a quick calculation. That meant Faith was around sixteen when she'd given birth to the boy—young, indeed. Ross may shed some light on this ... or even Stoney Maloney, if I dared to broach the subject with him.

Shane calling from downstairs to join him for a cup of tea, stirred me to shut down the computer.

We chatted without speaking on the pitfalls of snooping, and went to bed with no love lost between us. Still, sleep for me did not come easy as my renewed interest in Faith's sordid past fought a battle with my conscience.

5

Leo bolted upright, heart pounding from the dream that had woken him. Confused by the room's darkness, he checked the bedside clock and discovered night had fallen during his afternoon nap.

He dropped his legs over the edge of the bed and walked across the carpet to the open sliding door. Stepping onto the balcony, the terracotta tiles were cool underfoot and the breeze fresh against his bare skin. He inhaled deeply and viewed the wide and vacant beach, the ink-black sea hemmed with breakers foaming iridescent white in the moonlight. Though the growl of the waves drowned out the thrumming in his ears, the ache in his head and stomach remained.

He massaged the gnarly scar above the waistband of his shorts. His nightmares often included the jungle ambush, but sometimes they ended differently. Sometimes he would find his mates still alive on the track, joking and sharing a smoke, telling him he was a bloody sook for worrying. Other times, he'd been able to give aid and get them safely onto the chopper. Occasionally, Ned would live and Dodge would die, or the other way around. But tonight, the dream was more onerous. This time, the sniper grinning down through the foliage had morphed into Carl, and tugging his brother from the tree, Leo had pummelled the smirking face into a gruesome, meaty mash.

With a shudder, he returned indoors and hobbled downstairs to the kitchen to fetch a cold beer. Leaning against the marble-topped bench, he swigged from the bottle and noticed a piece of card poking out from under the fridge. He picked it up. An invitation. One he hadn't responded to. Surely his nephew had twigged to why he hadn't attended the photo gallery's opening. More than anyone else, he would have understood the difficulties involved in his uncle's return to Chances Crossing.

6

My parents dropped into the shop the next morning to deliver the gumleaf-green curtains Mum had made. Dad stayed to give me a hand while my mother dashed away to attend a CWA meeting in town to plan a market stall.

'You know, I've always had a hunch my great-uncle Fred was involved with this lot,' he said, examining a book about the razor gangs of 1920s Sydney. 'Worked as a wharf labourer, around that time, and lived at Darlinghurst, smack bang in crime central. Sure was a tough and shady character. He scared the crap out of me.'

I looked up from unpacking a box of tea towels printed with book quotes. 'Was he a violent sort?'

He shrugged. 'Well, nothing I was a witness to. But he had a deep scar running down the right side of his face and was missing an eye. To put the wind up me, he'd remove his glass eyeball without me knowing and add it to my stash of marbles while I was engrossed in playing. Then he'd laugh himself silly when I picked it up in horror. Bloody joker. Told me he'd lost his eye in the war, but when researching our family tree, I discover he'd never even enlisted.'

Dad got comfortable on the Chesterfield and cracked the book open to the first page. I knew by the way he sucked his bottom lip he was not to be disturbed. When my father's obsession with genealogy was piqued, no one could draw him back to the present in a hurry.

'Don't bend the pages,' I warned, and left him to it.

An hour later, he stood and stretched. 'Finished! No mention of Uncle Fred—not by that name anyway. Still, I reckon he was in the thick of it all.' He carefully displayed the book on a shelf, face out. 'If you want me to review it, I could, no problem. I could even critique more books, if you like. You could add my reviews to your blot.'

I pulled a face. 'My blot?'

'Yeah, on your website.'

'You mean my blog.'

'That's it. I could be your secret reviewer.'

'And you'd read whichever book you were given?'

'Of course. Crime, action, thriller, mystery. You name it, I'll read it.'

'How about historical romance, or chick lit?'

'Umm ... your mother could probably review those.' He took my hands in his much larger ones. 'I'm very proud of what you're doing here, Aberdeen. It's a big step starting your own business, and I want you to know I believe in you. I reckon the shop's going to be a roaring success.'

'Aww, that's so sweet.' I stretched up to kiss his cheek. 'Let me think about the reviewing idea and get back to you, okay?'

We both turned as the shop door flew open and my mother strode in.

'Time to make tracks, Robert. I've had enough crafty talk to last me a decade.'

'Here, Rose.' Dad passed her a glossy paperback he'd taken from a pile. 'Read this and give Abby a review.'

Mum took one look at the suggestive cover of the Sci-Fi erotica novel and grimaced. 'Are you sure?'

Dad peered over her shoulder. 'Er ... maybe not.' He snatched the book and dropped it back on the pile.

'C'mon Bobby,' she urged, tugging his sleeve. 'We need to get home. The lamb roast won't cook itself.'

Watching my parents leave, I thought on Donna not knowing who her real father was, or being able to have a relationship with him. I couldn't imagine not having my dad around to annoy me, encourage me, and shower me with affection. A surge of sadness for Donna's situation gave me a greater compulsion to find her father.

7

Serendipi-teas Cafe was packed with customers. This was not a deterrent, yet I found my patience waning as I waited in line behind a dithering bunch of seniors out for Saturday brunch.

'For God's sake, just pick something,' I muttered under my breath. How difficult could it be to choose an item from the menu? I was about to offer my recommendations when a nod in my direction from the attendant made me eagerly jump the queue to order. Waiting for my takeaway chai latte, I noticed an elderly man sitting on his own at a corner table, his impressive moustache trembling as he eyed the slice of Black Forest cake on his plate with a desire more suited to a bridegroom on his wedding night.

I sidled over. 'Hello, Stoney. You're just the person I want to talk to.'

He glanced up, his mouth open in preparation for the chocolate morsel balanced on his cake fork. 'G'day, luv, fancy seeing you here. How's the shop preparations going?'

'Good, I think. Things are coming along nicely.'

He shoved the cake portion into his mouth before asking, 'Well, what can I do ya for?'

I gnawed my lip. How to begin?

'Geez, girly, don't stand there like a stuffed galah. Pull up a chair, if you don't mind watching an old fella pig out on a sweet treat.'

I planted my backside on the seat opposite him. 'Of course I don't mind. I've ordered a drink, anyway.'

On cue, the cafe attendant appeared at the table and handed over the steaming glass of deliciousness. I offered her a grateful smile.

While Stoney ploughed into the rest of his cake, I ignored Shane's voice in my head warning me to 'leave things alone' and asked Stoney how well he'd known the Sweetman family.

'The Sweetmans?' he said, spurting cake particles out of his mouth and onto the tabletop.

'Yes. Carl and Faith Sweetman.' I brought up the photo on my phone and held it out for him to view. 'That's you, I take it.'

He squinted as he examined the image. 'By golly, that was a long time ago.'

'Forty years, actually. This was taken at their baby Donna's christening.'

'Ah, yes, at the church here in town. Cute kid. Dimples. Orange peach fuzz for hair. Wonder what happened to her.'

Between sips of my drink, I briefly filled him in on Donna's life and that she'd married and returned to Shadow Creek to run the antique store in partnership with her husband, Ross.

Cappuccino froth lingered on Stoney's whiskers like sea foam as he wrenched his coffee cup away from his mouth. 'Strike a light! Are you saying that nice lady in Fine 'n Dandy is baby Donna?'

'Yes, all grown up.'

'That's a surprise and a half. I often drop into that shop looking for a bargain. Bought a smashing little bowler hat recently. What in the world led her back to Shadow Creek?'

'Knowing she started life here was a draw card. And when the business came up for sale, I guess she deemed it fortuitous and made the move.'

'And her mother ... Faith ... is she here, too?'

I gathered by his fiddling with the bowl of sugar sticks, making sure they were all standing up the same way, that this was a concern for him.

'No. As far as I'm aware she hasn't visited since they've relocated here. Too busy travelling. Anyway, back to my first question. How did you know the Sweetmans?'

Stoney mentioned he lived out at Chances Crossing for several years and his property shared a common boundary with the Sweetman's. Also, owning a virile and award-winning Santa Gertrudis bull at the time, he had been in regular business with Carl who ran a small herd of breeding cattle. Stoney provided the stud, while Carl provided cash for services rendered.

'What type of man was he?' I asked.

'Let's see. Hard-working, driven, opinionated. A chip off the old block. Old Len, Carl's father, was the same. No sense arguing with either of those blokes.'

'And Faith? What was she like?'

He crossed his arms over his ample stomach and parted his freckled lips in a slow smile. 'Well, a good-looker for starters.'

'Did you meet her at the farm?'

'Nope, in town. Saw her getting off the bus. A stranger, all dolled up in her Sunday best.'

Shadow Creek, September 1977

Stoney watches from the shade of a Moreton Bay fig tree in front of The Axemen's Arms as a young woman steps off the bus and out of the path of boarding passengers. Checking her wristwatch, she drops a small suitcase at her feet on the pavement and scans the street. Not wanting to be caught perving at a stranger, Stoney eases back so he's partly concealed by the tree's broad trunk.

The woman searches through her shoulder bag, dabs on lipstick, sprays her wrists and neck with perfume, and pops a strip of gum into her mouth. Catching her reflection in the butcher shop window, she removes whatever is keeping her hair caught up in a bun, and releases dark tresses that fall to the waist of her bright orange jumpsuit. She then smooths down the flared legs of her outfit, lifts a foot, and examines the cork sole of her platform shoe. Had she stepped in something offensive, like dog shit? No surprise if she had, stray mongrels were common around town. After checking the time again, she folds her arms and shakes her head. She's not happy, that's for sure.

Stoney decides it is time to step out from the shadows.

He crosses the bitumen and sidles up to the woman. 'You look a little lost, luv. Need a helping hand?'

The woman scowls while eyeing him from head to foot. Under her gaze, Stoney is aware of his average height, stocky build, and shock of straw-coloured hair. He runs his fingers through his ginger-streaked moustache and reaches for the packet of Winfield Red stuffed into the rolled-up sleeve of his checked shirt, then changes his mind. Better wait to see if he can be of assistance before he lights up another cancer stick.

'I'm looking for someone,' she says. 'He was supposed to meet me here and take me to his farm at Chances Crossing.'

Stoney flashes a winning smile. 'You don't say. I live out that way. What would this fella's name be?'

'Carl Sweetman. Do you know him?'

Stoney cocks one bushy eyebrow. 'Well, it's your lucky day. He's a neighbour of mine. I could give you a lift if you like.'

The woman gives the street a glance in both directions, as if checking for other options. 'I should call first and find out what's kept him.'

Stoney nods towards the red phone box standing outside the post office. 'That phone's stuffed. You'd have a better chance of sending smoke signals. How about I run you out there? If we come across Carl on the way, I'll stop and hand you over.'

When she utters a tentative, 'O-kay', he thrusts out a meaty hand. 'The name's Stoney Maloney.'

The woman's handshake is stronger than expected. 'I'm Faith Crosby.'

He points to her suitcase. 'Is that all you've got? Not staying long, I gather.'

'Er ... no.' Her face flushes a light pink. 'Just the night, I think. We'll see how it goes.'

He sniggers. *Carl Sweetman, you sly old dog.*

Both seated on the front bench seat of the battered ute, Faith grasps the dashboard for support, her bangles jangling when the vehicle jolts over the corrugated dirt road leading through lush countryside. Stoney gives her a quick rundown on the history of the area dotted with farm houses and grazing cattle, but suspects by her frequent licking of her lips, that she's too nervous to take in any information.

He drives past the entrance to his own property and veers the ute through the gates of the Sweetman farm. Trees lining both sides of the driveway usher them uphill until the ute stops in front of a weathered timber house skirted by a wide verandah. Stoney lets the engine idle as he waits for Faith to get out. When she hesitates, he pats her knee and asks if she's all right. She nods, though the uncertainty in her eyes hints she may demand to be driven straight back to town.

On hearing a shout, they both peer through the front windscreen to spy a boy waving from the verandah.

Faith cracks a smile and leans out through her side window. 'Hello, young Simon!'

When she opens the door and slips out, Stoney passes her the suitcase. 'Don't forget this.'

'Thanks so much, Stoney. I really appreciate you helping a girl out.'

'My pleasure. Glad to be of service.'

Leaning over, he pulls the passenger door shut and watches Simon rush down the stairs with his border collie in tow. While the boy greets Faith with lively chatter, the dog sniffs her legs and wags its tail, a sure sign of approval.

About to drive off, Stoney sees Carl appear from the direction of the work shed. 'G'day, mate,' he calls, edging out of his window. 'Just dropping off a delivery for you.'

Carl doesn't return Stoney's wink and grin. 'Thanks for that. Just lost a calf to tick fever. I'll wait a couple of days before burying it, so you'll have to put up with the ruckus, I'm afraid.'

'No problem.' Stoney's ears prick to a bellowing coming from the paddock alongside his property: the cow mourning her loss. Carl's right, best to leave burying the carcass until the cow accepts its death rather than her madly searching high and low for the missing calf.

With no more conversation between them, Stoney drives away, leaving Carl to properly welcome his pretty visitor.

～

Stoney slurped down the remains of his coffee. 'A city girl in a country town stuck out like a sore toe back then. She smelled real nice too. Fancy perfume, like what a lady wears to impress a fella on their first date. I should know,' he smirked, 'I've been on plenty of them.'

'And you dropped her off at the Sweetman's?'

'Yep, and left her to it. Though I sure was interested in seeing how it all played out.'

'And how did it?'

'Well, she and Carl were engaged within a month, so I reckon it worked out a treat. A honeypot for a starving bear.'

'So, Faith wasn't the boy's mother. Who was she, and what happened to her?'

'Carl's first wife passed away a few years before. Irene ... no, hang on a tick ...' He fingered his moustache, twisting an end into a point. 'Eileen. Yeah, that's it. Carl had to bring up the kid on his own, with limited help from his mother, Alice, before she went into care. Simple Simon. A funny kid. The shy type. Got on well with Faith. No surprise there, with her not being an ugly step-mother. I have a notion he had a hand in Faith and Carl meeting up. No computer dating in those days.'

I slid my phone across the table. 'Tell me about these other people.'

Stoney picked it up and eyed the screen. 'Well, that's Carl on the right. Leo, his brother, is on Faith's left. A real larrikin before he drew the short straw and got sent off to Vietnam. Returned banged up pretty bad and had trouble settling into normal life. After what he'd been through, I don't blame him.'

'Did the brothers get on?'

He gave a snort. 'Like chalk and cheese, always having a barney over something ... like most brothers. Their fights got worse after Leo's return. I reckon Carl was banking on Leo helping with the farm, but when he turned out to be as unreliable as a two-bob watch, he resented him.'

'What about Leo and Faith? How were they with each other?'

'Okay, I guess. Though Leo was hardly around during that time.'

'What about the Reverend fellow?'

I jumped along with the crockery when he slapped his hand down on the table. 'A skinny God-botherer with a gaggle of feral kids and a wife who could talk the legs off an iron pot. I couldn't stand those do-gooders. Not after the Rev refused my offer of a jolly good time at the pub, friendly local lasses included. No community spirit, that one.'

I rolled my eyes, easily imagining the conversation. 'And the woman with short hair?' I asked, tapping the phone screen to bring the photo back to life.

Stoney enlarged the image with his fingers. 'Well, whaddya know, that's Nat-the-cat.'

'Nat-the-cat?'

'That's what I called her. Had these slanted feline-looking eyes. A little petting had her purring like a kitten.'

His cheeky grin had me smacking his arm. 'You old rogue.'

'Yep, that's me. Natalie Harper she was. Her parents ran the pub here. I took a real shine to her and thought she felt the same way until she suddenly up and married the butcher, Vince Schilling. As dull as dishwater, he was, with an ugly mug to boot. What she saw in him, God only knows.' He grunted and handed me the phone.

'Schilling? You mean Natalie is Lester's mother?' Lester was one of the local realtors, who I knew well—a little too well, unfortunately.

Stoney nodded. 'He's made a proper name for himself, raking in all that dosh from carving up Shadow Creek.'

I fidgeted with the phone, passing it from one hand to the other. I needed to get to the point of this conversation. 'So ... Stoney. What can you tell me about Donna's father?'

'Carl? I've already told you about him.'

I sucked in a deep breath, swiping aside a vision of Shane wagging a warning finger at me, and dived right in. 'No, not Carl. Her *true* father.'

Stoney leaned forward, dropping his voice. 'Now, how did you get wind of that?'

I exhaled, relieved he'd taken the bait. 'Donna told me. Her mother let it slip a few years back.'

He pushed back in his chair. 'Did she now? And who was he?'

'I thought you could enlighten me.'

'But you just said Donna told you.'

'Not his identity. Just that he was someone other than Carl.'

'So, Faith hasn't spilled the beans.'

'No, she hasn't. Donna believes Faith had an affair and is too embarrassed to elaborate. She's resigned to the fact that it will remain a secret.'

Stoney's gaze drifted to an area above my left shoulder. 'What a shame.'

When thirty seconds later his attention hadn't shifted, I swivelled around. Other than a toddler in a highchair painting her face with a custard tart, and a woman re-applying lipstick by studying her reflection in a silver teapot, there was nothing deserving of Stoney's concentration.

I swung back. 'Were you ever attracted to Faith?'

The crevices in Stoney's forehead deepened. 'What do you mean?'

'Well, you're not reticent in sharing your exploits with women. Maybe you beguiled her with your charming ways.'

'Me beguile her?' A laugh shot from his mouth. 'Love-a-duck!

We're talking about Faith here, a woman way out of my league. I was near on twenty years older ... an old fart in my forties. I certainly helped her out a couple of times, and we had a few laughs. She liked my jokes,' he added with a wink. His expression turned serious. 'But an affair, well then you're barking up the wrong tree. At any rate, why are you so damned interested?'

'It's Donna's fortieth birthday soon. I thought I'd surprise her with some answers about her father.'

'And you hoped to squeeze them out of me?' He jutted out his chin. 'I wasn't privy to everything Faith Sweetman got up to. Have you spoken to her about this?'

'Faith? No. If she won't tell her daughter, then she's certainly not going to confess to me.'

'Then maybe you should just let sleeping dogs lie.'

I slumped in my seat. Was he channelling my husband? 'Well, tell me this. Did Faith and Carl have a happy marriage?'

He brushed cake crumbs from the table top onto the floor. 'I'd imagine living with Carl, who was saddled with running the farm on his own after his dad died, wouldn't have been a walk in the park for a free-spirited woman like Faith.

'How did his father die?'

'A nasty accident. A tractor rolled on top of him.'

'That's awful. And Carl? He drowned in a flash flood, is that correct?'

'Yep. It'd been pouring all weekend. He went to check on the cattle and got caught out, swept away by flood water. They found his body in nearby bushland a few days later.'

'Really? An old newspaper article I read stated he was discovered in the creek, close to town.'

'Is that right? My mistake, then. Long time ago. Fewer brain cells,' he said, tapping his skull.

'Faith didn't hang around for long after that, I believe.'

'She did a runner down south, while Leo stayed on a bit and looked after young Simon. Leo leased the property rather than sell it when they moved away.'

His comment about Faith's departure lined up with my knowledge of Donna's early life. She'd spent her childhood in Melbourne and was back there again, hopefully de-stressing.

Stoney glanced at his watch and jumped to his feet. 'Hell's bloody bells! I'd best be off. Beryl will be spitting chips wondering where I've got to.'

Though Doris was Stoney's live-in lady friend, Beryl Erbacher was the co-ordinator at the craft shop where he volunteered, and I knew it was her he feared most.

Retrieving his black Akubra from the back of the chair, he shook it in front of my face. 'Be careful, Abby luv. You don't want to be opening a can of worms. There might be a good reason for Faith not wanting the truth to come to light.' A chill washed over me as he added, 'She might not be the only one to get hurt.'

Stoney's dire warning caused me to fumble with the simple task of inserting the key into the door at Ringtales.

A hand clutched my shoulder, and I spun around, knocking my elbow into the firm belly of Reverend Graeme Roper.

'Sorry, Abbs.' He grinned down at me. 'Didn't mean to startle you. I was at The Axe and thought I'd pop in to see how things were going.'

I caught a whiff of beer breath from the church minister—more friend to me than spiritual adviser—and wasn't shocked. Drinking alcohol mid-morning was not unusual for him, or a matter for concern. It was well known he liked to down an ale or two while chatting with locals at The Axemen's Arms—Shadow Creek's heritage-listed hotel named in honour of the area's timber getting history. Sometimes the discussions turned into heated political debates, or competitions in telling the biggest yarn. Other times they went Graeme's way and he could share of the epiphany that caused him to leave a biker gang, settle down with a tolerant wife, and become an ordained minister.

I seized the opportunity to show him the christening photo.

He scratched his bushy beard as he viewed my phone's screen. 'Family pic?'

'Well, yes, but not mine. I'm doing family research for ... someone else.' No need to tell him it involved Donna. The fewer people who knew about my venture, the better.

'This was taken in front of our church. What year was it?'

'1979.'

'Forty years ago. Geez, check out the minister. Thank God I don't have to wear that get-up all the time.'

I compared the pictured reverend's ministerial robe and stole, with Graeme's regular outfit of black T-shirt, jeans, and biker boots. A silver cross pinned to the lapel of his leather jacket being the only sign he was a man of God. Times sure had changed.

I slipped the phone into my pocket and asked, 'Can you find out the old minister's name? I'd like to get in contact with him.'

'Hmm ... not looking to have me replaced, are you?'

'No way. Your drinking buddies would have me lynched.'

'Okay, it shouldn't be too hard.' He peered into the shop through a gap in the window curtaining. 'How's the setting up going?'

'You can come in for a look, if you like.' I successfully turned the key in the lock and opened the door. Graeme followed me inside.

I watched as he eyed the strewn boxes, scattered books, piles of merchandise, and disarray of chairs that gave the impression the shop had been recently ransacked.

'Stunning throne chair,' he said, stroking the ironwork. 'Still, there's a lot left to tackle here. How many days until the grand opening?'

'It's this coming Saturday.'

'Oh, well … I guess you have a plan.'

'I sure do.' I squirmed within. I really needed to get my act together and curb my curiosity—especially in matters unrelated to me or my shop.

'Don't worry, Abbs. It'll all come together in the end. I'm pretty busy myself, but if you find it's getting on top of you, give me a whistle. I might scrounge up some helpers for you. Julie might even lend a hand if she's not rostered on at the medical centre.'

'I'm sure I'll be fine,' I said. 'Now get out of here so I can go back to work.'

I pushed his hefty frame towards the exit and he wished me good luck with the sorting and decorating.

Overwhelmed by everything needing to be done, I collected junk mail that had been fed through the door's mail slot, and flopped onto a wingback chair purchased from Fine 'n Dandy. Flicking through a bunch of leaflets, a glossy brochure advertising a new photographic art gallery just out of town stood out from the rest. The name of the owner, 'an award-winning photographer', had my stomach turning somersaults.

Simon Sweetman.

Was fate showing her cards, or was it merely a coincidence? I had to find out.

8

Nestled in a valley, Shadow Creek can be reached by either of two roads from the Brisbane surrounds: one from the east, cutting through the range, and the other from the south passing Tulipwood, the acreage estate where my parents lived. A third, smaller road led west out of the village to a more rural area, Chances Crossing, named after a route used by timber getters to ford a stream coursing down from the mountain heights.

Travelling this road after my day's work, I observed more properties sub-divided into smaller hobby farms or business ventures. The area already boasted a rose farm, boutique horse stud, and hillside vineyard with cellar door, yet I only slowed when I sighted a metal sign fixed to post and rail fencing advertising, '*Sweet Art - Photographic Gallery*'.

I drove through open wrought-iron gates and parked on a gravel drive in front of a modern corrugated iron structure coloured a deep grey. Stepping from my VW, I spotted other buildings on the same property: several farm sheds further back, and perched on a rise a white-painted Queenslander-style house.

A dam edged with waterlilies lay to the left of the gallery, though no animals dotted the lush paddocks. Long gone, I presumed.

Neat garden beds directed me to the gallery entrance, and I stopped briefly to admire the healthy-looking lavender, marigold, salvia, and assorted daisies before standing before a pair of wide glass doors. I pushed one and walked into an open-plan interior lit by several skylights.

A quick scan revealed cream walls lined with intentionally spaced photographic art, their canvases attached to thin wire cables hanging from stainless steel tracks. I could see no one so I called out a hello, only to be greeted with silence. Unsure what to do next, I walked the polished timber floor, my footfalls echoing as I perused the eclectic mix of artwork.

On the rear wall I viewed powerful landscapes along with images depicting humanity's struggle to tame this great southern land: rusted farm machinery, derelict homesteads, bleached animal bones. As I leaned close to examine a striking print, my skin prickled at a sense of being watched.

I twisted around and discovered a dozen faces staring back at me. From a dividing wall, images of people—old, young, and in their prime—conveyed truths in their features and secrets in their eyes. Mesmerised, I moved near, straining to catch the whisper of a life story.

'Can I help you?' came a firm voice.

I jolted and turned to see a tall, slim man standing directly behind me. His wavy-blonde hair shot with silver hinted at him being in his late-forties.

'I'm ... er ... admiring the photos,' I said, my voice coming out thinly.

A clutch of crinkles formed at the corners of his grey-blue eyes as he smiled. 'That's exactly what I want people to do here.' He extended a tanned arm, the sleeve of his white linen shirt rolled up to the elbow, and offered me a sinewy hand to shake. 'I'm Simon Sweetman. This is my gallery.'

He looked strangely familiar, and my heart fluttered with an instant attraction as our fingers touched. Startled, I diverted my gaze to the floor and noticed his rubber-soled loafers, the reason he'd been able to sneak up on me.

I forced my eyes to meet his. 'Sorry, I know it's late in the day, but I saw your brochure and wanted to check you out.' A pesky blush warmed my cheeks. 'I ... I mean, check out the gallery.'

He gave a wry grin. 'Well, now you're here, what do you think? It's only been up and running for a few weeks. A staggered start of sorts, seeing I'm only now getting around to advertising.'

'It's lovely. Good job.' This comment, accompanied with a two-thumbs-up, made me sound like a parent encouraging her child at his first attempt at finger painting. I fanned away a second blush with the collar of my shirt.

'Thank you,' he said. 'Are there any that particularly interest you?'

I cleared my throat and attempted to sound knowledgeable. 'That's a tough question. They are all brilliant. Highly evocative.'

'Excellent. Allow me to show you something else. I want your honest opinion, now.'

Simon removed a large cloth-covered frame from behind the counter, and I followed him to a bare spot on a side wall, between an image of a lighthouse and another of a field of red tulips. 'Now shut your eyes,' he urged.

I did as instructed. Robbed of sight, another sense came to the fore, and I picked up Simon's earthy aroma, reminiscent of a disturbed herb garden. After a few dizzying moments, I was told to open my eyes.

A sigh eased from my mouth at the sight of a close-up photo of a pair of dragonflies, blue skimmers, entwined with wings in motion, mating. I noted the shady pond in the background. 'Where was this taken?'

'At a rock pool near here. A lovely spot teeming with life. Dragonflies are a devil to photograph but when you get a perfect shot, its magic.'

'I have a fascination for dragonflies,' I said. 'I rescue them all the time from indoors. It's a shame they only live a few days.'

'That's not actually true,' he said, squinting. 'As nymphs, they can live from two months to three years below water. After metamorphosis, the adult dragonfly can survive up to four more months, in the larger of the species, anyway.'

'I wasn't aware of that. Still, if I was a dragonfly, I'd rather spend what time I had soaring the skies over fields and streams than being trapped behind window glass and watching the world go by without me.'

'Don't we all. Are you a photographer, too?'

'No,' I laughed. 'Just an admirer.'

'So am I. As a kid I collected bugs, coins, feathers, you name it, before I learned how to capture beautiful things with a lens.'

'And you do it so well. How long have you been photographing?'

'Let's see.' He stared above, as if searching for an answer in the high raked ceiling. 'I got my first camera on my eighth birthday, a Pentax Spotmatic, and I pretty much haven't stopped taking pictures since.'

'I got a wig for my eighth,' I blurted out.

The look of concern that flashed across his face inferred he most likely thought I'd suffered from alopecia or, God forbid, a rabid case of head lice. An explanation was necessary.

'One year my mum had my hair cropped short to control the frizz. I hated it. What I wanted was long, swishy, fairytale hair. So, for my birthday I asked for a wig. Must have looked dorky strutting around the neighbourhood showing off my synthetic tresses to my friends, but I felt gorgeous.'

'So, this abundance of curls is real?' Simon asked. A zap of electricity darted through me as his fingers alighted like a sparrow on top of my head before fluttering away.

I blinked hard and warded off another flush. 'The colour might not be, but the hair is definitely all mine.'

'Well, if you dreamed of having long hair, you'll probably like that print up there.' He pointed to a framed image on a wall near the exit and, intrigued, I shuffled over for a better look.

It was an outdoor shot of a young woman dressed in blue jeans and a crocheted top, sitting cross-legged on grass. Though a floral bandana covered her head, the length of her dark hair was visible in the way it cascaded over her shoulders to fall into her lap. With piercing blue eyes and a wide smile enhanced by dimples, she wasn't just beautiful, she was enchanting.

'That's Faith,' I gasped.

Simon came alongside. 'You know her?'

'Sort of. Her daughter is a good friend of mine.'

'Her daughter?'

'Yes, Donna.'

He opened his mouth, however, a burble of noise followed by a group of four walking through the gallery doors stopped him from commenting. As the visitors spread out to view the artwork, Simon bent down, his lips brushing against my ear. 'Let's talk again, when it's more convenient.'

I withdrew a new business card from my shoulder bag and handed it over. 'Drop into my bookshop in Shadow Creek. I'm not open to the public yet, but I'm there most days getting ready for the opening next Saturday.'

He studied the card. 'Okay. I better go mingle with the natives.'

I gripped his arm, halting him from walking off. 'Simon, I have to confess something. I actually came here to ask you about Faith.'

His eyes widened. 'I'll visit tomorrow, if that's all right.'

I nodded, and he hurried away. On my way out, I photographed Faith's picture to share with Ross.

The sudden scrape of the verandah sliding glass door made me almost drop my iPad.

Shane stepped out and sat in the chair beside me, nodding towards the lit screen. 'Who's that?'

I cringed and glanced back at the picture of Simon Sweetman on the homepage of Sweet Art's website. I hadn't mentioned my visit to the gallery that afternoon, or the reason for seeking Simon. 'The owner of Sweet Art,' I said.

'Sweet what?'

'A new photographic gallery at Chances Crossing.' I tapped on a tab that opened to a page displaying samples of Simon's work and showed Shane.

After a few grunts of approval, Shane folded his arms behind his head and stretching out his legs to rest his heels on the deck railing. 'I didn't know you were keen on photography.'

'I'm interested in all kinds of art ... and any new local business popping up.'

'Competition, hey? Ringtales could do with a decent website.'

'It's getting there,' I said, annoyed at his remark. 'I'm planning to work on it tomorrow.' I went back to the website homepage.

'About time.' Shane pointed to the screen. 'Not a bad-looking fella. Looks a little like that actor ... you know ... from that movie.'

I gave a sigh. 'More info?'

'*American Sniper*, that's it. Brad what's-his-name.'

'Brad Pitt?'

'No, the other Brad. The one who is going to be in the remake of *A Star Is Born*.'

'Bradley Cooper?' I studied Simon's headshot and saw the similarities. That's why he'd looked so familiar. It took all my energy not to enlarge the image and run my fingertips over it.

Shane coughed. 'What compelled him to open a gallery out this way?'

My stomach knotted as I considered how much to tell. 'He grew up in Shadow Creek.'

'A local, then?'

'He moved away when young. According to this blurb, he attended Brisbane Boys' Grammar, got an Arts degree at university, then moved to Sydney as an intern with a music magazine. This took him overseas, and after a few years he went out on his own.'

'So, what brought him back here? Shadow Creek's not quite New York.'

That's for sure. 'Maybe he wanted to return to his roots. His property at Chances Crossing seems to have stayed in the family.'

'Any relatives still in these parts?'

I shrugged and teetered on confessing all when Shane dropped his feet down and stood.

'Want a cuppa?'

'That'd be great,' I said, 'make mine an Earl Grey.'

Taking a step inside, Shane swung around. 'I just had a thought. What if you asked this Simon to take photos of you in the shop for your website? I'd recommend getting a quote first. With his background, he'd most likely charge the earth.'

Shane's idea was tempting. Though Stan Gruen had photographic skills, Simon's level of expertise was out-of-the-ballpark brilliant. Not to mention, posing for an attractive man with sparkling eyes and loads of charisma would be a more pleasant experience.

9

A morning swim worked a treat. Exhausted, yet invigorated, from bodysurfing for an hour, he located his towel spread out on the beach, and shook it free of sand before drying himself. Releasing the tie from his ponytail, he ruffled his dripping hair and popped on a cap.

Hot white sand squeaked underfoot as he shuffled towards the timber stairs leading up to the park.

A surfboard appeared at the top step, followed by its owner.

'Hey,' said the tanned surfer from the previous day as he brushed past Leo. 'How ya doing?'

'Oh ... yeah, good. Couldn't be better.' Leo winked.

The young man grinned. 'Sweet.' Jogging across the sand, he waded into the water, flopped onto his board, and paddled through breaking waves to a bobbing line of his buddies.

Leo's eyes stung as he watched. When he wiped his cheek, his fingers came away wet and glistening in the sunlight. Dread swept over him like a dust storm. Pent-up memories and emotions had been surfacing more often of late. If he lacked the strength to rally them back into the darkness, was it time to set them all free?

Back home, he pinpointed an old photo album in the living room bookcase and dropped onto the sofa to flick through the stiff yellowed pages. He stopped when his eyes fixed on an image of Ned posing bare-chested in front of their section tent at Nui Dat, a Russian flag held above his head. Piled at his feet was a cache of weaponry pulled from a VC tunnel. Stumps of rubber trees left from the site being cleared years before dotted the scene, while far in the background were the hills where Ned would lose his life.

Leo quickly turned the page and discovered a photo of him and Dodge sitting at a table in a US army hotel in Saigon, happily drinking cans of beer at the beginning of a two-day leave. They'd really let their hair down during that stint—not that he could remember much, as they'd been blotto for most of the time.

Another snap—one that always caused him to tear up. This picture showed two flag-draped caskets being transferred from a hearse to an aeroplane. Ned and Dodge had a full military send-off that day, but Leo was absent from paying his respects due to being stuck in hospital waiting to return to Australia on a separate flight. His last few hours on Vietnamese soil were spent writing letters to his mates' families, reporting on their bravery, telling them they were sons to be proud of. Dodge's family had responded soon after with a thank-you letter, while Ned's, he'd heard indirectly, had been too grief-stricken to reply but were grateful all the same.

After several minutes of contemplation, he closed the album and got up. Crossing the room, he stooped to retrieve a photo that had drifted to the floor. His chest tightened. Without hesitation, he stuffed the picture of a smiling baby between the sticky pages and shoved the album into the space on the bookshelf.

10

The stepladder at Ringtales wobbled precariously as I sorted titles on a high bookcase. Steadying my balance, something dark and leggy launched out from the top shelf and dropped down the front of my shirt. A wriggle against my skin and a bunch of tiny hairy legs waving from my cleavage caused me to almost lose my footing, and I flapped my shirt to dislodge the creature.

A voice startled me further. 'Need help?'

I twisted around to find Simon Sweetman had once again snuck in without warning. 'A spider,' I cried, 'I've caught a huntsman.'

He stared at me, frowning. 'Inside your shirt?'

'Yes!' I clamped a hand over a spot of discomfort at my waist and hoped I hadn't squashed the wretched interloper to a bloody pulp.

Simon rubbed his hands together. 'Okay, what do you want me to do?'

I struggled to come up with an answer that wouldn't embarrass either one of us, and felt a nip. 'Ouch! It bit me.'

'It's harmless. No need to panic.'

'I'd like to hear you say that after it's wriggled inside your underpants awhile,' I said, reefing my shirt out of my jeans and shimmying my upper body.

When the eight-legged critter plummeted to the floor and scurried away, I re-tucked my shirt and stepped down to floor level, giving a shiver. 'Ew, that was an experience I don't want to repeat. Sorry about the mess here, I'm still sorting things out here.'

'No worries. I know exactly how you feel. There's a lot to do when opening your own shop.'

I cleared the sofa chair of paper gift bags. 'Take a seat. Do you want a cold drink? I have bottled water in the fridge.'

'No, I'm good. Just had lunch at Mulga Bill's. A great little restaurant. Have you been there?'

'A couple of times.' I stifled a grin and flopped into the wingback chair across from Simon. With my connections and discounted rates, my visits numbered in double figures.

He looked trendy today in a pale blue Ralph Lauren polo shirt and chinos. Spreading out on the sofa, his voice took on a serious tone. 'So, Abigail ... you wanted to talk to me about Faith?'

'Nope, you've got it wrong.'

He cocked his head. 'But yesterday you said that's why you came to see me.'

'No, I mean, it's not Abigail. It's Aberdeen. But everyone knows me as Abby.'

'Aberdeen, hey? That's ... er ... different.' He leaned forward, hands clasped between his knees. 'Tell me, *Abby*, how you know Faith?'

My mouth went dry, and I wished I'd gotten some water from the fridge. 'I haven't met Faith in person. I am ... um ... helping Donna with some family research. More precisely, Faith and

Donna's time here in Shadow Creek.' I removed my phone from my skirt pocket and showed Simon the group photo.

'Oh my God,' he gasped. 'I haven't seen this for years.'

'It was taken at Donna's christening.'

He glanced up. 'I took it, with that camera I told you about. Faith bought it for my birthday. You could say it was she who got me interested in photography. Did you get this from Donna?'

I squirmed in my seat. 'In a fashion.'

'So much has happened since that day. Where is she now?'

'Donna? Right now, she's holidaying in Melbourne. But normally she's here, in town. Donna and her husband own the antique store down the street.'

'You're kidding me. I've been there. Don't tell me she's that friendly redhead?'

I nodded, and he slapped his forehead. 'I don't believe it. She was a baby the last time I saw her. And Faith, where is she?'

'New Zealand at present. She's an avid traveller. Not keen on staying in one place very long.'

Simon nodded as if this was no surprise to him. 'And she's well?'

'Faith? I guess so.' I reached for my phone and tapped on the Facebook app to bring up Donna's page. 'There should be a recent photo of her here.'

I jolted at the sound of the shop door being wrenched open.

'Hey, I'm sick of walking around this dump of a town,' came a shrill whine.

In the doorway stood a girl of fourteen or fifteen, her lips drawn tightly, eyes hidden beneath a thick fringe of jet-black hair.

'Oh, hello. Can I help you?'

Simon also stood. 'Abby, this is my daughter, Keira.'

Shocked by the fact his website hadn't mentioned children, or even a wife, I snuck a look at Simon's bare left hand and ring finger before brushing past a tower of boxes.

'Hi there. I'm Abby.'

The girl thrust out an arm and pointed a finger adorned with a black varnished nail at me. I followed its direction and discovered the huge huntsman spider now encircled my upper arm like a black mourning band. I squealed and jiggled until the spider tumbled off and crawled under the throne chair—most likely to plan its next attack.

Unbothered by my reaction, Keira stuffed her hands in the pockets of her fashionably ripped jeans and eyed her father. 'I'm bored. Can we go home now?'

'Give me a few more minutes, will you, Keira?'

'You're welcome to hang here and look at some books.' I forced a smile. 'I'm sure you'll find something of interest.'

She groaned, disbelieving someone of my vintage would have a clue what a girl her age would find entertaining.

'I have heaps of fantasy books and graphic novels, if that's what you're into.' My suggestions seemed to hold no sway with her. 'How about *101 Uses for a Dead Cat*?' The new edition was a hit with Elliott, and he'd laughed himself silly—but then he was a dog person. By the sullen look on this teen's face, I was pretty sure she shared neither proclivity: a sense of humour or a love of canines.

'I'll get an ice-cream.' She held out her hand.

From his pocket, Simon pulled out a credit card and passed it over. Her dark bob bounced as she spun on her black combat boots and trudged out the door.

'My apologies. My daughter's in a bit of a mood,' Simon said, returning to the sofa.

'That's okay. I've been through two teenagers myself.'

'Her mum and I are separated, talking about a divorce. Keira is staying with me for a few weeks while Genevieve cruises the Pacific with friends from her modelling days. It hasn't been all fun and games, I can tell you.'

'The separation?'

He gave a fleeting smile. 'That too. I meant Keira's time with me. She has school work to do, but I think she's completed most of her assignments. My motivation for moving back to Chances Crossing was to offer her an alternate way of life. After living with her mum in a three-story house at Milton within earshot of the city clamour, I thought she'd appreciate the lack of pace here in the country. Even bought her a flashy mountain bike to use, but she's hardly looked at it. Thought we'd have a better relationship than ...' His eyes darted away.

Than me and my dad, is that what he was about to say?

I broke the awkward silence that followed. 'How did your father meet Faith?'

'I introduced them. It started with a visit to the Brisbane museum. The old one at Bowen Hills.'

Brisbane, August 1977

Simon barely notices the other children climbing over the German first world war tank, Mephisto, captured by Australian soldiers in the first world war. The life-sized dinosaur replicas don't even rate a second glance as he hurries from the sunny hedged garden into the shady portico of the Queensland Museum. Passing the poor old lung fish lying in the murky waters of its glass tank, he enters the cool interior of the historic brick building and inhales pungent odours of long ago. This is not his first time he has visited the nearly-hundred-year-old structure styled with domes and pillars and loads of arched windows, and not the first time he has scanned the myriad of antiquities on display, his stomach lurching with excitement. Maybe one day, when he grows up, he will be a famous collector of strange and beautiful things.

He glides by hundreds of exhibits including large-scale dioramas of Aboriginal life before white settlement, stuffed and moth-eaten lions and tigers, toothy shark jaws, and a gargantuan sperm whale. Locating the undercarriage of Bert Hinkler's Avro Avian bi-plane suspended from the tall ceiling, he hopes the cables will hold while he's here. Then hurrying up the wide flight of stairs to the next level, Simon weaves around clumps of visitors and races down rows of display cabinets, drawn once again to the largest collection of winged insects he has ever seen. Pressing his nose close to the glass cabinet, he admires them anew.

'I like the Ulysses butterfly the best,' says a voice to his right.

He cocks his head and sees a lady in a pale green dress smiling at him. Her dark straight hair reaches down to the silver belt at her waist.

'Such an exquisite blue, don't you think?'

He's not sure what 'exquisite' means but he nods anyway.

The lady moves close. 'Which is your favourite,' she asks, her sugary-sweet perfume wafting around them.

A difficult decision. He searches the cabinet and taps his finger against the glass.

She bends to view where he is pointing, her long hair falling around her like a wizard's cloak. 'The Mueller Stag Beetle,' she says, her drop earrings shimmering with the same green-pink iridescence as the beetle. 'Good choice. It would make a lovely brooch to wear on my dress, don't you think?'

He warms to her friendly nature. 'I have a collection at home,' he confesses.

'You do? Beetles?'

'Heaps of things. Lots of insects.'

'Do you pin them to boards like this?'

'Sometimes. Or I just keep them in a box.'

She scrunches her nose. 'I think I'd rather watch them flying around than catching them to stick a pin through their middle.'

Simon feels bad, like when he got caught with a mouthful of aniseed balls pinched from his father's private stash. He moves to a standing glass cabinet filled with stuffed birds, and another with snakes. Stepping to another row, he views a line of mannequins wearing military uniforms. One soldier's outfit includes an old gas mask.

'My grandfather was gassed in the first world war,' the lady says, following him.

'Did he die?' Simon asks.

'Not then, but his lungs were damaged from the mustard gas and he passed away not long after my dad was born.'

Simon nibbles his lip before saying, 'My mum died because she couldn't breathe.'

'Oh.' The lady looks sad. 'I'm sorry to hear that.'

'Not mustard gas. She couldn't breathe and the car hit a tree.'

She blinks hard. 'Do you still have a dad?'

'Yeah, he's over at the hospital. My gran had a stroke and might have to go into a special home. He's coming back at two o'clock to pick me up.'

The lady checks her wristwatch. 'That's a whole hour away. Do you want to hang around with me? My date didn't turn up, the dirty sod. He mustn't like museums like us.'

Her smile and inclusion of him makes Simon feel good inside. 'Do you like rocks?' he asks. 'There's some beaut ones that look like dinosaur eggs I could show you. They're not dead and pinned to a board,' he adds with a smirk.

'Well, lead on, my friend.'

Sometime later, while studying a shrunken head in a glass case, Simon hears his name shouted. He spins around. Within a shaft of light coming from one of the high arched windows stands his father, stiff as an Egyptian mummy, tanned face scowling through a mist of shimmering dust motes.

'I said, two o'clock, young man. You were supposed to be waiting downstairs at the entrance. Had a devil of a time finding you in this rabbit warren of a place.'

Simon rushes forward. 'Sorry, Dad. I've been showing a lady around the museum.'

'A lady?' His father's hazel eyes sweep the vacant corner. 'What lady?'

'This one,' the woman says, springing out from behind a collection of Zulu shields. 'Simon's been a wonderful guide, very informative. He stepped in to help when my date stood me up.' She holds out her hand. 'I'm Faith.'

Simon's father rakes his fingers through his dark crop of hair before giving her hand a polite shake. 'I'm Carl ... Sweetman.'

His neck flushes a deep pink above the collar of his shirt when Faith croons, 'Sweet ... man,' really slowly, like she's tasting each syllable.

'Can she come visit us?' Simon asks.

'What?' His father's eyes shrink to narrow slits. 'No ... no, I don't think that'd be suitable.'

'Please, Dad,' he begs, 'She's never been out to Chances Crossing ... or even Shadow Creek. I could show her heaps of stuff. The cows, the creek, how clever Patch is at catching sticks—'

A firm hand clamps down on Simon's shoulder.

'Sorry,' his father says to Faith, 'excuse my boy, he gets a little excitable at times. Thanks for keeping an eye on him.' He shoves Simon towards the stairs, but before they reach the landing, Faith calls out.

'I'd love to come.'

His father halts, and turns, one eyebrow cocked. 'Really?'

She nods and walks over, the heels of her sandals clicking on the floorboards. 'I'd enjoy seeing the farm. Simon told me a lot about it. If you like, I could give you my phone number, and you could give me a call to arrange a time.' She flashes a wide toothpaste-commercial smile.

The man clears his throat. 'Well ... no harm in getting your number, I suppose.'

Faith removes a small spiral notebook and a pen from her shoulder bag and writes something down. When she hands the page to his father, their fingers touch and linger until his father pulls away.

'I'll catch you later, Simon,' she says with a wink, and then skips down the stairs ahead of them.

Simon's dad clips him over the head. 'What the hell have you done, boy?'

'A few weeks later, Faith turned up at the farm and stayed for the weekend. She and Dad must have been phoning each other. She came out to visit a few more times over the next couple of months, and on one of those visits they announced their engagement. It was pretty quick, but I couldn't have been happier. They got married mid-December, and we celebrated Christmas Day as a new family.'

Fast, alright. I'd be horrified if my daughter married someone after such a short time. 'Was your Mum an asthmatic?' I asked, puzzled by his earlier comment.

He answered with a nod. 'She was trying to get her puffer when she lost control of the car. We crashed into a tree not far from home.'

My stomach sank. 'You were in the car with her?'

'Yep,' was all he said.

I changed the subject. 'What was Faith like as a mother?'

Resting back, he stretched out his long legs. 'More like a big sister. Being only five when my mum died, my memory of her was different to how I saw Faith. She seemed too spirited to fill that role.'

I compared his opinion to the Faith I knew through Donna—restless, distant, and complicated. I guess age does that to a person … or sorrow … or regret.

A ping sounded from his phone and he checked the screen. 'It's Keira. I better go. I'm supposed to be spending quality time with her, which is rather difficult when you're running an art gallery.'

Simon's sudden departure left me disappointed and kicking myself. I still hadn't mentioned the mystery of Donna's conception.

11

Two text messages interrupted my afternoon: one from Ross Clarke inquiring if I'd gotten his previous text about dropping into Fine 'n Dandy for a chat and a coffee, and the other from Graeme Roper asking if I could meet him at The Axe for a chinwag over a pot of beer. *What to do?*

In the end, I chose to meet Ross first and delay the conversation with Graeme till just before heading home.

Ross thrust a coffee into my hand as I stepped in the antique store. Ushering me to a parquetry table, he sat me down and placed an embroidered coaster on the table top for my mug.

'How's your investigating going?' he asked, his eyes bright with interest.

I slurped the beige liquid and shuddered at its weak taste—definitely instant. Instead, of putting my foot down and halting our silly venture, I mentioned what Stoney had said—which wasn't much more than what Ross already knew—and told him about my meeting with Simon Sweetman. I even showed him the photo I took of the image of young Faith, which surprised and intrigued him.

Though I shared my concern about digging up a hurtful past, Ross suggested if something malicious or distressing had happened, then bringing it to light might help mend Faith and Donna's rocky relationship.

That made sense. We could become orchestrators of healing rather than perpetrators of destruction.

Ross offered to search for more clues in the old photos, and I said I'd keep him in the loop if I discovered anything else of worth.

A row of shiny motorbikes parked outside The Axe showed the pub was doing a roaring trade.

I spied Rev Graeme sitting at a corner table, his shaved head reflecting the flashing, coloured lights of the nearby poker machines. Today he was holding court with a ragged bunch of leather clad bikers. To a casual observer, it would have looked like a hearty discussion between fellow enthusiasts—drinking beer and raucously talking shop. But to someone in the know, I guessed there was a greater depth to their conversation.

Rather than disturb them, I sat at the bar, twisting on a stool and wondered if Graeme had information about the church minister. With luck, Faith may have confided her troubles to her spiritual adviser and shared her pregnancy situation. I wasn't too sure about the confidentiality protocol, but maybe there was a chance I could persuade the old reverend to divulge what he knew.

A scraping of a chair caused me to look up to see Graeme strolling over.

'Hi Abbs, sorry to keep you waiting.'

'That's okay. A fine bunch you've gathered together today.'

He glanced back at the rowdy mob. 'Turns out I know a couple of the blokes. We used to ride together in the old days. Good times back then ... and plenty of bad,' he added with a raspy chuckle. 'Want a beer? My shout.' He waved to the bartender. 'The same again, thanks Trev ... and she'll have a ...' He raised his eyebrows at me.

'Lite ale ... and a packet of chips to help soak it up.'

Trev tugged a packet from a shelf and flung it my way, then lifted two glasses from the drying rack and pumped out our order.

'What's the news?' I asked Graeme, now seated on the stool alongside.

'I have details on the minister who was here in the seventies.'

I swivelled around to face him. 'Who was he?'

'A Wesley McKenny.'

'That's great. What else have you got for me?'

He swigged from his glass and wiped froth from his beard. 'Well ... there's good news, and then there's bad. Which do you want first?'

My shoulders slumped, 'I hate that question. Let's get the bad news out of the way.'

'Okay. Wes's dead.'

My chips exploded from the packet and into my lap. 'Dead? No!'

'Yeah, sorry about that. A brain haemorrhage took him out two years ago.'

'Damn.' I gulped down a mouthful of ale. 'Well, that's stopped me in my tracks.'

'Wait, you haven't heard the good news yet. His wife lives in Spring Hill, with their daughter. I have her contact details.'

I hadn't considered on going any further than questioning the reverend. Now he had passed, his family might shed some light on the Faith matter.

'What's this all about, anyhow? You seem very secretive, Abbs. Anything I should be concerned about?'

I swallowed a potato chip. 'It's to do with Donna Clarke. Were you aware she was born here in Shadow Creek?'

'No, I wasn't. I thought their move here was a lifestyle choice.'

'The photo you saw the other day, the one I dropped, was taken at Donna's christening.' I chose my next words carefully. 'I'm helping Ross do some research for Donna's fortieth birthday and thought if we found the minister, he might offer some memories of that time.' There, that would have to do for now.

'Well, Mrs McKenny could help you out. She probably has more to tell you than her husband would have. You know how observant women are.'

Being one myself, I certainly did. And I was intuitive enough to realise he was being polite. What he really meant was how prone women are to gossip. I took no offence at that.

He fished inside his shirt pocket and removed a slip of note paper. 'Call her and let me know how it goes.'

The snake tattooed around Graeme's forearm seemed to wink at me as I took the paper from him.

I made the phone call to Linda McKenny as soon as I got back to the shop. The high, childlike voice confused me until she confirmed I was speaking with the correct person. Linda seemed pleasant, and I fibbed yet again, saying I was researching on behalf of Rev Roper about the history of the church and wished to talk to her about her and her husband's time in Shadow Creek. She sounded keen to meet up, and I arranged a visit for mid-morning the following day. I had to go into the city to collect an order of shop gifts, anyway.

. . .

I went to collect my dinner from Sam's Pizzeria and found Lester Schilling waiting on a bench outside. Pristinely dressed, as usual, in designer shirt and tie, and polished leather shoes, his fingers flittered over the keys of an iPad. Another real estate sale negotiation, I assumed.

'Hi, Lester, how are things?'

His eyes darted up from the screen. 'Oh, hello, Abby. Things are terrific. Business is going gang-busters. Sold a million-dollar property up your way on the weekend.'

'Good for you,' I said with a pang of envy. 'How's the family?'

'Fine. Kids are good. A little too good, I reckon,' he added with an eye-roll.

'And Karen? All good between you two?'

'Yes ... of course.' His botoxed features attempted a frown. 'What's it to you how well we're doing?'

I easily raised my eyebrows at him.

He coughed and patted a recalcitrant strand of hair into place. 'Don't go there, Abby. I've apologised already. It's all in the past. Never going to happen again.'

Thank God! 'How's your mum, then?'

'My mum? Doing okay. Looking after Dad. Why?'

'I'd like to have a chat with her.'

'What about? You're not planning to bring up what we—'

I held up my hand. 'Hell, no. I just wanted to find out what she can remember of Shadow Creek from the '70s. I've met a few people she might recall.'

'Oh, that all. Mum likes a good natter. You should phone her, or drop in. She could do with a distraction. Gets a bit tiring caring for Dad.'

'How's his Parkinson's?'

He gave a shrug. 'Getting worse, more's the pity. I'll text you her number.'

'Lester, your order is ready.' An attractive and shapely blonde appeared in the shop doorway with an armful of pizza boxes. 'I made sure they included extra pepperoni and jalapeños on the Supreme. I know how you like it hot,' she said, grinning.

As she offloaded the boxes to Lester, mine were not the only eyes drawn to the printed words stretched across her tight black T-shirt: *Mmm ... Tasty.*

Lester flashed her a toothy smile. 'Thanks, Lois, you're the best.'

She fluttered her false eyelashes and disappeared back inside the shop, while I stared at Lester, shaking my head.

He shot me a look. 'What?'

I tut-tutted and moved inside to see if I too could get some free extras on my pizza.

12

Leo glanced up from his plate of scrambled eggs and sausages to view Simon's invitation now returned to the fridge door. The typed words *Chances Crossing* stood out from all the rest.

Chances Crossing, January 1978

He arrives at the farm early in the morning after driving six-and-a-half hours straight from Port Macquarie for his mother's funeral. Her sudden death from a major stroke had taken them all by surprise. None the least Leo, who hadn't seen her since a fleeting visit to Brisbane over Christmas, that hadn't included a trip out to Chances Crossing.

He parks his station wagon next to Carl's ute and walks to the rear of the house, hoping to slip in through the back door. Adjusting his backpack, he falters at the sight of a figure in his mother's vegetable plot. He shakes aside the thought she'd risen from the dead to say goodbye, and diverts around the Hills Hoist clothes line to cross the lawn. His breath lodges in his throat for a second time. The woman crouching and digging in the soil, dark hair falling to her waist from beneath a wide-brimmed bamboo sunhat, sets his heart thudding and his vision dims.

Tackling mozzies and leeches, the platoon wades through a rice paddy, passing a buffalo working with four children on its back.

The kids wave and shout, 'Uc dai loi! Uc dai loi!' Land down under —their name for Australians. They climb off and come over, pestering the soldiers for lollies and cigarettes.

Back in the scrub, the platoon comes across a man and a cart, the women and kids alongside selling soft drinks. This is supposed to be a war zone, yet they can't seem to get away from the locals.

The men spread out, and Leo and Ned enter a small clearing centred by a vegetable garden. Among rows of greenery and stick tripods entwined by growth, black and gold fowl scratch the earth looking for tasty morsels. To one side crouches a woman, her face shielded by a traditional bamboo sunhat. They watch as she plucks leaves, snaps stems, and unearths roots, dropping them into a woven basket at her feet.

Leo calls a greeting and she looks up. She is young and beautiful with almond-shaped eyes that blink back at him. He holds out a packet of smokes and her smile reveals perfect white teeth.

He draws closer and halts when she tips over her basket and jumps up. With a chilling shout she raises a rifle to her hip, but Ned and Leo both beat her to the shot.

'Hello, there.'

The gentle voice draws Leo to 1978.

The woman in the vegetable patch is standing and brushing

dirt from her baggy black pants and loose linen shirt. She walks over to the wire fence and tilts back the sunhat he now recognises as the one he sent his mother from Saigon years before.

'You're Leo, aren't you?'

He nods and sees the dark-haired beauty is no more Asian than him.

Azure eyes glint like jewels as she smiles and offers a soiled hand to shake. 'I'm your sister-in-law, Faith. Sorry we didn't invite you to the wedding. It was just a registry office ceremony.'

13

I purchased bookish knick-knacks from a busy little store—a treasure trove of gift ideas—and arrived earlier than expected at the inner-city suburb of Spring Hill. Not wanting to seem too eager, I parked my car across from Linda McKenny's house and walked the hilly, jacaranda-lined streets, admiring the profusion of heritage-listed workers' cottages as I searched for a coffee vendor.

According to my father's genealogy research, my great-great-grandmother worked as a laundress in these parts back in the 1880s. I imagined her in one of the tiny houses, sweating over a boiling copper or wielding a heavy coal-fed iron, and appreciated that laundering was now less labour intensive.

On Wickham Terrace—noted for its health services—I ducked into a cafe on the ground floor of a high-rise tenanted by medical specialists. Sipping my takeaway cappuccino, I crossed the road to a park and peered up at the oldest surviving stone building in Queensland.

My first memory of The Old Windmill Observatory was viewing it during a primary school excursion and learning of its dark and brutal history. Built by convict labour in the 1820s when Brisbane was known as the Moreton Bay Penal Settlement, a harsh punishment for the repeat offenders sent up from Sydney Cove was to work the treadmill to grind maize into flour while wearing leg irons. After free settlement, the mill's hilltop position overlooking the town centre and serpentine river allowed it to become a signal station and an observatory from which panoramic sketches, paintings and, later, photographs were made to chart the town's growth.

The school history lesson had been informative but, as a ten-year-old, what had interested me more was hearing the legend of two Aboriginal men hanged at the windmill for killing a surveyor and his assistant and whose ghosts were claimed to haunt the tower. I remember studying the small glass windows below the observation deck, hoping to glimpse a troubled spectre. Today, as I scanned for apparitions, I pondered on what else haunted people other than the dead. Terrible secrets kept out of fear of recrimination or hurting love ones could also bring torment. I mulled this over. Did Faith ever have trouble sleeping? What would compel her to tell Donna the truth?

I checked the time. If I didn't hurry, I would be late for my appointment.

The same shrill voice I'd heard on the phone greeted my door knock.

'If that's Abby Eaton, you can come in!'

I turned the knob and stepped into the entry of a cottage larger on the inside than it appeared from the road. I peeked into a sitting room on the right which resembled a florist shop—one that had exploded. Flowers were everywhere, in the curtaining, upholstery, carpet, framed prints, and spilling out of an abundance of vases. I strangely detected no floral fragrance, only a hint of burnt toast.

Expecting a diminutive woman to match the voice, I flinched at the sight of Linda McKenny's giant frame filling a recliner chair. Not only was she rotund, she was also tall and broad-shouldered. With wild frizzy hair, a broad nose, and sprouting eyebrows, she looked like an Amazonian gone to seed. Her tracksuit, blue Crocs, and thick ankles encased in compression stockings did nothing to soften her appearance.

'Welcome,' she said with a flourish of a massive hand. 'Sorry, can't get up. It's taken me ages to get into this contraption and unless you want to see an old girl thrashing around like a fish out of water, I'm not moving. Take a seat.' She nodded to a regular armchair across from her.

I sat awkwardly, sharing the seat with two over-stuffed cushions.

'Biscuit,' she grunted.

'Pardon?' I removed a stash of magazines from behind one of the cushions.

'An Iced VoVo? A Ginger Snap?' She indicated a jar on the coffee table.

I shook my head. 'No thanks, I'm fine.'

'Well, be a dear and pass me the jar.'

I did as I was told.

'My daughter Chantelle lives here with me,' Linda said, pulling out a handful of biscuits and lining them side by side on the mound of her stomach. 'She's forever telling me to eat healthy, but I have such a sweet tooth.'

Watching her shove a whole ginger biscuit into her mouth and munch away, I wondered if I had to wait until she'd consumed the whole row before starting our conversation.

Linda coughed a mouthful of crumbs onto her chest. 'So, Abby, how can I help?'

I shuffled to the edge of my chair. 'As I said on the phone, I'm helping Reverend Roper chronicle the history of the Shadow Creek church by contacting past ministers and noting their recollections. We aim to put a book together ... a memoir of sorts.' My nose itched. Was it growing longer because of my lies? 'So sorry to hear your husband has passed away.'

'Yes, two years next month.' She let out a sigh. 'I'm happy to offer reminiscences because I was there too, you know.' Her grin revealed biscuit remnants had settled between her top teeth like grouting.

Before I could pull a notebook and pen from my bag, Linda was off and racing.

'It was Wes's first posting, and we were only there for six years. 1973 to the end of '79. He took up a position in Maryborough after that, a much bigger parish. More people to care for.' She pointed to a framed photograph hanging on the wall between two ink drawings of a young man and woman, presumably Mr and Mrs McKenny in their youth. 'Such a devout and dedicated man, my Wesley. A loyal servant of God.'

I stared at the portrait behind glass of a man with thick grey hair and a narrow face. He looked to be around my father's age, though more weathered with age spots and furrowed cheeks.

'He's about to receive a posthumous award from the diocese, in recognition of his tireless service to the community. I will, of course, be receiving it on his behalf. A proud moment for all of us.'

'That's nice,' I said, flipping open my notebook, eager to move on. 'And how did you find the people of Shadow Creek?'

She rested her hands on her belly. 'A mixed bag that lot. On the whole, friendly folk, welcoming and ready to roll up their sleeves and give a hand when the call came. Then there were those who kept to themselves. There were also plenty of the sort who wouldn't step inside a church if you paid them. One such rude fellow enjoyed pushing Wes's buttons. He once tried to hustle my poor husband into the hotel and force a few questionable ladies on him. A disgusting man.'

I stifled a laugh. *Gladstone Maloney, you certainly made a lasting impression.*

'Anyway,' she continued, 'we had a good turnout most Sundays. A full house at Christmas and Easter. No room to breathe then, I can tell you. And the women's fellowship had a decent following. Those country women love to bake. One lady, Mildred Rosethorne—'

Geez, this could take forever. I skipped several planned questions and butted in with, 'Do you remember the Sweetman family at all?'

She blinked twice. 'Sweetman, did you say?'

'Yes. They had a property at Chances Crossing. Len was the father's name, but I'm not sure if he was still alive when you were there.'

She shook her head. 'Don't recall a Len.'

'His wife was Alice. They had two sons.'

'No, sorry. Doesn't ring any bells.' She fidgeted with the front of her top, as if searching for leftovers.

I took my phone from my bag to show her Donna's christening photo.

She brushed her hands free of crumbs before taking it. 'A photograph? You'll have to fetch my reading glasses if you want me to view it properly. I think they're on the kitchen table. Get me a glass of water while you're there.'

I got up and went into the hallway. Opposite was another sitting room, this one decorated in beige and a light shade of aqua

—more soothing to the eye. Down the hall, I passed a bedroom on the right fashioned with gaudy florals, and another on the left with the decor of a beach house—shells and driftwood included. It was as if mother and daughter had divided the house between them, right down the middle.

The modern open-planned dining room and tidy kitchen were obviously the daughter's domain, with pencil drawings of sea creatures adorning the walls. I found Linda's glasses on the table, sitting between a daily devotional book and a dog-eared romance novel with a cheesy cover of scantily clad lovers. Taking a glass tumbler from the drying rack on the sink, I filled it with water from the tap and returned to Linda.

She gulped her drink down in one go, and putting on her glasses, studied my phone. 'What's this, then?'

'A christening photo. Your husband is there, I believe.'

Her voice rose an octave. 'Why, yes he is. My word, how young he looks. Very handsome.'

'Do you recognise the others?' I asked, testing her memory.

She squinted hard. 'Good God!' An Iced VoVo slipped from her lap to the floor. 'There's that infernal rascal who tormented my husband. What's he doing there?'

'He was a neighbour of the Sweetmans.'

'This is a Sweetman christening?'

'Yes. The baby's name was Donna. Her parents were—'

'Carl and Faith,' she cried. 'That's them there. I remember now.'

At last, I was getting somewhere. 'Well then, what is your memory of Carl?'

'Carl?' She played with a tuft of hair growing out of her chin. 'Serious ... a hard worker. Came to church when he could.' She waved the photo at me. '*Whatever you do, work at it with all your heart, as working for the Lord.* That's a bible verse, dear, Colossians 3:23.'

'Oh ... okay.' Unsure if I should thank her for this nugget of wisdom, I kept my focus. 'What do you recall about his wife, Faith?'

She nodded. 'Hmm ... Faith. It's slowly coming back to me. She attended a number of church committee meetings and caused a bit of a stir, if I remember rightly. Wanted to make changes to move with the times. Well, we couldn't have that. Newcomers have to earn their place in a country town. Yes, a little too worldly for Shadow Creek.'

'In what way?'

Linda's nostrils flared as if alerted to a scent—my nervous energy or an opportunity for gossip? I hoped it was the latter.

'Let me just say,' she paused to lick icing from her bottom lip, 'Faith was overly friendly with the menfolk. I had to take her to task on several occasions for her impropriety. She settled down after having the baby. No time for socialising then, that's for sure. I should know.' She pointed to another wall, and more framed photos. 'Five children. Conceived in quick succession. They kept me on my toes, well and truly.'

Among this array I spotted an aged photograph of her children together—all pudgy redheads with freckled faces and corkscrew hair.

'Your wife shall be like a fruitful vine within your house, your children like olive plants around your table,' Linda proclaimed. 'That's from Psalm 128.'

I imagined myself germinating like a triffid, while Gemma and Elliott sat at the dining table sprouting leaves and eating from bowls of fertiliser.

'Anyway, what's this got to do with the church's history?' Linda slid her glasses down the bridge of her nose. 'It all seems odd to me.'

Crunch time. I swallowed hard. 'Linda, I have to confess there's another reason for me being here. Donna, the Sweetman baby, is a friend of mine. She's about to turn forty and for her birthday present I am helping to put together her life story. That's how I came across the christening photo.'

Linda groaned and listed sideways, dropping one arm over the side of her chair. I thought she might be having a stroke until I heard the flick of a lever, and a squeak of the chair's footrest as it descended.

She planted her size twelve feet on the floor and folded forward. 'The baby is now forty? How can that be? But then again, a few of my children are nearing fifty, so that makes sense. How time flies. Where is she living?'

'Shadow Creek. She and her husband moved there a couple of years ago to run the antique store.'

'And Faith?'

'She travels a lot, but owns a luxury waterside apartment in Hamilton with a quick commute to either the cruise terminal or the airport. At the moment she's holidaying in New Zealand.'

Linda slumped back, looking more relaxed, so I ventured on.

'Was it a happy marriage?'

She narrowed her eyes. 'Ours?'

'No, Carl and Faith's.'

'Oh ... I guess so. But they weren't married long. Carl drowned in the farm dam.'

'Er ... no, it was in the creek,' I corrected. 'He got washed away in a flash flood.'

Her lips puckered. 'Are you sure?'

'Most definitely.'

'Well, same outcome. I think Faith and the child left the area soon after. All for the best, I suppose. Do you have a photo of Donna all grown up?'

I searched my phone and found one of her and Ross taken at a recent party we'd attended together. 'Ignore the outfit. She's not normally a fortune teller.'

Linda glanced at it. 'And her husband isn't normally a ... what is that ... a bear?'

'A werewolf. It was a Halloween party.'

She grimaced with distaste and studied the photo. 'Donna's a redhead?'

'Yes. Had the most wonderful fiery curls as a toddler.'

Her eyes darted to the photo wall. Her sallow complexion seemed to pale further. 'You need to leave,' she said, pushing up from the recliner. 'I have things to do.'

Surprised by my curt dismissal, I stood and found Linda towered over me like a mighty behemoth. I encouraged her to call me if she remembered anything else about the Sweetmans, and handed over a business card.

Linda was pensive as she steered me to the front door, and I feared I'd taxed her too much with my questioning.

'Thank you for your time,' I said, as the door slammed shut, leaving me standing alone on the porch.

I stepped down to the path and faltered when a wail burst from inside the cottage, followed by the noise of breaking glass.

Hurrying back up the stairs to see if my help was needed, I froze on the coir doormat as a shout reverberated through the door panelling.

'*The evil that men do lives after them. The good is oft interred with their bones!*'

I noted that Shakespeare had trumped the Word of God this time. With a glance to make sure no neighbours were peering over

86

fences, I crouched and pressed my eye against the keyhole, hoping to spy a clue as to my next move. Wes's picture sprawled on the hall floor among shattered glass, and an outburst of profanities coming from Linda's sitting room gave me my answer.

I was in my car and driving off in less than a minute.

14

The sea breeze brought with it a drop in temperature and the melodic clang of a brass wind chime. From the deck chair on his balcony, Leo located the sound to the apartment below, tenanted by a couple of young high-flyers relocated from Brisbane and dipping their toes into the coastal property market. Attuning his ears, another wind chime came to mind from the past.

Chances Crossing, January 1978

Sitting on the front verandah of the farm house in January of 1978, he notices a recent acquisition of his new sister-in-law hanging from a rafter. Made of bamboo, with a painted dragonfly knocking a wooden disc against hollow pipes, it stirs a horrid flashback.

The platoon spreads out as they patrol yet another rice paddy. Leo climbs onto a grassy mound that bears the tombs of the dead. As is the custom, villagers bury their relatives on raised ground in the centre of the paddy fields so the departed can watch over their work and bring good fortune and fruitfulness to the family crop. He rests on a crumbling edifice and props his rifle between his knees as he surveys the area that is more swamp than field. Leo removes a packet of smokes and a fold of matches from his shirt pocket, and he lights up.

It is restful here. He mops his face with the sweat rag draped around his neck and takes a long drag of nicotine.

A noise. Movement over his shoulder.

Gripping his rifle, he swings around, surprised to find a young girl standing behind him. Where'd she come from? She is twelve or so, fine-featured, with dark hair falling like a waterfall to her waist. Round eyes stare at him from under her bamboo hat. She is mixed race. Part Aussie or Yank? Something glints in her hand, a pocket knife. He stiffens and spits out his cigarette.

'What's that?' he demands, pointing to her other hand.

She uncurls her fingers to reveal a fine wooden object. 'Con chuồn chuồn,' she says, tapping it with the blade of the knife and miming what Leo recognises as whittling. 'I make'. Then, holding it above her head, she moves the blue-painted piece through the air. 'Fly.'

'Oh ...,' he grins, 'you make dragonfly.'

'Yes. Make drag-on-fly.' She presents it to him. 'You want?'

'Sure.' Though when he reaches for it, she draws her hand back.

'Cigarette,' the girl says with a wide smile. 'You give cigarette.'

He laughs and offers his packet of smokes in exchange for the carving which he examines closely, admiring the girl's craftsmanship. 'You have more?'

She nods and pulls a second one from beneath her loose shirt, this one painted red.

Leo pats pockets and shakes his head. 'No more smokes.'

'Photo,' the girl says, pointing to the camera slung over his shoulder. 'You take photo. Send back home.'

He obliges and takes a snap. 'I'll tell my family about you and your
... chwan chwan?'

'Con chuồn chuồn. Is good luck. I make more. You pay.'

'You're a smart cookie. Okay.'

A sharp whistle from one of his platoon, and he is motioned back.

Faith suddenly appears on the verandah and catches Leo swiping away tears. She sits with him and draws him into a gentle conversation. Under her spell, he opens up about his time in Vietnam and losing his mates. He even confesses to shooting the woman in the vegetable patch and Faith does not recoil. However, when he jumps up, rips the dragonfly from the wind chime, and tosses it into the yard, Faith's look of dread sends him inside to the safety of his bedroom.

Later, when Leo assumes everyone has gone to bed, he creeps from his room and slouches at the kitchen table intending to drink his way through a six-pack of beer. But Faith walks in when he is only halfway and demands an explanation for his violent action. With hands trembling, he tells her about his meeting with the young Vietnamese girl in the rice paddy, and the incident that followed, imploring her to not tell a soul.

That afternoon their section sets up a claymore mine ambush beside a paddy field. All is quiet until rifle fire blasts the night apart. Ned says he heard noises in the bushes nearby and given the sneaky bastard a taste of his M16. At daybreak, a search in the scrub reveals a dead chicken.

'Maybe it was a Viet Cong scout,' someone jokes.

The following evening after another ambush set up, Leo and Dodge are on piquet duty together. They study the stars and the beauty of the velvet sky, and talk about home, God, their fears, and dreams for the future. Once again, an uneventful night makes them wonder if the villagers are giving away their position. How in the hell are they supposed to know who to trust? Just before dawn, Leo hears rustling in the bushes. Chickens scratching for bugs? Then come voices— Vietnamese. He sprays the scrub with bullets. Silence.

When the sun rises, they find the body of an unarmed village boy of about fourteen. A bloody trail leads them to a girl, face down in the dirt. On the ground beside her, in a splatter of colour, are several carved dragonflies.

Faith's attempt at consoling him falls flat. 'You weren't to know the voices belonged to kids,' she says. 'You did what you were trained to do. Defend. Survive.'

He hurls a beer can at the wall and stomps out into the dark.

Leo rose from the deck chair and gripped the balcony railing of his apartment till his knuckles turned white. Surviving also brought guilt, and triggers which turned a person into a pathetic wreck or an angry drunk. *Peacetime* was what they called the intervals between wars. Yet for those, like him, who witnessed the horrors, tranquillity was as elusive as a dream upon waking. Forty-seven years and Leo was yet to dispel the thought that if it wasn't for him taking an interest in the dragonfly carvings, the Vietnamese girl may have survived that futile war.

15

Driving into Shadow Creek, I noticed Graeme Roper's motorbike parked out the front of the church, the chrome flashing with reflected sunlight. Had he discovered any additional information on Wes McKenny? I needed to find out.

I parked my VW behind the bike and crossed the footpath. Unlatching the iron gate, and stepping up to the arched doorway of the century-old building, I found the door ajar and slipped inside. A hush greeted me. Light filtering in through stained-glass windows enabled me to view the colourful cloth banners hanging on three of the four timber-panelled walls. Made by children from the Sunday School and depicting well known Bible stories, one creative account had me chuckling. Among the varied animals entering Noah's Ark were a pair of tyrannosaurs and two yellow Minions.

Much had changed in the five years since Graeme had ridden in to town on his throbbing steed and taken over the ministry of this church. But not the message—only the way it was delivered.

Several wall-mounted floodlights, a video projector bolted to the ceiling, and a drop screen above the raised platform testified to modernisation. An upholstered bar stool—most likely pilfered from The Axe—standing centre stage behind a microphone stand was another indicator. However, as far as I was aware, only a few of the old guard had kicked up a fuss at being ushered into the 21st century way of doing church, and all of them had been men. Graeme could do no wrong in the eyes of the female parishioners. I put it down to his rugged charm and winning smile—and his eagerness to sample their culinary delights.

To the right of the stage was the vestry, now used as an office, in which I hoped to find Graeme. I headed in that direction when the sound of sniffing had me swinging around and squinting to make out a figure in the back row, hunched against the wall. Deliberating whether to offer compassion or leave them in their sad contemplation, a loud sob had me rushing over.

A head lifted at my approach and I recognised the face now streaked with black eyeliner.

'Keira? Are you okay?' I moved into the row before hers.

'What do you think?' she snapped, sniffing and blinking away tears.

I pulled a handful of tissues from my bag. 'Sorry. Here, these might help.'

She snatched them up. 'You're that spider woman,' she said, and blew her nose.

'Pardon? Oh ... yeah,' I grimaced, recalling my wimpy response to the eight-legged critter's sudden appearance. 'Is there anything I can do? I'm a good listener.'

Her thick hair swayed as she shuffled further into the corner. Another sob came out as a hiccup. 'Why would I want to talk to *you*?'

'Well ... I've weathered the storm of two adolescents who've now reached adulthood relatively unscathed. I'm sure whatever you say will not surprise me.'

She frowned. 'You've got kids?' Then she eyed my left hand resting on the back of the pew. 'You're married?'

'Most definitely,' I said, taken aback at her disbelief. 'Have been for twenty-five years.'

'Then why were you hitting on my dad?'

I cringed. 'Your dad? At the shop? I wasn't hitting on him. We were talking about his childhood ... when he lived out here.'

Her eyes bore into mine. 'Is that all?'

'Pretty much.'

'My mum's coming home soon,' she said, throwing back her head.

'From her cruise?'

'Yep. We've missed her like crazy ... Dad and me.'

That's not the impression I'd gotten from Simon. 'And you'll all live at Milton ... together?'

She scowled and fidgeted with the hem of her shirt, bunching it in her hands, then smoothing it out. 'Do you believe God hears our prayers?'

'Sure,' I answered truthfully. 'I reckon God ... the Universe ... whatever you want to call the higher power, hears every prayer. Though whether they're answered in the way we expect is another matter. Sometimes what we want isn't the best outcome for the situation.'

'I want my parents to love each other again,' she said.

I felt sorry for the poor girl. 'Whatever happens, their love for you won't change, you know that, right?'

'Life's shitty,' Keira hissed. 'I miss the city. Miss my friends. Another week before I go back to school and I'm bored stiff.' She inhaled a deep breath and let it out. 'I had a big fight with Dad at the post office, shouting and stuff, and he drove off without me. Who does that to their kid? He texted me and said to call him when I was ready to apologise and come home.' She chewed her bottom lip so hard I expected to see blood. 'What if I'm never ready?'

I reached down and gently squeezed her knee, surprised she didn't pull away. 'We can't have you wandering around Shadow Creek like a stray dog. How about you come back to my shop for a bit? I could do with some help.'

She narrowed her smudged eyes. 'What sort of help?'

'Giving me a hand in setting things up. My grand opening is hurtling towards me and I'm nowhere near ready.' An idea sparked. 'Have you had any experience with data entry? I have loads of book titles you could enter into the system. It's time-consuming, so it'd free me up to do other things.'

'I helped my dad list his pictures. That was easy enough.'

'Good.' I turned at a noise coming from Graeme's office, chair legs scraping on floorboards. 'Look, I need to catch up with the Reverend. I'll meet you at the shop in, say, ten minutes and show you the programme I'm using. You could tell me if the job is something you'd be interested in.'

'Will I get paid?'

'Hmm ... we'll work something out.'

I saw her smile for the very first time. 'I'll buy a cold drink,' she said, and eased out of her row. 'Thanks ... er ... Abby?'

'Yep, you got it.'

Keira walked outside while I headed towards the vestry office. I lifted my fist in readiness to knock on the door when it burst open.

'By crikey!' Graeme cried, lurching back and ripping earbuds from his ears. They dangled from the phone he held in his hand. 'How long have you been here, Abbs?'

'Not long. I've been talking with Keira.'

'Who?'

'Keira Sweetman. You may not have met her yet. Her father has opened a photographic gallery at Chances Crossing. Sweet Art.'

He scanned the interior. 'Where is she?'

'She's gone now. Was a little upset. Family problems.'

'Sorry.' He tapped the phone's screen several times. 'Been listening to a podcast. Can I help you with something?'

'I've just been to visit Linda McKenny, the old minister's wife, and I wondered if you'd come across any other info on Wes's time here.'

'You're in luck. Found a box of church records he kept. Minutes of meetings, details on church members, things like that. They might include something of interest to you. I'll just get it.'

He disappeared into his office and returned a few seconds later to drop a cardboard archive box at my feet. 'It might take a while to go through, but something helpful might turn up.'

I studied the box bursting with bound books and assorted stationery. No doubt I'd need several mugs of coffee and an entire block of chocolate to get me through this lot.

Keira arrived at the shop five minutes after me.

I showed her the software programme and let her have a play. She knew her way around a computer—no surprise there—and quickly picked up the inventory management section.

'Too easy,' she said, with youthful nonchalance. 'Scan and alphabetise.'

I waved my hand over the room littered with cardboard boxes. 'There are still quite a lot of books to enter.'

'I got nothin' better to do.' She stepped from behind the makeshift counter consisting of a sheet of ply balanced on two sawhorses and lifted a box from a pile.

I glanced at my watch. 'I've arranged to meet somebody. Will you be okay here by yourself for an hour?'

Keira rolled her eyes. 'I'm not a kid. I don't need babysitting.'

'If you haven't done so, you might want to give your dad a call and tell him where you are.'

'Yeah,' she shrugged, 'maybe.'

16

Scenes, as vivid as when they occurred, drift into Leo's dreams during his afternoon nap.

Chances Crossing, January 1978

Music wakes him. Leo slides out of bed and staggers to the bathroom, his head fuzzy from the previous night's binge drinking. He splashes his face with cold water and stares at his reflection in the tarnished wall mirror, unsurprised he looks like hell because he feels like he's downed shots with the devil. A jackhammer pounds within his skull to the beat of the infernal racket coming from ... *where?* He turns and faces the window. *Outside?*

On the verandah, Leo notices an electrical cord leading downstairs and across the yard. Intrigued, he follows, and is guided towards the rose garden. Before rounding a screen of leaves, the music stops. So does he. A few seconds of silence, and then it starts up again, a more tender tune this time.

He peeks through thorny branches and spies a record player resting on a wrought iron garden table, the black vinyl spinning and gleaming in the morning sunshine. A figure flutters past, gauzy blue wings suffused with flashing silver. Faith is a magical creature come to mesmerise him with her graceful moves as she dances to the song's lilting rhythm and haunting vocals.

When she sees she is not alone, Faith doesn't pull up and gasp as one would expect at being discovered, but smiles back at Leo, pirouettes, and curtseys.

'So, you're out of bed, sleepyhead,' she says, her kimono robe as sheer as gossamer settling gently against the satin nightgown worn beneath.

Leo turns his gaze away from the clinging fabric and steps from behind the rose bush. 'The ruckus woke me.' He thumbs towards the garden table.

'Ruckus? Have you no appreciation for Fleetwood Mac?'

'I'm more of a Creedence Clearwater kind of guy.'

Faith sighs and glides over to the record player to flick the lever and raise the needle from the vinyl. The music ceases.

'Another rough night?' she asks.

Leo pulls a face and folds his arms across the stained T-shirt he hadn't bothered to change out of before going to bed last night.

'Where'd you learn to move like that?' he says, changing the subject.

'Always loved to dance. Formal ballet as a child. Jazz ballet as a teenager. Had dreams of becoming a choreographer. Took some lessons, but ...' She shrugs. 'Life happened.'

'You could run dance classes in town, for the local girls. Earn a little cash for yourself. Put on performances.'

She nods towards the house. 'Yeah, like that would ever happen.'

'Surely Carl wouldn't stop you from doing that.'

'I'm his little bird in a gilded cage.'

Leo chuckles, then realises she is serious. 'He's not your jailer. You're a grown woman. You can do as you please.'

Now it's her turn to laugh. 'Believe whatever you like, Leo.' Unplugging the record player, she picks it up. 'Can you bring that cord with you when you come in?'

Then she floats away.

March 1978

For some odd reason, Leo returns to Chances Crossing earlier than planned.

He and Faith sit side-by-side on the front steps drinking iced tea. The planting of a jacaranda tree and assorted varieties of native grevillea has been a welcome task and come spring, when masses of flowers bloom, honeyeaters will thank them for their labour.

Leo rests back on his elbows and offers his bare chest to the afternoon sun. Today he is content, his mind free of the buzz of agitation. He closes his eyes and breathes in scents of tilled earth and Faith's exotic sandalwood perfume. Working alongside her has given him a sense of comfort, a hint of normality, a glimpse of a life he'd always yearned for.

He flinches at a stab of coldness and discovers Faith bending over him, running a shard of ice over his chest. She trails it over his abdomen and stops just below his ribcage where the shrapnel scar lies pink and puckered like a gruesome crooked smile. Stroking it with her pinky finger, her eyes lift to meet his.

He frowns. 'That doesn't disgust you?'

She pops the ice remnant into her mouth and shakes her head. 'Not at all. It's part of you, so why would it? The scar is a reminder that you cheated death.'

Conflicting emotions compel him to turn away. 'But why me? Why not Dodge or Pete? I wasn't any better than them. They were good blokes.'

'No one knows why some are chosen and others aren't. That's fate. I guess all you can do is make sure it wasn't all in vain. Don't waste this gift of life, Leo. You were saved for greater things.'

He turns back. 'Me?'

'Yes, you. Sure, tragedy tears you apart, but it also offers a chance to reinvent yourself. That way you can put yourself back together any way you want. A do-over, if you like. Dwelling on the horrors of the past just drags you down.'

There's a tremor in her voice, a flash of pain in her sea-blue eyes. What horrors had once held her captive?

'You've got to live life to the full,' she urges. 'Live it for Dodge and Pete.'

Leo grits his teeth. *How in hell was he supposed to do that?*

'Don't sell yourself short,' she says. 'You are more amazing than you realise.'

A scoffing laugh catches in his throat when Faith reaches up and smooths hair back from his face, the soft skin of her wrist brushing against his cheek. He focuses on her dimples, her mouth, the tip of her tongue as it slips out to moisten her bottom lip. *God, she is stunning.* Even her hair twisted into a granny's bun and her frayed singlet worn with grubby denim overalls take nothing away from her beauty, only enhancing it. If she wasn't his brother's wife …

Footsteps on floorboards.

Leo twists and peers up to see Carl at the top of the stairs. Dressed in a pressed white shirt and good trousers, he looks to be heading into town to the pub.

Faith distances herself from Leo. 'Carl, how long have you—'

'Get inside,' he demands, nodding towards the door.

She rises and thrusts her shoulders back. 'What's your problem, Carl? We were just talking.'

'You heard me, get inside. Leo and I need to have a chat.'

Faith sneaks a troubled look at Leo before dashing up the stairs, purposely knocking against Carl as she stomps past.

When his brother descends, Leo leans forward and grips his knees in readiness for the admonishing he is about to receive.

Carl stands in front of him and kicks Leo's foot with the toe of his polished boot. 'So, you piece of shit, what game are you playing at?'

Leo shakes his head. 'Not playing any game, Carl.'

'I'm not an idiot. I know what I saw.'

With his chest puffed out and fists clenched, Carl is busting for a fight. But he's not getting one today, not if Leo can keep his cool. Even the gold signet ring, inherited from old Len, glints from Carl's right middle finger, the flashing bloodstone goading Leo, reminding him who was the preferred son. Still, he holds his tongue.

'You're doing it again,' Carl snarls. 'Faith isn't Eileen. She's not weak. She's settled. Happy. So, leave off.'

'Happy?' Leo gives a wry laugh. 'Are you sure about that? I've heard the arguing.'

'All couples argue. It's nothing.'

'Punching holes in walls isn't nothing. A wife smashing china and throwing vases isn't a sign of contentment.'

Carl scowls back. 'And you think you know everything about marriage, do you, brother? Don't see you married. Can't even remember you ever having a serious girlfriend. So you have no idea how relationships work.'

'I know women don't respond well to being treated like possessions. Not Mum, not Eileen ... no one. I guess, once again, you're following Dad's lead.'

'That's a crock of shit. Mum was happy. Everything she wanted was here. The house, the farm, us.'

'You don't think she dreamt of something more? She was a head teacher at a girl's school when she met Dad. You can't tell me her aspirations died once she tied the knot. And Eileen would have been more fulfilled if you hadn't discouraged her from going back to nursing. Maybe she wouldn't have taken off and got herself killed if you'd given her what she needed.'

Deftly catching Carl's fist before it smashes into his face, Leo sees the bloodstone wink at him, as if impressed by his quick reflexes. 'Now, now. You don't want to put on a show. Faith is probably watching, and her opinion of you might plummet even further. Then I might have to offer her a shoulder to cry on .... or something more satisfying.'

Carl yanks his hand back and leans in, his mouth only inches from Leo's ear. 'Touch her and you're a dead man. I mean it, Leo. I won't think twice about stringing you up and watching you bleed out while the dogs fight over your severed balls.'

Leo shoves him away. 'Well, don't keep Faith so caged up. Give her what she wants.'

'And what would that be?'

'Freedom to soar. To live without constraints.'

'Hah! You know nothing, Leo. What she wants, I can't give her. And that's the catch.'

The rasped words surprise Leo. Watching Carl stride away, he hears a noise from behind and spins around.

'Everything okay?' Faith asks, rushing down the stairs.

He stands so they are at eye-level. 'Yep, just Carl letting off steam.'

She clutches his arm, her fingernails biting into his flesh. 'We can't let that happen again, Leo.'

'Let what happen?'

She gives a puzzled look. 'Didn't we just—'

'We?' he butts in, and wrenches her hand away. 'I didn't do a thing.' Then he hurries upstairs to pack his bag.

17

Natalie Schilling welcomed me into her house with a flurry of excitement similar to a puppy greeting its owner after a long day left alone. She led me to a dining table bearing home-baked goodies and a 'crazy tea set'—purposely mismatched china cups, saucers, and side plates—and told me to sit.

My concern rose when this woman, so dissimilar to her self-assured son, struggled to pour tea into the delicate china teacups without spilling. I noted her wobbling head and trembling hands. Was Natalie's anxiety because of my visit? Maybe she didn't get many visitors.

'Thanks so much for allowing me to drop in for a chat,' I said, my eyes drawn to her blouse incorrectly fastened with the top button not having a hole to feed into. 'No need to have gone to all this trouble.'

'No bother,' she said with a twitchy smile. 'Vince is away for the day at respite, giving me more time to do other things. You wish to talk about the past?'

'Yes, that's right.' I took a scone from the plate pushed in front of me, broke it in two, and dolloped strawberry jam on each half.

Natalie pointed above my right ear. 'My parents owned The Axeman's Arms for a spell.'

I twisted around and viewed a framed photograph of the hotel hanging askew on the wall behind. The orange coupe parked out front—a Holden Monaro GTS, just like the one my uncle had spent years restoring—gave a clue to the photo being taken in the 1970s.

'I got to hear a lot about the goings-on in this town. Not on purpose, mind,' Natalie added with a facial tic.

So, she's a mine of information. I'd come to the right place. 'Actually, I'd like to know about the Sweetman family.'

'Len and Alice? Lived here for many years. Len bought—'

'No,' I interrupted. 'I mean Carl and Faith. You were at their daughter's christening.' I removed my phone from my bag and tapped the screen to bring up the photo.

The phone shook in her grasp as she squinted to focus. 'How did you guess that was me?'

'A friend told me. That's him standing with you.'

'Oh.' She looked up. 'Gladstone Maloney is your friend?'

I nodded and Natalie slid the phone back across the tablecloth so fast it would have collided with my teacup if I hadn't blocked it with my hand. Had I hit a nerve?

'What do you remember about Carl and Faith?'

Natalie licked a smear of cream from her bottom lip and studied me through narrowed eyes. 'Why are you so inquisitive?'

'Their daughter, Donna, is also a friend of mine. I'm helping research her family history and thought you might be able to fill in some gaps.'

'I see.' Her eyes softened. 'Well, I went to school with the

Sweetman boys, but Faith was only here a couple of years. She was Carl's second wife. He and Eileen had a son, Simon.'

'Yes, I'd heard that. What kind of person was Faith?' This was becoming a mantra.

'A fish out of water living here. She came to the pub with Carl on the odd occasion and we struck up a friendship of sorts.'

'Of sorts?'

'Faith noticed me. She didn't look down her nose at a girl working hard pulling beers for her parents. Showed an interest. Asked if I was happy and if I dreamt of a life away from Shadow Creek.' Another twitch of her mouth. 'Things like that.'

'And did you dream of living somewhere else?'

She rested her elbows on the table and steepled nail-bitten fingers. 'Of course I did. I wanted to become a famous author and write bestsellers.'

I coughed. 'You wanted to be a writer?' I hoped she hadn't tweaked to my surprise.

'I gobbled up romance novels like sweets. Tried writing my own and thought I might be the next Jackie Collins.'

'And do you still write?'

'No.' She twisted the gold ring on her left hand as if trying to tug it free. 'Life got in the way.'

'Are you aware that I'm opening a bookstore in town? Ringtales. I wouldn't mind reading some of your work.'

'Oh, dear, I'm not very good.'

'Who says?'

'Me. I wouldn't dare let anyone else read what I've written. A load of rubbish, most likely.'

I reached over and patted a hand that felt like crêpe paper. 'You are your own worst critic, you know. I could at least give a second opinion.'

Her cheeks flushed pink, and she slid her hand out from under mine. 'Maybe I could dust something off and pass it on.'

The chiming of a wall clock had me checking the time. Best to move on. 'Now, back to Carl and Faith. Did they have a happy marriage?'

'Let's see.' Rolling her eyes as she considered this, she reminded me of a creepy google-eyed ventriloquist doll my dad once owned which scared the pants off me and my sisters when we were kids. 'They were happy at first, like all newlyweds. But then, about six months into their marriage ...'

I leaned in with eager ears as Natalie recounted the event.

Shadow Creek, May 1978

Starting her shift at The Axe, Natalie does a double-take when she recognises the young woman seated at a corner table behind a potted philodendron. Usually calm and collected, Faith Sweetman is swaying like a palm tree in a tropical storm.

'How are you, Faith?' Nat says, taking three empty beer glasses from the table and stacking them on the tray she brought with her.

Faith squints through hair fallen free of its clips. 'Oh ... hello, Nat. I've seen better days.' She goes to take a sip from the half-full glass she holds when her elbow slips and the glass shatters on the floor. 'Oops,' she says and giggles.

Nat squats and picks up the larger shards of glass which she places on the tray. 'C'mon, sweetie. You're already sozzled. I have no idea why my dad served you so many drinks. I'll be having a word with him later.'

Faith shakes her head. 'I'm not drunk. Az-a-madder-of-fact,' she slurs, 'I do this *all* the time. Just not here.'

Nat steadies Faith as she tilts sideways. 'There you go, how about a cup of coffee? That should set you right.'

'No way.' Faith points towards the bar. 'I'll have another beer, thanks, Nat-ar-lee.'

'Why are you drinking alone? Only galahs drink by themselves.'

'Hey, I'm not alone, you're here with me.' Faith pats the metal chair beside her. 'Pull up a seat.'

Nat clutches her hand. 'I think you should go home. Where's Carl? I could go fetch him.'

'Hey, I need a beer,' shouts a man in overalls banging his fist on the bar.

Natalie catches his eye. 'Give me a sec, won't you, Reg?' Turning back to Faith, she asks, 'Does Carl know where you are?'

'He's buggered off again to buy more cattle, leaving me alone for a few weeks with the kid. Sometimes I feel like a live-in nanny. Anyway, how am I supposed to get pregnant if he keeps running off? It takes two to make a baby, right?'

'I didn't know you were ready for that. Where's Simon? Not home on his own, I hope.'

'No, he's at the showground with school friends. I ... I couldn't stay.'

Nat pulls a face. 'I don't blame you. The crowds. The noise. Those annoying carny folk talking everyone out of their hard-earned cash.'

'That's why I came here.' She clutches Natalie's hand by the wrist and squeezes tight. 'It was awful. I had to get away ... get away from ...' There's terror in her eyes, red veins stark against the white.

Natalie offers Faith a handkerchief from her apron pocket to mop the tears now trickling down her cheeks. 'Get away from what?'

'Hey, I'll pour my own bloody beer, will I?' shouts Reg from the bar.

Nat gives him a glare that shuts him up and turns back to Faith. 'Look, luv, you're in no fit state to drive. How about I go ask Dad to man the fort so I can give you a lift home?'

Faith drops her head into her hands and moans. Natalie takes this as a 'yes' and dashes off to locate her father.

Returning minutes later, she finds Faith is nowhere in sight. A search around the pub, the beer garden, and the ladies' toilet proves fruitless.

'If you're looking for that good-looker who was full as a tick,' Reg says, swivelling on the bar stool, 'then I have to tell you she's scarpered.'

Nat hurries to the doorway and scans the dark street for Faith's station wagon. Perturbed that it is not among the few cars parked kerbside, she groans. 'God, don't tell me she's driving back to Chances Crossing.'

Reg stands alongside her, his hand wrapped around a schooner of beer he must have poured himself. 'Nope. Stoney Maloney dropped in. They had a little natter and then left together. He probably thought he'd won the jackpot with that pretty young thing.'

Natalie clenches her jaw. 'For your information, that pretty young thing is a married woman who knows better than to give a bloke the wrong idea.'

'Maybe if she was sober.' Reg gives a sly wink.

Nat spies Stoney's dilapidated ute parked three cars down. Living on a property next to the Sweetman's, he'd surely just been neighbourly in offering to drive Faith home in her car—nothing more.

Then why did Nat's stomach squirm like a sack filled with rats?

Because she knew darn well he'd try his best to get lucky on a Saturday night.

~

I frowned and reached for the jam dish. 'What are you implying, Natalie? That Stoney saw an opportunity to get more friendly with Faith while Carl was away?'

Now it was Nat's turn to lean in. 'I found out a few days later from Jenny Bailey, who lived across the road from the Sweetman's, that she saw Stoney sneaking down their driveway at the crack of dawn the next morning.'

'That doesn't mean anything lewd happened. Maybe he just stayed on to make sure Faith was okay.'

'But he was shirtless, dressed only in trousers and boots. Not even a hat. Hardly ever saw him without a hat, you know.'

'Simon would have been there. Surely nothing would have gone on with the kid around.'

'Well, the thing is, the boy stayed at the Thornton's that night. Jenny's son, Craig, also attended the sleepover.'

My heart skipped several beats. 'So, Faith and Stoney were alone.'

'All night,' Nat added, with a click of her tongue.

I had to admit it sounded suspicious. Still, I couldn't wrap my head around the idea that Stoney would lie to me about his relationship with Faith. 'Would Faith have wanted Stoney to ... er ... comfort her in her loneliness?'

'She may not have had all her wits about her at the time. She was very drunk, and vulnerable, and he could be a real charmer. Maybe Stoney took advantage of the situation.'

'Took advantage? You don't mean he ...' I couldn't even say the words. The jammy spoon dropped from my hand to clatter on my side plate. Stoney might talk about being a rogue in his younger days, but he wouldn't have assaulted a woman. 'Did you ever ask Faith about that night?'

'I didn't have the gumption. I had no desire to embarrass her into a confession.'

'What if she'd been coerced? She might have appreciated a listening ear, a friend's compassion.'

Natalie jumped up and began to stack the used crockery.

I took this as a hint that our conversation had ended.

I thanked Natalie for her hospitality and encouraged her to drop a sample of her writing into the shop. Both remarks were met with silence. Yet when I opened the screen door to step outside, she dragged me back in.

'Beware of Stoney Maloney,' she croaked, shaking her knobbly finger in my face like an old crone. 'He's not all he seems.'

The skin on my arms goose-bumped. 'Natalie, did Stoney ever … um … take advantage of you?'

She surprised me by dropping into the hall chair, her body crumpling like a deflated blow-up doll. 'I … I've told no one of this.' Her left leg juddered, causing glassware in the hall cabinet to tinkle. It was then I noticed she wore two different shoes—a slipper on one foot, a low-heeled court shoe on the other. A problem with bunions? She grasped my hand. 'Stoney raped me.'

Shock smashed into me like a tsunami, and the room spun. I tugged my hand from hers and pressed it against the wall to steady myself.

'It happened a week or so after Faith was drunk at the pub,' Nat continued, her voice steady, monotone. 'It was a busy night. Stoney followed me down into the cellar to check on stock. We had a habit of flirting with each other, but I never trusted him enough to go out with him. So, when he tried to kiss me, I objected. The next thing I was on the ground and he was fastening my hands together with his belt. He ripped off my skirt and wrapped it around my head and face to stifle my screams. I couldn't see a damn thing. Then he wrenched the rest of my clothes off. I struggled, but he was too strong.'

She hugged herself as if trying to cover her envisaged nakedness.

'Afterwards, with neither a sorry or thank you, he went back upstairs, leaving me to sort myself out. When I returned to the bar, I discovered him having a drink and a laugh with some other blokes, as if nothing had happened. As you can imagine, I didn't finish my shift.'

I was dumbstruck. *Stoney was a rapist.* When I found my voice, it came out as a whimper. 'Did you tell anyone?'

'Of course not. I was ashamed. Who'd believe me, anyway?'

'And he never tried it again?'

'I asked Vince, just an acquaintance at that stage, to hang around after the evening sessions. He became my bodyguard without knowing it.'

'Oh, Natalie.' I squeezed her bony shoulder. 'I'm so sorry that happened to you.'

She looked up at me, her eyes brimming with tears. 'When Faith told me she was pregnant a month or so later, it got me wondering.' She shifted in her seat. 'Abby, it's very likely that your friend is Stoney's child.'

I jolted back, bumping against the cabinet and further unsettling the glassware.

I'd never thought of myself as gullible—quite the opposite, in fact. Now, with the revelation of Stoney's true nature, it appeared my discerning ability wasn't as sharp as I'd believed.

18

Keira proved to be helpful. She added a good number of titles into the system, while I took my mind off Stoney and his wicked ways by shelving books alphabetically in genre groups.

When four o'clock came, I suggested to Keira that I drive her home to Chances Crossing rather than have her father come in to town to collect her. She showed her agreement with a 'thumbs up', and I suggested she choose a book as payment for her efforts. Without hesitation, she surprised me by choosing *The Little Prince* by Antoine de Saint-Exupéry.

When we reached the Sweetman property, Keira directed me to drive uphill and park near the house in the shade of a massive jacaranda tree. Getting out of the car, I found the height offered outstanding views of the farm. Nearby, an ancient iron shed leaned at an angle that defied gravity, while below, in a paddock to my left, rusting farm machinery looked to be grazing in the verdant field like ageing oversized beasts. A paddock to my right held a circular dam, its water reflecting hues of pink and gold from the setting sun. Edged by weeping willows, it also boasted a timber jetty and a white-painted gazebo alongside. With many picturesque backdrops to choose from, had Simon considered hiring the property out as a wedding venue?

Keira offered to give me a hand in the shop again the following day and then rushed up the front stairs of the sprawling Queenslander. Shouting to her dad that she was home, I gathered she'd already offered an apology to him by phone.

I followed her up to the verandah and discovered Simon leaning against the doorframe.

'G'day, Abby,' he grinned.

Shirtless, his well-defined chest glistened with perspiration. A drop of sweat slid down my cheek as my eyes drew left of centre to a tattoo resembling a gaping rip in his flesh. From this realistic gash crawled a cornucopia of inked insects: beetles, butterflies, caterpillars, and a lone dragonfly. Shane had recently gained an intricate arm tattoo that I rather liked, but this one took creativity to a whole new level. It took all my nerve not to reach out and stroke it.

'Hi,' I said, lifting my gaze to his face. 'Keira's been a great help in the shop. She's saved me a couple of hours of mind-numbing work.'

'She can be a great little worker when she wants to.' His eyebrows bucked beneath strands of sweaty hair. 'I guess she mentioned we had an altercation.'

I shrugged. 'She might have mentioned something.'

'Bloody teenagers think they know everything.' A twitch of his left pec brought the colourful swarm to life. 'I've been building a new garden bed down by the gallery. I could do with a cold drink. Want to join me?'

'Sure. I have some time to spare.'

As Simon pressed flat against the open door and ushered me

inside, I tried hard not to sideswipe anything bare, moist, or squirming with bugs.

In the hall, he lifted a shirt from a wall hook and fed his arms through the sleeves. 'Wine? A cheeky chardonnay?'

'Oh, that kind of drink. Perfect.'

'Why don't you head out to the back verandah. Through there,' he added, thumbing over his shoulder. 'I'll meet you outside in a tick.'

I walked through a lounge and then a dining room, surprised by the outdated furnishings. With the gallery being so modern, I assumed the same decor would have extended to the house, or at least matched the era built, circa 1910 by my calculations. Yet it seemed I'd returned to the 1980s with tones of peach and mint and faded florals doing little to enhance the white wicker and Baltic pine furniture. I made a mental note to set aside several books on redecorating to aid Simon in giving the house a much-needed makeover.

French doors opened onto a wide verandah overlooking a yard dappled with afternoon light and planted with native shrubs and rose bushes. Beyond this, I glimpsed a paling fence with gate attached attempting to deter a dense forest of bracken and eucalyptus. I chose one of two deck chairs separated by a small glass-topped table, and was about to sit when Simon appeared with a cheese platter and wine glasses. I relieved him of the bottle wedged under his arm and placed it on the table.

While he uncorked the wine and filled the glasses, I loaded a cracker with a wedge of brie and waited for him to start the conversation.

'As you've probably noticed,' he said, sitting in the chair alongside. 'I still have to whip the house into shape. Genevieve has all the good furniture. I'm using what the last tenants left behind. My priority has been setting up the gallery.'

'How long has your family owned the property?'

'My grandfather bought it in the fifties. Ran it as a dairy farm before subdividing it, and then downsized to a small herd of beef cattle in the sixties. Grew corn and barley too, I believe. Dad and uncle Leo had to help each day, before and after school.'

'Did they get along, your dad and Leo?'

'Like most brothers. Dad ran the farm single-handed after my grandfather died, and continued with his grass slashing business. He hoped when Leo finished his armed service he'd partner him, but Leo didn't want a bar of it. The farm was okay to visit from time to time, but not somewhere to settle down. Whereas Dad got his love of the land from pop, a tough old bugger. Leo getting called up to do his bit in Vietnam gave him a means of escape, I reckon.'

'He was wounded there, right?'

Simon nodded. 'Yep, though he was one of the lucky ones. It must have played on his mind because he drank heavily back then and had trouble sleeping. He'd be up at all hours of the night listening to the radio or smoking in the dark. I'd walk past his room on my way to the loo and see the red glow of his cigarette. Sometimes he'd call me in and ask me about my day, and we'd end up chatting. But I was hesitant to ask him about the war. Maybe it was the look in his eyes.'

'What sort of look?'

'Haunted ... pained. Faith seemed to have the right approach, knowing when to ignore him and when to show interest. Not like my father. Leo in a sullen mood would disgust Dad and end in a shouting match. I remember him saying he thought fighting in the war would make Leo a stronger man, but it had sent back a fucked-up bludger.'

'That's cruel.'

'You bet. Leo put in plenty of work around the farm when he

was here. He was just inconsistent with his visits. He'd take off for months and then return hung over and bruised from fights. Then he'd work flat out for days before taking off again. He changed after Dad's death, what with the responsibility of looking after a kid.'

'I heard your father drowned in a flood.'

'Yeah.' Simon clenched his jaw and a tendon on the side of his neck became as taut as a length of rope. 'It'd been raining full on for days. He went for a walk to check on the cattle or something and didn't return. His body turned up the next day a few kilometres away, lying in a field of water-flattened sunflowers.'

A field of sunflowers? Yet another version of events. 'And you and Leo stayed on here?'

'Until the end of the year. Then we moved closer to the city, and I started school at Brisbane Boys Grammar. If it wasn't for Leo, who knows where I'd be.'

Good on Leo for pulling himself out of his woes to care for his nephew on his own.

Simon refilled his wine glass. 'We have a more distant relationship now. He hasn't visited here yet. Too many bad memories.'

'Did either of you keep in touch with Faith?'

'Not at all. Leo was just as shaken up as me when she split. My guess is he couldn't forgive her for running off so soon after Dad's death.'

The need to broach the subject of Faith's great secret niggled like a whining mosquito at bedtime. While Simon sipped his wine, I jumped in before I lost my nerve.

'So, you didn't see Faith as a replacement for your mother?'

'As I said the other day, she was more a big sister, or maybe an aunt. She was only twenty-two when she married Dad. We had a lot of fun together, Faith and I.'

'Doing what?'

'Before coming to live with us, she worked in a city record store and owned an impressive collection of albums. When Dad was away, she'd turn up the stereo and teach me dances like The Twist and The Nutbush. We'd also go on adventures around the property, pretending to be on safari, tracking wildlife. Not to kill, but to observe. The truth is, I had a little crush on her.' His eyes glinted with a hint of mischief. 'But then I wasn't the only one.'

My interest kicked up a notch. With any luck, I wouldn't have to bring up the subject about Faith's affair at all. Simon might even serve the answer I sought on a silver platter. 'Who else?'

'Well, Reverend McKenny, for starters.'

My hand jerked, spilling drops of wine on my blouse. 'How did you know that?'

'Kids notice way more than people realise. They may be advised to be seen and not heard, but they are never told not to watch.'

'Is that your excuse for being a little perv?' I joked.

He chuckled. 'Well, being an only child, I spent a fair bit of time in the presence of adults, which proved informative on occasions. That and peeking through the odd keyhole. Anyway, Faith got involved in local church stuff, charity fund raisers and such. Sometimes they'd have meetings at our place and the Reverend always hovered around Faith, scribbling stuff down in his notebook. Once I caught him alone in the lounge room giving a discarded cardigan of hers a good old sniff. A pretty weird thing to do, right? I told Faith, but she just laughed it off.'

'Sounds creepy to me. Linda said she and Wes were blissfully happy.'

'Linda?'

'Wes McKenny's wife.'

The blue of his eyes deepened. 'You've met her?'

'Earlier today. She lives at Spring Hill with her daughter. Wes went to heaven two years ago.'

'Why were you visiting her?'

Should I tell Simon the lie about doing research on the church, or the one about helping Donna with her family history? He probably wouldn't believe either of them.

'I'm looking for Donna's real father.'

A beat, and then he answered. 'You know about that?'

'Donna shared it with me. Faith told her a few years ago Carl wasn't her dad. It came as quite a shock.'

'So, it's true, then.' His face stiffened. 'Who was he?'

'No idea. Donna doesn't even know. Faith refuses to tell.'

Simon got up and leaned over the railing. 'Poor kid. That's cruel of Faith not to tell.'

'Got any ideas?' I placed my glass on the table before shifting forward in my chair.

He remained staring out at the garden. 'Faith shooting through with the baby devastated me. I thought we were a family, and she up and abandoned me. As I got older, I realised there had to be more to it, especially since she never contested Dad's will leaving his half of the farm to me alone, not divided between any living offspring. When I suspected Donna wasn't his kid, Faith's desertion made sense.' He turned around to face me. 'She'd left because she had no real ties with us.'

Simon arched backward and closed his eyes, his fluttering lashes resembling two winged creatures trapped between folds of skin. He wasn't merely attractive, he was strikingly handsome. What made someone more perfect than another? The shape of their nose, their mouth, their eyes? Or facial symmetry, how well the features fit together?

His eyes flew open, and I looked away, praying I hadn't been caught gawking.

'Have you any leads on who the father is?' he asked.

I groaned, not ready to share my suspicions about Stoney. Not until I'd confronted him first. 'Still searching. I hoped to have some answers by the time Donna returned. Thought it might be a nice surprise for her.'

'Nice surprise?' Simon's glare made my stomach knot. 'What would be nice about finding out you were conceived from a sleazy one-night stand? Or the reason your parentage was in question was because of too many potential suspects?'

He stepped close and bent over me, his hands gripping the arms of my chair. 'Would you like to learn your mother was a horny little slut?'

My eyes darted from his gritted teeth to his heaving chest, where the bugs seemed to scurry out through the gap in his shirt. I clutched his arms to push him away when I heard footsteps. Twisting around, I saw Keira standing at a distance.

Her eyes landed on mine before moving to her father's. 'What's going on?'

Simon straightened and flicked hair from his face. 'Just having a friendly chat, that's all, honey.'

Friendly be damned. 'I best be off,' I said, rising.

Simon placed a hand on my shoulder and eased me back down. 'Give us a few more minutes, Keira. Then you can help me with dinner. I guess that's why you've slunk out of your room.'

With a huff, she spun and disappeared inside.

'More wine?' Simon asked calmly and refilled my glass before I had time to reply.

What the hell? Where had that rage come from? More importantly, where had it gone?

I looked towards the sliding door. Could Simon have actually been talking about his wife? Was he worried Keira might find out the truth about her wayward mother? There had to be a story behind his reaction. Best left alone for now.

I steadied my breathing, yet my voice came out shaky. 'You intimated there were others infatuated with Faith. Who else besides Wes McKenny ... and you?'

He gave a fleeting smile. 'I can't provide names. I only remember Dad accusing her at the dinner table of being overly friendly with the local men, and Faith getting all feisty and saying he was from the dark ages. He punched a hole in the kitchen wall that night.'

I rubbed my arms in response to a cool breeze picking up ... or the thought of such fury. 'What about Gladstone Maloney? You remember him, don't you?'

'Stoney?' He nodded slowly. 'He lived on the property next door, where the winery is now. A burly bloke with a huge moustache who liked to crack jokes. You know him?'

'I do. He lives in town now.'

'What age is he? Got to be seventy-odd.'

'More like early eighties. Was he an aggressive sort?'

'Aggressive?' He shook his head. 'Just rough around the edges. He helped Dad after Pop died. Don't tell me he had the hots for Faith, too?'

I ignored that question. 'Does anything stand out in your memories about him and Faith?'

'Let's see ...' His eyes drifted skyward before flitting back to mine. 'There was ... no ... I'm not sure.'

'You're recalling something?'

'I have a memory of catching Faith with some guy. She was upset, yelling and shoving him out the back door.'

'You think it was Stoney?'

'Not sure, it happened pretty quick. But I saw a bushy

moustache like his, and he wore a hat. A floppy cap, very mod at the time.'

I cringed. Stoney and his bloody hat obsession. 'Did you ask Faith about it?'

'I wouldn't think so. What kid would? Anyway, I was more concerned about my arm.' He gripped his left wrist. 'It got burned. I still have the scar.' He held it out for me to see.

I studied the zigzag of puckered flesh on the inside of his wrist. 'How did you do that?'

'I did nothing. Timmy Thornton used a stick to stir a fire and then got cocky, pretending it was a light sabre. Seared me good and proper.'

'Timmy Thornton?'

'A school friend. A few of us kids stayed at his place for a sleepover and we built a campfire in his back yard. Cooked marshmallows and stuff.'

'A sleepover?' Words from Natalie Schilling's conversation with her gossiping friend rang in my ears.

'We'd been to the Shadow Creek Show that afternoon. I must have got dropped off home the next day and that's when I walked in on Faith and this bloke ... Stoney?'

Sadly, Simon's story fell in line with Natalie's. 'Did he have a shirt on? Shoes?'

'Geez, I don't remember. What's that got to do with anything?'

'Well, was it early morning? Before breakfast?'

'Not likely. Mrs Thornton made the best pancakes, so I reckon I'd had a proper feed before being dropped home.'

Maybe Stoney returned to talk about what had happened the previous night, to apologise. I really needed to have a serious chat with him.

The sound of screeching overhead. I looked up to see a wave of fruit bats flapping through across the darkening sky in search of something ripe to feast on.

'I should make tracks. It's dinnertime.' I reached for my bag. 'Well, give it some more thought and see what else you remember.'

Simon walked me to my car.

'Sorry for losing it back there,' he said, holding the door open as I slid behind the wheel. 'You hit a nerve or two. All this talk about Faith dredged up things I assumed I'd dealt with.'

My thoughts flipped again—perhaps Faith *was* the slut he referred to. I turned the key in the ignition. 'What about Leo and Faith? Catch any intimacy between them?'

'Nothing out of the ordinary comes to mind. He hardly spoke of her after she left, nothing positive anyway. Probably angry because he had to step up to the plate and rear me in her place.' He tapped his hand on the car roof. 'Drive carefully now. You don't want to miss a bend in the dark. Trees don't jump out of the way out here.'

I laughed. Simon didn't. *Shit! His mother died crashing into a tree.*

He shut the door, and I drove away, cringing at my blunder.

Other than having to confront Stoney about instances of sexual assault, something else gnawed at me on the way home. Why was Simon told Carl's body had been found in a field of sunflowers? Was it a fib to hide the gruesome truth from a kid? It shouldn't matter, Carl had drowned all the same.

19

'Donna's phone,' said a husky voice.

It was seven in the morning, and still in bed, I'd called Donna to see how she was doing. Not expecting a strange man to answer my call, I viewed the phone screen. I'd definitely rung the correct number.

'Hello ... is anyone there?' came the tinny voice from my hand.

I sat up, thoughts tumbling into one another. Where was Donna at this early hour? Why had a man answered her phone? Who the hell was he?

Lifting the phone to my ear, I stuttered, and then hung up just as the door of the en-suite slid open and Shane emerged from a cloud of steam.

I mentioned what just happened.

'Stop getting your knickers in a twist over things that don't concern you,' he said, pulling out a cupboard drawer and searching through folded underwear. 'Maybe he's an old acquaintance. Or a new friend. A neighbour, even.'

'Visiting so early? Why didn't the man hand the phone to Donna?'

He dropped his towel and stepped into a pair of black briefs. 'Maybe she wasn't even there.'

'Where would she be without her phone?'

Shane shuffled through the next drawer, plucking out thick grey socks. 'She could have been on the loo.'

'He should have called out and told her I was on the phone.'

'Did you give your name?'

'Er ... not quite.'

'What do you mean, not quite?'

'I didn't actually say anything.'

'What, nothing? He probably thought you were a nuisance caller, or a telemarketer. You didn't breathe heavily, did you?'

'Umm ... maybe.'

'No wonder he didn't fetch Donna. He was protecting her from a crazy person.'

Shane collected his work pants from the chair in the room's corner and gave them a sniff, deciding if they were good enough to wear. He pulled them on, yet when he tested the shirt he'd worn the previous day in the same way, he screwed it up and dumped it on the floor with the towel.

'There are clean work shirts hanging up,' I said, pointing to the wardrobe.

'I know, I washed and ironed them myself.'

'And you did such a wonderful job. You should do the laundry more often.'

He removed a shirt from its hanger and slipped it on. 'I only did it out of desperation. You haven't been on the ball in the housework department of late.'

I eyed the patterned water glass on my bedside table. If it wasn't a precious Mother's Day gift, I would have hurled it at him.

'Well, if you haven't noticed, I've been rather busy with the bookstore and all.'

'Aren't women supposed to be experts at multi-tasking?'

'I am, thank you very much. But I can't do everything.'

'No, that's right, you can't. Maybe you should start prioritising and dropping things that aren't so important, like messing around in other people's business.'

My back stiffened. 'What are you saying?'

'Well,' he pointed to my phone, 'the whole Donna thing, for starters. I know you haven't abandoned the idea of finding her father.'

I stared, open-mouthed. 'How'd you find out?'

'I can smell it. You exude a certain odour when you're meddling.'

'Odour? Really?'

Shane rolled his eyes. 'Ross texted me this morning by mistake. He wants you to meet him at Fine 'n Dandy to talk over what you've both found out.' He gave a scowl that would send a wild dog scurrying with its tail between its legs.

'Hey,' I snapped. 'I'm helping a good friend discover her family roots.'

'Without her consent.'

'I have Ross's permission. That's close enough.'

'What about Faith's?'

I paused, then threw up my hands. 'She's kept this secret far too long. It's about time this cold case was reopened, for Donna's sake. Anyway, we already have some leads.' A disgusting one involving old mate Stoney that I needed to tell Ross about.

As if reading my thoughts, Shane responded with, 'What if it was something worse than a secret love affair? What if it wasn't consensual, have you considered that?'

If only he knew this very thought caused sleep to elude me most of the night.

'So, Miss Nosey-Parker,' Shane added, picking up the wet towel and soiled shirt. 'That's what I meant about someone getting hurt. You could do more harm than good by opening up old wounds.'

When he stomped from the room, I fell back against the pillows. The last thing I wanted was to cause further pain. I seriously contemplated pulling the plug on my investigations.

After Shane had left for work, I decided to give Donna another call. It was now half past eight, a more reasonable hour. I took my phone onto the sunny back deck, and planned what I would say to her.

A wallaby on the grassy slope below nibbled on fresh shoots, her joey climbing from her pouch to feed alongside. Their ears twitched as lorikeets flying overhead alighted on the branches of a flowering gum to feast raucously on blossoms. A kookaburra laughed. A magpie we had dubbed 'Dawn' because of her regular morning visits, landed on the railing and cocked her head to study me. It was like being in an Aussie Disney movie. I breathed in clean mountain air and phoned my friend.

No answer. I was diverted to message bank.

Unsure how to explain my earlier non-verbal call in a ten-second message, I hung up. Had Donna, or someone else, purposely turned off her phone? For what reason other than not wanting to talk? I cringed at an unsettling prospect. What if they didn't want to be disturbed?

I jolted when the phone buzzed in my hand, and quickly answered the call.

'Abby! Are you at home or on your way into town?'

I recognised the voice belonging to the manager of Mulga Bill's restaurant.

'Hi, James, I'm at home. Still in my PJ's.'

'Well, you might want to bring a bucket and some cleaning products with you when you come. I was just opening up and noticed someone has graffitied your shop windows.'

'Graffitied?'

'Yeah. There are some rude drawings and a few choice words you'll want to get rid of in a hurry. I'd do it, but people are queuing up for breakfast.'

'No, it's okay. I'll get down there soon. Thanks for giving me a heads-up.'

I kicked a railing post. *Bloody local kids!* No respect for property or literature.

20

A rmed with warm water, vinegar, and razor blades—as per a Google search on how to clean off spray paint—it took a good two hours to rid the bright orange graffitied obscenities and images of male genitalia from the shop windows. I could have done with Keira's help but, for whatever reason, she was a no-show. However, there were plenty of people who stopped to give assistance by way of unwelcome critiques and advice.

'That one looks like a large schnoz and eyeballs,' one road worker remarked, balancing handfuls of paper-packaged treats purchased from the bakery.

'Nah, more like a pork sausage and two blobs of mashed potato,' came his bearded mate, hoeing into a dripping meat pie.

'Is that an eggplant?' asked a man pulling up his mobility scooter at the road's edge. 'I hope this is a new fruit shop. I could do with some decent artichokes.'

'Ooh, mind those razorblades, luv,' warned one old dear pushing her pug-nosed pooch in a pet stroller. 'Don't want to cause yourself a nasty injury. Not like my Ralph when he—'

My insides squirmed as she prattled on, giving a vivid description of her husband's bloody mishap while shaving his mole-dotted face.

Next, a mother and middle-aged daughter sidled up. 'Filthy words,' the older woman said. 'Disgusting. But that one's not too bad.' She pointed to the word I was having trouble scrubbing away.

'The C word?' gasped her daughter. 'Mum, that's the worse word of all.'

'No, it isn't,' she cackled. 'Your father taught me that word on our honeymoon. I use it all the time when playing online Scrabble.'

'Oh, Mum!' The daughter quickly steered her mother away.

Scraping away the last phallic taunt, my eyes shot daggers at three giggling kids who should have been at school already. When I asked for their names, they bounded away like startled wallabies, almost knocking over Natalie Schilling as she tried to dodge their escape.

Her hands flew to her face. 'Oh my!' she cried shrilly. 'What happened here?'

I downed my tools. 'Graffiti. Kids having a lark, I suspect.'

'Oh, yes. That would be it. Do you need a hand?'

'I'm pretty much done. Thanks all the same.'

I remained tight-lipped as I emptied the bucket into the gutter and collected my cleaning equipment. How was I to continue a conversation with Natalie after what transpired at our last meeting?

Moving into the shop, I found Natalie following right on my heels. 'Can I help you with something, Nat?'

She slipped a hand into her shoulder bag and removed a well-thumbed exercise book. 'Here,' she said, thrusting it under my nose. 'Just like you asked.'

I eyed the worn cover that had 'Natalie Harper' written in the name section. On the subject line was, 'Book One.'

'Oh, one of your stories.' I dropped the empty bucket and took it from her. 'I'll give it a read sometime. I'm pretty busy at the moment.'

'That's okay,' she said, with a head twitch. 'Whenever you get a chance. It's been hidden this long so I'm sure a few more days won't matter.'

Days? More like weeks. 'Sure,' I nodded. 'I'll take good care of it.'

She clutched my free hand so tight I thought my fingers might snap. 'Thank you, Abby. I trust you.'

After several seconds, I tugged my hand away. 'Was there something else, Natalie?'

She stared at me and blinked, her fast-fluttering lashes sending out a strange code I couldn't decipher. 'What I told you the other day about Stoney wasn't the worst of it.' She wiped perspiration from above her top lip. 'He got me pregnant.'

The room swirled. 'W-what? Stoney got you pregnant, too?'

Natalie nodded.

Holy crap. Just when I thought her story couldn't get any worse. 'What did you do?'

'I let Vince believe he was the father, and we married well before Lester was born.'

'Lester?' I jolted as hundreds of invisible needles pricked my flesh. 'Lester is Stoney's kid?'

'I gave birth a couple of weeks before Faith had her baby. Being small, it was easy to pass him off as premature.' She lunged, once again taking hold of my hand. 'No one must know. It would kill Vince, I'm sure of it. And Lester ... well, he just wouldn't cope hearing he was the result of a rape.'

'And Stoney? Is he aware?'

'Certainly not! He's never deserved to know he fathered a son. It has to remain hush-hush, Abby. My family will not be ripped apart by someone blabbing secrets.' With a swish of her skirt, she spun around and scampered away.

My stomach clenched. If this news was such a huge secret, why had Natalie just blurted it out to me, a virtual stranger?

I fed the exercise book into my bag and went outside in search of a restorative coffee.

At my window seat in Mulga Bill's, with a clear view of the street, I chatted to James and thanked him for alerting me to the vandalism.

'No probs,' he said. 'A least there was no permanent damage done. Would have been worse if they'd thrown a rock through your window.'

'I guess so. Though it wouldn't be me paying to replace a pane of glass. That's the beauty of leasing a property, right?'

He smiled and took a step backward to allow the young attendant to hand me my jumbo-sized cappuccino. 'Still, it'd be bloody inconvenient. Thank God we've had nothing untoward happen here, touch wood.' He tapped his head. 'Wouldn't want anything to interfere with our excellent track record.'

'Well, aren't I the unlucky one. The shop's not even open and I'm getting targeted by local scumbags.'

James gave a sigh for my benefit and went to greet a trio of young mums with bubs as they walked through the door in a rabble of noise.

I sipped my coffee. What had happened to Keira? Had she accepted a better offer, or had Simon's need of her eclipsed mine?

'Mum, what are you doing here?'

I glanced sideways as Gemma pulled out a chair alongside,

and pointed to my mug. 'Medication, Mum?' I nodded. 'I saw your Facebook post about the graffiti. Little weasels up to no good again, hey?'

'Guess so. Why are you here? Coffee break from work, or,' I winked, 'a more personal reason?'

A month ago, Gemma had moved in with James's son, Benji, the chef here at Mulga Bill's. 'Just friends sharing the cost of renting a place in town,' she'd said. 'Nothing else.' I had my suspicions, which normally I wouldn't have minded, but the scenario of them being romantically involved presented complications.

Gemma held up her re-usable drink bottle filled with something green and mushy and disgustingly healthy. 'An energy drink to help kick-start my afternoon. Delivering bulldog pups by caesarean at two-thirty.'

Benji appeared as if by magic. As usual, he was a treat to behold—dark wavy hair, smouldering eyes, lips like two soft cushions. If I was my daughter, I'd be smitten.

He squeezed Gemma's shoulders from behind. 'Hey, housemate, are you home for dinner tonight? I want to try out a new recipe on you.'

'I don't mind being a guinea pig,' I said. Benji's skills in the kitchen equalled any TV celebrity chef.

'It's a vegan dish.'

'I like vegan food.'

'But Gem is a proper vegan. I value her opinion. Er ... not that I don't value yours, Abby,' he backtracked. 'But if it doesn't get Gem's tick of approval, it won't appear on the menu.'

'Oh, I see.' I was only slightly miffed.

'Be home by six, Gem,' Benji urged. 'I'll make it really special.'

As he dashed away, I gave my daughter's arm a nudge. 'Hmm ... how special? Candles, champagne, mood music?'

She shook her head. 'You're a worry, Mum.'

A bleep sounded from inside my bag, and reefing out my phone, Natalie's exercise book slipped to the floor.

Gemma reached down and picked it up. 'What's this? Who's Natalie Harper?'

'She's Natalie Schilling now. It's her manuscript.' I frowned at the text message from Ross: *'Are you coming to visit me today or what?'* Geez, Ross, don't get your jocks in a bunch. I sent him a reply.

Gemma sucked noisily from her bottle. 'Is she Lester's mother?'

'Yep, one and the same.' No need to tell her of the bombshell Natalie just dropped about Stoney being Lester's father. 'Turns out she used to write. She wants an assessment of her work.'

'Have you read it?'

'Just got it. I'll glance through it when I have some free time.'

Gemma peeled back the cover to the first page. '*The Publican's Daughter*. Nice.'

God, is that what she's called it? Still, it'd sit well among other contemporary titles.

Clearing her throat, Gemma read aloud from the neat handwriting. '*For Lucinda Braidwood, being the daughter of the local publican wasn't all beer and skittles. On days like this, it took all her strength not to pop her cork when her father demanded she serve behind the counter. Life as a bar wench pulling beers for Wattle Gully rednecks was not the future she planned for herself. She had dreams of joining a theatre troupe, or a travelling circus, and seeing the world. That was until a tall dark stranger glided into the pub and asked for a whisky as smooth as a woman's thigh.*'

I clutched my face. 'Well, that's going to the bottom of my reading pile.'

'Why? It sounds fun. I could give it a read. I like soppy romance.'

'Be careful,' I warned, nodding towards the kitchen door. 'It may soon present itself on a silver platter. Or in your case, a compostable eco-friendly bowl.'

'I'm off!' She pushed up from her chair and tucked the exercise book under her arm. 'If you're nice, I'll let you in on what Lucinda Braidwood gets up to.' Then she was out the door, power walking across the street and around the corner to the veterinary clinic.

I too needed to get back to work. I also needed to see Ross and fill him in on some mind-blowing revelations. However, at the sight of Beryl Erbacher standing in the craft shop doorway, I put both actions on hold.

21

Beryl forced a jar into my hand. 'More tomato relish for your hubby?'

'Well, now that you mention it. Make it two. It doesn't last long at our place.'

'Anything else? Some lovely rosella jam and lemon butter just came in. Estelle's products are hot buys, so you'd better be quick.'

'No, just the relish. But I have a question regarding a person from Shadow Creek.'

Beryl perched her elderly self on a stool behind the counter. Folding her arms, she peered over the purple frames of her glasses and changed hats—metaphorically—transforming into Beryl Erbacher, President of the Shadow Creek Historical Society. 'Okay, young Abby. What's the name?'

'Carl Sweetman from Chances Crossing.'

She leaned back, her steel-grey eyes darting as she delved into the archives of her mind. 'Hmm ... son of Leonard?'

'Yep, that's him. Carl drowned in a flash flood.'

'Correct. What did you want to know about him?'

'Where they found his body.'

She cocked a wiry eyebrow. 'Now why on earth would you want that information?'

'Well,' I took a deep breath, 'a friend of mine is his daughter, or at least she was led to believe she was. Now she's discovered she probably wasn't, and I'm helping her find out the truth. I've spoken to several people and they have quite different memories of where Carl's body was found. So, I'm wondering if his death had been recorded locally, say in an issue of The Talk of the Town, or one of its predecessors.'

She shook her head. 'No predecessors. It's been called The Talk of the Town since its inception in 1958.'

'Well then, is it possible to check if an article was written concerning Carl's death?'

'Of course. We've scanned every past edition of the magazine.' She sprung off the stool and rounded the counter. 'I'll look on the office computer. Do you recall what date he died?'

'End of February 1979.'

'Do you mind holding the fort while I nick out back? You know how to use an EFTPOS machine, don't you?'

I checked the machine on the counter, relieved to find it was the same type as the one I'd be using at Ringtales. I nodded and took her place on the stool.

In Beryl's absence, I sold a colourful knitted beanie with a pom-pom on top to a lovely old lady smelling of Red Door, my mum's favourite scent.

'My granddaughter will love this when the weather cools,' she crooned.

It was only after she'd paid and exited the shop that I realised, on reading the removed price tag, that she'd actually purchased a tea cosy. How long would it take for her granddaughter to discover the two side openings were not for ears but a spout and a handle?

Beryl returned from the office, smiling. 'Success! Here you are, Abby.' She handed me a printed copy of the front page of the March 1979 edition of the town mag.

'*DEATH OF LOCAL MAN. FLASH FLOOD CLAIMS A LIFE,*' was the headline.

I read the article aloud.

'*On the afternoon of 26th February, a body was discovered caught in tree roots at a bend in Shadow Creek near Jock Buchanan's property. Identified by Dr Peake as Carl Sweetman, 35, from Chances Crossing, the man had been missing since a flash flood surged down the eastern range the previous evening. Steady rain falling in the area for three days caused waterholes and streams to overflow and swell the creek, carrying a good deal of timber, farm produce, and an occasional dead beast towards town. Though the rain had ceased by mid-afternoon of Sunday the 25th, a wall of muddy water was seen descending on Chances Crossing around 6 pm. When Mr Sweetman, who had been checking on his cattle, had not returned home by late evening, his concerned family alerted the police. A search party was organised on the morning of the 26th, and his body was located just before dark. A second-generation farmer, Carl Sweetman is survived by a wife and two young children.*'

So now I knew.

'You should talk to Bernard Peake,' Beryl said. 'He'd be happy to give you more information. The doctor likes a chin wag.'

'Dr Peake is still here in Shadow Creek?'

'Semi-retired. Works a day or two per week at the medical centre just to keep his hand in.'

His hand in what, I thought, cringing.

'What's today? Thursday? I think he'll be there. Let me give the centre a call.' She lifted a mobile phone from the shop counter.

Before I could object, she was pressing keys and talking to someone called Mim.

'So, Bernie's there ... right now ... not busy? Good, make an appointment for Abby ... er ...' Beryl shot me a questioning look.

'Eaton,' I said, 'I haven't been there before.' I preferred to continue seeing our family doctor back in the northern suburbs. Not that I saw Dr Prentice much, just for the annual check-up and flu injection. That reminded me, I needed a skin cancer check, essential for living in the Sunshine State.

'You've got half an hour to kill before your appointment,' Beryl said, slipping a third jar of relish into my shoulder bag and pushing me towards the doorway. 'This one's free. I was a tad heavy-handed with the chilli making that batch.'

'Thanks,' I said, 'I'll let you know how I—', but she had rushed back to the counter to answer the ringing phone.

22

'R oss, I'm here!' I called, stepping into Fine 'n Dandy and discovering it devoid of anything with a heartbeat.

'In the office,' he called from out back.

I slipped behind the curtains and found him sitting at the desk, his computer screen displaying multiple spreadsheets.

'By the way, numbskull,' I said, prodding him in the chest, 'you sent your earlier text message to Shane's phone.'

'Oops, my bad,' he shrugged, unconcerned by the pickle he had gotten me into with Shane. 'I just wanted us to catch up on where we're at with the Faith thing.'

'Well, what have you discovered?'

'Nothing more. I've been busy.' He nodded towards the screen.

And I haven't? 'In other words, you wanted to hear what I alone turned up.'

'That's right. Give it to me.' He rubbed his hands together and pointed to a wooden stool stacked with manila folders.

I dropped the folders onto the floor and sat to relay my

conversations with Linda McKenny and Natalie Schilling, leaving the details of Nat's assault at the pub to the very last.

'Shit-a-brick,' he cried. 'Gladstone Maloney is a rapist? You have to confront him.'

'Why me? Wouldn't it be better if you had a man-to-man talk with him about this?'

'But you heard it firsthand. It'd be hearsay from me. Anyway, you know him better, so it should be easy for you to get him to confess.'

'You're wrong. That just makes it more difficult.'

A jingle of the shop doorbell. Ross went out to see who had entered.

He returned moments later with a smile spread across his smug face. 'Hey presto! Guess who just walked in?'

My stomach plummeted ten floors. 'You're kidding me. Not Stoney?'

'Yep, in living colour.' He pulled me out of the room and shoved me through the parted curtains. 'Go get him, Abby.'

'Coward,' I hissed over my shoulder as Ross disappeared behind the swaying velvet.

Stoney was in a far corner studying a tobacco pipe collection. To anyone else he looked like a fussy old man weathered by life, a typical grandfather sort. Yet, if what Natalie said was true, he was also someone capable of despicable acts.

Alerted to my presence—or the laser beams of anger shooting from my eyes and into his back—he spun around and flashed a grin. 'Hello, pretty lady. What are you doing here? Need some additions to your shop? Or maybe a new outfit?' He nodded towards a rack crammed with outdated women's clothing, the metal bar bending under the weight. 'There's a fur stole complete with fox head you might want to try on.'

I grimaced at the idea of a mummified carcass hanging around my neck and walked over. 'No, I've ... er ... come to chat with Ross.'

Stoney removed a mauve cloche hat adorned with a jewelled brooch from a mannequin's head and slipped it onto mine. 'You sure? This cute little number looks fetching on you.'

He pushed me in front of a lengthy wall mirror and I squirmed from the grip of his hands around my waist. For the first time since we'd met, he gave me the creeps.

I returned the hat to the mannequin and changed the subject. 'I've met Simon Sweetman.'

Stoney squinted. 'Simon Sweetman? Carl's son? Where'd you dig him up?'

'He's opened a photographic gallery at Chances Crossing, on their old property.'

'That's news to me. They've leased the place out for decades. I thought it was high time it was sold. So, he's returned too, has he? Geez, all we need is Faith and Leo to show up and we'll have the whole bloody lot of them back in town. How is the young fella?'

'Doing okay. He has a daughter.'

'A daughter? Well, blow me down, he's all grown up. Makes a fella feel mighty old.'

I chewed my lip. How on earth was I to segue into a conversation about rape? I cleared my throat. 'I also had an enlightening chat with Natalie Schilling.'

Other than a twitch of a craggy cheek, Stoney showed no sign of interest. He lifted a straw boater with a ribboned band from a hat stand and examined it closely. 'How is the old girl? Don't see her around much, what with her hubby being so unwell.'

'She's getting by. Vince goes to respite now and again.'

'I bet she appreciates the break, poor luv.'

Poor luv, indeed. 'She ... um ... told me about an incident between you two at the pub.'

Stoney gave me his full attention. 'And which incident might that be?'

Which one? How many had he been involved in? I glanced around and made sure there was a clear path to the front door in case a quick escape was necessary. 'A disturbing occurrence in the cellar, about forty years ago.'

I caught it: a blink, a flash of colour to his cheeks. I didn't know old people could blush.

'Oh ... that's letting the cat out of the bag.' He hung the straw boater back on the stand. 'What made her bring up that juicy bit of information?'

Juicy? 'Good God, you admit to it?'

'We were only having fun. Youngsters get up to worse things than that these days.'

'Rape is not fun, Stoney. Sexual assault is a criminal offence.'

His eyes grew to saucer-size. 'What the flamin' hell are you talking about, girly? What Nat and I got up to in that cellar was definitely not rape.'

'In your eyes,' I said, my fury escalating.

'No, in nobody's eyes,' he scowled. 'What did she say to you? How did she describe it?'

I repeated Natalie's version of events.

Stoney smoothed down his moustache and chuckled. 'I admit to binding her hands together, though a length of rope was used, not my belt. And yes, there was a blindfold of sorts. But it was Nat's idea, not mine. I just followed her down into the cellar to give her a hand in bringing up some crates of beer. She's the one who surprised me by smooching like there was no tomorrow and asking me to tie her up. She even produced the items she'd previously stashed behind a barrel. I thought, okay, this is a little kinky, but if she's offering, then I'm willing. What happened down there in the dark while the locals satisfied their thirst above, I can assure you, was done by mutual consent. She asked if I wanted to try other things that I'm too much of a gentleman to mention, but I passed them up. There's only so much a bloke can handle after downing a skin-full of beer.'

'So, your version is the truth?'

'Bloody oath it is. I like women, always have. But I've never forced myself on any of them. Never needed to.'

I was tempted to tell him about the result of that racy tryst: a child, who now managed the real estate business that was 'carving up Shadow Creek'. Instead, I launched further into my interrogation.

'What about that time you took Faith home from the pub because she was too drunk to drive herself, and you bolted home the next morning partially dressed? Anything you want to tell me about that?'

Stoney's face fell. 'Geez Louise. That sure is one gossip mill you've been listening to. If you must know, I drove Faith to her place in her car, got her settled, and must have drifted off myself. I left at first light and then hitched a lift into town to get my car. Just a mate looking after another mate.' He came near and eyeballed me with a look that had me sucking in a sharp breath. 'If anyone thinks I went around molesting women,' he growled, 'then they're bloody well lying or sick in the head.'

I eased my hands onto his trembling arms and spoke softly, hoping to soothe his rage. 'I'm sorry, Stoney. I really am.'

He shook my hands away. 'Yeah, well, so you should be. I don't appreciate being grilled. Nat got her wires well and truly crossed telling you that story. She was a real goer back then, everyone knew that. Getting hitched to Vince Schilling was the best thing for her. It settled her right down. So why is she shooting her mouth off about it now, hey? I reckon she's losing her marbles.'

I considered Natalie's mismatched tea set, the odd shoes, the wrongly buttoned blouse, her nervous tremors and twitches. Maybe Stoney's assumption was correct. Was Lester aware of his mother's mental state? Graeme Roper's wife, Julie, worked at the medical centre and, if asked nicely, she might slip me some info on Natalie's condition.

Disinterested in browsing, Stoney left the shop to meet Doris at the hairdresser's while I searched for Ross.

I found him skulking behind a coat rack. 'Did you hear any of that?' I snapped.

'A fair bit, actually. Good work, Abby.'

I punched him in the shoulder. 'Not good work. It was horrible having to quiz Stoney about his past liaisons. He could have suffered a stroke. At least he didn't do what Natalie accused him of.'

'That's his story, anyway. What now? Back to the drawing board?'

'No way. I'm having a break from the whole Faith and Donna thing. All this, and the graffiti incident, is doing my head in.' I started for the door.

'Graffiti?' Ross cried. 'What graffiti? Those rotten local kids been at it again?'

I nodded and checked my watch, I had only five minutes until my appointment with Dr Peake.

23

Walking the exposed rock formations below the headland, Leo was careful not to lose his balance on the uneven terrain. A black dog neared, following a small blue soldier crab as it scuttled sideways and slipped into a crevice to hide.

'Hey, there,' Leo said, patting his thigh, drawing the poodle-mix over.

The dog sniffed his hand and allowed him to run his fingers through the curly hair matted with wet sand and strands of seaweed.

'Having fun, are you? Where's your owner?' Leo glanced around and sighted a fair-haired boy busy on the sand, collecting washed up treasures and dropping them into a plastic bucket. A dog leash slung over his narrow shoulders swayed with each movement. What Leo wouldn't give to be a kid again—young and carefree.

Chances Crossing, May 1978

Almost two months since his last visit, Leo rolls into Chances Crossing unannounced, relieved to find Carl has gone to Kingaroy to buy more cattle. Simon and Patch greet him with the usual enthusiasm, while Faith is frugal with her attention, giving off vibes of annoyance. Has whatever she once felt for him cooled?

Leo gets to work mending the barbed-wire fencing, with Simon assisting and chatting about having attended the Shadow Creek Show the previous weekend, followed by a sleepover at a friend's place.

'We had fairy floss and choc-top ice-cream, and later on at Timmy's we had a bonfire. I got burned,' he adds, showing Leo his seared arm. 'But I didn't cry. Only sooks cry.'

He also fills Leo in on all the things he's been adding to his collection of rocks, old coins and, importantly, insects. Leo tells Simon he must have been a bower bird in a former life. Simon considers this and agrees, saying that a bird gathering pretty things was better than being an Egyptian king or a famous explorer.

Every time Leo sneaks a look at the house, he catches Faith watching from the verandah, probably just checking on their work. Yet, like a siren luring a sailor to his demise, she sets his pulse racing and mind whirling with salacious thoughts. He is glad of Simon's distraction, even though their talk unleashes ghosts from his past.

'Did you kill anybody in the war?' Simon asks, eyes wide and brimming with interest.

Leo's skin prickles. 'Don't know,' he shrugs.

'But you got hurt.' Simon points to the ugly scar seen through Leo's gaping shirt. 'Didn't you see who did that to you?'

'No. It was a grenade thrown from the bush. I never had time.'

An upside-down face bobs into his mind: dark hair, slanted eyes, sallow cheeks, and a mouth leaking blood. Leo shoves it back into the shadows.

'You never shot anyone? Seen them die?' Simon falls to his knees. Clutching his stomach, he groans, feigning injury before lying spread eagle in the dirt, his eyes rolling back in his head. Patch scampers over and begins licking the boy's face.

Leo cringes as more spectres appear. He kicks Simon's leg. 'Get up, you silly bugger. You've been watching too many spaghetti westerns. Here,' he hands him a spade, 'see how good you are at digging holes. I've got to replace a few old posts.'

A figure walking towards them interrupts their task.

Faith has changed her outfit, replacing baggy shirt and trousers with a long-sleeved cheesecloth dress and leather cowboy boots. With the sun behind her, and the dress billowing in a cool breeze, the outline of her shapely legs is visible through the fine fabric.

'Lunch,' she announces, stopping in the shade of a golden ash and laying down a tartan picnic rug. Removing sandwiches and cans of soft drink from a wicker basket, she sits cross-legged and waits for them to join her.

As they eat, Leo lets Simon prattle on about building a tree house with odd bits of used timber, while he fights the urge to brush breadcrumbs from the tight embroidered bodice of Faith's dress, or stroke the silken hair falling over a shoulder into her lap. Even the smooth skin of a bared knee entices him.

Mark Twain hit the nail on the head when he said, *"There is a charm about the forbidden that makes it unspeakably desirable."* God knows where he'd read that, but it fit—especially today.

'Can you fix the chicken coop?' Faith says, stirring Leo from his yearnings.

'What's wrong with it? Don't tell me that Taj Mahal for

chickens you had me knock together the last time I was here has already fallen to bits.'

'No. The wire mesh has come away from the frame at one end. Forced open by our resident goanna pushing through to snatch eggs, probably.'

'Old George still hanging around, is he?'

'Yes, he's rather a menace. Also, I noticed when I went for a walk yesterday that the rear gate behind the vegetable patch has broken from its hinges.'

'Most likely rusted. Were you going for a swim?' He imagines Faith skinny-dipping in the rock pool like he has done many times, the clear water swirling around her nakedness.

'Don't be stupid, the water's too bloody cold right now.' Reminded of the weather, she rubs her arms to warm herself.

'There are heaps of dragonflies around the water lilies in the mornings,' Simon says, stifling a burp with his hand. 'I found a blue skimmer the other day and brought it home.'

Leo nudges him with his elbow. 'Not for your insect board, I hope.'

'Oh, no,' Faith jumps in, 'Simon doesn't do that since we had a chat about hurting innocent creatures. You caught it with the bug catcher I bought you and set if free after, hey, Simon?'

Simon's cheeks pink up. He tosses a sandwich crust to Patch, who snaps it between his teeth and gobbles it down. 'Yeah, I let it go, just like I promised.'

Faith reaches for Leo's paper plate. 'So, the coop and the gate?'

'I can check them out after we've finished here, in about an hour.'

'I could be your helper, this time,' she says, her fingers lingering on his.

A prolonged look passes between them that stirs hope in Leo. A hope that Faith wants him as much as he wants her.

Faith collects the other items and drops them into the basket. Playfully ordering Leo and Simon to get to work, she leaves them to it.

'Okay, mate,' Leo says, forcing his gaze away from Faith walking back to the house in a cloud of cheesecloth, 'what really happened to that blue skimmer?'

The boy digs at the earth with the spade. 'It died.'

'You don't say. And where is it now?'

Simon glances up, and Leo catches a hint of menace in his nephew's cold stare and steady voice as he says, 'Pinned to the board with the others, of course.'

24

'You've got fifteen minutes,' barked Mim, the practice manager of the medical centre, stabbing a finger towards the hallway.

Good Lord, somebody needed to work on their people skills.

I followed the signs and reached Dr Peake's room by going out the back door and down a ramp to an annex built beneath the building, well away from the rest of the centre. At whose request, I wondered.

With trepidation, I knocked on the timber door and it opened with an eerie creak.

Dr Peake wasn't at all what I expected. At roughly six-foot-five, with a wide girth, a mop of grizzled hair, and a florid face scattered with whiskers, he was a bear of a man in his mid-seventies. However, his voice had a more mellow tone than a fearful growl.

'Come in, come in,' he grinned. 'I don't get many visits from healthy young people like yourself. You are healthy, I gather,' he asked, with a waggle of sprouting eyebrows.

'Ah … yes, I think so,' I said, feeling a twinge in my gut that I prayed was not symptomatic of something diabolical.

'Good, good. Bernard Peake's the name. Take a seat.'

As I started to lower my backside onto the chair in front of his desk, Dr Peake wrenched me up and directed me with a gentle shove towards a leather sofa beneath the window.

'There you go, that will be comfier for you.'

I sat where shown and watched as Dr Peake eased his massive frame into a wingback chair opposite, folding his long limbs in like a startled spider.

He eyed me with amused interest. 'So, how can I be of assistance?'

I said I wanted to inquire about a past patient, Carl Sweetman.

He cleared his throat. 'It is imperative I inform you I am obligated by patient confidentiality not to divulge personal information.'

'Understood,' I gushed. 'I'm not here for his medical history. Beryl Erbacher suggested you might shed some light on the facts of his death.'

He tapped his bristled chin with a stubby finger. 'His death, hey?'

'Yes. I'm doing some family history research on behalf of a relative of Carl's and I've come across several inconsistent versions of the discovery of his body. So, who better to ask than someone who was on the scene?'

'You want to know where we found him? Well, let's see what I can remember.' He leaned forward, and I heard an odd squeak I hoped was the chair upholstery straining against his weight and not a sneaky fart. 'Carl had gone missing the Sunday night a flash flood roared down from the hills. When he hadn't turned up safe and well the next day, many thought he'd been swept away in the flood. We formed a search party, and later that day discovered him downstream from his farm.'

'Near Jock Buchanan's property.'

'That's about right, at a bend in the creek. We found the poor fellow caught in exposed tree roots.'

'Dead.'

'Most definitely. He wasn't in a good way, that's for sure.'

'Can you expand on that?'

He frowned and rested back. 'Are you sure?' I nodded, and he continued. 'Well, I hung around during the preliminary police examination, before they transported Carl's body to the city morgue. I saw many lacerations and abrasions to his face and limbs, injuries consistent with coming in contact with all manner of debris—branches, barbed wire, rocks, you name it.'

'So, no suspicion of foul play?'

He cocked his head. 'Why would you ask that?'

'Er ... just covering all bases.'

'Death by accidental drowning, was the ruling. The coroner confirmed lungs filled with creek water, evidence of haemorrhaging in the sinuses and airways, that sort of thing. Yet ...' He rested his hands on his belly and twiddled his thumbs. 'There was one thing that had me puzzled.'

I edged forward, my heart doing star jumps.

Dr Peake glanced at the closed door and dropped his voice to a stage whisper. 'Between you, me, and the fencepost, I reckon he'd had a stoush before he died.'

'A stoush? You mean a fight?'

'Yeah, a proper punch up. Had a haematoma here.' He touched his face just below the left eye socket. 'Some may argue it was an injury gained while travelling a fast-flowing creek filled with god-knows-what, but I'd put my money on it being made by one of these.' He held up a hand curled into a tight fist. 'You see, a contusion requires blood to flow into injured vessels and then spread. Therefore, an injury after death, when blood is not flowing, will not produce such a bruise. The colouring and swelling of the one I saw on Carl's face indicated it had been obtained pre-mortem. Most likely on the same day he died.'

'Oh ...' Weighted thoughts ricochetted around my brain like billiard balls. *Who had Carl been fighting before his death? And why?* 'Did you mention it to anyone of importance?'

He pulled a face. 'Hell, no. I was a rookie in the medical field. A young country GP, wet behind the ears.'

I thought on the local magazine's report. 'The Talk of the Town at the time, stated that Carl had been out checking on the cattle when the flash flood occurred.'

'Well, unless those beasts had gotten loose and wandered off, I'd be asking what he was doing down by the creek.'

He had something there. I recalled my visit to the Sweetman's. The paddocks were nowhere near the creek, more on the flats down from the house. Maybe he'd gone to view the rising water level. But that didn't explain the bruising.

'I saw Carl at church that Sunday morning and he looked none the worse for wear,' Dr Peake said. 'His daughter was christened during the service. *His* daughter, I say dubiously.'

My interest rose to a new level. 'What are you implying?'

'Now, I'm not usually one to spill the beans, but Carl could no more father that child than I could have been the first man to step on the moon.'

What did he know? I had to tread carefully. 'But he already had a child. Simon.'

'Well, the boy is his. Let me just say,' he said with a glimmer in his eyes, 'there are several viral infections that can cause infertility in previously productive adult males.'

I was about to ask for specifics when a buzzing came from his desk phone. A scratchy voice sounded through the aged intercom.

'Doctor, your two-thirty patient has arrived.'

Dr Peake unfurled his limbs and got to his feet. 'I'm afraid our time is up. Mim will chuck a wobbly if I'm lagging behind.'

I stood with reluctance and thanked him for clarifying a few issues.

'My pleasure,' he said, ushering me to the door. 'Off you go. You don't want to get Mim offside, I can assure you.'

Filing Dr Peak's comments into my already crammed brain, I walked back up the ramp, narrowly avoiding an elderly woman with a patch on one eye as she zigzagged down.

I passed through the waiting room and sidestepped a toddler upending a basket of toys onto the carpet, only to have my exit out the door blocked by Julie Roper.

'Hi, Abby.' Her clinical eyes flicked over me, assessing my physical wellbeing. 'What are you doing here?'

'I've just seen Dr Peake.'

'Dr Peake?' She grimaced. 'Why? Doctors Newbury and Dhawan are way more proficient. More in touch with 21st century medicine, if you get my drift.'

'I'm not sick, or looking for medical advice. I came to ask after an ex-patient of his.'

'Ex-patient?' Julie pursed her lips, obviously uncomfortable with the notion of me quizzing Dr Peake on patient matters.

'The death of one, actually. I'm gathering information on someone who died decades ago.'

'Has this got anything to do with Donna?'

I gasped. I wasn't aware Julie knew about Donna's complicated parentage. When I asked how she knew what I was up to, she said Graeme had mentioned I was helping Ross put together something for Donna's birthday. Thank God, she wasn't aware of Faith's infidelity.

'Are you formulating a family tree for Donna? You'd be good at that, with your nosey ways.'

My back stiffened. 'It's called research, Julie.'

A scream drew our attention to the kid on the floor, who was now struggling to remove a large Lego brick from his right nostril.

'I'll leave you to it,' I said, hurrying outside.

I walked around the corner to my shop. What debilitating virus had rendered Carl infertile? If he had discovered Faith had cheated on him, could he have accosted the perpetrator mere hours before his own death and gotten into a fistfight? On the other hand, maybe he'd confronted Faith about her adultery and she'd given him a taste of her powerful right hook. Though, of greater importance, how did Carl end up being washed away in a flooded creek?

A weight bore down on my shoulders. How in the world was I to find any of that out?

25

I added more titles to the computer programme Keira had worked on, and rearranged furniture. Scattering bookish gift items around the store for easing viewing, I came across the archive box Graeme had passed on to me. A quick search through the stash of bound books uncovered one of interest, and curling up on the throne chair, I flicked through Wes McKenny's 1978 journal.

Standard entries noting church life—sermon plans, home visits, prayer points—bored me, until a jotting concerning Faith Sweetman leaped from the page.

'*Carl Sweetman brought his new wife to church today, a rather modern young woman from the city. I cautioned Linda for being envious of her fashionable outfit, yet I too experienced a twinge of envy. Carl is one lucky man.*'

Poor Wes. No, poor Linda having a husband with a roving eye. I pencilled an asterisk in the margin and moved on, making additional marks with each discovery.

'Faith Sweetman has shown an interest in joining our church fundraising committee. What an asset she'll be with her fresh ideas.'

'Met Faith Sweetman in town today. Our inspiring conversation challenged my views.'

Good on Faith for being intelligent enough to question his philosophy.

'Cancelled a visit with Faith Sweetman due to Peter falling off a swing and breaking his arm. Another visit to the doctor for this clumsy child.'

'Fundraising meeting held at the Sweetman's tonight. Such a tidy, welcoming home. Linda could learn a thing or two from Faith.'

So, Donna inherited being a neat freak from her mother.

'The Church fete was a huge success thanks to Faith Sweetman's ingenuity. The dunking machine was a hit. Because of the excellent aim of many townsfolk, I've caught a cold from all the soaking.'

My pulse ramped up a notch at the next entry found. 'Faith Sweetman stayed back again after today's meeting. Does she enjoy our times together as much as I do? I hope so.'

I flipped more pages and chanced upon another tantalising admission. Faith's name—who else could it be—now reduced to just initials. 'Thoughts of FS hinder prayerful contemplations.' Followed a few pages later by: 'I plan to visit FS soon. I pray my yearnings will not be met by resistance.'

An entry a fortnight later had me even more perturbed: 'How can I call myself a man of God and encourage the flock to holy living when all I can think about is FS and that glorious day.'

Glorious day? I studied the dates. What had happened during that first two weeks in May to stir his emotions into such a frenzy? Had he visited Faith as planned and experienced something sufficient to cloud his mind and question his calling?

A text message from Shane took precedence over my apprehension. 'When are you coming home?'

I checked the time. Six o'clock already? The darkening sky outside confirmed it. I carried the archive box out to the car and hoped for a chance to read more that night.

26

Leo ate the Cornetto ice cream before the heat and breeze robbed him of his treat. Sitting on a grassy verge on the headland, in the shade of a pandanus, he searched the rocks and beach below for the boy and his dog. Long gone. Probably back home with his family or tearing around the streets with his mates. His thoughts again go to Simon, the closest thing to having a child of his own.

Had he yearned for a kid? Maybe once, briefly. However, he'd never obsessed over creating a new life to carry on his genes, to give him a future. To be honest, he'd hardly had the opportunity. There'd been relationships—some indeed bordering on love—but those commitments had never eventuated to the next step of considering children.

Disappointed? He didn't think so. He'd done all right, eventually landing a permanent job as a motor mechanic, which led to running his own business for twenty-five years. It was only now, in his retirement, that he occasionally wished he'd had grandkids to annoy him with never-ending questions about the olden days, or tease him, calling him an old fuddy-duddy. Simon had Keira. But Leo rarely saw her, what with Simon's wife being such a stuck-up bitch.

He shook his head. What Simon saw in Genevieve other than a damn near perfect body was a mystery. Marrying her because a baby was on the way was a big mistake on Simon's part.

'A dream come true,' Genevieve once said to Leo, referring to her pregnancy.

When he'd asked how her relationship with Simon rated in comparison, she'd given a fleeting smile and changed the subject. Leo wondered if the kid was even Simon's. Sometimes a woman's desperation to become a mother overrode propriety.

Chances Crossing, May 1978

Faith is a no-show at the chicken coop. Leo even lingers at the rear gate, taking his time in replacing the rusty hinges. After an extra ten minutes sorting through his tools, with only Patch as company —the dog more interested in snapping at flies—Leo realises he must have read Faith wrong. She had no intention of helping, let alone meeting up for a dalliance. Though dark clouds massing overhead and a distant rumble herald an unseasonal storm, he figures he has time for a dip in the creek's icy waters to exorcise his primal urges.

Patch joins him as he follows the worn path through dense bush interspersed with silky oaks and lemon-scented gums. Halfway down, he comes to a clearing where a massive Moreton Bay fig tree holds court, the spreading branches and dense foliage giving wide shade. A flash of colour catches his eye. Stepping close, he tugs a wad of purple silk partially buried beneath a buttress root, surprised by its weight. When unfolded, the fabric reveals an ornament that fits into the palm of his hand. He recognises it as a piece from his mother's china collection, The Madonna with Child. *What is it doing here?*

Leo circles the tree and finds more articles hidden among the thick buttress roots. A painted babushka doll with all five nestled pieces intact, a leather marble bag filled with wishing stones—grey stones, each with a single perfectly unbroken stripe wrapped around it—and a floral pencil case wedged too tight in a crevice to remove. What has he stumbled upon, a secret treasure trove of his mother's? After her initial stroke, she'd started doing some bizarre things. Maybe this was just another of her odd eccentricities ... *or somebody else's.*

He replaces each one as he found them and continues down to the water.

27

By the non-existent smell of food cooking, I gathered Shane had not thought to start dinner without me.

Dropping the archive box at the bottom of the loft stairs, I followed the blare of the TV and walked into the living room to find Ross Clarke sitting on the couch next to Shane, both engrossed in a football game.

Ross turned suddenly and grinned. 'Here she is.'

Shane jumped up. 'Great, we're hungry.'

'You could've put dinner on,' I scowled.

Shane glared back. 'I didn't know you were going to be so late.'

'Well, I didn't know you'd invited a guest.'

'I wasn't invited,' said Ross. 'I was lonely for company and sick of ready-made meals. Shane mentioned you were roasting a chicken with all the trimmings and I said count me in.'

'It's not a roast. It's chicken schnitzels and pasta with bottled sauce.'

'That'll do just fine,' he said, patting his stomach.

'Shane.' I nodded towards the kitchen. 'Want to lend me a hand?'

'Sure, no problem.' He passed the remote to Ross. 'Watch whatever you like. This game's all but over, and we don't need a crystal ball to tell us the outcome.'

Shane and I worked in tandem to cook the meal, with me boiling water for the pasta and tossing a salad, while he placed the frozen schnitzels in the air fryer and opened a jar of pasta sauce.

'A productive day?' he asked.

I placed frozen garlic bread on a tray and slid it into the oven. 'You could say that.' No need to mention finding out Stoney Maloney had raped Lester's mother, then discovering he hadn't. Or that Donna's dad—who wasn't her father after catching some god-awful disease—got into fisticuffs with an unknown assailant who may or may not have had something to do with getting Faith up the duff.

I turned at a cough coming from the kitchen doorway.

'So,' Ross said, walking in and winking at me, 'what else have you to report, comrade?'

I gave him a death stare that he must have failed to comprehend, for he broke into a smile and nodded in expectation.

Shane looked from one conspirator to the other. 'What's this?'

I kept my mouth shut, but Ross barged right in. 'Surely Abby's told you about us trying to find Donna's real father.'

'She's told me,' Shane said, a stern look on his face, 'and knows exactly what I think about it.'

I tried to stop Ross from saying more by miming the act of locking my lips, but the dumb-arse just frowned at me and continued. 'Well, she's found out some highly interesting stuff.'

I winced and waited for another reprimand from Shane.

Instead, he tossed the jar lid into the sink. 'Pandora's Box,' he snapped, giving Ross a stiff shoulder nudge as he stomped out.

Ross stared at me. 'What the hell, Abby. He's not a happy camper about this, is he?'

'To put it mildly.' I was conflicted. My head advised me to honour my husband, yet my gut informed me I was in too far to give up. 'Let's see if we can eat dinner without riling Shane any further, okay? No more talk of our plan in his presence. And for future reference,' I lifted my hand to mouth and repeated the mime, 'this means, shut the hell up.'

When Ross finally left for home, I lugged the archive box upstairs to the loft. Disappearing into the bathroom, I filled the tub with hot water and a dash of rose-scented bubble bath. Once I slipped under the scented foam, I reached for Wes's journal and searched for where I'd left off.

I almost dropped the book into the suds when the bathroom door burst open and Shane entered. He'd pretty much ignored me over dinner, so I expected him to hurl another dart of rebuke.

'What's that you're reading? Doesn't look like a novel.' His calm voice unsettled me.

I closed the cover and rested the book on the edge of the bath, with my thumb keeping my place. 'It's an old journal someone lent me to read.'

'Why would they ask you to do that?'

I dared not tell him the truth. 'Just boring family history stuff. But I said I'd give it a glance.'

'Well, I'm about to head off to bed. Though ... I could stay awake if you wanted me to.'

Why would I want that? I wasn't in the mood for discussing the whole Donna thing. Then I caught his eyes lingering on my wet naked bits bobbing above the waterline. 'Oh, so we are friends now, are we?'

'I wouldn't say that, but I could pretend everything's fine for a good fifteen minutes or so.'

'Well, if I'm not there in ten minutes, start without me.'

He gave a groan and walked out.

I slunk back down and looked for more clues to Wes's dilemma.

Another day, another comment. *'Sweet FS. I am like a madman. Your perfume lights the match, your image fuels the blaze. Consume me again and again, O beautiful fire.'*

Intriguing, and slightly cringey, but not as riveting as a scribbled inscription a few days later: *'Have mercy on me, O God, according to your unfailing love; according to your great compassion blot out my transgressions. Wash away all my iniquity and cleanse me from my sin.'*

A prayer? A bible verse? I took my phone from the ledge behind my head and googled the first phrase. My innards twisted as I read the notation on the screen. Wes had quoted verses from Psalm 51. Words written by King David after he'd committed adultery with Bathsheba.

An avalanche of bubbles slid from my skin as I sat up straight. Is that what Wes meant by *'that glorious day'*? Had he and Faith succumbed to their lust?

The next entry did little to allay my fear. *'Like a witch, FS has beguiled me. Dear God, will I ever be free of this torment?'*

Then, to top it off, two months later, words underlined three times: *'Faith is pregnant.'*

I counted on my fingers the number of months from May to February. *Nine!*

Shane's call dragged me from my disgust. 'I'm going to bed now, Abby.'

My constricted throat hindered me from answering.

I slithered out of the tub and wrapped myself in a towel.

Leaning back against the washbasin, I flicked through the rest of the journal only to be disappointed, frustrated, and annoyed at finding no more references to Faith or her predicament.

I slapped my forehead. Of course, Donna was born in February of the next year.

I tried not to slip from wet feet as I raced down the hall and up the stairs to the loft. A rummage through the archive box uncovered the journal for 1979, and I skimmed its pages until I came across a brief account of Donna's christening.

'February 25th - Christening service held today for Donna Sweetman, daughter of Carl and Faith. A blessed event. Many in attendance.'

Surprisingly short and sweet. I searched diligently, yet the only other remark about the Sweetmans was: *'March 3rd - Funeral service for Carl Sweetman. A very sad occasion.'*

I found it strange that there was no mention of Faith leaving Shadow Creek, or how Wes felt about her sudden departure. Cold and emotionally detached from his earlier jottings, had he found forgiveness for whatever sin he'd committed and washed his hands of Faith? Or had her fleeing town released him from his torment? I had to share my discovery.

It was far too late to phone Ross. Snores wafting up from our bedroom revealed it was also too late for make-up sex, so I made a cup of tea and copied Wes's incriminating journal entries into a notebook for easy reference.

Had I stumbled upon the identity of Donna's father, a married church minister, for pity's sake? No wonder Faith had refused to confess. A thought sprung up. What if Carl had cottoned on, and confronted Wes McKenny about his transgression on the day of the christening? What if they fought and Wes was the one who gave Carl a shiner?

28

I woke before Shane had even stirred and went for a walk to clear my head from a troubled sleep. After getting dressed, I stepped outside and into a day breaking to low-lying fog—an indication the temperature would skyrocket with the promise of an afternoon thunderstorm.

Navigating the swirling mist, I descended our street to the cul-de-sac at the bottom and took a dirt path between two properties that led into bushland. Careful not to go off course and step through the wall of grey mist to plummet over the edge of the escarpment, I followed the track until I reached a rocky outcrop. One could normally see a vista of the valley and Shadow Creek township from this vantage point. This morning, however, thick cloud blanketed the view, so I rested against an enormous granite boulder and listened to a cicada orchestra warming up. When a pied butcherbird launched into a melody with its fluting call, I closed my eyes to focus my thoughts and breathed in the aromatic smells of eucalyptus and flowering wattle.

Three days until Ringtales opened. Three days to finish setting up for the grand reveal. How was I to accomplish this?

Running a bookstore, and proving my ability as a sole-trader, was a big deal. So why had I complicated matters by messing around in other people's affairs? Shane was right, I had to get my act together. I needed to forget about lifting Donna out of her depression and concentrate on my own concerns, like bolstering my own self-worth. Later on, when the shop's fanfare had settled, I could return to helping Donna find her father. Or better yet, pass the information and baton on. After all, it was *her* family secret to uncover, not mine.

I visualised putting everything I'd discovered about the Sweetman family into a wooden box, sealing the lid shut, and pushing it to the back of a deep cupboard. Now I could move on.

A scuffle through leaf litter.

A wallaby? A goanna? A scrub turkey? I opened my eyes to find Otto, my neighbour's fox terrier, staring up at me. I cringed and pinched my nose. If he'd gone through with the pamper package the other day at the vet surgery, then its benefits had been negated by whatever decomposing thing he'd just rolled in.

'What the hell are you doing out here,' I growled. 'Have you done another runner?'

He ambled close, cocked a leg, and casually peed onto the boulder.

'Well, that's a lovely how-d'ya-do,' I said, jumping out of the way of the trickle. 'C'mon, let's get you back to Jean before she calls emergency services.'

Stinky McStinko kindly followed at a distance as I hiked back through the bush to the cul-de-sac. He still trotted behind as I walked up the street, its length now visible because of the dissipating fog. Though it wasn't necessary for me to open the gate and walk him to Jean's front door, for Otto snuck through a gap under the fence and scurried across the manicured lawn all by himself. Scared of getting into trouble? No, keen to gobble down some breakfast, more like it.

My stomach heralded its own need for nourishment and I hurried down our driveway and opened the door, just as Shane staggered from the bedroom. Blinking, he scratched his pyjama-clad backside and asked where I'd been so early in the morning.

'Changing tack,' I said, making for the kitchen. 'Got time for bacon and eggs before you head off to work? Or something tastier,' I added, with a sly wink.

Shane's eyes widened. 'Geez, someone woke up on the right side of the bed. Can I have both?'

'Which first?'

He stripped off his pyjama shorts. 'Guess.'

Shane drove off to begin a residential paving job at Tulipwood, near my parents' place, while I returned Wes McKenny's journals to the archive box. When I pushed it into a corner of the loft, I noticed a bulky manila envelope wedged between two lever arch files. I tugged the unsealed envelope out and peeked inside, surprised to find it contained a length of fabric. Drawing it out like a magician's trick, I discovered it to be a brightly-patterned silk scarf with one end tied around a silver bangle. On examination, the bangle bore an inscription on its inner surface: *To she who walks in beauty.*

I checked the outside of the envelope, but no name or address gave a clue to who owned the items. Yet another search within offered a hint in the form of a greeting card. With *Happy Anniversary* printed on the front in gold lettering, Wes had penned inside, *To my dearest Linda, here's to a new year of love and devotion.*

Why had the gifts not been given? Had Wes experienced a

change of heart, his affections having transferred to another woman? Or had he simply forgotten about them and gifted Linda something else, such as dinner out, or a bunch of long-stemmed roses. Maybe even chocolates—which she would probably appreciate even more.

I replaced the items and shoved the envelope back into the box. Not my concern now.

Still the items in the envelope played on my mind. When I arrived at Ringtales for another day of preparation, I phoned Linda McKenny. If the gift and card were bought for her, she needed to receive them. With Wes's passing, they might offer her comfort in knowing how he felt back then.

She answered on the fourth ring.

'Hi, it's Abby Eaton.' I used my most pleasant voice. 'I dropped in the other day to talk about the Sweetmans.'

'I know who you are,' she said, her voice gruff and heavy with annoyance. Maybe she'd had a rough night wrestling with heartburn from eating too many biscuits.

'Well, I'm phoning to tell you I've come into possession of a box of stuff from your husband's time at the Shadow Creek church, mostly old books and journals. But among them I found a gift Wes intended to give you for your wedding anniversary.'

'Wedding anniversary? Which one?' Her tone had a lighter, more melodic lilt to it now.

'No idea. There is a card but no date. Maybe he forgot to give it to you .... or misplaced it.'

'Oh ... it's just like him. So forgetful.' A sniff followed. Was she crying?

'Do you want me to tell you what it is, or would you rather wait until I can drop it in? Not sure when that will be, I'm very busy right now.'

'No, you can tell me, dear. I'd love to know.'

'Well, there's a stunning silver bangle with an engraving and a silk scarf.'

'A silk scarf?'

'Yes, very pretty. A floral design, big yellow sunflowers.'

Silence.

'Hello, Linda?'

'The bangle,' she sounded stern again. 'What does the engraving say?'

'*To she who walks in beauty.* Quite lovely, don't you think?'

A growl shot through the phone ... or maybe a burp. Whatever it was, it didn't sound healthy.

'Linda, are you okay?'

'Don't ever contact me again,' she yelled, and hung up.

I held my phone at a distance. What the hell! Why was she so angry? Unless ... the gift wasn't meant for her.

I brought up Donna's christening photo on my phone and studied Wes as he stood with the small group. I could understand his enamour with Faith, but it couldn't be anything more than a one-sided attraction, not with his lack of physical appeal. But then again, he may have had a power over Faith that was too strong to repel. Cult leaders gained followers not because of their good looks and athleticism, but their ability to influence and persuade. Take Charles Manson, for example. Wes could have exuded a strange charisma that elicited devotion in certain people, vulnerable women in particular.

I swiped the image away, only to see it replaced with the photo I'd taken at Sweet Art of Faith sitting cross-legged on the grass.

'It's your fault I'm having trouble getting things done,' I snapped, and went to put my phone down when I noticed the pattern on the scarf tied around her head like a bandana. *Sunflowers*. How in the world had Faith gotten her hands on the scarf Wes bought? I bit the inside of my cheek. What if it was the other way around?

Gemma entering the shop interrupted my task of flat-packing cardboard boxes.

'Morning, Mum, thought you could do with a heart starter.' She handed me a large takeaway cup I hoped contained a triple shot cappuccino.

'Thanks, Gem, you're a lifesaver.' I took a swig and almost choked. 'What the hell is this?'

'A turmeric latte made with almond milk. Healthy and filled with zing.'

'Tastes like seasoned dirt.'

'Well, it'll get your blood flowing.'

I tempted another sip and guessed I could grow to like it.

Gemma fanned herself with an old exercise book I recognised as Natalie Schilling's. 'It's great you have air con in here. It's a shocker outside.'

'Have you finished Nat's story? What did you think?'

She flopped onto the chaise lounge. 'Well, it turns out *The Publican's Daughter* isn't a soppy romance after all. It's way worse, or better, depending on the way you look at it.'

'Really?' I dragged over the wingback chair to sit across from her. 'How would you describe it?'

'Let me see ... imagine *Fifty Shades of Grey* crossed with *Sweeney Todd* and in need of a good edit.'

'No!'

Gemma nodded. 'Actually, I had trouble putting it down. It had enough thrills and chills to keep me reading non-stop till the very end, which was utterly mind-blowing.'

She had me intrigued. 'So, give me a rundown on the story.'

Gemma took a gulp of her green goop and set the cup on the floor near her feet. 'In short, that dude at the bar, Preston Black is his name, sweeps Lucinda Braidwood off her feet. Smitten, she ignores her father's warnings and plans to run away with Preston to the city. Days before their departure, she discovers he's stolen money from nearly everyone in town, including her father, and is already married. Lucinda confronts Preston and tells him to hit the road without her.'

'Way to go, Lucinda!' I cheered.

'Preston responds by tying her up in the pub cellar and raping her. Daddy finds out, and with the help of the local butcher, they string Preston up, hack bits off him until he bleeds out, and then hide his assorted body parts in a barrel of ale. They then have the barrel delivered to a city establishment owned by Preston's father, a chief of police, and he and his cronies drink the night away none the wiser.'

'That's disgusting, but good payback.' I started to rise, but Gemma signalled me to stay seated.

'The story continues. When Lucinda realises she's pregnant, she marries the butcher and gives birth to a son who grows up to become the village priest.'

'Wow, I see what you mean. Natalie didn't pull out any stops with that story.'

'But wait, there's more. A beautiful woman comes to town who seduces Lucinda's son, the priest, before confessing she is his sister from another mother. Horrified, he stabs her to death with a crucifix and then hangs himself in the church bell tower. The end.'

Gemma waited for a comment, but this time I was too stunned to speak.

'Anyway, I better get to work,' she said, jumping up and handing me the exercise book. 'I'll let you tell Natalie what I thought of her story. You never know, it might be a bestseller, especially around here.'

That wouldn't surprise me, after what I'd recently learned about folk from Shadow Creek.

'Hey, Gem, before you go. How was your romantic dinner last night?'

'It was a meal,' she said flippantly, 'nothing else. So leave off, will you?'

I held my hands up in an act of surrender. 'Okay, I'll say no more.'

And I didn't, even when she tripped over a box, knocked into a pile of books, and pushed rather than pulled the door to open it. Someone seemed a little flustered.

I remained on the chair, dwelling on Natalie's story. Not because of its diversity and shocking nature, or that skittish Natalie hid a dark underside, but that it mentioned the tying up and rape in the cellar. Had she used Stoney to add authenticity to her narrative? Or did having deviant sex with Stoney inspire her to write the story? Whichever, her addled mind seemed to be playing tricks, making her unable to sort fact from fiction. If that was the case, her disclosure about Stoney being Lester's father might also be a fabrication.

29

I printed out signage for shelves and a poster detailing the shop opening hours, then planned my window display. Amid trying to decide if I should go with a rustic theme or something bold and on trend, my new EFTPOS machine arrived, delivered by a keen young geek from the bank. I listened intently to his animated instructions on setting it up. He even got me to do a dummy run of a sale while offering encouragement similar to a parent cheering a toddler on in taking its first steps.

Afterwards, I walked to the grocery store to buy something healthy to eat for lunch—if I was able to swallow a turmeric latte, I'd be able to stomach a ready-made bean salad. Gemma was right. It was like a sauna outside and the light cotton dress I wore soon stuck to my sweaty ribs and thighs.

Inside the store, I made a beeline for the refrigerated aisle to cool off and found Stoney Maloney checking out the dairy produce.

I sidled up for a quick chat. 'Hey, Stoney.'

'Hey, yourself,' he said, without a hint of a smile.

'Natalie Schilling handed me a manuscript for a story she wrote many years back and guess what?'

'What? Not that I really care.'

'A character in her story ties up a woman in the cellar of a pub and assaults her.'

He narrowed his eyes. 'So?'

'So, I reckon, like you said, Natalie got her wires crossed when she talked to me and blamed you for attacking her. My theory is she either enticed you down to the pub cellar to use you as a guinea pig for a scene she was writing, or added what you did together to her story later on. Of course, she changed consensual sex into a violent rape. What do you think?'

He drummed his fingers on the block of cheddar he was holding and gave a nod. 'You know, I have a vague memory of her doing some story writing back then. Weird stuff. Maybe you're onto something.'

I smiled with relief. 'It would certainly explain things.'

Stoney clicked his tongue. 'Poor Natalie. She sure has some screws loose in that old noggin of hers. I just wish she'd stop spreading those filthy lies. Could give a fella a bad reputation.'

We both turned at a loud clatter to find Natalie Schilling standing beside a collapsed tower of canned vegetables and grasping her face.

'Natalie,' I cried. 'We were ... um ...'

Before I could expound further, she let out a groan and took off, disappearing down the cereal aisle.

'Bloody hell,' Stoney said, frowning, 'do you think the silly old bat heard us?'

'I'd bet on it. Though how much ...' I gave a shrug.

Stoney dropped the cheese block into the fridge. 'See what meddling does, girly?' With a shake of his head, he left me wallowing in remorse.

. . .

I waited in the checkout queue to pay for my tuna and quinoa salad when a tap on my shoulder made me turn.

'How's things?' Simon Sweetman asked, his arms loaded with a barbecued chicken balanced atop a twenty-four pack of toilet paper.

'Busy,' I chose from several answers I could have given but wasn't willing to share. 'You?'

'Getting by.'

'Hello, Keira,' I said, spying her standing behind him and fidgeting with her phone. 'I could still do with your help at the bookshop if you're looking for something to do.'

'Nope, I'm good,' she said without lifting her eyes from the phone screen.

'Hey,' Simon nudged me with his elbow. 'Will you be selling used books in your shop? I found a box of old titles in the shed at home that might interest you. In pretty good nick, too.'

'Well, yes, I'm considering selling quality used books. I've a lovely old bookcase I can use to showcase them.'

'Great. Want to drop by and check them out?'

'What, now?'

'No. How about tomorrow? I'll whip up a tasty meal to make the trip worthwhile.'

'Oh ... might be tricky. I still have a lot to do. Only three days to the opening, you know.'

'But you take a break for lunch, don't you?' He eyed my plastic food container and bottle of kombucha. 'No need to hang around long. How about it?'

Keira poked her head out from behind her father. 'But, Dad, you were going to take me shopping tomorrow? I need new boots.'

'We can do that another day.'

Keira grumbled and pushed past, then stomped out through the automatic sliding doors.

'Kids.' Simon grimaced. 'So, tomorrow. Can you make it around twelve?'

How could I resist a rest from the tedium of getting the shop ready, or those grey-blue eyes imploring mine? 'I shouldn't ... but ... if it's just a quick visit.'

'Short and sweet, I promise.' His wide grin had my stomach flipping.

'Next,' called the checkout operator.

I paid for my lunch and told Simon I'd see him the following day.

Rather than return to Ringtales, I strolled down to the park by the creek, hoping it would be cool enough to sit and eat in the shade.

Choosing a bench seat under a Moreton Bay fig tree, I ate my salad while listening with expectancy to a storm bird calling in the rain. 'Go for it, little eastern koel,' I encouraged.

I set my empty containers aside and walked to the water's edge to gaze upstream. If tree roots much further up hadn't caught Carl's body that fateful afternoon, the flood may have dragged it right into town. What if someone standing on this very spot had seen him swirl past? It wouldn't have been as beguiling as watching The Lady of Shalott drift solemnly by. His twisted and battered corpse bobbing among forest debris would have been a gruesome sight.

I shivered and turned away from the creek.

When I checked my phone, I saw with surprise that a post from Donna had popped up on Facebook: 'Loving Melbourne.' Attached were photos of her posing at tourist spots—Federation Square, Captain Cook's cottage, Hosier Lane with brick walls covered in remarkable graffiti art, the Shrine of Remembrance.

These were not selfies. Someone had taken the photos for her. Someone whose reflection I could see in a glass shop front in The Block Arcade—a tall man in a bulky jacket. The final pic—a crowded rooftop bar without Donna, this time—showed a tall man wearing a military style jacket standing under a line of naked lights. Smiling for the camera, his handsome face bore a close-shaven beard. Was this the husky-voiced male who'd answered my phone call to Donna?

Concern reared its head. What was my friend up to?

I commented on her post: 'Hope you're not having too much fun?' On second thoughts, I added a smiley face to add a note of levity to my words.

Desperate for air con, I disposed of my lunch rubbish and headed back uptown.

I hurried past Fine 'n Dandy, hoping not to engage with Ross. With Donna's happy snaps flicking through my mind like a show reel, I couldn't trust not to blurt out something that would incriminate my friend. I needn't have worried. From my quick glance through the store window, Ross was nowhere in sight. Good for me, but not so good for the group of people waiting at the counter clutching their intended purchases.

Had he also seen Donna's Facebook post? Was he busy searching online for the identity of his wife's mystery man?

At Ringtales, I pulled up with a start. There was no need for a forensic analysis to tell me what somebody had smeared over the front door. I'd stepped in plenty of dog poo in my time to recognise that distinctive stomach-churning odour. First graffiti, and now dog shit. If I ever caught hold of those little rotters, I'd rub their noses in some of the same.

Out came the bucket, gloves, hot soapy water, and disinfectant.

Anger and bewilderment empowered me to scrub away the offensive calling card before anyone came by to make some smart-arse comment.

I'd only just finished and was packing away my cleaning equipment when Shane strode into the shop.

'What are you doing here?' I growled.

He took a step back. 'I'll go out and come back in again when you've taken your chill pill, shall I?'

'Sorry, it's not you. Some lowlife just shat over the door.'

He twisted around to study it. 'How did a person manage that?'

'What I meant was, someone smeared dog poo over it.'

'Why?'

'How the hell do I know?' I yelled.

Shane gripped my shoulders and pushed me down onto a chair. 'Settle down. Do you need a glass of water? A cup of tea?'

I folded my arms and shook my head. 'I don't think I can do this.'

'What? Run a bookstore?'

I nodded, my eyes smarting.

'Aw ... come on, Abby. Don't be like that. There mustn't be much left to do here. Anyway, I have something that might cheer you up.'

'Overseas airline tickets?'

'The shop counter. It's outside in the ute. I'll need a hand lugging it in.'

That made me spark up. I assisted Shane and his trolley to move in the timber shelving, and then the counter top. Lifting the polished redgum slab onto its base was a mammoth task, but we got it done with only minor injuries—a crushed thumb on Shane's part, and a wrenched shoulder on mine.

I ran my hand over the glossy timber and breathed in the heavenly scents of wood and polish. 'It's beautiful. Thank you so much.' I planted a kiss on Shane's cheek and he caught me around the waist and pulled me close.

'Want to christen it?' He grinned suggestively.

'Don't be silly,' I said, smacking his arm. 'It's still daylight and we can't chance those graffiti artists and crap-slingers coming by and catching us in *flagrante delicto.*'

His brow puckered. 'What's that? I had in mind popping a bottle of Prosecco and downing a seafood basket from Merv's Fish 'n Chippery. Throw a few paper serviettes on this little ripper and we can celebrate in style. Got any wine glasses handy?'

'No, but I do have some paper cups somewhere.'

'Great. I've got to finish bricking a retaining wall a street away, and then I'll pick up our dinner. Got enough to do here?'

'Hah! I'm sure I can find something to fill in the time.'

Slipping out to collect an order of gift bags delivered to the post office, I tackled a strong breeze playing havoc with my hair. A distant rumbling. I looked skyward at purple clouds bearing the promise of rain and sighted veins of lightning zip across the dark expanse like fireworks.

Back at the shop with my delivery, I set up the new counter, stacking office stationery and gift bags on the shelves underneath, while the laptop and EFTPOS machine I placed on top. Gift items and a couple of picture books were perched on display stands. By the time I finished, the sky had darkened to the extent I had to switch on the lights, even though it was only four thirty in the afternoon.

I jumped as a lightning bolt dashed earthward in the near distance, followed soon after by an ear-splitting crash that rattled the shop windows. The lights went out. Sliced open, the clouds released their load and water descended in heavy drops that clattered like reindeer hooves on the tin roof sheeting until the shower became a torrent, filling roadside gutters and rushing in waves down the bitumen.

I hoped Shane was under cover and not caught out, soaked to the bone.

About to shut the door, I noticed a figure standing under an umbrella on the footpath across the street. I squinted. Was that Lester Schilling watching me through the grey shower? I gave him a wave, yet he offered no response. He just stood there, staring.

My skin prickled. Had he spoken with his mother? If so, what had Natalie told him about me ... about Stoney?

The lights flickered back on and I locked the door and drew the curtains. Taking refuge on the throne chair, my heart beat a frantic drum solo as I waited for Shane to arrive with or without dinner.

30

Again, I couldn't sleep. After an hour of tossing and turning and struggling to talk my mind into turning the hell off, I surrendered. Creeping out of the bedroom so as not to disturb Shane, I made a cup of tea and retreated to the loft to write a list of jobs in need of doing before Saturday's grand opening.

When I switched on the light, my eyes fell on Wes's archive box in a corner. What was I supposed to do with the scarf and bangle now? Sending them on to Faith it would only open up a fresh can of worms. Best to leave them in the box where they'd been hiding for over forty years.

A few minutes later, I dragged the box to the centre of the room and tugged out the envelope. A peek inside revealed I'd removed a similar cream envelope by mistake. This one contained pages of pencilled drawings, which I eased out. My jaw dropped as I flicked through a handful of finely detailed sketches of Faith Sweetman as a young woman.

One drawing showed only half her face, a hint of a smile, and long hair falling over her right shoulder. Another she sat on a wicker chair in a floral dress, her face enraptured by something to her left. In a third she looked wistful, holding a teacup while the next had her sitting on a fence railing in jeans and a sweater and laughing like she'd just heard a cracking joke. The signature scrawled at the bottom of each page verified the artist was Wes McKenny. I was impressed with his talent as he'd captured her likeness to perfection. Were they drawn from a memory fuelled by infatuation?

My thoughts drifted back to my visit with Linda and the artwork hanging on her walls. If I'd looked closer, would I have discovered Wes's signature? A further search inside this envelope disclosed a worn sketchpad the same size as the pages I'd found. I dropped it into my lap and flipped it open.

I spent ten minutes viewing page-upon-page of drawings, though these were partials—hands, legs, feet, arms, a shoulder, the jut of a hip bone, the curve of a thigh, taut muscles—as if Wes was trying to perfect his artistry and the technique of shading to add depth and form. I suspected his wife was the inspiration for plump buttocks stippled with cellulite, and robust breasts centred by puckered nipples. Tufts of paper caught in the spiral binder hinted additional pages had been ripped out.

I located the original envelope containing the scarf and bangle and included the pictures of Faith and the sketchpad before placing it on my desk. Then I lifted the heavy box to return it to the corner of the room when a sharp twinge in my back made me lurch and trip on the curled edge of the floor rug. I fell hard, the cardboard box crumpling beneath me, and rolled sideways, groaning and checking for damage—not to the contents strewn over the floorboards, but to my aching torso. An examination under my pyjama top showed a blooming welt across my rib cage.

I'd have to find another archive box now to store Wes's rubbish. Maybe I could just dump it as no one but me was interested in all this historic crap.

An attempt to stand revealed a sheet of paper had adhered itself to my left knee. I peeled it free and stared wide-eyed at yet another, though more shocking, sketch of Faith. She was drawn standing naked in a large seashell with lengths of windswept hair barely covering her modesty, just like Botticelli's Venus on the occasion of her birth.

A rummage through the debris at my feet unearthed loose pages fanning from a dog-eared manila folder. I scooped it up and flopped onto the sofa to view pencilled reproductions of other famous artwork: Lady Godiva astride her horse; a woman holding a splayed oriental fan with her robe slipped down to expose a shoulder and a glimpse of side boob; and a bare-breasted mermaid combing her hair near a rock pool—all familiar to me, even if I couldn't recall the artists. In each, Wes replaced the facial features and hair colouring with Faith's, for his salacious pleasure, no doubt.

I went to the desk and brought back my laptop. An internet search to compare the sketches with images of the original artwork showed Wes had enhanced the women's figures, giving them fuller breasts, narrower waists, and flatter stomachs. He'd even slimmed down the legs, except for John Collier's Lady Godiva's which Wes must have seen as a perfect representation. Had Wes improvised, drawing what he imagined Faith looked like nude, or had he, by chance, spied her like that? *Was Wes, in fact, a filthy perve?*

I eyed the bottom corner of each sketch where Wes's signature lay. The one of Faith holding a fan included a scribbled date. So did the mermaid picture. *May 1978.*

I fell back against the sofa cushions. Did this mean Wes visited Faith that day in May, as mentioned in his journal, with the purpose of drawing her in these suggestive poses? Or had the idea come up during their conversation and she'd agreed to model for him, removing her clothing for art's sake? A more vexing scenario popped into my head.

What if something happened during that visit which enabled Wes to conjure up Faith's naked image at whim?

Again, I viewed the sketches. This time I noticed a piece of cloth floating mid-air beside Faith's Venus: a scarf patterned with sunflowers. It also appeared draped over the neck of Lady Godiva's horse. I peered across the room to the large envelope resting on my desk and felt sick. Wes must have pocketed the scarf as a memento of 'that glorious day' and added it to his drawings as a motif.

What had they done?

I got up and paced the floor. Surely Faith hadn't found the spindly pastor attractive enough to have sex with. But then again, Wes may have held sway over her. Through mind control, or whatever, he could have lured her in until she'd succumbed to his sordid demands. That way he'd been able to draw her true to form in whichever pose took his fancy.

I kicked an old hymnal out of my way and sent it skidding under the sofa. That's ridiculous. I had difficulty in visualising Faith getting down and dirty with Wes McKenny.

In his 1978 journal, Wes mentioned he'd struggled with his feelings for Faith after this May visit. Would sketching her naked —however that came about—have been sufficient to inflame his passion and have him struggle with temptation? Nothing else needed to have taken place. Also, according to Wes's jottings, his torment trailed off after Faith became pregnant. Maybe the news of her impending motherhood had been the splash of cold water necessary to cool his fantasies and restore sense to his troubled mind.

I chose to believe this version of events. It made more sense.

Hiding the incriminating evidence in a desk drawer, I hurried downstairs in search of something stronger to drink that might knock me out before dawn.

31

On Leo's way back to bed after a midnight leak, he sighted the full moon through the sliding glass door in his room. Fascinated by the clarity of the celestial globe, he stood entranced, watching clouds drift in shadowy strands across the pockmarked surface. A memory surfaced of long dark hair as cool as silk sliding over his fevered skin, while the twinkle of stars brought to mind eager eyes reflecting flashes of light. He'd fallen hard for Faith—so young and beautiful, with resilience beyond her years—which made her deceit so painful.

Chances Crossing, May 1978

Dinner, after Leo fixes the gate, is awkward.

Faith's iciness has returned. Barely uttering a word to him, she loads his plate with mashed potato, home-grown vegetables, and patties made from lentils and grains. His brother would have had a fit if she'd served him such a meal.

He can see him now. 'Where's the flamin' meat?' Carl would rant, banging his fist on the table and pushing back his plate.

Faith whisks Leo's empty plate away and replaces it with a large bowl of apple crumble and ice-cream. Tapping her foot, she scowls and waits for him to finish before snatching the bowl and tossing it into the sink. He offers to wash up, but she demands he get out of her kitchen and shoves him out the door.

What is going on with her?

Bored watching TV on his own, Leo retreats to his room with a book taken from the crammed bookcase and lights up a smoke.

A few pages into John Wyndham's *The Chrysalids*, a photograph drops onto his chest. It is a Polaroid snap of Faith reclining seductively on an outdoor sun lounge, wearing only a string bikini. An interesting bookmark, for sure.

Leo ogles her curvaceous figure—the length of her legs, the cinch of her waist, the swell of her breasts straining against small triangles of material. He flips it over to look for a notation and his jaw drops. This side has a pencil sketch of Faith in the same pose —minus the sun lounge and bikini. Whoever drew this has given attention to detail, using their imagination to picture her nude. Unless Faith has a secret penchant for art and this is a self-portrait.

He draws his attention away and slips the photo under the bed mattress for safekeeping. Unable to concentrate on reading, he lights another cigarette and lets his mind wander.

The storm heralds its arrival with a lightning strike that robs the house of electricity, sending Leo cowering in a corner of his room—darkness around him, dark within.

A touch wrenches him back from the terrors of war. Cradled within slender arms, he allows whispers to soothe, and silken hair to caress. When a flash of light allows him a glimpse of his ministering angel—her beauty, her compassion—he realises he cannot live without her.

He shudders at a clap of thunder.

'It's alright,' Faith says, holding him tight. 'I'm here.'

No, it's not all right. He is in love with his brother's wife. Leo pushes her away and hears a crash accompanied by a groan. Another lightning flash reveals the overturned bedside table and Faith crumpled on the floor, face contorted, hand clutching her head. He shuffles over in the dark and finds her, sits her up. Locating her face, he strokes cheeks wet with tears.

'I'm sorry, I'm sorry,' he says.

Rain pelts the tin roof like bullets and Leo's trembling returns. Tempted to curl into a ball and cover his ears, his hands are caught and pressed against soft breasts covered by slippery fabric. Warm puffs of air buffet his throat as his fingers glide over this satin barrier, the flesh beneath responding instantly. His thumb eases a thin strap down and his lips glance her shoulder before moving up to follow her collarbone, skim her neck, brush an earlobe. A flutter of lashes tickles his cheek and his mouth finds hers.

Freeing Faith from her nightgown, Leo sheds his pyjama shorts. No thought is given to his brother, the consequences of his actions, or that young Simon is only the thickness of a wall away. All he can think of is his desperate need for the woman coiling around him and setting his whole being on fire.

Sex is urgent, and for Leo, bordering on spiritual. Glimpsed in bursts of light, they take delight in the forbidden, their cries muffled by the deluge until, sated, they lie entwined on the floor rug, listening to the storm pass.

Leo is the first to break hold. He fumbles for his cigarette lighter on the floor and sparks the flame. Faith gets up and stands unabashed before him—her skin flushed and glistening in the flickering light, her hair a tangled cape falling down her back. His eyes sweep over her, drinking her in. The artist's impression of

Faith in the nude was inaccurate. In reality, her features are even more breathtaking.

He flicks off the light and bows low, resting his forehead on the top of her feet. It is easy to worship at Faith's altar, for she has saved him from himself. Verging on grateful tears, he feels her hand on his head, her fingers in his hair. But instead of lifting him to his feet, she moves away.

The bedroom door creaks open.

'Wait,' he calls, but brisk footsteps fading away tell him she has gone.

A door bangs further down the hall.

Leo rises to follow when a noise coming from the back verandah forces him to move to the window. He pokes his head out at the sound of footfall on weathered decking. 'Who's there?' he cries.

No answer.

Leo grips the lighter and rushes out to the verandah, yet the only movement visible is the gentle sway of hanging plants and their dancing shadows. He creeps around to the front stairs where moonlight seeping through scattered clouds affords him a monochromatic view of the property with the dam shining like a giant silver medallion. He attunes his ears. Water drips. Frogs chirp. A cow bellows. A curlew screams its haunting call. However, it is the clang of metal followed by a dog's yelp that has him worried.

He dashes around the verandah to the rear of the house and considers venturing into the yard when a coldness on his leg makes him flinch. He peers down and sees the shimmer of a moist black nose. The last time he'd seen the dog, he was curled up at the foot of Simon's bed.

'Holy shit, Patch, what are you doing out here? Been out for a piss, have you, mate?' The sight of a metal chair knocked over has him adding, 'Come across a feisty possum, hey?'

The dog blinks up at him, wispy eyebrows waggling.

'C'mon, back inside.'

Leo first checks on Simon, finding the boy wrapped in his blanket and breathing soundly in sleep. Patch leaps onto the mattress and gets comfortable beside him.

Outside the main bedroom, Leo's turn of the door knob is met with resistance. He knocks lightly and calls Faith's name. When there is no response, he presses his ear against the timber panelling and hears the squeak of bed springs and the sound of sobbing.

At daybreak, Leo is on the highway, travelling to the north coast.

32

The next morning at the shop flew by without interruption, and I was soon driving to the Sweetman's eager for a respite from the monotony of allocating books to shelves.

Simon met me at the house front door, not shirtless this time, but fully dressed in a T-shirt and khaki shorts. He took me into the lounge room where a cardboard box sat in the middle of the coffee table. I looked inside and read the spines. Some titles were familiar to me: *The Faraway Tree*, *A Little Princess*, *Black Beauty*, and *The Wind in the Willows*. There was even a copy of *The Island of the Blue Dolphins*. I hoped they were in excellent condition for resale value.

'Were they yours?' I asked.

Simon pulled a face. 'No. I was more into comics. Though I enjoyed reading *Doctor Doolittle*, and later on Jules Verne and Tolkien novels. I think these were my mother's.'

That sounded feasible. I pulled out a dog-eared copy of *A Picnic at Hanging Rock*, flipped open the cover, and gave it a good sniff. Ahh ... the scent of years gone by. Penned words on the title page piqued my interest: *To Faith, happy fourteenth birthday, love Mum and ...* A coloured pencil had been used to cross out the other name. It could have been Mike or Midge. It certainly wasn't *Dad*.

I showed the book to Simon. 'This was Faith's. Did she have any siblings?'

'Not as far as I know. Never met any of her family, not even at Donna's christening. I assumed they were estranged.'

I slid the book back into the box. 'Maybe Keira would like to read these.'

'I asked. She doesn't. Are you ready to eat? I have bread rolls and iced tea. Some fresh fruit too. We could go down to the creek for a quick picnic, if you like, and I can show you where I photographed those dragonflies having sex.' His lopsided grin made me smile.

'Okay. But I only have an hour to spare. An hour and a half, tops.'

He disappeared into the kitchen and returned with a backpack.

'I invited Keira to tag along, but she said she'd rather hang out in her room and listen to music.'

'Oh well, her loss,' I said, and followed Simon out to the back verandah.

We crossed the yard and walked through a gateway leading into thick scrub. A worn path led us downhill to a clearing where an ancient Moreton Bay fig tree stretched out its thick branches and offered us two choices to continue our journey. Without hesitating, Simon chose the path on the left, and five minutes later we stood on the banks of a gentle flowing creek where water diverting around semi-submerged boulders created small rock pools.

We sat on the grass beside the creek, and Simon unpacked our lunch.

Handed a bread roll, I noticed mine was chock full of tasty greens and smears of tomato relish, while his also looked to contain sliced ham and boiled egg. When I mentioned he'd forgotten to add the extra ingredients to my roll, he was quick to apologise.

'Sorry, Abby, I thought you were vegan.'

I cocked my head. 'What gave you that idea?'

'Yesterday. The salad you bought?'

'Oh, well, I'm an occasional vegan. My daughter is the hardcore one.'

He took the lid off his bread roll. 'Want some of my ham?'

'No. I'm good,' I said, trying to extract a bean sprout from between my teeth with my tongue.

Red and blue dragonflies played around us as we ate—darting among reeds, skimming water, and hovering in the bright morning air before alighting on lily pads. I watched with fascination while Simon, having finished eating before me, squatted and clicked his camera.

He'd told me, when we met at the gallery, he enjoyed collecting stuff as a kid. Then, when Faith bought him a camera, he captured objects on film instead. Was taking photos—freezing events, places, and living things in time—his way of keeping them forever, without fear of loss or decay?

I lifted my face to the sun. What's a few more freckles at my age?

Another click, close by. I turned and found Simon flashing a broad grin.

'Got a good one,' he winked, raising the camera for another shot.

Horrified, I jumped up, skidded on wet grass, and slipped knee-deep into the creek's reedy shallows, my feet sinking well above the ankles in mud. Struggling to release myself from the sucking ooze, I cried, 'Give me a hand before I lose my balance and fall in arse-first.'

Simon took his time lowering his camera, probably taking a candid shot of my predicament.

'Try to pull one foot out,' he suggested.

I wriggled and pulled without success.

'Well, untie your joggers. That'll free your feet.'

I bent down and got stabbed in the eye by a reed stalk. On my second attempt, I shoved my hands into the squelchy muck and discovered wet and slimy shoelaces were near impossible to undo. Defeated, I straightened and shook my hands, flicking mud in Simon's direction.

'Hey, watch it,' he growled, examining his camera, 'It's a new Canon EOS 80D.'

'I don't give a stuff about your bloody equipment,' I cried. 'Just get me out of here.'

Simon placed his camera in its bag before returning to the water's edge. He reached out, gripped my forearms, and tugged, to no effect other than almost wrenching my arms from their sockets. Next, he dropped one foot in the water, grasped me under the arms, and pulled until my left jogger released from the mud. I stood one-legged, flamingo-like, and urged him on. However, freeing my second jogger resulted in Simon falling backwards onto the bank with me on top of him.

I don't know who was more aghast.

I rolled off Simon to crouch on all fours and catch my breath. 'Thank God, I might have remained stuck here all day.'

'That would have given me a few more good shots for my display,' Simon said, laughing.

I poked my tongue at him and was about to stand when I was pushed down flat on my stomach. My leg was grabbed and fingers clawed the back of my thigh just below the hem of my shorts. I kicked out and shrieked when my flesh was pinched.

'What the hell are you doing?' I said, twisting around and sighting something black and plump wriggling from Simon's fingers.

'Got you, you slimy little sucker,' he said, and waved the engorged leech at me before flicking the satisfied bloodsucker into the bush.

I heard a sickening *thwack* as it landed among dry leaf litter.

Rubbing the itchy moist spot below my buttock, I winced as my fingers came away smeared with blood.

'You'll be right. It'll coagulate in a few minutes.' He caught me off guard by licking his fingers and massaging saliva into the leech bite. 'I thought you were accustomed to the delights of country living.'

A blush burned my face. Bar the wildlife, I was isolated with a male hottie rubbing body fluids over me. I sat up and wrestled slimy joggers from my feet.

Simon plonked down beside me. 'I've had another memory about Faith.'

'What, just now?'

'No. Last night. You imploring me to search my memories got me delving deep into my subconscious.'

'Geez, that sounds scary.'

'Puzzling more like it. One memory took ages to unravel. I'm still unsure if it makes sense.' He rested back on his elbows, his grey eyes glistening as he related the event.

'It was a stormy night. I'd woken in fright and found Patch, my dog, missing from the foot of my bed. I went in search of him and discovered the house lights weren't working. The power must have gone off. I went out to the back verandah and spotted someone standing outside Leo's bedroom window. It was just an outline, a silhouette, but I knew it was a man, and it wasn't Leo. I rushed back inside and saw Faith hurrying down the hall ahead of me. The odd thing is, she was starkers.'

'You saw her naked? Are you sure? It was dark.'

'Moonlight coming in through the windows, perhaps. Anyway, I ended up in my room, hiding under the covers. Patch came back at some stage.'

'Did you mention this to anyone the next day?'

'Can't remember. Probably just thought it was weird.'

'Why was a man spying on Leo?'

Simon raised his eyebrows. 'Maybe it wasn't just Leo he was watching.'

'You mean Faith could have been with Leo? Where was your father? Are you sure it wasn't him looking through the window?'

'I think he was away on one of his many trips getting stuff for the farm. Anyhow, the man had a more solid build than Dad, and he wore a cap.'

I sucked in a breath. 'Was it a floppy cap like the one worn by the man Faith pushed out the back door the day you returned from the sleepover? The guy you said could have been Stoney?'

'Something similar. But the guy on the verandah was tall, his head level with a plant pot hanging from a rafter.'

'So, it might not have been Stoney who Faith was arguing with. It could have been this guy. How could you not have remembered all this earlier?'

'Hey, I bet you can't recall every life event. Sometimes it takes a good prod to bring them to the surface. Like hypnotherapy.'

I gulped iced tea from the drink bottle Simon had given me earlier. Though now tepid, it was still thirst-quenching. 'You said Leo has never mentioned having an affair with Faith. Maybe she'd been getting up to mischief with the man in the cap. They could have been frolicking outside in the rain.'

Simon took a swig from his own bottle. 'Then why was he looking in Leo's bedroom window?'

'Checking to see if he was awake, and if they'd been seen? The guy was definitely stocky, not slim?'

'If my memory can be trusted. Though he could have been wearing a thick coat, a raincoat. That would have bulked him up.'

'And no clue as to when this happened?'

'Not really. There's a chance it was the night a big ol' gum tree in the front paddock got struck by lightning. Dad chopped it up and we used it for firewood that winter. Faith loved an open fire, so that would have made it ... 1978.'

My heart beat faster. May, when Faith got pregnant, was the last month of autumn in Australia. 'You've mentioned your dad getting angry with Faith for flirting, do you think he ever suspected her of cheating on him?'

Simon arched back, and seemed to search the sky for an answer. 'Well, he bailed me up once. Made me watch Stoney's bull service the cows while he gave me the sex talk. Nice, hey?'

I shuddered. My mum handed me a book with lovely cartoon pictures when I'd asked about the facts of life. A well-endowed bull mounting a cow was not an illustration I recalled seeing on any of those pages.

'Then Dad asked if I'd ever seen Faith do that. I remember being shocked and saying, With a bull? He called me stupid, or something, and said he meant with a man, someone other than him. I probably took too long to answer, still trying to wrap my head around the whole disgusting business of procreation, because he shoved me up against the barbed wire fence that bit into my back like a bitch and asked me again. I must have said I hadn't, for he related a Swedish folk tale about dragonflies being sent to look for bad souls, sneaking up on children who told lies and stitching their mouths, eyes and ears shut.'

'Hooly dooly, that's a lovely bedtime story to tell your kids.'

'Well, it scared the shit out of me. Anyway, when Faith announced she was pregnant, it gave me the horrors, thinking she'd suffered the same fate as those poor cows. I couldn't fathom how anyone would enjoy sex. Of course, I know differently now.'

I averted my eyes from his and glanced at my watch. 'We'd better go. I need to get back to the shop.'

As we packed up our rubbish, Simon suggested I return for another visit.

'I'll take you to an old pine forest on the other side of this creek. It's quite remarkable. Planted in the fifties, it's still untouched. Though you'd have to cross a rope bridge to get to it. A wooden one the timber-getters used rotted and collapsed awhile back, so I've fashioned this ingenious rope structure.'

'How high up is it?'

'Only five or six metres. It's quite sturdy.'

'Sorry, you won't catch me up there. I can't stand heights. I'd be bawling like a baby in no time.'

Walking the trail back up to the house, I bravely put a question to Simon. 'Your father obviously had anger issues. What if, on the day of the christening, he discovered Donna wasn't his child and got into a fight?'

'With Faith?'

'Or someone else.' I felt like a short distance runner about to push off the starting blocks. 'Have you ever considered Carl may not have been caught out by the flash flood but had drowned on purpose?'

Simon narrowed his eyes. 'Are you suggesting he killed himself?'

'Now that's an interesting theory I hadn't thought of. No, what if Carl had argued with someone in the morning who turned up at the farm later that day, saw an opportunity, and pushed Carl into the flooded creek on purpose?'

'Murdered him, you mean?'

'It's a possibility, right? No one witnessed him being accidentally washed away. Well, no one admitted to seeing it happen. I guess you wouldn't if you had a part to play in his death.'

Simon's face fell and then broke into a grin as he laughed. 'Man, you have a wild imagination. You should write books, not sell them.' Then he strode off, his pace so quick I had to jog to keep up with him.

Keira was in the lounge watching TV when we arrived back at the house. Once again, she took no notice of me, so I ignored her.

I thanked Simon for lunch, picked up the box of books, and exited.

Driving away, I had a hunch Simon knew more about his father's death than he'd let on.

33

Back at Ringtales, I fixed my hair and makeup in front of a mirror and saw that I'd lost an earring. This normally wouldn't have bothered me; however, the rose gold tear drops were a recent gift from Shane for our twenty-fifth wedding anniversary. I hoped it would turn up before he noticed its disappearance.

Opening the curtains, I saw something poking out of the mail slot in the door and tugged it free. It was an unaddressed envelope. Promotional material for another business? Torn open, it revealed a strange note. One whose brief message was created by pasting words and phrases cut from a magazine or book onto the page:

Stop sticking your nose into other people's affairs or there will be hell to pay. This is not a threat. It is a promise.

I dropped the page as if smeared with anthrax powder. Who would want to harm me? Who had I offended enough to seek revenge?

I considered the graffiti, the dog poo, and this threatening letter. Was the same person behind them? I thought on people I might have irked. Stoney. Linda McKenny. Natalie Schilling.

Lester. Simon. Shane? Not Faith, she didn't know what I was up to ... unless Ross had spilled the beans.

Rushing outside and down the street, I went to storm into Fine 'n Dandy when I read a note taped to the door: *Closed till Saturday.* I pressed my face to the window. All dark inside. No movement.

On my return to the bookshop, I phoned Ross, only to hear the call go straight to voicemail. 'Where the bloody hell are you?' was the message I sent.

Puzzled, I flopped into the throne chair. What had forced Ross to close shop at such short notice, and without notifying me? I hoped he wasn't unwell. I felt a little sick myself—could he have discovered his wife had been spending a lot of time with another man? He might have drunk himself into a stupor.

I wondered if I should drive to their house and see if he was okay. Though what could I say to ease his worries? I was as flummoxed by Donna's actions as him. Better to wait for Ross's response to my text.

I looked over at the threatening note on the counter. What was I supposed to do about that? I locked the door, pulled the curtains, and tried to keep busy, though fear trussed me in a restrictive shroud.

Hypervigilant, a blast of a car horn made me jump; a clatter on the roof had me trembling; a bang on window glass caused me to cower behind the counter. Who was out there baying for my blood?

Maybe it was time to phone the local police. Newly promoted to sergeant, Will Feather would be happy to help.

I stretched up to locate my phone on the counter when my hand brushed against the note, knocking it over the edge to land at my feet. Flicking it away, I noticed two of the pasted words had come unstuck and lay on the floorboards. I picked them up and found other words printed on their flip-side. '*Buxom*' was on one, '*fondled*' on the other. Intrigued, I peeled back a phrase stuck on the note—being careful not to remove it entirely—and discovered '*his hot breath*' on the reverse side, proving the cut-outs had come from something far juicier than a literary publication.

I slapped the side of my head. *Natalie Schilling.* Of course! Had she lost her mind, thinking I'd let slip her imagined secrets to Stoney, that I'd told him about Lester? I needed to put things right before she did something crazier.

Feeding the note back into its envelope, I collected my bag and hurried out of the shop to a street bustling with traffic. A dazed pigeon huddled at the foot of the display window and a powdery smudge of feather markings on the glass above it revealed what had made the banging sound that scared me. Large seed pods scattered on the footpath from an overhanging flame tree showed what had clattered on the roof. Relief infused me as I walked to the car.

Natalie answered my knock after the first rap.

'What do you want?' she hissed, poking her head out through the narrow gap between door and jamb.

'Who's that?' barked a deep voice from the lounge room.

Over Natalie's shoulder, I saw the TV screen flashing through channels. Vince must have returned from respite.

'Never you mind,' she called to him, her blinking eyes never leaving mine.

'I've received your note, Natalie, and there is no need to threaten me.' I lowered my voice. 'Stoney doesn't know about Lester.'

Her brow creased like a paper fan. 'What are you on about?'

'The note. The one with the cut-out words saying I'll regret my actions if I keep sticking my nose into other people's affairs.'

'You're mistaken. I never sent a note.'

'But the words came from a book, a racy romance, by my calculation. Much like Jackie Collins.'

She puffed air through her lips. 'I might be stroppy with you, but I did no such thing. It must be from someone else you've been gossiping about.'

Her contempt worsened my guilt.

'I'm sorry you overhead my conversation with Stoney. I didn't mean to hurt you. Like I said, I never told Stoney about Lester. But I think you may have got your memories mixed up. Stoney assured me he hadn't assaulted you. He said he would never—'

Natalie's head disappeared just before the door slammed shut.

Unopened windows and no car parked in the driveway at the Clarke house showed Ross was also not at home. I phoned him again, but didn't leave a second message when it went unanswered. Bewildered, I returned to Ringtales and found another delivery of books had arrived. Manoeuvring the heavy boxes inside, I thought hard on what to do next about the note and its dire warning.

I needed to talk to someone. But who? Not Shane, for obvious reasons—one being I wanted to keep our marriage intact. Not Stoney, already miffed by my meddling. Gemma knew about Natalie to some extent, though not my search for Donna's father. Did I really want to involve her in all of that? Elliott and his clever brain had helped sort out some issues a few months back when I researched a lost relative, but he was probably too cool now to help his old mum out. Graeme Roper might prove helpful, yet his bike parked outside the pub meant he was ensconced inside, in deep discussion with his drinking buddies.

That left only me. I'd gotten myself into this mess, so I had to get myself out.

Hitting a roadblock as to my next move, I slit open the delivered box of books and plunged my hand into the sea of Styrofoam packing peanuts.

The first paperback withdrawn, entitled *Belles and Whistles*, bore a cover image of a tanned and muscular confederate soldier —coat and shirt unbuttoned, cap askew—cradling a ringlet-haired beauty dressed in a décolletage-revealing crinoline gown. I skimmed the back cover blurb and cringed. Just as I thought, a trashy romance novel sent by the distributor to entice me into including this type of novel in future orders. Tossing the book aside, my breath caught in my throat. I'd seen a similar styled book recently, but where? Clues slowly emerged from my memory bank.

A book on a table, in a small kitchen. A pair of reading glasses alongside. Yes, a sleazy paperback owned by ... *Linda McKenny*.

I removed the envelope from my bag and slid out the note. Had Linda been the one to drop off the menacing message? Had she suspected Wes cheated on her during their time in Shadow Creek? Being told about the scarf belonging to Faith, and the bangle with engraving—which I now realised wasn't a gift intended for Linda —would have offered proof in her mind of her husband's indiscretion. She would definitely have motive for warning me off if she feared I'd use this information to defame Wes, right before he received a posthumous award.

Linda needed to know Wes hadn't engaged in an extramarital affair with Faith, he only had her pose for his life drawings—still my belief.

I used the new shop phone rather than risk Linda recognising my personal phone number and ignoring the call.

She answered with a pleasant, 'Hel-lo.'

'Please don't hang up,' I urged. 'This is Abby Eaton. I've received your threatening note, but I have to—'

'Sorry. Did you say I sent you a threat?'

Don't tell me the old dear had forgotten already. 'Yes, a note with words cut out from a book warning me to keep my nose out of things. I have to tell you I've found something of Wesley's that might explain what happened between him and Faith Sweetman. It was rather shocking and, to be honest, a little creepy, but—'

'Mum!' Her screech pierced my eardrum like a hot needle. 'There's a woman on the phone implying Dad had an affair!'

Holy crap! It wasn't Linda, it was her daughter.

'Yes, with a Faith Sweeper,' she called out. 'She says she has proof.'

'No!' I cried into the phone. 'You've got it wrong.'

'What's that?' the daughter asked me. 'Not Faith Sweeper?'

'No, Sweet-man, but—'

'A sweet man? Mum, scrub that, she says Dad had been carrying on with a bloke.'

Oh God! I face-palmed. 'Look, um ... sorry, what's your name?'

'Chantelle.'

'Okay, Chantelle, can I speak with your mother. She sent me the threat. She knows what I'm talking about.'

'Mum knows? Everything?'

'Well, sort of. I've called to explain things. To set her mind at—'

'Mum, you knew about this?' She must have put the phone down, or dropped it, because after a bang, I heard muffled sounds: angry words, yelling, something smashing.

What had I done? My attempt at defusing the situation had escalated into a slanging match between mother and daughter—not at all what I expected, or wanted.

I hung up.

Just when I thought things couldn't get any worse, my phone pinged. I picked it up and discovered it wasn't a text from Ross but an email from an address I didn't recognise. The subject read: *Gotcha!* But there was no message, just two image attachments.

I viewed the first one and my world tilted. In glaring colour and focus was a picture of me lying on top of Simon on a grassy verge. The second image showed me now on my stomach and Simon bending over me with his hand up my shorts.

My knees buckled, and I folded onto the floor.

Taking deep breaths, I forced myself to reply: 'Who are you?'

A long minute later, I got my answer. *'Your worst nightmare.'*

34

The bedroom door burst open and light flooded in.

'What's going on here?' Shane asked. 'Why are the curtains drawn? It's only five in the afternoon.'

I shielded my eyes and waved him away. 'Get lost.'

'Have you got a migraine?'

'Yes,' I whined, covering my head with a spare pillow.

The mattress dipped as Shane sat beside me. 'Can I get you anything? Painkillers? A cup of tea?'

'No.'

'Want me to make dinner?'

'Yes.'

'Did you have something in mind?'

I lifted the pillow a few centimetres. 'Diced chicken and vegetables in the fridge. Jar of sweet and sour sauce in the pantry. Rice to be cooked.'

'Right, I'm onto it. Had a tough day?'

If only he knew. I gave an extended moan.

He patted my leg. 'Well, you rest up. A big day tomorrow

finishing the setup, and then, *ta-da,* the grand opening on Saturday.'

'Nope.'

'Nope, what?'

'Not opening.'

Shane laughed. 'Don't be silly, of course you are. Can't get this far and give up. It's just nerves. I'll come down tomorrow and give you a hand. It'll be exciting, you'll see.'

Exciting? Someone was out to destroy me. If they succeeded, my life would be reduced to rubble—my reputation, my marriage. Words of warning came back to haunt me:

'You don't want to be opening a can of worms.'

'Faith might not be the only one who gets hurt.'

'You could do more harm than good by opening up old wounds.'

'Pandora's box, that's all I'm saying.'

'See what meddling does, girly?'

I groaned and sank my face into the pillows to stem the tears dribbling from my eyes.

Left alone in the dark, I thought on who was stalking me this time. Who had followed me out to Chances Crossing, and down to the creek to hide in the bushes and take sneaky snaps? What would Shane say or do if he discovered pics of me 'rendezvousing' with another man? I hadn't told him I'd met with Simon for lunch, or that I questioned him about Faith's past actions.

Guilt twisted in my gut like a switchblade. Not physically unfaithful to Shane, I'd been disloyal, flouting his advice.

A beep sounded from my phone on the bedside table. I flinched. Another horrid email? I gingerly reached for it and found I'd received a text message from Ross Clarke. A tap on the screen and a photo appeared: a shot of Melbourne's iconic Flinders Street railway station with its distinctive facade and green copper dome. Had Ross flown down for a brief encounter with Donna, or a confrontation about her impropriety?

I forced down a plate of stir-fry and took the unfinished shiraz out to the back deck. Swigging straight from the bottle, I leaned back from the railing and stared up at the starry sky, wishing I was floating amid space junk and not down here, tackling self-made problems. Secrets. It was all because of stupid secrets. Why couldn't everyone tell the bloody truth?

The scrape of the sliding door caused my muscles to tense in preparation to flee.

'You okay?' Shane said, and placed his hands on my shoulders. 'Are you still worried about the shop, or is something else troubling you?'

I sucked in a deep breath. Time for the big reveal. Swivelling to face him, I opened my mouth.

'Hey, I'm back!' came a voice from inside the house.

Shane spun around and Elliott appeared in the doorway.

'Oh, there you are,' he said, and stepped onto the deck. 'Sorry, were you two having a moment?'

'Your mum is anxious about the shop opening.'

'Aw, Mumski.' Elliott wrapped me in a bear hug. 'You'll blitz it. I'm staying over so I can help out tomorrow, and then we'll all be with you on the day to give you a boost. Anyway, I have a surprise that will cheer you up.'

He dashed back inside, leaving Shane and me to shrug at each other.

Elliott returned with a shopping bag which he handed to me. I pulled out a light pink T-shirt from the top. Printed on the upper left, in the place of a pocket, was a logo comprising two possums entwined around the letters of the shop name and grasping golden rings—exactly like the shop sign.

'Turn it over,' he urged, 'there's an even bigger logo centred on the back. I've got shirts for us all, though Dad's and mine are a more manly black.'

'Thanks so much.' I gave him a hug and kissed his cheek. 'Have you had dinner?'

He grinned. 'What do you reckon?'

Shane draped his arm around Elliott's shoulders. 'Come on, boy, let's feed you up before you waste away.'

For my family's sake—and my own—I delayed my truth-telling.

35

Alexandra Headland 2019

Leo woke before dawn, his mind clear, his resolve strong. The difficult phone conversation he'd had with Simon the previous night gave weight to the decision he knew was for the best.

Searching a high shelf in his walk-in wardrobe, he found an old biscuit tin and lifted out a small carved object. Then he moved downstairs to the living room, where he removed two photos from an album. A third photo, taken from a shoebox kept in a cabinet drawer, showed Carl sitting at a table set for Christmas lunch, a brightly coloured paper crown perched on his head. It was the last picture Leo had of his brother and it transported him back in time.

Chances Crossing, Christmas Day 1978

To not tempt a repeat of that thunderstorm tryst, Leo stays well away from the farm and tries to forget it ever happened. Yet when he hears Faith is pregnant, he panics.

'Carl is definitely the father,' she assures him during a phone call he makes from western Queensland, during a stint working as a machinery mechanic for Mount Isa Mines. 'No doubt about it.'

He is occasionally sent photos of Faith's growing stomach, while Simon writes random letters telling of his excitement in gaining a new brother or sister and the games they'll play. As for Carl, he seems content enough.

When the holiday season comes around, Leo has an urge to visit Chances Crossing. He invites a girl he's dated on and off and they arrive on Christmas morning in time to exchange gifts.

Simon is rapt with the microscope Leo gave him and Faith loves her opal earrings and the soft toy koala bought for the baby. Even Carl cracks a smile, but that was probably because of the bottle of Bundaberg Rum he's been gifted.

'She's lovely,' says Faith, pulling Leo aside. 'Perfect for you.'

'Is she?' He glances over at Tess, who is short and blonde with a straight-up-and-down figure. Nothing like Faith, whose shape has blossomed further since her last photo.

'You're looking well, Faith.'

'About ready to pop, I reckon.' She rubs her distended stomach through the stretched cotton of her shirt dress. 'Only a couple of weeks to go, now.'

Tess comes alongside, carrying her overnight bag. 'Where do I put this?'

'In Leo's old bedroom,' says Faith. 'He'll show you the way. I'm sure you won't mind sharing a single bed.'

'Well,' Tess says, 'if it's too cramped, I'm sure the floor will do nicely. More room to thrash about,' she adds, chuckling and bumping her hip against Leo's.

He shoots a glance at Faith and catches a blush rising from

beneath the collar of her dress, guessing she too is recalling what they got up to in that room one stormy night.

They enjoy a festive lunch with all the trimmings on the rear verandah, and after cleaning up, go their separate ways around the farm. Tess jumps at the chance of a horse-riding lesson with Carl, while Leo leaves them to it and ambles around the gardens with another beer in hand and reminisces.

Sticky with sweat, he changes into board shorts and heads to the dam for a quick swim to cool off. Halfway down the hillside, Simon, with Patch in tow, runs into him. With his camera slung around his neck and a pouch bulging with god-knows-what hanging from a rope belt, there's no need to guess what the kid's been up to.

'Did you dig lots of panda pits in Vietnam?' Simon asks.

Leo pulls a face. 'What? Oh, you mean, punji pits.'

'Yeah, the ones with spikes at the bottom.'

'Had I told you about them?'

The boy nods. 'And you covered them with branches so the VC would fall in and get stuck.'

'It was more like the other way around. The Viet Cong built them first. I fell in one. Did I tell you that? Lucky for me, the bamboo spikes were rotten and snapped under my weight rather than piercing my guts. Still, my bruised ribs hurt like hell.'

'Can you show me how to make one?'

Leo cocks his head and studies his nephew. 'For what purpose?'

'To catch wild dogs. They've killed some of our chooks.'

'So have carpet pythons, I bet.'

'Please, Uncle Leo. I don't want to lose any more hens.'

'Better than going after them with a rifle, I suppose. Let me think about it, eh?'

The boy nods and rushes away with Patch bounding close behind.

When Leo reaches the water, he finds Faith has had the same idea. Floating in an inner tube of an old tractor tyre, she waves from the centre of the dam and calls him out. He wades through reeds and swims over to reach her.

'Be careful of eels,' she says, 'I just felt one brush against my butt.'

He rests his elbows on the tube and sees she is wearing a sarong tied around her chest. Her legs, exposed from the knees down, hang over the edge with feet skimming the water.

'Can you get me back to shore? My paddling just turns me in circles.'

Leo swims behind her, and kicking his feet, pushes the tube towards the reedy shallows. Once there, he grips one of Faith's feet and drags her and the tube onto the grassy slope. He helps her out, and she collapses onto the grass, wringing tea-coloured water from the soaked lower half of her sarong.

Leo flops down beside her and ruffles his wet hair.

'Well, that was more exhausting than I imagined,' Faith says, resting back on her elbows, her dripping ponytail dragging on the ground. 'I don't know how I'd have gotten back if you hadn't turned up.'

Leo can't take his eyes off the firm ball of flesh poking out through the parted sarong. A dark line travelling from the knot of the belly button right down to the top edge of bikini bottoms marks Faith's lightly tanned skin.

'Ooh,' she gasps and sits up. 'That was a hefty kick. Do you want to feel it?'

Before he can answer, she grabs his hand and presses it against the left side of her stomach. Within seconds something prods his palm. He smiles and fingers the tiny hummock until it retracts.

'That's amazing. Was it a foot?'

She nods. 'Or an elbow. I love being pregnant, growing a human being inside me. Not sure about the birth, though, I hear it could be a tad painful.' She laughs and covers his hand still on her belly with hers. 'I reckon it's a girl. Got any suggestions for a name?'

Why ask him? He's not the father. He grunts and pulls his hand away.

'Would you be a dear, then, and get me the suntan oil?' Faith points to a drawstring bag on the jetty.

Leo fetches the bag and returns to find Faith has removed the sarong, the entirety of her baby bump now on show. He is startled by how delectable she looks for a woman in the last stage of pregnancy, and forces his eyes away from the overflowing strapless bikini top.

She lies flat. 'Squeeze a few drops on my tummy, will you? It's made from coconut. The best thing for avoiding stretch marks.'

He removes the plastic bottle and kneels beside her. Dribbling the aromatic oil over her stomach, he breathes in the familiar scent of a summer beach packed with sunbathers, and watches as trickles snake down the mound of flesh like golden syrup on a steamed pudding.

'Now rub it in,' she says.

He balks. 'Nah, I'll let you do that.'

'Don't be a chicken. The baby won't burst out and attack you.'

That's not what he's afraid of. Just the thought of his fingers slipping and sliding over Faith's warm, swollen body causes his pulse to race.

When he can't be persuaded, Faith sits up cross-legged and smooths the oil in herself.

Leo grabs the opportunity to ask the question that has niggled him for a long time. 'Why did you run off?'

She cocks her head. 'When?'

'After we made love. I heard you crying.'

'Oh ... it's complicated. You wouldn't understand.'

'Try me,' he snaps, his desperation surfacing.

Faith groans and her face crumples as if she is about to break down and blubber an explanation. Instead, she cradles her stomach and lets out a sharp cry.

'What's wrong?' Leo clasps her shoulder. 'Can I help?'

Faith shakes her head and begins panting. Then inhaling deeply, she releases a long breath.

'Shit! You're not in labour, are you?'

'Braxton Hicks,' she moans, stretching out her legs. 'I've been getting them for a while now. Practice contractions. The uterus getting ready, that's all.'

'How do you know these aren't the real thing?'

'Because they're easing right off.' Her breathing steadies and her body relaxes. She waits a few minutes before asking Leo to help her up. 'I really need to pee.'

He assists Faith to her feet, but can't seem to let her go. Drawing her close, her stomach knocking against his, he lifts her chin and stares into eyes reflecting the vibrant blue of the sky. His heart and body ache for her. 'Faith, I have to—'

She presses her fingers against his lips. 'Don't, Leo. I'm happy. Carl and I are getting along famously. The baby is doing wonders for our marriage.'

Could that be? He searches her face for a sign she is suppressing the truth. Nothing.

Faith steps out of his embrace and retrieves her sarong and drawstring bag. 'It's time you found your own happiness. I'm sure Tess will gladly help.'

Leo keeps his distance from Faith for the rest of the afternoon, choosing to hang out with his nephew.

In the evening, when Tess gets frisky in bed, Leo recalls his last night spent in this room. Not wanting to spoil those vivid memories, he pulls the cover off the bed and leads her outside.

While they are getting intimate in the rose garden, Leo's ears prick to a sound that squeezes his heart. Wafting from the open window of the main bedroom are cries of passion he recognises only too well.

Leo placed the collected articles side-by-side on the TV cabinet. Lighting a scented candle, he knelt before the line-up of faces and a red-painted dragonfly, and unburdened his soul. He offered an apology in turn to Dodge, Ned, Carl, and the Vietnamese girl, and asked for their forgiveness.

Old bones creaked as he pushed up from the floor and went outside into the fresh morning air.

Crossing the quiet street, he stood on the boardwalk at the top of the stairs to watch the sun sneak a peek over the horizon, its newly birthed rays spreading gold, orange, and pink into the clouds. He inhaled the beauty of the sunrise and stepped down to the empty beach, finding the sand cool underfoot.

A breeze ran icy fingers through his hair and over his bare chest, goose-bumping his skin, as he walked to the water's edge and slipped out of his pyjama shorts. Wading naked into the sea, briny waves buffeted his body, attempting to return him to the beach. Yet he continued, ploughing through breakers until his feet lifted from the seabed and he floated on his back. Limbs splayed and eyes closed in surrender, he allowed the pull of the rip to draw him out to the depths until nature's force sucked him under and cleansed him of his sins.

36

Shane, Elliott, and I went to Mulga Bill's for breakfast before tackling the last day of setting up Ringtales. Gemma, not working at the vet clinic till the afternoon, joined us.

James was his usual friendly self, though Benji didn't once stick his head out of the kitchen. It could have been due to a busy morning ... or something else.

'How are things between you two?' I asked Gemma.

The spoonful of berries scooped from her acai bowl stopped just shy of her lips. 'What do you mean?'

'You and Benji. Or is there another coupling I'm not aware of?'

Gemma's blue eyes bore into mine. 'There's no coupling going on anywhere.'

'Oh, yes there is,' Elliott murmured through a mouthful of beef sausage. Three sets of eyes focused on him and waited while he finished chewing. 'I may have met someone.'

I leaned over my smashed avocado on toasted sour dough. 'How'd that happen?'

'Quickly,' he smirked. 'She's a girl from uni. Real smart, studying speech therapy.'

Elliott had broken up with his high school girlfriend over the Christmas break. An amicable decision, we were told, the result of different visions of the future—whatever that meant.

'I thought you planned to concentrate on your studies this year.'

'Hey, I'm not going to ignore the power of attraction.'

'Or your raging hormones,' Gemma scoffed. She held up her watermelon frappe. 'Here's to Mum and her new shop.'

Elliott lifted his glass of freshly squeezed orange juice, while Shane dropped his brekky burger to raise his coffee mug. 'Yes, cheers to Abby Eaton. Bookseller extraordinaire.'

I squirmed in my seat. 'Well, not sure about that, yet. Let's just hope it all goes to plan.'

'Why wouldn't it?' Shane said. 'We're all here to make sure you don't stuff it up.'

I cringed. They weren't aware I had already missed my footing by forcing secrets into the light. Life for me could be about to get very messy.

At the shop, Shane opted to stick the decal of opening times to the display window, while Elliott commandeered the work laptop to fine-tune Ringtales' new website and Facebook page that I'd created with limited knowledge. This freed me up to visit the bank and withdraw cash for the shop till.

Turning away from the cashier with my stash of notes and coins, I bumped into Lester Schilling as he entered the bank. I apologised and went to move aside when he clutched my arm and pulled me close enough to catch a whiff of citrus in his choice of cologne.

'What are you up to, Abby?' he hissed.

I tugged my arm free. 'Getting cash for the shop opening tomorrow.'

He shook his head, his gelled hair showing no sign of life. 'I meant with Mum. You've rattled her good and proper. She can't seem to think straight, let alone sit still since meeting with you. Gone all jittery, she has.'

I coughed to mask a laugh. Nat's nervous tension was evident before I upset her. 'You'll need to have a serious chat with your mum if you want to know what caused that reaction.'

Then I escaped before Lester quizzed me further and I blurted out a secret that was not mine to tell.

Hurrying back up the street, I yelped when a figure lurched out of a narrow lane between two cottage shops and tugged me into the shadows.

Dr Peake looked like an excited puppy, sparkly eyed, panting, and jigging from one foot to another. Foam collected at the corners of his mouth as he spoke. 'I've remembered something else about Carl Sweetman's death.'

'Oh, you have?'

He nodded rapidly. 'Don't know why it slipped my memory. When I had a squiz of Carl's body before the cops carted it away, I noticed his right trouser leg was torn open. In the bared flesh were puncture wounds, each roughly a centimetre in diameter. Here, here, here, and here,' he indicated, jabbing his index finger into the outer side of his right thigh. 'They were evenly spaced in a direct line.'

'Could the injury have resulted from Carl being hit by debris when he was washed away in the flood?'

'That's what the medical examiner must have concluded because they weren't mentioned in the coroner's report. But now, the more I think about it, it makes me wonder.'

'Wonder what?'

'Well, the only other time I've seen an injury like that was when some poor fellow I treated had a run-in with a pitchfork.'

'A pitchfork? You think that along with being punched, Carl was attacked with a pitchfork before he drowned?'

He shrugged. 'Maybe. Anyway, I better go. Got a cyst to lance in fifteen minutes.'

'Wait!' I gripped his arm to stop him moving away. 'What dreaded virus did Carl have that made him infertile?'

'Orchitis, a result of contracting mumps. Carl suffered a severe case after his son was born.' Then, giving a nod of satisfaction, Dr Peake stepped into the sunlight and loped up the street.

Hooly dooly. Someone must have surely had it in for Carl to attack him with a farm implement.

I thought of the people I knew who'd been in his sphere of influence: Stoney; Faith; Leo; Wes and Linda McKenny; Natalie Schilling. Then there were the people I didn't know. Carl had anger issues so there was a high chance he'd offended others, made enemies. Had any of them held a grudge against Carl, a resentment so strong they wanted him dead?

What if a person I hadn't yet met had harmed Carl and gotten wind of my snooping? Could they have wanted to scare me off, or worse?

What if Leo wasn't the caring, innocent man Simon had made him out to be? Just because I hadn't yet talked with him didn't mean he was oblivious to my investigations. I wondered what level of contact Simon had with his uncle.

A shiver ran through me. How much danger was I facing? If my curiosity wasn't reined in, then like the proverbial feline, my existence could be cut short.

37

The 100 km journey seemed to be over in a blink of an eye. After his ritualistic cleansing early that day, ridding his burden of guilt, it was as if Leo had travelled to Shadow Creek on the wings of an angel.

He parked his car roadside and took a stroll before heading out to Chances Crossing. As expected, the town was inhabited with ghosts. Everywhere he looked, phantasmal scenes came into play.

There was the butcher shop where ruddy-faced August Schilling and his son Vince always added an extra sausage or two before wrapping the order with blood-streaked fingers. The bakery whose pink-iced vanilla slice was the best he'd ever tasted. The post office, which old Gertie Collins ran with military precision. *'No licking the stamps, young fella. Use the moistened sponge.'* The milk bar, now a fish and chip shop, had been a child's idea of heaven with ice-cold milkshakes served in anodised containers, and glass cabinets stacked with jars of lollies. A Queenslander house that had been a solicitor's office had become a restaurant, a popular one if the crowd on the verandah was anything to go by.

He shielded his eyes and looked to the top of the street to an establishment he'd spent more time than he should have. Still guarded by two ancient fig trees, the Axeman's Arms seemed unchanged, and the thought of swilling down one of their cold brews made his mouth water. Crossing the street, he stared over the chain wire fence at the white-painted timber church and stiffened as memories swirled around him like an eerie mist.

Shadow Creek, 25 February 1979

Arriving late, Leo has to sit in a back pew of the crowded Shadow Creek church and watch the christening proceedings from a distance. Of course, he'd received the good news just hours after the birth, but out of respect for the bonding needed for a new family, he'd waited until today to visit.

When the minister takes the baby from Faith, douses the small head with water from the font, and gives a prayer of blessing, Leo inches forward on the pew and squints for a clearer view of the infant. Once again, he experiences niggling doubts about Faith's reassurance.

First, there is the child's ginger fuzz that reminds him of his own baby photos rather than Carl's—his brother inheriting their father's dark hair while Leo bore the strawberry blond of their mother's. When Simon was an infant, he'd had similar coloured hair to Carl's, ringing his scalp like a monk's tonsure until it fell out and was replaced with fair curls like Eileen's.

Second is Carl's behaviour. Shouldn't a father be joyful at producing another child to love, a sweet little girl to protect? Instead, he looks to be suffering from a raging hangover. It wouldn't take much for him to crack a smile every now and again instead of standing glum with his hands shoved in his pockets.

Then there is the choice of name: Donna *Leonie* Sweetman. That set alarm bells ringing.

After the required photographic session and small talk with guests, Leo searches out Faith by following the cries of a baby to the cramped room off the church hall used for a nursery.

'Sorry, I'll come back later,' he says, catching Faith wrestling with the squirming child as she changes her nappy. 'When she's settled.'

Faith beckons him in. 'It's okay. Stay.'

He enters, his eyes drawn to the room's circus theme seen in the wall frieze, hanging mobiles, and scattered fluffy toys. Clowns, tigers, lions, elephants, and monkeys are everywhere. Faith sits in a bentwood rocking chair and points to a child's plastic stool in front of her.

'Sit,' she commands like a ringmaster, and he obeys, finding his knees come level with his chest. 'How are you, Leo? Sorry to hear about your break up with Tess. I liked her.'

'Yeah, well, that's life.'

He's taken aback as she casually unbuttons the bodice of her yellow frock and peels down her maternity bra to reveal a blue-veined breast twice the size he remembered. As the baby's miniature mouth latches onto the dark nipple and sucks, a memory of doing the exact thing to Faith sends a buzz of electricity through him and he shifts in the plastic chair, causing it to creak.

'What a relief,' Faith says. 'I thought I was about to burst. She should have been fed an hour ago, but with all the goings-on ...' She shrugs. 'How long are you staying this time, Leo?'

Was there an edginess to her tone? A trace of sarcasm?

'As long as I'm needed,' he says, hoping she catches his intent.

Her eyes move to the baby. 'Isn't she gorgeous? A dream come true. Even though she was overdue, in the end.' She caresses the tiny head, and the child responds by kneading the breast with her toy-like hand.

'Does Carl know what we did?' Leo asks.

Faith glances up and scowls. 'How would he? I've not told him, and it's going to stay that way. We're doing fine.'

'Fine?' Leo gives a wry laugh. 'Carl's not bloody fine, anyone in their right mind can see that today. What's up with him?'

'I think he's jealous of Donna. My time isn't his anymore. I have someone else to consider. Someone who needs me more than he does right now.'

Leo doesn't buy it. Carl isn't just jealous, he is angry, about fit to explode. He'd barely said a word to Leo during the obligatory photo taking.

The baby pulls away, mewing, tiny fists pumping. Faith lifts her to her shoulder and pats the small back, releasing a burp. 'Do you want to hold her?' She passes the baby over.

Donna fits easily into the crook of Leo's arm. Cornflower-blue eyes blink up at him, and a squeak slips from the rosebud mouth along with a line of milk bubbles. A twinge tugs at his heart when he breathes in her scent. Loving her would be easy.

The baby wriggles, her face scrunching and turning an alarming shade of red as she grizzles. He passes her back to Faith, who offers a fresh breast to suckle.

This time Leo lifts his eyes to an image on the wall of a pair of smiling trapeze artists meeting in mid-swing, one gripping the wrists of the other. 'Do you ever think about us?'

'About what we did?' Faith clicks her tongue. 'All water under the bridge. We had a moment, that's all.'

Only a moment? Is that all it was for her? She had changed his world, instilled hope, given him purpose. Just being with her now, in easy reach, ignites his need of her.

'Are you in love with Carl?' he rasps.

'Love? Yes, I guess you'd call it that.'

'But you deserve better. I could give you so much more. Let you follow your dreams.'

'Oh, Leo.' She lays a hand on his knee. 'I'm living my dream. And you ... well, you're my brother-in-law ... nothing else.'

A knife stab of pain jabs between his shoulder blades. He has to know. 'Tell me the truth, Faith. Is Donna mine?'

There's a beat before she replies. 'Do you want her to be?'

He shocks himself with his answer. 'Of course I do.'

A sigh. A roll of her eyes. 'How many times do I have to tell you I was already pregnant? There's no better contraception than being up the duff.'

'Were you aware of it when we were together that night?'

'Well, no. The doctor confirmed it later on.'

'But the name ... Leonie.'

She laughs. 'Don't be ridiculous. We chose her middle name in honour of your father. Look, face the facts, she's not yours and what happened between us was, to put it bluntly, just sex. Physical urges being met.'

'I don't believe you.'

'Well, it's the truth ... on my part, anyway.'

He jumps up from the chair and kicks it across the room. 'In that case, you're a slut. You used me to get your jollies. I probably wasn't the only poor schmuck you screwed while Carl was away.'

Her glare seems to last forever.

Leo drops his gaze to the baby who is now asleep, the mouth detached from the breast yet still making sucking movements. Faith does nothing to cover herself, as if flaunting what he can't have.

'You disgust me,' Leo snarls.

They both flinch as a voice calls from the hall. 'Faith? Are you here?'

Leo strides out the door, colliding with Wes McKenny. 'She's all yours, Reverend,' he says, and storms off.

Outside, intending to walk up to The Axe and get blotto, he rounds the back of the building and discovers Simon sitting on wet grass under a tree, crying.

'Hey, what's going on here?' he asks, squatting beside the boy. 'Are you feeling crook?'

Simon looks up, eyes red and streaming. 'Patch is dead.'

'Bloody hell! When did this happen?'

'Yesterday. He got real sick. Dad said he must have eaten a bait put out to kill wild dogs.'

'Did you take him to the vet?'

He shakes his head. 'Dad said he wouldn't make it. He made me shoot him. Said it was my dog, so I had to be the one to do it.'

Leo cringes, remembering his father telling him much the same thing when he was a boy. 'Your dog, your responsibility.' Then handed a rifle to put his border collie, paralysed from a tick bite, out of its misery.

'I hate him!' Simon groans, punching the ground. 'We should've taken Patch to the vet like Faith said. He wasn't ready to die. I could tell by the way he looked at me before I—'. He hides his face with his arms.

'Oh, mate.' Leo squeezes the boy's heaving shoulders. 'At least Patch didn't have to suffer any more.'

Simon curls into him and sobs into his chest.

When the weeping slows, Leo suggests they swing by the milk bar on the way up to the pub. 'I'll shout you a soft drink and an ice-cream.' He hands Simon a hanky from his trouser pocket.

'Now blow your nose before you leave more snot trails over my good shirt.'

Leo shook off those memories. Passing a low-set office building advertising Lester Schilling Real Estate, he wondered if the owner was related to the old butcher. Across the street he saw an antique store that looked to be closed, a gift shop, and a chemist. Further up was a shop that used to be a drapery store in his childhood, where his mother bought fabric and patterns for sewing frocks for herself and shirts and shorts for her sons. The signage on the awning and the window display hinted it had transformed into a bookstore.

38

It turned out to be a real family affair at Ringtales when my parents arrived. Dad produced a bottle of bubbly and popped the cork, while Mum blew a party trumpet that sounded more like an elephant in a bucketload of pain.

'Thought we'd celebrate a day early,' Mum said, enfolding me in a Red Door hug. 'You'd probably be too busy tomorrow to notice we were there.'

I forced a smile and crossed my fingers. 'Here's hoping.'

'I made you a cake and some other nibbles.' She nodded to Dad, who removed plated food from a picnic basket and lined them up on the timber counter top—jam drop biscuits, cheese scrolls, fudge squares, sausage rolls, and a huge lamington sponge.

'We won't be needing lunch, that's for sure,' Shane said, loading up a paper plate.

Elliott followed his father's lead. 'If there are any leftovers, I might take some back for my housemates.'

'Got any glasses, luv?' Dad asked.

I found my stash of plastic cups and handed them out. 'Fill mine right up. I could do with some Dutch courage.'

Soon after, the shop door opened, and a man walked in.

He stood just inside and gazed around as if searching for someone. Tanned, with long grey hair tied in a ponytail and a bristly beard, he looked to be in his late sixties. Trying to recall if I was expecting a delivery, I put down my plate of goodies and hurried over.

'Hello, can I help you?'

'Thought I'd have a bit of a browse, if that's okay.' He moved towards a bookcase.

I rushed after him. 'Sorry, but we're not actually open.'

He frowned. 'You aren't? But ...' He eyed the shenanigans going on over by the counter—Elliott sitting on the throne chair and stuffing his face, Mum boxing up the remains of the cake, Dad flicking through a glossy coffee table book with Shane peering over his shoulder and cracking jokes about what they viewed.

'The shop has its grand opening tomorrow,' I blurted. 'My family came in to help me set up and celebrate in advance.'

'I see,' he nodded. 'Well, the shop looks wonderful. I'll return for a proper look at a later stage, then.'

'Please do that. Do you live locally?'

He seemed to consider this question and then shook his head. 'I did once. Years ago. In my day, this was a drapery store.'

'Yes, I've heard that. The shop's gone through a lot of changes, as has most of the town.'

'I've noticed. Just had a wander and couldn't believe my eyes.'

'When were you here last?'

He shrugged. 'It's been thirty-five, thirty-seven years. Something like that.'

'And you lived here in town?'

'No, a little way out, at Chances Crossing.'

'I know the area well,' I nodded. 'Sort of, anyway. There's a lovely winery out there now, and a new photographic gallery, Sweet Art. Well worth a visit.'

'That's good to hear,' he said, grinning. 'Happy to pass that on to Simon.'

My jaw dropped. 'You know Simon Sweetman?'

'Sure do. He's my nephew.'

My nerves fizzed as I studied him. Wavy hair, easy smile. *Of course.* 'You must be Leo.'

'I am. How did you guess?'

My chest tightened as dread replaced delight. *Leo was here.* Thoughts scurried around in my brain, colliding and bouncing off one another like circus clowns. 'I ... er ... um ...' I had no idea where to begin.

Shane poked his head over my shoulder. 'Abby, sorry to interrupt. What do you want me to do next? Take rubbish to the tip?'

'I'll leave you all to it,' Leo said, backing away. 'Hope you have an awesome opening ... Abby.'

Had I heard a sinister inflection in his mention of my name? 'Thanks,' I said, and watched him walk out the door.

Shane squeezed my arm. 'Who was that?'

'Ah ... someone who'd come in to browse.'

'Did you tell him to come back tomorrow and bring a horde of his mates?'

I gave a hint of a smile. 'Could you stick those *Opening Tomorrow* posters in the windows? Don't want anyone else making the same mistake.'

He saluted and went in search while I remained rooted to the spot.

So, Leo Sweetman was in town. Was he visiting Simon by chance, or had he come by request? What if dropping into the shop wasn't an accident but a ruse to check me out? What if Simon wasn't on my side and arranged for someone to take those nasty photos of us to throw me off the scent? The scent of what, in particular?

My desperation to interrogate Leo about Faith overtook the necessity for safety. Hang the consequences, I had to get some answers.

First, I needed to complete my task list and make sure Ringtales was ready for its big debut.

39

Leo was pleased to see Chances Crossing had moved with the times. Still rural, there was an air of sophistication in the horse stud, flower farm, and other new ventures. Approaching a hillside winery, he rounded a bend and by habit glanced at a weathered tree stump at the edge of the bitumen. Once a stately silky oak bearing brilliant golden flowers in spring, it met its demise after Eileen's car rammed into it. Carl moved the written-off Datsun to their property and returned with a chainsaw, felling the innocent tree and sawing the trunk into logs that were left for pickup by passers-by.

Poor Eileen. A plain but sweet local lass whose nursing career ended when she got pregnant in the back of Carl's ute and was pressured into a shotgun marriage by well-meaning but moralistic parents. Carl's insistence that she become a stay-at-home wife, as his mother had, and help around the farm caused Eileen to turn to Leo for support and the odd scrap of comfort he was stupid enough to offer. This only made matters worse. Carl's jealousy and fits of rage persuaded her to leave the marriage one night with their child in tow. She would have succeeded if, in her panic, she hadn't suffered an asthma attack only a kilometre from the farm and missed the sharp bend.

How much did Simon remember of the night his mother died beside him in the wreck? At such a young age he'd lost his mother, then his father, followed by Faith's abandonment. Now, with Genevieve threatening divorce, was it the right time to give Simon another taste of grief's lash?

He steered the car through the signposted gate and bypassed the carpark alongside the fancy gallery shed to continue uphill to the old house. Parking in the shade of the now enormous jacaranda tree he'd planted with Faith decades ago, he slid out and surveyed the property.

The terrain was the same, however, the grass in the paddocks looked to be slashed by machinery rather than ripped up by bovine teeth. The ugly stockpiles of rusted farm machinery had disappeared, and the barbed wire fencing of old replaced with a post and rail design. The dam, still boasting a jetty, had gained a small timber gazebo to offer respite from the elements. A good spit and polish had improved the property no end.

Leo inhaled familiar smells, and a gamut of emotions jockeyed for position. Some had questioned why, if he wasn't keen to remain, he hadn't sold up after Carl's death. But he couldn't. Though Simon had been a minor, he was legally half owner. Leo waited until the boy reached twenty-one before suggesting they sell the property, but Simon was determined to keep the farm. Years later, when financially able, he paid Leo out for his share and continued leasing it until he saw fit to return.

At least it wasn't necessary for Simon to lock horns with another sibling or a step-mother over its use. Faith hadn't contested Carl's will that stated Simon alone was the beneficiary of his share of the property. Once she'd received her spousal inheritance, she'd taken off interstate, cutting all ties with the Sweetmans.

Batting away depressing thoughts, Leo ambled down the conifer-lined drive towards the gallery, only to falter at a clanging coming from the old shed. He swung his head around and spied a loose sheet of corrugated iron banging in the strong breeze.

25 February 1979

Bringing Faith and the kids home because Carl wasn't ready to leave the pub, Leo rustles up some lunch while the baby is changed and fed yet again. Things are frosty between him and Faith, and it is a relief when she goes for a nap.

Leo creates a lanyard out of a length of cord and Patch's scuffed name tag, which the boy had kept. As he hangs it around Simon's neck, the boy's face beams with delight.

'It's just like your army dog tags,' he grins, fingering the metal disc engraved with the dog's name.

'That was my aim. Maybe one day we can add a second medallion engraved with your name.'

Simon gives him a tight hug before rushing off.

Leo passes the main bedroom and hears the baby gurgling. A peek inside reveals Faith spreadeagle on the bed, deep in sleep, while Donna is wide awake in the cot and contentedly sucking her fist. He tiptoes over and lifts the baby out. Fashioning a sling from one of Faith's silk shawls, he places Donna inside and ventures outdoors.

Clouds hang dark and heavy in spite of the area having had more than a month's worth of rain in three days, according to Stoney. Tree branches dance in a gentle breeze. Dandelion seeds drift past like tiny paratroopers blown off course. Underfoot, the sodden lawn is spongy and mud squelches up the sides of Leo's rubber boots as he admires blossoming shrubs festooned with liquid jewels. He introduces Donna to the Double Delight—his mother's favourite rose—and pinches off a petal, holding it to her nose. One day she'll appreciate its heady scent.

A clanging from the shed draws him down the drive. Expecting to find Simon tinkering with a new project, he is startled to find Carl standing behind the timber workbench with a can of Fourex raised to his mouth.

'Hey,' Leo says from the doorway.

Carl's hand jerks, spilling beer down the front of his shirt. He scowls at Leo. 'What do you want?'

He walks in, stepping over several crushed beer cans to reach the bench. 'I thought you were still at the pub wetting the baby's head.'

'I got a lift back with Stoney. You didn't hang about long. That's not like you.'

'Someone had to bring your family home.'

Carl staggers from behind the bench and belches as he eyes the shawl slung across Leo's chest. He leans forward and peeks inside. 'She's got you babysitting now, has she? You're so piss weak.'

'Just helping out.'

'Is that what you're doing, giving Faith a hand? I bet you're itching to give her more than that, mate. If you haven't already had your itch scratched.'

The dirty look he gives Leo alarms him. 'What are you on about?'

Carl chuckles. 'What do you take me for? I'm not stupid. Just look at her.' He nods towards the baby. 'The spit of you, I reckon. You just couldn't keep your dick in your pants. What is it about you that attracts women? Your don't-give-a-shit attitude, your puppy dog eyes? I don't get it. Eileen was infatuated with your compulsion to break with tradition until you nicked off to Viet-bloody-nam. But Faith—' His voice catches. 'I've fallen for her, hook, line, and sinker. I love her like you wouldn't believe. So, why did you have to lure her away?'

Leo grunts. Lure her? Faith was no more his than Simon ... or Donna. 'I did no such thing. She doesn't want me. I'm nothing to her.'

'Yet, you're the child's father.'

'I'm not,' he snaps. 'Faith was already pregnant when we—.' He cuts his words short.

Carl smashes the beer can on the workbench. All manner of tools jump and clink. 'You bastard. I knew it. How long has it been going on?'

'It was just the once. It was wrong of me, and by God, I regret it, but, I'm not Donna's father, you are. Faith was adamant about that.'

'Well, she's a liar!' Carl yells.

'No, she isn't. When we ... when I ...' Words wedge in his throat like lumps of gristle.

'Go on, say it. When you fucked my wife.'

Leo recoils at Carl defiling what they'd done. He'd loved Faith, worshipped her even. 'Faith was already pregnant, though she wasn't aware of it at the time. So, Donna is definitely yours.'

Carl throws back his head and laughs, the noise resounding off the shed's tin sheeting. 'That's impossible.'

'Why not? You two have sex often enough. The house walls are paper thin, you know.'

'That's not the issue.' Carl twirls the bloodstone signet ring on his middle finger, a tell Leo recognises as nervous energy. 'I'm sterile.'

'You bloody well aren't. Have you forgotten about Simon? Or are you going to tell me he's also not yours?'

'Of course he's mine. But I've been shooting blanks since I got mumps a few years back. You probably never heard how crook I was, busy serving your beloved country overseas and all. When Eileen and I struggled to have another kid, tests showed my sperm count had dropped significantly, meaning my chances of fathering another child were pretty much nil.'

Thoughts tangle in Leo's brain. 'Does Faith know this?'

'I haven't had the guts to tell her. She told me from the outset she was desperate to have a child of her own. And I desperately wanted her, so I kept quiet about it. If I now let on why I know the baby isn't mine, she'll say I led her on, letting her believe we were both eager to expand our family. If she mistakenly thinks she was pregnant when you had sex, when in fact it was you who planted the seed, I'll have to live with it.' His Adam's apple bobs as he swallows hard. 'I couldn't bear her running off on me, too.'

'But Faith said the doctor confirmed it.'

'Doctors can be wrong. Unless Faith is a sly bitch and neither of us is the baby's father.'

Leo recalls Faith's words: *It was just sex. Physical urges being met.* Maybe he wasn't the only one with whom she'd found sexual release while Carl was absent.

As if he'd heard Leo's thoughts, Carl kicks a beer can lying at his feet and it rebounds off a dusty Victa lawn mower. 'I swear, if I ever find out who the mongrel is, he's a dead man.'

'Does that mean I'm in the clear?'

Carl snatches a nail gun from the workbench and aims it at Leo's chest. 'You deserve to die.'

Leo shields the baby with his arms. 'What I did to you was a dog move. I admit it. But I can assure you it will never happen again.' He flinches when the gun's muzzle is jabbed against his forehead.

'Promise me you'll keep your cock the hell away from Faith,' Carl demands.

'Yes, I promise.'

The muzzle jabs harder before Carl lowers the nail gun. 'I'll hold you to that, little brother.'

A clang of metal. They whip their heads around to view the shed entrance, only to see the door still latched back. A pitchfork knocked from its wall hook onto a sheet of iron on the ground, and tin sheeting rattling above show the wind is picking up.

Donna wriggles in the sling and Leo offers her a gnarly finger to grasp. 'If you suspected me of being the baby's father, why didn't you confront me earlier?'

'I was waiting for you to slip up and mention something by mistake, which you sorta just did. Then again ... maybe I hoped to catch you both rooting like rabbits, giving me cause for payback. Something really ugly.'

'You're mental, Carl. How will you cope knowing Faith slept with someone other than me?'

'It won't be easy, that's for damn sure.' He waves the nail gun towards the sling. 'I'm reminded of Faith's betrayal every time I look at this little one. But what can I do? If I say anything, all hell will break loose, and what good is that? Best to keep dark truths buried, eh, Leo? Isn't that your motto?'

Leo winces. Has Faith broken her promise, divulging his secret about the Vietnamese girl?

Carl drops the gun onto the bench. 'Life was much better before. If only I could snap my fingers and have this kid disappear. Dad used to drown unwanted kittens in the dam. Shame we can't do that for one of our own.'

Leo slams his fist into his brother's face.

Carl falls back, crashing into the workbench and sliding to the ground. He clutches his left cheek just below the eye and stretches his jaw. 'Christ almighty, that's a mighty right hook you've got there.' He gets to his feet and says he's off to cuddle up to a bottle of Scotch.

Watching Carl stumble out of the shed, a loathing for Faith seizes Leo, looping around him like a python, crushing the air from his lungs. He shakes out his stinging hand and makes a vow. Faith has to pay for what she's done to them.

40

'Hey, Leo!'

The shout interrupted Leo's recollections. He caught Simon waving from the gallery door and jogged down the drive to meet him. Giving his nephew a hug and a slap on the back he asked, 'How's it going?'

'Great. Glad you finally made it, ol' boy.'

'Well, your phone call last night was rather convincing.'

'Then come on in. I'll show you around.' Simon waved Leo inside.

Aromas of newly hewn timber, fresh wall paint, and floor polish tantalised Leo's nostrils. Lit naturally by ceiling skylights and occasional strip lighting, the gallery was brighter than expected. Simon's tour was swift with brief explanations of the displays, yet the artwork and ingenuity impressed Leo.

'Too clever for his own boots, that kid,' Carl used to say, though the remark had sounded critical rather than complimentary.

'I'm really proud of you, mate,' Leo said to his nephew, blinking moisture from his eyes.

'Thanks.' Simon smiled and nudged him with his shoulder. 'I appreciate that. I've got a bit of paperwork to do, so why don't you have another squiz around and I'll meet you up at the house. We can catch up over a few beers while Keira tries her hand at cooking curried prawns.'

Leo gives him a thumbs-up. 'Sounds like a good plan.' It would give him time to drum up the nerve to disclose some information to Simon that might knock the buzz out of his excitement.

Left alone, he took a proper wander through the gallery, noting the extent of Simon's travelling in the evidence on the walls. Not only had he photographed Australia's diverse landscapes, there were plenty of images from his visits to the Pacific Islands, New Zealand, and South East Asia.

He stopped in front of a portrait shot of an elderly Asian woman sitting on the steps of a market shop, her back hunched like a question mark, face scored by a criss-cross of lines. Though her shrunken and toothless mouth lacked emotion, her steely gaze spoke of the horrors she'd seen in her long life.

Moving on, a photo of an abandoned vehicle in bushland drew him to a sudden halt. Aged by time and weather, the rusty brown of the corroded car body contrasted with the verdant green of surrounding foliage and an azure sky above. He leaned in for a closer look, focusing on the front passenger door now broken off and resting against the front wheel. It wasn't his recognition of Eileen's old Datsun that chilled him, but the item hanging from the side mirror.

Whispered words had him turning to find no one there, only static faces peering from walls. Were they smirking at him? He envisaged one of them parting its monochrome lips and shouting, 'Surprise!'

He glanced back at the rusted car. What he'd seen had the potential to change everything.

On his way out, Leo flinched when he caught Faith watching him from the picture above the doorway. When he'd last seen her, she was packing her brand-new Holden Gemini in preparation to leave Chances Crossing for good. Simon had clutched her arm and pleaded through snot and tears for her to stay.

'Let her go,' Leo had demanded, tugging the boy back. 'She's made up her mind. She doesn't want us.'

Soon after, Faith and the baby were driving away, the car leaving clouds of dust behind as it sped down the hill and out onto the road.

41

At last, I was alone. After all the hours spent planning, setting up, and worrying, there was nothing left to do to prepare for tomorrow.

Making slight adjustments—repositioning a chair, adding a book to the window display, moving a couple of the helium balloons Gemma had dropped in—I took some photos. Then, after saving another dragonfly, I collected the cash box and laptop and turned off the lights.

Walking out and locking the door, I checked the sky. The sun, still a distance above the horizon, meant I could nick out to Chances Crossing, speak with Leo—or arrange a more convenient time—and be home for dinner. I loaded the items into my VW and was about to phone Simon to give him a heads-up about my visit, when I changed my mind. It would be better to arrive without warning and catch them off-guard, rather than allow them time to hatch a dastardly plan to outsmart me.

A black cockatoo screeched overhead as it flew by. Hoping its cry wasn't a call of foreboding, I shrugged off concerns and slid behind the wheel.

I slowed my car at the intersection at the top of the street and noticed Graeme Roper and Lester Schilling sitting at a picnic table outside The Axe. Engrossed in a serious discussion over pots of beer, Lester gesticulated frantically, as if trying to get his point across, while Graeme shook his head. Whether he was disagreeing or commiserating, I couldn't tell. As I turned right and passed by, Lester suddenly dropped his hands and bobbed up from his seat like a meerkat. Our eyes met briefly before Graeme tugged Lester's arm and pulled him back down.

I sneered at Lester's image in the rear-view mirror. From his reaction, and the scowl he'd just given me, I gathered I was the subject of the fiery conversation. Shaking off my irritation, I headed out to Chances Crossing.

42

Instead of waiting inside the house for Simon, Leo walked around to the backyard.

He edged through a row of straggly rose bushes, passed a vegetable garden in need of a good replanting, and aimed for the rusty iron gate. Stiff hinges creaked like old knees as he pushed it open and stepped through. A shudder ran through him at the top of the path leading down to the creek. Did he have the nerve to purge himself of every dark memory of that fateful afternoon in 1979?

There'd been a time, many years ago, when he'd declined an invitation to travel back to South Vietnam with a bunch of ex-army mates and revisit locations from their tour of duty. He'd reneged out of disillusionment. What use would it be to view sites seared into his memory and find them unrecognisable? He'd heard the former runway and vast helipad at the Nui Dat Task Force Base had become a street and soccer field, and the Cu Chi tunnels—the intricate, subterranean hiding place of the Viet Cong

—had transformed into a theme park of sorts, where visitors had an opportunity to experience the tiny hideouts, fire war-era weapons at a gun range, and study VC booby traps that maimed and killed allied forces and their own people. Many in the group returned, saying it was an enlightening trip. Still, Leo wondered what terrors his psyche would have unleashed if he'd visited.

Now, as he dug deep for the strength to continue walking, he feared the same. Steeling himself, he placed one foot in front of the other and followed the path through the bush.

Memories launched from his mind like attacking wolves.

25 February 1979

Clothes damp from perspiration and sprinkles of rain, Leo returns from the old timber bridge with a new determination. Taking the trail above the swollen creek, a cry cuts through the sound of rushing water. An owl? A possum? *A call for help?*

He follows its direction and catches a flash of yellow through the lush green foliage. A gap between branches affords him a better view. Faith, still dressed in the frock she'd worn to the christening, stands ankle-deep in the creek's overflow. What in God's name is she doing?

A jet engine-roar startles him, and he reels at the sight of a swirling mass of brown water bearing down on Faith. A warning shout would be lost within the tumult, so he slides down the muddy incline and lunges, grasping Faith around the waist. Dragging her back from the torrent that would have swept her away, he shoves her uphill to the safety of the rise where they collapse amid rain-soaked leaf litter.

Leo untangles himself from Faith. 'What were you doing down there?' he yells.

She responds by slapping his face. 'Where is she?' she screams, beating him with her fists. 'Where is she?'

Leo dodges a smack to the head and grips Faith's wrists. Kneeling over her, he pins her arms to the ground. 'Who? What are you talking about?'

She writhes, eyes wild, chest heaving. Two wet circles on the bodice of her dress show her breasts are leaking. 'What did you do with her, you bastard?' The thrust of her hip jabs him hard in the groin.

He buckles, yet his knees remain planted in the dirt. 'You mean Donna?'

'You better not have harmed her.'

'Harmed her? What the hell, Faith?' He could never hurt a child. Not again.

'Carl said you had her.'

'I did. I took her for a walk while you were napping, but I put her in the bouncinette before I came down here. Is she missing?'

Faith nods and her body goes slack. Tears trickle from her eyes. 'I don't know what's going on.'

Leo releases his hold and slips to her side. 'Did Carl say I'd run off with Donna?'

'You were the last one seen with her. Simon thought he saw you go through the rear gate and Carl suggested we head down to the creek to look for you.'

'I've been at the timber-getter's bridge, having a think on my own. You gotta believe me.' He scans the bush, his gaze moving down to the fast-flowing water and the forest debris hurtling along with it. 'Where's Carl?'

Faith pushes up to stand with leaves and twigs sticking to the skirt of her dress like filthy ornaments. 'We had a fight, and he walked off. I heard a baby crying and thought it was Donna. But when I got down here, I discovered it was just one of those green catbirds.' She snatches Leo's shirt sleeve. 'We have to find her. She can't have run away by herself.'

Leo's mouth goes dry. What if Carl has done something to Donna? He was pissed to the hilt and angry. His mind could have snapped. An image of kittens in a weighted sack dumped into the dam chills him.

He jumps to his feet and clenches Faith's hand. 'C'mon, it's almost dark. Let's go back to the house and get some answers. If Donna isn't there, we'll formulate some kind of plan.'

They reach the clearing as a downpour hits. Sheltering under the old fig tree, they huddle close, clothing drenched and plastered to their bodies. Faith's hair hangs in wet ropes that sway as words shoot from her mouth in rapid-fire.

'When Carl and I went looking for Donna, he was drunk and ranting and accused me of cheating on him. He said he knew about you and me. Did you tell him? You must have. He said he wasn't Donna's father, and I said he was crazy, of course he was. Then he confessed something dreadful. He told me he—'

'Can't have any more kids?' Leo interjects, shocked that Carl had confessed his big secret.

She stares open-mouthed. 'You knew?'

'Just found out today.'

'Is it true or only rubbish?'

'True, I reckon. Seems he had a serious case of the mumps a few years ago.'

'Yes, he mentioned that. But it doesn't make sense. He got me pregnant.'

'Did he? Are you sure about that?'

'Dr Peake's calculations showed he had.'

'Dr Peake isn't Einstein. He could have made a mistake.'

VICKI STEVENS

'But that would mean Donna didn't arrive late like we thought but early ... or on time.' She turns away and groans.

A hummingbird beats within Leo's chest. 'So, there's a chance Donna's my daughter after all.'

Faith swings back sharply, wet hair whipping Leo's arm. 'I ... I can't be sure. My cycle was out of whack with all the stress.'

'You can't be sure?' There's a bitter tang in his mouth. 'You've been with someone else, haven't you?' He wrenches a crumpled photograph from his hip pocket and holds it up for her to see. 'Is this him? Is this the guy you've been screwing?'

'Where'd you get that?' She tries to snatch the photo, but Leo holds it at a distance.

'It was in a floral pencil case wedged between buttress roots right here, under this tree. There were other pictures and bits and pieces inside, a few old joints. How had I not guessed that you smoked weed? We could've had even more fun together.'

She narrows her eyes at his sarcasm. 'How did you find the pencil case?'

'I saw it a few months back when I stumbled across some other stuff hidden around the tree. At first, I thought my mother had stowed objects here. Then I suspected it was you, a woman longing for a child.' Her silence compels him to continue. 'I left the pencil case alone then, but this afternoon, when I was angry with you, I wondered if it contained secrets. So, I dug it out and proved my assumption correct. I've been sitting on the bridge trying to work out what to make of it.'

Leo gives the photograph another glance. 'You two look pretty chummy snuggled up close like that.' Flipping it over, he reads words scrawled in pen. '*Thanks for everything sweet F*'. He searches her face for a glimmer of culpability.

'He's my brother,' she blurts. 'Half-brother. My mum had a child to

254

another man before she married my father. Dad made her put him up for adoption, but he came back into my mother's life when he was eighteen. Dad was dead by then, and he ended up living with us. Mum doted on him, yet I hated him from the very start. He was pure evil. I tried to support mum, but I couldn't stay after he ...' A twitch tugs a corner of her mouth. 'After he raped me on my sixteenth birthday.'

'He raped you?' Leo touches her arm, but pulls his hand away when Faith flinches. 'So why did you keep in contact with him? This photo is recent. I've seen you in that outfit.'

'It was taken at the Shadow Creek Show last year. I almost died from shock when I saw Mitch working at a Knock'em Down stall. He recognised me before I could run off and got a roving photographer to take a Polaroid snap of us. I wasn't happy, no matter what it looks like.'

'Mitch?'

'Mitchell Shepherd.' She wraps herself in her arms. 'Someone must have told him where I lived because he came by the next morning, the Sunday of the Show. He said he wouldn't let me go now he'd found me ... said he'd tell my husband ... tell Carl ... we'd been lovers. That was a lie, Leo. I swear it. I sent him away with some cash to shut him up, but he mailed the photo to me a few days later as a taunt, and then ...' She brushes past him to move out from under the tree. 'We have to get back. The rain has eased.'

Leo steps in her way. 'There's more to it. What else did this Mitch do? Did he demand more money?'

'He returned a fortnight later, but this time he ...' Her eyes dart away and she chews her bottom lip. 'Mitch said if I didn't have sex with him, he'd hurt Simon. His threat was real. He was a psychopath. I couldn't let him harm Simon, so I ...' She covers her face. 'Oh God, it was horrible.'

Faith staggers, and fearing she might be about to faint, Leo clasps her shoulders to steady her.

'Sonofabitch! Did this happen before or after we were together?'

'The day after, in the morning.' She uncovers her face. 'Simon had caught the bus to school. Mitch told me he'd camped the night in the bush nearby ... waited until I was alone.'

Leo heard noises outside that night, after they'd made love. Footsteps on the back verandah, the clang of metal, the dog yelping. Maybe Patch hadn't fought with a possum, after all.

'And that was the end of it? He never came back?'

Faith shows no emotion when she says, 'No ... he's dead. I killed him.'

Leo's world spins. Had he heard correctly? 'You did what?'

'When Mitch had ... had finished with me, he demanded I make him a cuppa. While he sat at the kitchen table drinking tea and eating biscuits like he'd just popped in for a friendly visit, I grabbed a jaffle iron from the pot stand and hit him over the head. Once I started, I couldn't stop. I smashed his skull until it became mush.'

Leo freezes, ice travelling through every artery. He couldn't have been more stunned if Dodge had suddenly jumped out of the bushes and danced a jig. 'What did you do with him? Where is his body, for Christ's sake?'

'You don't need to know. He's gone. We got rid of his motorbike too.'

'We? Bloody hell, Faith, don't tell me you got Simon involved?'

'No. I phoned Stoney and begged him to help. The body is buried where no one will ever find it.'

'You can't be sure. If it's on our property then—'

'It's not,' she butts in. 'It's well hidden.'

'And you involved Stoney in this mess?'

'He won't tell. He promised.'

Leo paces in the mud. Was all this true? Was Faith capable of murder? His heart ached with the realisation that he didn't know her at all. 'And you think this animal ... your brother ... could be Donna's father?'

'There's a possibility now, isn't there? When Dr Peake told me how far along I was, I felt relieved. It ruled out the possibility of being pregnant to Mitch.'

'Or me,' Leo says with a sting of disappointment. 'Did you tell Carl what your brother did to you?'

'Just before? I tried, but he refused to believe I'd been forced to have sex. He called me horrid names. Said he'd forgive me if I gave Donna away. He even offered me that bloodstone ring he was wearing if I agreed, said it was valuable, worth thousands. As if I'd put money or my marriage before my child.' She clutches her chest and moans. 'I have to find her. She'll be desperate for a feed.'

'Where is Carl now? Did you do something to him? Did you ...' He can't say it.

Faith stares, her eyes wide and haunting in the failing light. 'I told him to go to hell. Told him he couldn't have me without Donna, and once she was found I'd be leaving. He tried to change my mind. Things got physical, violent, but I fought him off and bolted. That's the last I saw of him.'

When she races away, Leo takes a moment to gather his wits before following.

Slipping and sliding, they tackle the miry path leading up to the house.

Leo and Faith step through the gateway just as Simon appears to the left of them, mud-splattered and panting. All eyes drop to the backpack cradled in his arms. A backpack that is squirming and making a racket.

Faith snatches the pack and drops to her knees. Unbuckling the flap, she peels back the canvas and reveals a wailing baby, face beetroot red, tiny fists punching the air. She clutches the child and dashes to the house.

Leo seizes Simon and frogmarches him across the yard and up the verandah stairs.

They join Faith in the lounge room where she is sitting onto the sofa and tugging the bodice of her dress free of its buttons. Pressing the small head to her breast, the bawling is replaced with noisy suckling.

'Where was she?' Leo yells, shoving Simon against the wall so hard that hanging picture frames rattle on their hooks.

'In the car,' the boy whimpers, his face pale.

'What car?'

'Mum's car.'

Leo scowls. 'That rusted wreck? Is it still down by the Bunya pine?'

Simon nods and rubs his eyes, smearing muddy streaks across his face.

'What are you two talking about?' Faith says from the sofa.

'Eileen's crashed car that Carl dumped in the bush to rot.' Leo pokes Simon hard in the chest. 'You hid Donna there? What stupid game were you playing at, you little shit?'

Simon's upper lip quivers. 'It ... it wasn't me. It w-was Dad. He said he wanted to trick Faith. Pay her back for hurting him.'

'When did he do this?' Faith cries.

'When you were sleeping. Uncle Leo had gone for a walk. Dad took Donna outside and came back later without her. He told me what he'd done, where he'd hidden her. Told me not to say anything.'

'You didn't care how frantic I was when I discovered her missing?' Faith's hand trembles as she smooths down Donna's damp curls. 'You led me to believe it was Leo who'd taken her.'

'I had to. Dad was really mad and scary. When you were all taking so long to come back, I got worried and went to find her.'

'I suppose I can thank you for that.' Faith's eyes snap back to Leo. 'So, Carl pretended to be concerned and watched me going out of my mind with fear. Did he even intend to bring Donna back? If it wasn't for Simon ...' Tears zigzag down her cheeks to trickle under her chin. 'Does Carl hate me that much that he'd let my baby die?'

Leo kneels in front of Faith and offers comforting words he's not sure he believes. 'He wouldn't have let it go that far. I think he just wanted to give you a fright.' He glances at Simon now slumped on the floor in a crouch, watching, listening, and lowers his voice to speak from his own heart. 'The idea of you sleeping with another man, let alone having that man's child, is driving him crazy. He adores you, Faith. He can't bear losing you.'

'Well, he has,' she sneers. 'I won't stay with anyone who'd hurt a child.'

Her glare pierces his soul. Was she including him in that statement? Surely, he'd made it clear he hadn't killed the Vietnamese girl and her brother by intention.

Leo stands, tempted to flee out to his car. In less than a minute, he'd be gone, speeding away from all this stupid crap. Instead, he sucks in a deep breath and slowly releases it. 'Well, I guess I better go look for that mad bastard and knock some sense into him.'

'Take the kerosene lamp from the shed,' Faith urges. 'You'll need light.'

Leo opened his eyes to see the bush swirling like a spinning top. He gripped a slender tree trunk to ease his wobbling and breathed in fresh eucalyptus scented air. The events of that night in 1979 had turned his life on its head and forced him to make a desperate decision. A decision that took all his courage to conceal just so he could protect the ones he loved.

Now he was ready to bring everything out into the open.

43

Finding Sweet Art gallery closed, I parked my car and walked up the drive to the house.

My knocking on the front door went unanswered, probably drowned out by the music coming from a room nearby. So, I moved around to the side verandah, only to pull up when sharp voices drifting from the rear deck suggested a serious conversation was taking place.

'Well, spit it out Leo,' I heard Simon say. 'Why'd you really come here?'

A clink of glass on glass. A bottle set down on the outdoor table?

'I came to explain what actually happened the afternoon your father went missing,' said the older male.

Hooly dooly! Talk about sneaking in at the right moment. I pressed against the outside wall and edged as close as I could without being seen.

'Remember when Faith and I bumped into you returning with

baby Donna in your backpack, after you fetched her from your mum's wrecked car?'

What the hell? Donna in a backpack?

'Of course I do,' said Simon. 'I remember everything from that day.'

'Good.' Leo again. 'You said your dad told you he'd hidden Donna there out of spite. A cruel joke to get even with Faith for cheating on him.'

Carl knew of Faith's affair? Why had Simon failed to mention that to me yesterday?

'Well, I didn't know what she'd done at the time, just that she'd hurt Dad badly.'

'And he made you promise not to tell. So, when Faith woke from her nap and discovered the baby missing, you told her I'd taken Donna, when in fact I'd gone for a walk on my own after fighting with your dad.'

An exaggerated sigh. 'I've explained my reason for lying, Leo. I'd have received a thrashing if I'd blabbed. Why are you digging this all up again?'

'Stay with me, Simon. You said your dad and Faith went in search of Donna, and when everyone took too long to return, you worried for the baby's safety and went in search of her. You found her still in the old Datsun and you brought her back home. Is that correct?'

'If that's what I said, then that's what I did.' Simon's sarcastic tone revealed his irritation.

'Okay. As you know, I ran into Faith down by the flooded creek. She and your dad had come looking for Donna and me. They'd argued and he'd stormed off, leaving her in a mad panic. I persuaded her to return home, and that's when we encountered you with the baby. Now your dad was the one missing.'

'Because he'd been caught in the flash flood. We all know this story. What's your point?'

Silence, followed by a throat being cleared.

Leo spoke again. 'I went looking and came back hours later saying I hadn't found him. The truth is, I lied. I came across him half-buried in mud down by the creek on our property.'

A grate of chair legs on timber decking. 'Our property? But he got washed away.'

'Not until I pushed him into the water.'

I gasped. *My theory was correct.* Carl had been murdered by being shoved into the flooded creek.

'Holy shit!' Simon was as shocked as me. 'Dad was still alive when you found him?'

'No ... he was already dead. When I struggled to drag his body out of the mud, I discovered he was stuck in a hole with his leg pierced by wooden spikes planted in the ground, very much like a punji pit.'

What in God's name was a punji pit? Wooden spikes. That might explain the pitchfork type of injuries Dr Peake mentioned.

'I had to use all my strength to free him. I reckon that's how he drowned. Stuck in this efficient trap, he couldn't get out when the flood came.'

A thud and a clatter. A chair kicked over?

'You should have told me, Leo.' Rasped words filled with pain. 'How could you have kept this from me?'

'Because I wanted to protect you. I didn't want to reveal to a kid that something he built to catch a fox, a wild dog, or whatever, accidentally trapped his father and led to his death.' Leo's voice cracked as he added, 'I ... I couldn't let you carry the guilt. More than anyone, I knew how it messed with a person, stuffed up their life. That's why I made it look like the flood had caught your dad out and swept him downstream.'

'And you tell me this now? Why?'

'Because it's time you knew the truth. Also, I need to free myself of the burden of carrying this secret.'

'Fuck!' Simon cried. The tread of boots pacing floorboards.

Bloody hell! My heart ached for Simon, for Leo, for poor Carl—what a dreadful accident.

Another scrape of chair legs. Softer footfalls. 'The worst of it is, Simon, I reckon you've known all along your dad died in the pit.'

A dry laugh. 'Don't be ridiculous. I was told his body was found in a field.'

'You knew because you have your father's signet ring. I saw it just before, in the photograph.'

'What photograph?'

'In the gallery. The one of the rusted car in the bush. Your mother's car. No one else would probably give the items hanging from the side mirror a second glance. But I recognised the lanyard I made for you after Patch's death, and that along with the dog tag, it now bore your dad's bloodstone ring. Made me wonder if the shot was set up to represent loss—your mum, Patch, your dad.'

A short period of stillness was broken by Simon. 'So what if it was?'

'How did you get the ring?' Leo snapped.

'Dad left it to me. Like Pop left it for Dad.'

'Given to you after your dad's death?'

'Yeah, that's right.'

'The trouble is, mate, according to Faith, your father had it on his finger when they quarrelled in the bush before he ran off.'

'You've spoken with her?'

'Not recently. She told me that afternoon. Carl offered her the ring if she agreed to give Donna away. He said it was worth thousands, which it wasn't. When I obliterated all trace of the pit the next day, I didn't come across the ring. And it wasn't returned with his possessions after his body was found. So, unless, over time, it resurfaced, I think there's another scenario to be considered.'

More footsteps. The chink of glass. The glug of liquid being poured.

'Simon, my guess is on your way to get Donna from the car, you discovered your dad drowned in the hole. Maybe it was shock that made you lie about seeing him. Maybe it was sheer terror. What troubles me, is that you had the gall to tug the ring from his lifeless hand and pocket it as a keepsake.'

I muffled a cry with my hand. *Was Simon that cold-hearted?* I would have fainted or run screaming if I'd found my father dead in a flooded trench. Blood pulsed in my ears as I waited for Simon to respond.

'You're right, Leo. I stumbled across him on my way to find Donna. Of course it freaked me out. I tried to pull him free, but he was already dead. That's when the ring came off in my hand. I hadn't realised I'd put it in my jacket pocket until I found it days later.'

'Why haven't you ever told me this?'

'I intended to tell you. But when they found his body farther away, I felt vindicated. I went back a day or so later to destroy the pit and found no sign of it ever being there. It was as if God, or nature, had absolved me from building such a horrid thing and not finding Dad in time. So, I kept quiet, believing he'd gotten what he deserved.'

'What do you mean by that?'

'Dad intended to kill Donna.'

Kill her? My God, who were these people?

'When did he say that?' Leo's voice sounded strained.

'That afternoon, I heard you and Dad shouting in the shed, so I snuck in to see what was happening. You were holding Donna, and he pointed a nail gun at her. I heard him say he wanted to get rid of her like a sack of unwanted kittens.'

'But he didn't mean it. What he said was shocking, and I slogged him for it. He was drunk and upset, but he wouldn't have killed a baby.'

'I wasn't so sure. I was just a kid, for God's sake. That's why I ran off with Donna. I was taking her into town to tell the cops when she started screaming her lungs out. So, I hid her in the old car and went to get her bottle, but Dad and Faith saw me. To give me time to get away, I told them you had taken the baby, sending them on a wild goose chase.'

'Hang on. *You* hid Donna in the car? Then all that guff you told us about your dad paying back Faith was a pack of lies?'

A smack. A crash. A moan.

'You piece of shit!' Leo yelled.

'I did it to protect the baby.' Simon's voice seemed to have risen an octave.

'What about the punji pit? Did you really build it to catch animals, or had you hoped to trap larger game, and it paid off?'

'Only wild dogs, honestly.'

'How can I believe you?'

The sound of the sliding door opening.

'You can't tell Keira,' Simon urged. 'Our relationship is tenuous as it is.'

One of them stomped into the house. The other followed.

I slid down the wall to a crouch, feeling like a priest who'd just listened to a round of diabolical confessions. Confused as to what to do next, I noticed a pair of worn boots resting between two potted geraniums. They were frosted in parts with bright orange paint, the exact shade as the graffiti on the shop windows. I cringed. Why would Simon pull such a childish prank?

I crawled over. The boots were Doc Martens, size seven. *Keira.*

Had I upset her by hanging out with her dad? Had she thought something romantic was developing between us? Had she also smooshed dog poo on my shop door and taken pics of me and Simon by the creek?

Movement to my left.

I turned and saw the girl in question standing on the verandah and glaring back at me. She must have come out via the front door.

'What are you doing here?' she asked, hands on hips.

I held up a boot. 'You graffitied my shop.'

'And you've been eavesdropping.' Her smug smile proved she hadn't overheard everything I had.

'Keira! Where are you?' Simon called from inside the house.

'Out here,' she yelled, grinning and nodding at me.

I couldn't be caught snooping. What if they realised I knew their dreaded secrets?

Not chancing capture by Keira if I tried to reach the front stairs, I turned towards the rear deck and bolted.

In the backyard I faltered, and then aimed for the iron gate with no purpose other than a need to escape. Simon shouting my name propelled me into the bush.

44

The gigantic fig tree in the clearing loomed up like a gatekeeper. *Greetings, choose your path.* The track on the left led to the rock pool where Simon had taken me the day before, so I chose the one on the right.

This track followed a scrubby ridge. I may have been able to push through and cut across the farm paddock to reach the gallery car park if the bush wasn't so dense. However, I didn't trust my chances against the thickets of lantana and thorny blackberry. Spurred on by the whistle-and-snap call of whipbirds, I continued running in search of a break in the overgrowth.

Through the vegetation, I snatched glimpses of the creek below, its fast flow and constant burbling revealing last night's downpour coursed from the heights. Simon mentioned there was an old bridge upstream that timber-getters once used, which would imply there was an unused trail heading back to the road. From there, I could re-enter the property through the main gate and reach my car.

My hopes rose until a wall of green drew me to a standstill—

barbed wire fencing wrapped tightly in madeira vine. I breathed in a sour stench and noticed a gap low in the bracken. On closer inspection, I found it to be a burrow dug by a forest creature. White feathers scattered inside, along with small bones and a wizened fowl claw, suggested I had stumbled on a fox's lair. I scanned the brush and discovered a narrow path of flattened grass leading away from the lair and downhill. A way of escape. The fox's winding route soon brought me to the creek.

It was easy to see the water level had risen. No sight of stepping stones, and the scrub seemed to be growing out of the flow instead of the bank. Jutting out midstream was the derelict bridge, a ruin of rotted timber buffeted by foaming swirls. Once again it appeared I'd arrived at a dead end, unless ...

I peered above and spied the rope suspension bridge Simon said he'd constructed. It spanned the creek from a tall red gum this side to another on the opposite bank, and would have looked right at home in an Indiana Jones or Jack Sparrow movie. Where did Simon say it led? A state forest?

I flinched at a cry coming from a little way off. 'Abby, this is crazy. Get back here.'

This urged me to come up with three options. 1. Backtrack along the ridge. 2. Try and swim upstream against the surge. Or 3 ... I looked up and winced.

A set of wooden slats nailed to the tree trunk allowed me to climb up to a small platform and take in the full view of the hanging bridge. The rope handrails, netting sides, and timber decking looked sturdy enough, so I gripped the rope and launched out six metres above fast-flowing water and discovered the structure dipped and swayed more than expected. My vision blurred and my joints locked. Frozen with acrophobia, I wasn't going anywhere. Yet when the rocking slowed and another shout came from Simon—accentuated with expletives—I dusted off a yoga technique to ease my nerves. Taking long steady breaths, I focused on the slats at my feet rather than the drop, and tackled the bridge like a tightrope walker crossing Niagara Falls until I reached the other side.

Safe on solid ground, I heard Simon yell, 'I can see you!'

My eyes searched the bush across the water and locked on a figure standing on the creek bank. *Shit!* I sprinted away.

Leafy fronds curled like waves around my ankles as I dashed through a sea of ferns growing in profusion from the forest floor. Tall eucalyptus trees shedding bark in spaghetti strands surveyed as I sped by, wondering, like me, where the hell I was going. I scoured the surroundings for a trail leading to freedom. When none was visible, I pulled up with a stitch in my side to catch my breath. With a prickling sense of being watched, I jerked around and caught a face staring at me from a rotten tree stump—two gashes for eyes, fungi for lips, and moss for a beard. If only it could offer directions. I forged on, quickening my speed.

Cresting a rise, I found I had walked into a standoff. On my left, hundreds of pine trees stood to attention in perfect military rows as if awaiting their next order. While to my right, a scattering of grass trees wielding spear-like stalks appeared ready to protect the land of their ancestors. Not wishing to stir either army of warriors to life—though the idea of them coming to my aid was tempting—I zigzagged through ranks of pine soldiers until a large fallen scribbly gum in their midst caught my attention. The exposed root ball offered a shield for concealment, and I hurried over and dropped into the depression caused by the uplift of roots.

Air wheezed from my parched throat as I examined my branch-scratched legs and arms, relieved to find no ugly leeches imbibing on my blood. As a pine-scented breeze dried my sweaty skin, my panting lessened. It was strangely quiet, with the only noise being wind rustling through branches and the thrumming in my ears. Where were the birds, the lizards, the scrub turkeys? Were they also in hiding?

A twig snapping had me back on alert. The sound of dried pine needles crunching underfoot forced me to press flat against the tree base. *Please God, don't let Simon find me.*

I picked up a sharp stick and turned sideways in preparation to fight back. Something odd dangling from the mass of roots near my face drew my interest—a jaw bone with teeth attached. Protruding from the detritus alongside this was a long leg bone. Remnants of a dead cow? A wild pig? I studied the stick in my hand and realised it too was made of bone. I dropped my gaze to the clump of roots distending from the mud beneath my feet and saw they now resembled a section of a rib cage. Jolting back, my shoe butted against a curve of pale rock. Though I dreaded what would be revealed, I squatted and scrabbled in the damp earth until the left side of a skull appeared. A human skull, the eye socket packed with soil.

The shriek that tore from my throat sounded nothing like the perfect bloodcurdling screams uttered by Jamie Lee Curtis in any of her *Halloween* movies, nor the one let out by her mother Janet Leigh in *Psycho*, not even Macaulay Culkin's in *Home Alone*. No, it sounded more like Homer Simpson in a frenzy.

I crumpled, a marionette with its strings cut, just as Simon came into view at the edge of the depression.

He sported a newly split and swollen bottom lip, and his questionable cry of, 'Abby?' showed he was surprised the screech had come from a person.

I didn't care that I'd been discovered. There were worse things to fear. I pointed to the gruesome remains.

'Holy shit!' Simon leaned forward. 'What is that?'

'Well, it's not buried treasure,' I whimpered.

Heavy footsteps and huffing pre-empted a second pursuer, and Leo took his place beside his nephew.

'I'm too friggin' old for this nonsense,' he rasped, bending at the waist, his face bright red, hair loose and falling over his shoulders. He spotted me huddled in the hollow, trembling. 'My God, are you okay? Did you fall in? You might want to get out from behind that root ball, luv. These toppled trees spring back up on the odd occasion and we'd have a devil of a time getting you out before it crushed you to death.'

The thought of being buried under tree roots alongside that hideous thing had me crawling out in a flash.

'We've found a body,' Simon announced.

'A skeleton ... actually,' I corrected, pushing up to stand.

Leo watched wide-eyed as Simon pointed to each ghastly item as proficiently as a presenter on a shopping network. *Buy all four and receive a free pelvis.*

'I know who it is,' Leo said, his face now drained of colour.

45

Before elaborating, Leo questioned me on how much I'd overheard of their conversation back at the house.

When I answered, 'Everything,' Simon let out a groan, and punched his fist into his hand. 'I knew it.'

Leo released a long sigh. 'According to Simon, you are well acquainted with Faith and her daughter.'

I nodded in response.

'And that you've been digging for clues regarding Donna's real father.'

I nodded again.

The glare he gave me looked menacing, yet I felt no genuine fear. In stumbling upon a greater horror—one that Leo had previous knowledge of and possibly some involvement—I had secured my safety. Though if I'd had time to consider the situation, I may have suspected I'd dug myself a deeper hole in being privy to more of their horrid secrets.

Still, an alliance was formed when Simon and I listened to Leo recount what he'd been told by Faith on the afternoon Carl went missing. The more he related, the more it sounded like a badly written soap opera, or a story Natalie Schilling might have penned.

Apparently, at the time of the Shadow Creek Show back in 1978, Faith was visited by her half-brother who she later bashed to death with a vintage sandwich toaster after he raped her. A neighbour helped Faith dispose of the body but she'd refused to divulge to Leo where, saying it was in a place near impossible to find.

Leo pointed to the skull. 'I'm sure if we dig that out, the damage will confirm that here lies the remains of Mitchell Shepherd.'

'And the neighbour?' I asked. 'That wouldn't have been Stoney Maloney by any chance?'

He pulled a face. 'Don't tell me you know him too? Well, yes, he came to her aid.'

A shudder ran through me. *Bloody Stoney!* His involvement in this Faith fiasco kept popping up like rodents in a game of Whac-A-Mole.

'I reckon Stoney buried him in this plantation, and then planted a sapling over his grave,' Leo said. 'Maybe he believed planting a tree that wasn't a pine would stop the body from being discovered by loggers.'

Simon gave a scoffing laugh. 'They certainly hadn't considered that nature might betray them in the end.'

My imagination ran wild. 'Talking about trees, I'm going out on a limb here and suggest that this Mitchell who assaulted Faith may be the one who got her pregnant. It would make sense, her keeping it a secret for so long.'

Leo nodded. 'I think that's what Faith was afraid of.'

I envisaged myself presenting a boxed gift to Donna for her birthday. 'What's this?' she'd ask, removing the lid and lifting out a skull. 'Let me introduce you to your father,' I'd say with a wicked grin.

'Yet,' Leo fingered his beard, 'it could just as easily have been me.'

My jaw dropped. What was this, another confession? Simon throwing his hands up showed he was as surprised as me.

'So, you and Faith *were* screwing around,' he said. 'In all our conversations you never once hinted you two had an affair.'

Leo shrugged. 'There was no affair. It was a single occurrence. The night before Faith was raped, so I found out. A lapse in restraint, that's all.'

'A paternity test could prove it,' I said, a touch excited.

'I wouldn't get a test done without Faith's knowledge. Anyway, I can't see her wanting all this dredged up.'

'What do we do now?' I urged, wishing I'd gone straight home after work. I would have been preparing something mildly healthy for dinner instead of having this hideous discussion.

We all stared at what was left of Mitchell Shepherd until the despondent call of a crow high above broke the silence between us.

'I guess we should tell the police,' was my suggestion.

Simon scowled. 'Faith would be arrested for murder, or manslaughter at least. And Stoney would be charged with interfering with a corpse. Leo, you'd be in a shit load of trouble for withholding information regarding a murder.'

I thought of Donna finding out about her mother's actions. She'd be shattered and inconsolable. That black dog of depression wouldn't be just nipping at her heels but ripping her to shreds.

I now agreed with Simon. 'Okay, we can't go to the police.'

Leo clapped his hands together. 'Right. We'll have to rebury him and promise this horrible discovery stays between ourselves.'

Was that possible? Could *I* keep such a thing secret? Not

admitting to Shane I'd continued to nosey around was bad enough. Not telling him I knew of a killing and the whereabouts of a body was abhorrent.

'It all comes down to where our loyalties lay.' Simon said. 'Mine lies with you, Leo.' He gave his uncle's shoulder a solid pat.

'Well, mine lies with Faith,' Leo said. 'I saw the terror in her eyes when she told me about the assault. It wasn't the first time that bastard had forced himself on her, either. The punishment fit his crime, I reckon.'

Both men looked at me.

My loyalty didn't lie with Faith—I hardly knew her—it was with Donna, and Stoney who, I assumed, had just helped a mate out of a tight spot. 'My friends come first,' I said with conviction. 'I can't have their lives ruined by that filthy mongrel.'

And so, we made a pact to bury the truth—both metaphorically and literally.

46

'And what have you all been up to?' Keira asked Leo and Simon, hands on hips, boot tapping on the kitchen floor. 'Did you catch that nosey bitch?'

'Hey, mind your language,' Simon scolded. 'How's dinner going?'

She pointed to the pots bubbling on the stovetop. 'Probably ruined now. What did you do with her?'

'We gave Abby a good talking to about eavesdropping,' Leo said, 'and sent her on her way.'

'That's all you did? Then why did it take so long? Where'd she run off to?'

'Geez, what's with the inquisition?' Simon brushed hair out of his eyes, his filthy hand smearing dirt over his forehead. 'You sound just like your mother. I'm going to get cleaned up, then I'll help dish out.'

Leo washed his hands at the kitchen sink. 'Want me to set the table?'

Keira opened a drawer, took out the silverware, and dropped

them with a clatter on the bench. 'Knock yourself out, uncle Leo. The glasses are in the overhead cupboard.'

Leo chose three glass tumblers and placed them with the silverware on the dining room table, along with a jug of iced water. He then found placemats in a sideboard, noticing the display of framed photos on top included Simon and Keira, together or on their own, but not Genevieve. Had it come to that already? The Sweetman fellas had little luck where women were concerned.

'Think we can pull it off?'

Leo spun around to see Simon setting a steaming dish of curry on the table.

'You mean holding our tongue about you-know-what?'

Simon nodded.

'We have to.' Leo dropped into a chair, his body slumping with fatigue and age. 'We can trust Abby ... can't we?'

Simon shrugged. 'I guess so. I haven't known her long. Not even a week.'

'Damn.' Leo rubbed the creases in his brow he knew were there to stay. 'Oh, well, time will tell.'

Keira walked in and plonked down a bowl of cooked rice and a plate of partly burnt naan bread. 'Rice might be gluggy.' She eyed her father. 'But that's your fault. You weren't here to tell me how it's done correctly.'

'It'll be fine,' he said. 'We've eaten worse, haven't we, Leo?'

'Sure have. Yet we survived my cooking, as bad as it was.'

Leo drew Keira into some general chat while they ate, more to keep his mind in the present and not slinking back to the harrowing past or leaping ahead to the frightful future. He listened as she whined about her boring stay in the country, and how much she missed her mum and her school friends, while Simon stuffed his face and rolled his eyes at his daughter's complaints.

After dinner, Keira vanished to her room to watch a movie on YouTube, while Leo and Simon sat on the back deck downing beers and enjoying the cool of the evening.

'So, you and Genevieve are kaput?' Leo asked.

'Probably.' Simon twisted the top off another beer. 'She's holidaying with friends to think about whether she wants our separation to be permanent.'

'And what do you want?'

'I want her to be happy. I want Keira to be happy. If it means we have to live apart, then so be it. I'm not perfect. I've made plenty of mistakes. But at least, unlike Gen, I've put effort into this marriage.'

'*Always do your best, angels can do no better*, is what your grandmother used to say.' Leo stared at his hands, at the skin rubbed raw from digging a grave with the shovel Simon had gone back for to aid the process. He had to believe they'd done right in covering up the crime. 'I might hang around for a couple of days, if that's okay.'

'You're very welcome. That's if you can survive living with a sullen teenager.'

'Hey, I've done it once. I'm sure I can do it again.'

Simon flicked his bottle top at Leo. 'Rude bugger.'

Leo caught it. 'Sorry about punching you in the face earlier.'

'I deserved it. I should have told you the truth about seeing Dad in the pit years ago instead of being such a scaredy cat.'

'It would've saved me a lot of angst having to hide that secret from you. I can't imagine how you kept it to yourself.' Waiting for a response, he studied his nephew ripping the damp label from his bottle in strands.

'Well ...' Simon glanced up from his task, 'sometimes we push stuff down so deep we forget it's even there.'

'Until some nosey ... *woman* ... comes sniffing around.'

Simon sighed. 'Yeah, Abby's certainly like a dog with a bone.'

'Anyway.' Leo got up from his chair. 'I'm off to catch some shuteye.'

Simon raised his beer. 'Good luck with that. Don't let the bed bugs bite.'

Maybe not bed bugs, but Leo had an inkling that other things would gnaw at him and disrupt his sleep.

In his old room, he stripped down to his boxer shorts and switched off the light. Dropping onto the mattress, he blinked until his eyes adjusted to the darkness. Shadows flitted, curtains danced, and a breeze as light as a baby's breath skipped over his bare skin. A rumbling filtered through the wall from whatever Keira was watching, and the noise—similar to the roll of thunder—conjured up a scene from his past.

As real as when it occurred, Leo felt the silken glide of Faith's hair, the caress of her fingers, the warmth of her mouth. He smelt her perfume, tasted her sweat and desire, heard her gasp. Her cry, as their souls meshed, rang in his ears like a siren's song.

47

The drive home was a nightmare. Not only was I forced to dodge hares and wallabies, swerve around potholes, and straddle roadkill, I struggled to grasp the reality of the last two hours. I would have had less trouble believing I'd stumbled onto the film set of a horror movie. I thumped the heel of my hand on the steering wheel. What would it take to end the scenes playing in a loop in my mind?

Reaching for the stubby of beer I bought at the bottle-o in town as I passed through, I caught a flash of russet leaping out of the scrub to my right. I stomped my foot on the brake pedal and my VW screeched to a stop just before hitting a wild deer. No, not just a deer, a humongous red stag now standing on the road and eyeing me with majestic nonchalance, a length of electric fence tape entwining its impressive antlers like Christmas tinsel.

A beep of the car horn and a flick of high beams didn't alarm the stag out on the prowl in search of its mate. So, I wound down the window and unleashed several colourful words to urge it to move along. It took the hint. Giving its antlers a shake, it bounded across the road and up a grassy incline to disappear into the night to do more damage to property fencing.

I pulled the car over to the gravelly verge, twisted the top off the bottle, and gulped down the locally brewed ale. The alcoholic buzz shimmied around my brain. Would it settle my thoughts and steady my nerves as I hoped? I switched on the interior light and held out a dirty hand, only to see it trembling like a daddy-long-legs spider in fear of its life. Fine splinters were imbedded in my palm from wielding a tree branch to help dig a grave, while encrusted under jagged fingernails was enough evidence to send a forensic pathologist breaking into a dorky happy dance.

I poked my head out the window and inhaled deeply, only to find the rush of cool air worsened my dizziness. What I really needed was a soothing camomile tea, and the only place I could get a cup this late in the day around here was at home. Yet how would I explain my beer breath to Shane when I, supposedly, had been delayed by putting finishing touches to the shop?

'Sorry, got held up. Home soon,' was my reply to his four missed text messages before leaving the Sweetman's. *Yeah, held up by running away in fright and then reburying a dead man.*

A lint-covered mint in the bottom of my bag came to my aid, and I steered the car back onto the road, hoping Sgt Feather wasn't lurking behind a shrub with his trusty speed gun and breathalyser kit. In my tipsy state, there was a chance I'd lose control, drop my bundle, and confess what I'd just been up to.

'Hello, just going to get cleaned up,' I called as I entered the house, and rushed to the bathroom before being seen.

Shedding my filthy clothes, I stepped into the shower and lathered up. Hot water rained over me as I scrubbed away every trace of my forest escapade and then crouched, arms around my knees as I rocked on my heels. I'd never been much good at acting, even missing out on the smallest parts in school plays and Christmas pageants. So, I knew I would have to pull out something award-winning to keep that dreaded secret hidden.

I jumped up as Shane burst into the bathroom.

'You took your time,' he said, closing the door behind him. 'I figured there was nothing left to do at the shop.'

I turned off the water and got out. Taking the towel Shane offered, I wrapped my body burrito-style.

'Well, I rearranged a bookcase and moved some chairs around. Stuff like that.'

'Elliott and I have eaten. Want me to reheat your sausages and mash?'

'That would be great, thanks.'

He eyed me standing stock still with water dribbling down my legs and making a puddle at my feet. 'You okay? Still nervous about tomorrow?'

'Yeah.' That was one of the many emotions churning inside me like a whirlpool.

When I said nothing more, he gave a nod and walked out.

I dried myself and hurried to the bedroom to change into pyjamas.

While Shane and Elliott watched TV, I attempted to eat my dinner. Three mouthfuls in, I gave up and returned my plate to the fridge.

I stuck my head into the lounge room. 'I'm off to bed.'

'Finished your dinner?' Shane asked.

'Not much of an appetite, I'm afraid.'

'Too excited about your big day, hey, Mum?' Elliott asked, his eyes still on the TV screen, his hand inside a bag of Cheetos I'd stashed away for my own pleasure.

In the darkened bedroom, I slipped under the covers and

curled into a foetal position. How was I to sleep? I pulled the spare pillow over my head and tried to erase my thoughts.

I must have drifted off, because I was jolted from deep slumber by Shane shaking me by the shoulders.

'Abby, wake up!'

I squinted against the glaring light. 'Is it morning already?'

'No, just gone midnight.' He held out my phone. 'It's the police.'

I bolted upright. An icy shiver ran down my spine and back up again. *Oh God. Oh Shit!* Had our dastardly deed in the forest been discovered?

'It's Will Feather,' Shane grimaced. 'He says Ringtales is on fire.'

48

The drive down from Rosella Ridge was a blur. By the time we reached Shadow Creek, a filmy grey shroud hovered above the village centre. Turning into the main street, smoke billowed down from the top end to greet us. Even from this distance we noticed the quick responding fire brigade—who only had to drive their truck three hundred metres—had extinguished the flames.

Shane parked the work ute near the grocery store and he, Elliott, and I leapt out into air filled with the acrid odour of a barbecue gone wrong. We raced up the street and pushed to the front of a mob of spectators, some wearing pyjamas, many holding aloft their mobile phones. I stared wide-eyed and incredulous at the mess of charred timber and warped iron sheeting that had once been Ringtales. The gift shop next door looked to be only partially damaged, while the bookshop was gutted.

Shane gripped my hand, crushing my fingers, yet I didn't pull free. I needed an infusion of his strength to keep me standing upright.

Elliott received an elbow jab in the ribs from his father when he uttered, 'What a bummer. Filming the fire at its height would have made an outstanding video.'

'Mum!' Gemma clutched my arm. 'This is terrible. I can't believe it. How did it happen? Was it an accident? Faulty wiring?'

I turned my head robotically and stared into her blue eyes glinting in the flash of emergency lights. Unable to speak, I gave a shrug.

'It's an old shop,' Benji said, coming alongside her. 'We had an electrician check the restaurant out before we took it over. He found a mishmash of shoddy work done by amateurs.'

'Where's Will Feather?' Shane asked, looking around. 'We should talk with him or one of the firefighters. See what they can tell us.'

He tugged my hand, but I shook my head. 'You go,' I croaked, unsure if my jelly legs could walk even a few steps.

'Right. I'll be back as soon as I can.'

'I'll come with you,' Elliott said, pocketing his phone, while Benji and Gemma dashed away to make sure the restaurant was securely locked.

Graeme Roper took Shane's place by my side.

'What a bloody mess, Abbs. And you were about to open tomorrow. Such a damn shame. How are you?'

'How do you think? My world has just crumbled.' My eyes stung, and a sob lurched from my throat. Disappearing within his encompassing hug, I cried until my chest hurt.

Shane returned a little while later. 'Found Sgt Feather. He said forensics have to give the scene a good look over, but the fire chief highly suspects it was arson.'

'Arson? But who ... who,' I whimpered, sounding more like a barn owl than a person in shock.

Shane once again viewed the destruction. 'I don't get it. Why would someone do this to *your* shop?'

There was no need to guess. I'd stepped on somebody's toes one too many times, that's why. I scanned the crowd of gawkers. What if that individual was here watching and admiring their effort?

Searching the sea of faces, I recognised Stoney and Doris, Trev the bartender from The Axe, Beryl Erbacher—dabbing her eyes with a handkerchief at the loss of another heritage building—and standing at the rear, Lester Schilling with his arm around his mother's shoulders. Was that a smirk twisting the corners of Natalie's mouth, or just a nervous twitch?

'Look, there's nothing we can do here,' Shane said. 'Let's go back home and get some sleep.'

He started to direct me through the thinning throng, but I froze.

'I can't leave. I need to stay here.'

'And do what? You won't be allowed inside. The police have to do their thing if they're to catch the culprit. C'mon, let's just go.' He pushed, rather than led, me away.

We bumped into Gemma as we passed the restaurant.

'Mum, you probably don't want to go all the way home. Why not come back to our place? Have a cuppa and try to have a lie down. Then you'll be on hand in case you're needed early in the morning.'

Yes, my daughter understood. 'That would be great, Gem.' I fed my arm through hers and we began to walk away.

'Well, if we're not invited,' Shane called, 'Elliott and I will toddle home to snatch a few winks.'

I didn't have the energy to even wave goodbye.

Somehow, I'll blame it on the fragrant oil burning in Gemma's bedroom, or the gin and hardly-any-tonic Benji mixed for me, I fell sound asleep.

49

I stumbled out of Gemma's bedroom early the next morning, having no clue where she'd dossed down for the night. No extra bedding strewn around showed she'd already packed the linen away or ... I glanced towards Benji's closed bedroom door. So be it.

Gemma was in the kitchen serving up Spanish omelettes. With my dire situation splicing my heart in two, I couldn't be bothered to quiz her about her love life, or talk about the fire, so I ate my breakfast in the lounge room. Respecting my sullen mood, Gemma scoffed down her omelette and went for her regular morning jog.

While she was absent, I phoned my parents to inform them of the disastrous event. My father consoled me, said he really wanted to come into town to offer support but had concerns about Mum's difficulty in adjusting to her new blood pressure medication. I assured him I'd be fine and asked him to pass on my love to Mum. Then hanging up, I stepped outside to confront my new reality.

My weight felt as if it had doubled as I crossed the bitumen and lumbered up the street. I should be swinging wide Ringtales' door and welcoming excited hordes eager to browse and buy, not paying my respects to a shop recently deceased.

Shards of glass from the blown-out display window crunched underfoot as I stood on the pavement in front of the ex-shop. Kept from entering by police tape, I examined the site from my remote position. The smell of smoke was strong to the point of overpowering, and it was easy to ascertain by daylight that the interior had been damaged beyond repair. Though there was hardly anything to show what the shop had once been, one item was recognisable. Rising triumphantly from the centre of the blackened ruin like a scorched steampunk phoenix was the throne chair—a true survivor.

A lump formed in my throat when I discovered the shop counter's beautiful slab of polished redgum had been reduced to a length of charcoal. All that hard work put in by Shane to create a showpiece to be proud of was wasted. Thank God I'd taken photos of the shop before leaving yesterday and had proof of my venture, now dead before it was even born. I was also grateful for taking the cash box and laptop home. At least I had an inventory to help with the insurance claim.

'Abby, you poor thing!'

I turned and saw Donna rushing up the footpath, her face crumpled in pain, her arms outstretched. She gathered me into a tight embrace. 'This is horrible, absolutely horrible. Do they know who did it?'

I shook my head. 'No. Not yet.'

'I hope they catch the bastards. Bring back the stocks, I say. The entire town would relish chucking truckloads of rotten vegetables at them. Then we could shave their heads and strip off their clothes and drag them around the streets buck naked.'

I smiled briefly and stepped back. 'When did you return?'

'We flew in on an early flight. Ross was keen to get back to Shadow Creek. It seems there's something special to celebrate tonight.' Her grin slipped away. 'Sorry, that was insensitive. We should be celebrating both my birthday and your shop opening, but now ...' She studied the fried remains. 'Oh, God, it really is a mess, isn't it? There's nothing worth saving?'

'Doesn't look like it, except maybe the throne chair. The owners will have to tear the whole thing down and rebuild from scratch, I reckon.'

'Will you reopen when it's done?'

I winced. 'You've got to be kidding.'

'Insurance payout should cover stock and fittings. You'd have the means.'

'But not the drive. It's the last thing I want to do.'

'Such a shame.'

I nodded in agreement. 'How was your Melbourne holiday?'

'Bloody brilliant. I had a ball.'

'I saw your Facebook pics. You didn't respond to any of my comments or messages.'

'You sent messages? I must have missed them.'

'Enjoying yourself too much I suppose. Is that why Ross rushed down, to curb your enthusiasm?'

Her brows knitted together. 'He came down to join me on my last day. As well as check out a glorious Edwardian dresser that took my fancy.'

'Is that all you fancied?'

She cocked her head. 'What's that supposed to mean?'

Before I questioned her further, Ross arrived.

'Abby! Such a shock. Arson, right? You don't think they'll try to do it again? We should check our stock worth, make sure we have the proper insurance cover. Donna, honey, could you dig the files out for a proper look?'

'What, now?'

'Yeah. There are a few things I want to talk to Abby about ... in private.' He gave her a wink.

'Righto.' She touched my arm. 'I'll understand if you can't come to the party.'

'Of course I'll come. Anything to take my mind off all of this.'

'Only if you're up to it.'

'I'll be fine. I wouldn't miss the chance to welcome you into your fourth decade.'

She pulled a face and hurried away.

Though Donna was nowhere near, Ross dropped his voice to a whisper. 'Sorry to bring this up now, but how'd you get on with that Faith thing? Solved the riddle?'

I let out a groan. 'No.' Which was true. I had no concrete evidence, and if I did, I wasn't in the right headspace to share it with him. 'I think we should just call it quits and let sleeping dogs lie. If Faith wants her secret made known, then it's up to her to reveal it, and in her own time.'

'Oh ... okay. It would've been an incredible surprise, but ... *comprendo*. I better go, there's plenty to do before tonight. Hope we see you there.'

'You will,' I said, faking determination.

In fact, I'd rather have gotten the hell out of Dodge. A TARDIS, or a souped-up DeLorean would have proven helpful. Even an antiquated wardrobe leading into Narnia would have sufficed. With none available, I eyed The Axe at the top of the street and saw Trev opening its doors. Was 10 a.m. too early to drink myself into oblivion? Sense prevailed and, spying Stan Gruen from the Talk of the Town heading towards the crime scene with his trusty camera, I walked in the opposite direction to buy a strong coffee.

. . .

I sat on a bench in the communal garden alongside the craft shop to drink my espresso. Surrounded by flowering shrubs, the heady fragrance of a mock orange, and the hum of pollenating bees, I enjoyed the serenity until it was interrupted by a phone text from Shane.

'Coming in to town. Almost there.'

I texted back, telling him where to meet me.

Lifting the cup to my mouth, I jumped as a four-legged beastie burst out of the bushes, causing me to spill coffee down the front of my shirt.

Surprised to see me, Otto froze mid-prance, his lead dangling on the ground beside him. I glanced around for his owner and, finding no one resembling Jean, patted my thigh and called him over. Otto eyed me sceptically and stepped forward. I lunged, grabbing the plaited leather just as he started to dart away.

Pulled at speed down the path, we dodged shrubbery and a terracotta bird bath, and slammed into Sgt Will Feather scoffing a meat pie.

'Bleedin' heck,' he said, wiping a smear of gravy from his face. 'Abby Eaton. I was about to phone you. We need to have a little chat.'

I didn't like the sound of that. 'Um ... what about?'

He fed his half-eaten pie back into its white paper packet. 'I'd like you to view some CCTV footage that's come to hand.'

'CCTV?'

'Yes, of last night.'

'Oh, I didn't realise my lease included video surveillance.'

'I'm sure it doesn't ... or didn't. The footage came from a security camera mounted on the Schilling Real Estate building. It isn't aimed at your shop, but we have a footage of someone in that vicinity at the time of the fire.'

Otto tugged on the lead, and I jerked him back. 'So, it definitely was arson?'

'Yes. Someone wilfully set your shop ablaze. According to the fire chief, an accelerant was used, most likely kerosene, and a large pile of books was the point of origin.'

'How'd they get in?'

'Not sure at this stage. Broke a window or busted a door. Were the doors deadlocked?'

'The front one was, but not the back. Do you need me to identify someone?'

'That would be helpful. Er ... what are you going to do about that?' He pointed to the glistening turd Otto had just dropped.

'He's not my dog.'

Sgt Feather's raised eyebrows and tapping of his boot had me emptying the rest of my coffee onto the grass and scooping up Otto's smelly deposit. The soiled cup was dumped into a nearby bin, and I shadowed the officer across the street to the police station.

An elderly woman in hot pink Capri pants and orange shirt greeted us at the gate. 'Otto, you scallywag.' Jean crouched and the smarmy dog bounded into her outstretched arms, and attempted to lick the wrinkles from her face. 'Thank you, Sgt Feather, I was about to report a missing canine.'

'He was in the garden by the craft shop. Abby, here, found him.'

'I don't understand what happened. I left him tied up outside the store. It's not like him to go wandering.'

Otto snapped his head around, his beady eyes pleading with mine not to let his secret out of the bag. I scowled and refrained from informing Jean her precious pooch was, in fact, a serial absconder.

'Maybe a tracking device would come in handy,' I offered.

'No, I couldn't do that to the poor boy. It was just a one-off. C'mon snookums, I think you deserve a tasty treat after that big adventure.'

Jean took hold of the dog lead, and she and snookums trotted off without a backward glance.

'In here,' Sgt Feather said, opening the station door and directing me inside.

I followed as he moved behind the counter and crossed the carpet to a desk loaded with paperwork. He pulled the desk chair out and sat in front of the computer monitor while instructing me to sit on a wheelie stool alongside. A tap of the keyboard and a video file appeared on the screen.

'Before I play this, Abby, I need to know if you've upset anyone recently. Someone who might enact payback for you angering them.'

I gave a nervous laugh. Where would I begin? 'Not enough to set my shop on fire,' I lied.

He nodded and clicked the mouse to start the video.

I leaned in and watched as a black and white scene came into play, a side view of the display windows and entrance to Schilling Real Estate along with a section of pavement. As the street itself, and my shop directly opposite, weren't visible, I wasn't sure how helpful the video would be.

A group of men emerged from the bottom of the screen and staggered past the building, after a session at the pub, no doubt. One melded into the dark recess of the entry and reappeared moments later zipping up the fly of his trousers.

I peered at Sgt Feather.

'It's okay, I know who the pisser is. He'll be getting a fine.'

The men eventually moved out of shot and nothing eventful occurred over the next minute other than a possum scampering past. Sgt Feather fast forwarded the video briefly and returned it to normal speed as an effusion of light appeared on the left side of the screen.

'We can't see it, but that's a vehicle pulling into the kerb,' he said. 'Keep watching.'

The light went out and several seconds later a figure stepped onto the pavement: a tall man in a dark bulky jacket with a hood. He looked to be grappling with a weighty object between his feet. A container? A tin? Then the person disappeared.

'I won't bore you so I'll move ahead ten minutes.' Sgt Feather said, fast forwarding again.

While he did this, my phone bleeped. It was a message from Shane: *Where are you?* I texted back, *Police station*, and returned to viewing the computer screen.

The footage slowed again and I saw light flickering off to the left.

Sgt Feather answered my question before it was asked. 'Yep, that's the fire taking hold.'

The man reappeared with the container now under his arm, and the hood of his jacket slipped back from his head.

Sgt Feather pointed to the monitor. 'Watch closely.'

I stared unblinking and noticed the man make the mistake of glancing toward The Axe before vanishing from view.

'That was quick,' I remarked. 'Can you replay that bit?'

Second time around, Sgt Feather paused the video just as the man faced the camera. 'So, anyone you know?'

I shuffled forward, squinted, and then jolted. 'Oh my God!'

A ding of a bell had Sgt Feather turning around. 'Come through,' he said, and the next instant Shane was standing behind us and enquiring what was going on.

'Looking at CCTV footage of last night,' Will Feather explained. 'Do you recognise him?' he asked me.

I nodded, my eyes fixed on the screen. 'It's not a man.'

Will Feather leaned in, 'Are you sure? It looks like a guy to me.'

'It's Linda McKenny,' I said, my stomach churning.

He turned to study me. 'And who might she be?'

I sneaked a peek at Shane pursing his lips. How much I should divulge?

I related a watered-down version of events, telling how, when researching Donna Clarke's family history, I'd found a christening photo and decided to try and locate the people pictured, ask them a few questions. My search for Rev Wes McKenny led me to his wife, Linda, who somehow had gotten into her head I was out to defame her departed husband. I mentioned the threatening letter I believed she'd sent, and my attempt at defusing the situation, assuring Sgt Feather and Shane I was unaware her retaliation would go as far as destroying my shop.

They seemed to buy my story, so I withdrew Linda's warning letter from my bag and handed it over, along with her contact details.

Sgt Feather thanked me and said he'd follow this up. Told me I'd be required to provide a statement at some stage and he would be in touch.

It was only when I strode out of the police station with Shane in tow and headed up the street that he spoke.

'Well ... you've done it again.'

Shane's glare and snort hinted what was about to go down, and I steeled myself for the onslaught.

'I've warned you time and time again, Abby, and look what your meddling has achieved. I shouldn't have wasted my breath. Obviously, my advice means nothing to you.'

'Of course it does. I've followed your advice plenty of times, but ...'

'But what? Go on, tell me why you disobeyed me.'

I gasped. 'Disobeyed?' I dropped to my knees and bowed low. 'So sorry, master. Please don't punish me.'

'Get up,' he snarled, and stepped back.

I clutched his ankles. 'Don't go. I'll be a dutiful servant now, I promise.'

'Stop it, Abby!' Shane wrenched me to my feet. 'You're embarrassing yourself.'

I tugged free of his grip. 'I don't care! I've had enough of you. Had enough of this town. Enough of bloody everything!'

This time when I walked away, Shane did not follow.

50

Benji and Gemma were both at work, so I had the cottage all to myself.

I raided their alcohol stash and pantry, and spent the rest of the day mixing drinks, eating junk food, and watching TV, anything to take my mind off my reality.

When Gemma arrived home late in the afternoon and discovered me asleep on the floor, surrounded by empty glasses and bowls, she lost her cool.

'What the hell, Mum! Get up.'

I opened one eye. 'What? Stop kicking me.'

'I realise you're depressed, but drinking yourself into a stupor isn't the answer. Why hasn't Dad come for you?'

I sat up and rested against the sofa. Wiping drool from my face, I told her he had been in town, but we'd had a fight so he left.

'Fight? About what?'

'Everything,' I said, flinging my hands in the air. 'Life sucks.'

She gave me a dressing down. 'Well, Mrs Grumpy-bum, I'm

gonna get you cleaned up and then take you home myself so you two can sort out this mess.'

'No,' I cried. 'I have a party to attend.'

'What? Don't tell me you're still going to Donna's birthday?'

'She's my friend. It would be rude not to.' I tried to rise, but the room spun like a carousel. 'What time is it?'

'Five. That means you have one hour to get ready if you want to get there for the fancy appetisers Benji's created. If I can't talk you out of it, I recommend you have a shower while I try to find you something to wear.'

I didn't protest when she pulled me up and pushed me towards the bathroom.

'There's a fresh towel on the rack and you can use my toiletries.'

I shut the door and peeled out of my clothes, only stumbling once when a foot got caught in the leg hole of my undies. The hot jets of water were soothing and I could have stayed there for hours if Gemma hadn't hammered on the door telling me to hurry up.

Drying off, I blow-dried my hair and scrunched it into soft curls with mousse that may have been Benji's, while Gemma took care of my make-up.

'Here, this should do.' She held up a black knee-length lace dress with capped sleeves. 'I bought it online, but it arrived two sizes too big for me.'

It fit me snugly. To add a touch of bling, Gemma pinned a jewelled brooch to the bodice and handed me a matching set of earrings. A pair of strappy sandals, at a height my daughter thought I could handle, completed the outfit.

I grinned. 'I feel like one of your Barbie dolls.'

She grimaced. 'A bloody big Barbie doll.' Then she stood me in front of a full-length mirror. 'There, what do you think?'

I sighed. 'You're a magician. I'm stunning, if you don't look at my bloodshot eyes. Ever thought about changing careers?'

'Nope. Not right now. Too many things going on.'

'Hmm, such as?'

'Never you mind.' She fed a black clutch bag into my hand and led me to the front door. 'Oh, wait.' She hurried away and returned to spritz me with a rose and sandalwood smelling scent. 'Now go, Cinderella, the ball awaits.'

I took a step and then faltered. 'Oh, no! I don't have a present for Donna.'

Gemma dashed away for a second time and came back with a gift bag. 'This should do.'

I peeked inside and spotted flamingo bookends and a book by Brene Brown. 'Hey, I had these items in my bookshop.'

'I know,' she said, sheepishly. 'I took them yesterday with the intention of paying you later.'

'Well, at least something survived.'

I gave her a wave and stepped cautiously as I navigated my way to the footpath. Still light-headed from binge-drinking, I just needed to keep my balance for five minutes until I reached Mulga Bill's.

I walked into the restaurant to the tune of 'Boogie Wonderland' blaring from ceiling speakers. The rustic decor, reminiscent of Australia's colonial past, had been enhanced with colourful balloons, streamers, and shiny foil banners. A chocolate fountain on a circular stand spewed forth its decadent delight, while on a table against a wall sat a smattering of wrapped gifts. This is where I headed when Donna, blitzing a teal chiffon cocktail dress, greeted me.

'So glad you could make it, Abby.'

'Happy birthday, dear friend,' I said, handing over the gift bag. 'I intended to give you something way more exciting, but it didn't materialise in time.'

She peeked inside the bag. 'This is lovely. I wasn't expecting anything what with ... well ... everything you've been through. Is Shane here?'

I eyed the crowded room. 'No, it doesn't seem like it.'

She cocked her head. 'What's going on?'

'It's nothing.' I pointed to the decorations. 'This is wonderful. Did Ross do it all himself?'

'Until he got flustered, and I stepped into help.' She waved to a woman I didn't recognise. 'I better keep moving. Help yourself to some bubbly before it's all gone.'

Donna fluttered away, and I found the drinks table lined with rows of already-filled wine glasses. Throwing back two sparkling whites in quick succession, I picked up a third glass and hijacked James carrying a tray of hors d'oeuvres, grabbing a few and gobbling them up before he offered the treats to others.

'How's it going, Abby?' It was Lester Schilling, a glass of red wine in one hand, a cracker topped with a curl of salmon and a sprig of dill in the other. Tonight, he wore a tight-fitting burgundy suit with a black shirt and tie. His shoes were also black, yet he'd forgotten to wear socks—or was trying hard to show he was on-trend with the current fashion style. 'Sorry about your shop. I guess you've heard the owners aren't planning to rebuild.'

'They aren't?' I licked a smear of olive tapenade from the corner of my mouth.

'No. I've offered them a fair price for the block so, fingers crossed, I'll soon have another acquisition.'

I coughed up some flaky pastry. 'Good God, is there anything you don't own in Shadow Creek? They should change the town's name to Schillingsville. We could mount a statue of you in the park and lay wreaths once a year on your birthday. You'd like that wouldn't you?'

Lester scowled. 'That's a snarky thing to say, Abby. I know you're miserable regarding the fire and all, but if we're throwing darts ...' He took a slurp of his wine. 'I could say you're a prying bitch who doesn't care who gets hurt just as long as you get a story. Now you're unemployed, *once again*, you should consider applying for a job with a trashy gossip magazine. I reckon they'll snap you up.' He spun around and went to talk to a big hairy bloke resembling Santa Claus who'd swapped his traditional costume for chinos and chambray.

Stuff you, Lester. His snide comment tempted me to run over and inform him the word around town was he'd been conceived out of wedlock while his mother had S & M sex in the pub cellar. Instead, I guzzled down my Prosecco and replaced it with a stubby of beer from a waitstaff's tray as he passed by.

Julie Roper came alongside. 'Bloody awful about the fire, Abby. You must be devastated. Arson, hey? Have they caught the bastard who did it?'

'Not sure. But I think they have some strong leads.'

'A local? Some ratty kids?'

'They're looking into it,' was all I was prepared to offer.

'Bet it was a Worrall kid. The older one, Grady, is a real mongrel. Wouldn't put it past him to do such a thing. Anyway, take heart. Things can only get better.' Then she was off to speak with Karen, Lester's wife.

My beer finished, I stumbled over to the chocolate fountain and dipped in a finger. What would happen if I stuck my face under? Would anyone even notice?

'You're supposed to dunk skewered marshmallows and strawberries in there, not your fingers.' Donna moved me back before I plunged anything else in. 'I have to speak with you.'

I snatched another glass of wine before she pushed me into a shadowy corner.

'Don't try to console me, Donna. I couldn't handle any more pity.'

'No, I want to tell you a secret.'

'A secret?' I drank the cabernet in one gulp and pricked my ears.

She cleared her throat. 'I think I'm pregnant.'

Donna caught the glass that slipped from my hand before it smashed on the floor.

'What?' I gasped. 'Are you sure?'

'Pretty sure. I've peed on a handful of sticks today and three out of four gave a positive reading. My body is already changing.'

I eyed her from head to toe. 'Where?'

'Inside. I can feel it. It's magical. What you said the other day did the trick.'

'Geez, what did I say?'

'Keep believing in miracles.'

'Hah! I think you need to do more than that to make a baby. A little hanky panky, hey?' I gave an exaggerated wink. 'I know what you got up to in Melbourne, you naughty minx.'

Donna leaned in. 'What are you talking about?'

'I saw the guy you were with.'

'What guy?'

'The man who took all your photos: good-looking, with a beard. I phoned you the other morning, and he answered. Very sexy voice. What was he doing in your hotel room at such an early hour? No, don't tell me. You had a sleepover, didn't you?' I elbowed her in the ribs.

Her dimples deepened as she chuckled. 'Well, yes, we did.'

'Was it only the once?'

She shook her head. 'Four nights all up.'

I slapped her arm. 'I knew it. And where did you find him? A seedy bar? Tinder?'

'None of those. I've known Michael for years. He agreed to keep me company.'

'Michael, hey? You sneaky devil. And did you ask him to do a job for you? Step in and take over where Ross had failed?'

She arched her eyebrows. 'Well, he was helpful, and we had a marvellous time together.'

I snorted. 'I bet you did. Was he a former work colleague?'

'No, we met at high school.' She smiled wickedly.

'Oh, your first love?'

'Not quite. He went by the name of Michelle, back then.'

'You mean like a fancy French pronunciation?'

'No, just the standard Michelle. A girl's name.' She must have noticed my look of confusion because she added, 'He started transitioning a few years ago. It's amazing how much confidence he's gained since his gender reassignment surgery.'

This time I didn't just swipe a glass from a passing tray, but an entire bottle. I swigged down something red and fizzy. 'I guess that means Michael didn't get you pregnant.'

'Of course not. My husband is the only male to venture anywhere near my lady bits of late. Other than my gyno, that is.'

'So, Ross's teeny tadpoles finally reached a lily pad.' I fist-pumped. 'Way to go, boys!'

'Remember,' she put a finger to her lips, 'our secret. I'll tell Ross once it's confirmed.'

'Hey, I'm the queen of secrets,' I announced as she disappeared into the crowd.

Sucking from the bottle like an old wino, and nodding to the tom-tom drum beat of 'My Sharona', my light-headedness increased. So had the number of party-goers, many unfamiliar to me. This was a good thing because I wasn't up to talking with anyone else.

I winced when I spotted Shane sauntering into the restaurant. He'd chosen to dress in the outfit he'd worn for our wedding anniversary dinner the previous month. I'd commented then on how hot he looked in the navy-blue trousers and blue and white paisley shirt. He still did, darn it. Appropriately, Rod Stewart's 'Da Ya Think I'm Sexy' started playing.

Shane scratched his goatee as he scanned the surroundings without seeing me in the dark corner, and then strutted over to talk with Graeme Roper. Ross Clarke joined them and all three moved to a stand bearing a laptop, its screen flashing through images of Donna at different stages of her life.

I edged the wall and peered between the fronds of a potted ficus. Some pics appearing on the screen I recognised from the day I helped Ross with the PowerPoint. I flinched when the christening shot slid into view. *Damn you, photo. You got me into this mess.*

A tap on my shoulder. I swung around and the room swirled with me.

It was Benji in his chef's tunic and bandana. 'Why are you hiding and spying, Abby?'

I clutched his arm for balance. 'Am I spying?'

'You tell me. You're the one wearing foliage as camouflage.' He tugged a broad leaf from my hair, and bent close to sniff my neck. 'Is that Scandal by Night?'

'I don't know,' I shrugged. 'Are you a perfume connoisseur?'

'Not really. I bought some for ... for someone, that's all.'

My laughter sounded more like a duck quacking. 'The plot thickens.' I poked him in the chest. 'I'm onto you, Benji boy.'

He frowned and held me up from buckling. 'You might prefer

to take a seat.' He pointed to the tables set with silverware and place cards. 'The meals are coming out soon.'

I groaned. If I wanted to avoid a heated confrontation, I'd need to move my place card away from Shane's.

The volume dropped on Michael Jackson's 'Don't Stop 'til You Get Enough' and Ross clinked a fork against a wine glass to gain the crowd's attention.

As guests congregated in a clump and listened to him shower Donna with praise, I slunk between tables trying to locate a place card with my name on it. Having difficulty in focusing to read, I stumbled against a chair and knocked it over with a loud clatter. A tinny crash made additional noise when I bumped into a server and sent her silver tray, and the tiny bread rolls it held, flying across the room.

People turned and stared, and I dropped to my knees. Crawling and searching for a way of escape around chair legs, I heard my name called and stopped to look behind.

'So, you're here,' Shane said, a puzzled look on his face.

'Oh, am I? Thanks for pointing that out.' I scrambled to my feet and tried to act cool through my swaying.

'And you're drunk,' he added.

'If you say so.' I went to move past, but he stepped in my way.

'Let's go home before you create a bigger scene.'

'We haven't eaten yet. Benji's cooked up a real treat. It'd be rude not to partake.'

'It'd be rude if you upset the celebrations.'

I shoved him aside, and he clutched my arm. Attempting to pull free, my heels slipped on the polished floor and I rolled an ankle. A dagger of pain shot up my leg and I slapped Shane across the face.

An icy hush in the room was broken by a sudden cry of, 'Surprise!'

All eyes, including mine, darted to the entrance to see Faith Crosby in the doorway holding aloft a bouquet of helium hearts and a giant kiwi soft-toy. Looking fabulous in a leopard print jumpsuit and ankle boots, she burst into a melodious rendition of 'Happy Birthday'.

My stomach squirmed as I saw a vision of a younger Faith: eyes wild, teeth bared, and face spattered with blood as she belted the life out of a man with the aid of a jaffle iron.

I lurched and vomited over Shane.

51

Faith had earlier flown in from Christchurch. Dropping home to change into party wear, she'd thrown a few items into an overnight bag and caught an Uber to Shadow Creek. The hour-and-a-quarter road trip, sharing the back seat with a giant fluffy kiwi and a bunch of helium balloons, was littered with memories and mixed emotions.

Donna's birth had been the highlight of Faith's life. The joy of holding a healthy baby—one she helped create, one she could shape—surpassed the agony experienced in delivering her. She fingered the new greenstone pendant hanging around her neck, chosen as a talisman. Carved in a spiral, the Koru symbolised the fresh shoots of New Zealand's silver fern. The seller told her the coiling movement represented going back to the beginning, while the unfurling frond itself signified new life, growth, strength, and peace. Was the Koru her totem?

She firmly believed it was destiny that brought her to the Brisbane Museum that fateful day when she met the boy and his father. Drawn to Carl's strength, which balanced her flightiness, and Simon's sensitivity—mirroring her own—she'd accepted the hasty marriage proposal. Eager for a life that didn't include her spineless mother and a half-brother she despised, she'd happily put down roots, only to feel more hobbled than planted when Carl's insecurities arose. If she'd denied her desperation for a baby and uprooted sooner, could she have avoided the horrors that eventuated? Maybe now, the Koru would bring her the peace she craved.

Faith thought up suitable totems for the rest of the Sweetman family.

Carl's would have been a crab—hard on the outside, though with a soft interior. Physically strong, yet vulnerable when threatened, with the ability to attack.

Simon—an inquisitive and clingy child, she saw him having a monkey totem, representing his mischievous nature and yearning for love.

Leo's totem would have been a wave—coming and going, tossed to-and-fro by life's pull, yet wielding such power, as she'd discovered the night they made love. The experience had overwhelmed her, and if what occurred less than twelve hours later had not happened, she may have pursued her fascination with him.

Faith's thoughts detoured to Mitch, whose totem was definitely a scorpion—ruled by passion, dominance, and self-protection. Her ridding the world of this demon was both a victory and a defeat, for it turned her into a killer. An image came to mind of his gloating face transforming into a horror mask, and she recalled too easily the metallic smell and taste as blood spurted from his skull to cover her in crimson splatter.

Nightmarish scenes leap in turn from her memory: Stoney responding to her phone call and rushing over, his eyes wide and darting from her, drenched in blood, to the thing lying dead on the floor; being wiped down with a towel, and made to assist in carrying the body down the rear stairs; stripping Mitch of his clothes and placing him in a wheelbarrow along with a shovel; Stoney manoeuvring the wheelbarrow through the rear gate and into the bush, while she returns to the house and cleans the kitchen of gore; turfing the jaffle iron into the dam; wheeling Mitch's motorbike into the shed and hiding it under a tarp until Stoney can return the following day and sell it cheap as chips without licence plates to some bloke on the other side of town; peeling out of her bloodstained clothing and tossing them with Mitch's onto a pile of rubbish in the yard; dousing the pile with kerosene, lighting a match, and watching flames destroy evidence of a murder; Stoney returning and undressing to his jocks, throwing his overalls into the fire; being guided upstairs and into the bathroom to shower and put on fresh clothes; shots of whisky burning her throat, dulling the pain in her head and her heart.

It relieved Faith that no one came looking for Mitch, as if nobody cared he'd vanished off the face of the earth. Their secret had remained hidden for forty years, and she vowed to make sure it stayed that way.

When the car arrived at Shadow Creek, Faith instructed the Uber driver to let her out at the restaurant in the main street.

She hesitated on the porch of Mulga Bill's. How would her surprise arrival at the party be received? Would Donna greet her warmly, or did she still begrudge Faith for not revealing the name of her father? In truth, she hadn't chosen to keep that information to herself. It was simply she didn't know who he was. Some people would label her a slut. Others would deem her irresponsible. But Faith labelled herself 'a victim of circumstance'.

Inhaling deeply, she positioned the kiwi on her hip, held the balloons high, and stepped through the door.

52

Dragged outside the restaurant, Shane shoved me into the ute before getting in and driving away.

Silence and the sickly stench of vomit filled our trip towards home.

'Pull over,' I moaned midway, gripping the door handle.

'You're not gonna puke again,' Shane snapped.

'Just pull over, will you!'

Shane skidded the car to a stop on the grassy verge of a lookout, and I leaped out. Rushing over to the railing, I bent over and sucked in the dewy night air. I didn't need to be sick. I needed to quell my mortification. Not only had I embarrassed myself and disrupted Donna's celebrations, I'd assaulted my husband in public. All because I struggled to cope with the mess I'd gotten myself into.

I sank to my knees and sobbed, my blubbering loud and clear in the wide-open space.

The sound of a car door opening and footsteps coming near.

'I'm so sorry,' I cried, noticing a splotch of spew on Shane's left shoe as he stood beside me. 'What I did was unforgivable.'

'It was humiliating, that's for sure ... and hurtful.' He rubbed his cheek, and I had an urge to kiss it better.

'You should just throw me off this cliff,' I whined. 'Watch my body smash onto the rocky hillside below.'

'A tempting thought, but I'll give it a miss.' He laid a hand on my head and stroked my hair. 'You've had a pretty rough day. If you'd sailed through it without breaking down, I would've been more worried. As for me blaming you for meddling and making all this shit happen ... well ... that was wrong of me, and I'm sorry for acting like a tyrant. I was as disappointed as you that your dream literally went up in smoke.'

I patted his hand on my head. 'You were right, though. I went too far in helping Donna find her father. I should have kept my distance. In future, I'll heed your advice without question.'

'Bloody hell, don't do that. I'm not perfect, you know. C'mon, let's get home and out of these stinky clothes.'

'No, let me wallow in despair a little longer.'

'My pleasure,' Shane said, and retreated into the darkness.

How was I to survive this? Not only my despicable performance at the party, but the grief of losing my shop, my future, my purpose. Maybe I could hide in a mountain cave and wither away, my dried bones discovered years later by adventurous rock climbers. This sparked a vision of Mitchell Shepherd's grisly remains. Would they continue to haunt me, pointing bony fingers of accusation? I groaned some more.

A hand squeezed my shoulder. 'Time to go, Abby. I need a shower and a strong drink.'

Fatigued physically and mentally, I allowed Shane to pull me to my feet and walk me back to the car.

'Might be a good idea to apologise to some other people too,' he said, easing me inside and doing up my seat belt. 'Ross and Donna, for starters. How about you pop into town first thing in the morning with your tail between your legs?'

'Can you come with me? I don't trust myself to do it right.'

'I'll be your minder, as long as you promise not to slap me in the face for my efforts.'

'No more slapping ... or spewing over you.' I pinched my nose. 'I'll even pay for an interior car clean to get rid of this smell.'

'You'd better. Don't want anyone thinking I've upchucked because I couldn't hold my liquor.'

53

The first thing I did when we got to Shadow Creek the next morning was buy a bunch of flowers.

Writing a brief message on a gift card, *Sorry for upsetting you*, and signing my name, I had Shane drive to Natalie Schilling's. Doubting she would open the door to me, I placed the flowers in a shady spot on the porch and hoped she'd find them before they wilted.

Then we visited Fine 'n Dandy.

'Be with you in a minute,' Ross called from below the shop counter. Springing up, his welcoming grin slid away when he saw me standing there. 'Oh ... it's you.'

'I'm here to apologise for my deplorable behaviour last night. I want you and Donna to know I am mortified about causing a scene.' I looked around. 'Is she here by any chance?'

Ross shook his head. 'Donna's with her mother. Faith is staying for a few days.'

'Quite the surprise, her turning up like that.'

'Yes, indeed. Faith was the life of the party after you left.'

'Of course she was,' I snarled. Shane's foot nudging mine told me to keep my comments in check. 'All going well between her and Donna?'

'Mostly.' He removed his glasses and cleaned them with the hem of his shirt. 'Maybe Faith will set things right with Donna about who her father is.'

So, she might get her special birthday present after all, without our help. I snuck a look at Shane, and his arched eyebrows hinted he had the same thought as me: *Why hadn't I left well alone and let life play out in its own good season?*

'Would you like some birthday cake?' Ross asked, his friendly demeanour returning. 'Donna packaged up some leftovers in little boxes to give out.'

'That'd be great,' Shane said. 'I could do with something sweet.'

Ross went out back and returned with a gift bag containing two wedge-shape boxes.

I implored him to pass on my apology to Donna. 'I'll catch up with her later in the week, when she's free.' *After she's told you the news about the baby,* I was tempted to add.

Gospel singing wafted across the road from the church as Shane and I walked up the street. However, the lyrics of 'Oh, Happy Day' did little to relieve my melancholia as we neared what remained of Ringtales.

The residual odour of smoke drifted around us as we ducked under police tape and entered the burnt-out shell of the shop, our shoes crunching on splintered glass and charred bits of wood.

Examining seared skeletons of furniture and remnants of books that disintegrated when touched, I let out a groan. 'What a mess, what a waste.'

'At least we might save the throne chair,' Shane said, running his hands over the tarnished iron. 'With a thorough clean and a spray paint, it should come up okay. It would go well in the gazebo I'm intending to build in the back yard. Want me to ask Will Feather if we can take it home today?'

'Yeah, whatever.' I felt no joy. Eyeing the destruction only fuelled my depression. With the excitement of owning a bookstore now snuffed out, what was I to do?

Shane rubbed his sooty palms on the seat of his jeans. 'Want to get a coffee? We have cake to go with it.'

I nodded, and with a heavy heart I stepped away from the corpse of a dream.

As usual, Sunday patrons filled Serendipi-teas to overflowing, so we bought takeaway coffees and went to sit in the park by the creek.

While we ate birthday cake, we watched purple swamp hens bob for food in the reedy shallows and wood ducks waddle around the lawn in search of discarded treats. Across the water, a colony of bats hung upside down from tree branches like dark fruit, their incessant chatter as soporific as white noise.

'It's peaceful here. Life almost feels good.'

'There's always speed bumps and detours along the way, but you have to take the good with the bad.' Shane nudged me with his shoulder. 'You'll get through this, Abby. At least you gave your dream a shot.'

'But I didn't, not really. My dream was aborted, remember.'

'Still, you prepared well. You would have smashed it out of the ballpark.' He crushed his empty cake box and slid it back into the gift bag. 'I might see Sgt Feather and ask if we can move the throne chair. You okay to stay here, or do you want to come with me?'

'I'll stay.'

'I'll meet you back here, then.'

Left to contemplate my misfortune, my dark thoughts were interrupted by an elderly man stepping from the path to scatter chunks of bread around for the ducks.

Stoney glanced up, saw me, and hobbled over.

'Horrible about your shop burning down. It's a godawful mess. Have they caught the scoundrel?'

'Not sure. But they will soon enough.'

'Here's hoping.' He sat alongside and patted my knee with a hand mottled by bruising, typical for someone his age 'How are you doing, girly? Or is that too difficult to answer?'

'Yeah. Next question?'

He chuckled and stretched out his legs. On his left foot he wore a hook-and-loop leather sandal, while on his right a double-plugger rubber thong. I hoped Stoney wasn't going the same way as Natalie.

'What's with the mismatched footwear?'

'It's alright … I'm not going bonkers. I've a sore toe. A real bugger that flares up from time to time.'

'Bunions?'

'No, a freeloader. The little toe on the thonged foot is missing a joint. Over time its grown deformed. See?' He lifted his right foot and offered me a closer view of his crooked toe, bent sideways across its neighbour. 'Shoes rub it raw. Gives me real jip. My father had his toe lopped off, but I'm in two minds about that.'

'Your dad had the same problem?'

'And his father before him. It's a genetic thing. My sister has a freeloading *left* toe to balance out mine.'

I turned to face him, bubbles bursting inside my chest. 'Donna Clarke has a similar problem with her left little toe. Has trouble buying comfortable shoes.'

Stoney's brow crinkled. 'Is that a fact.'

'Is there something you wish to tell me?' I asked him.

'Something you forgot to share about your relationship with Faith?'

He averted his eyes and stroked his moustache. 'Like I said, there was no relationship between us, we were just mates.'

'Mates with benefits?'

A sideways glance. 'Maybe.'

'Maybe?' I poked him in the arm. 'Come on, spill *all* the beans.'

'Don't get all excited, it was only the once.'

My mouth gaped. 'So, you did have sex with Faith.'

'Well ... I guess so.'

'What do you mean, you guess? You know what sex is, don't you?'

He stared at me. 'Could Bradman hit a six? It's just that I don't have a strong memory of it.'

'Why, were you drunk at the time?'

'No.' He sucked in his bottom lip. 'More like off my head on weed.'

I jolted back. 'Marijuana?'

'I'd never smoked it before. Faith had a stash and talked me into giving it a try.'

'When was this?'

'The Saturday night of the Shadow Creek Show, after I took her home from the pub.'

'But you said no hanky-panky took place that night. You just put her to bed to sleep it off. Were you lying to me?'

'Not technically. I can't recall the finer details, just that the weed sent me stupid, and I woke up the next morning in bed with Faith.'

I shook my head, struggling to believe what I was hearing. 'Were you clothed?'

'I had my jocks on, but she was starkers. I found my clothes scattered around the lounge room.'

'Did you ask Faith what had transpired?'

'No, she was dead to the world, and I wanted to get the hell out of there. And later, well, we never spoke of it, and it sort of faded from my mind ... until recently. We could have just dozed off together.'

'With Faith in the nude beside you? Yeah, right. What do you recall happening?'

'Nothing vivid, only blurry snippets. Could have been a raunchy dream. Though I did find a bite mark on my arse.'

I clapped my hands to my face. 'Geez, Stoney. When was the Shadow Creek Show?'

'Same as it's always been. The second weekend in May.'

No need to count on my fingers how many months that was before Donna's birth. I studied the grey strands sticking out from under Stoney's tartan flat cap. 'What's your natural hair colour?'

'It was light ginger. Strawberry blonde, I think they call it on a girl. My dad was a full-on blood nut.'

'Donna's a natural redhead,' I said, shocked that the answer had been right under my nose all along. 'Stoney, you realise there's a chance you are Donna's father.'

He blinked once. Twice. Three times. 'Strike me pink! I do now.'

'Nevertheless, I suggest you get a paternity test done before you break out the cigars. Didn't you ever suspect?'

'As I said, I was confused about what had happened that night.' He removed his cap and scratched his head. 'Maybe I didn't want to deal with the horrid truth, that I'd accidentally bonked a married woman.'

I had no heart to tell him there was a possibility he'd also fathered a son. Or that I discovered he'd helped Faith cover up a murder. However, I mentioned Faith was in town.

His cap slipped from his fingers and dropped to the ground. 'Here? Now?'

'She's staying with Donna for a few days. With any luck you might bump into her.'

'Don't think that would be a good idea.' He retrieved his cap and gave it a shake. 'A lot of water's passed under the bridge since we last spoke.'

'Faith might want to catch up, especially if you get tested and it turns out you're a match. Then you can reminisce about the great sex you can't remember.'

He jabbed his elbow into my ribs. 'You're a worry, girly.'

I gave a sigh. 'My husband would agree.'

Shane met me on the main street.

'All good. Sgt Feather said we can take the throne chair. I've moved the car closer so we don't have to lug it down the street, but I'll need your help in lifting it onto the back of the ute.'

We headed up to the shop. 'Did he mention anything about Linda McKenny? Have the cops visited her yet?'

'Oh ... yeah. She and her daughter came in for questioning yesterday afternoon. Mrs McKenny confessed to setting the fire, but blames you for getting her riled up. You're needed to come in tomorrow to make a statement.'

Though relieved, I knew I'd have the awkward tasks of coming clean about my actions and divulging Wes's lascivious hobby.

My phone rang. It was a video call from Simon Sweetman. I tapped the answer button and his face appeared, looking very grim.

'Hi Abby, is this a bad time to call?'

'No.' I stepped into the shade of the chemist shop. 'I'm just walking through town.'

'Sorry to hear about your shop. Someone must have rocks in their head to want to burn it down. Have they been caught?'

I nodded. 'Yes.'

'Who was it?'

I signalled to Shane to keep going while I finished the conversation. 'An old woman who got her wires crossed over something I said. Feared I was out to harm her husband's reputation.' Simon's look of puzzlement had me adding, 'I'll fill you in about it sometime.'

'So, what are you going to do now? Start over?'

'No way. Couldn't put myself through all that. I may just go to bed for a few months.'

'Well, before you do that, there's something you need to hear.'

Keira appeared alongside him, her eyes downcast. 'I ... I wanted to apologise for the graffiti on your shop windows,' she said with a sullen pout. 'And for rubbing dog poo on the door.'

'So, it *was* you,' I said, unsurprised.

'Go on.' Simon urged Keira with a nudge.

'Also, for taking photos of you and Dad down at the creek.'

Annoyed, I responded coldly. 'And you're my worst nightmare, are you?'

'I thought you were coming on to Dad. I didn't want you two hooking up.'

Simon focused the camera on himself. 'I found the photos on her phone and ripped into her.'

Keira's voice: 'You shouldn't be searching through my phone, Dad. That's an invasion of privacy.'

'Well, you shouldn't be making threats without first checking the facts. As if I'd try anything on with Abby.'

Simon's eye-roll sliced through my ego. *Was hooking up with me such a horrible concept?*

'Can I go now,' Keira asked.

Simon gave a nod.

'Hang on, Keira,' I said, and her face reappeared. 'I want to say that I accept your apology. What you did was childish and destructive and caused me a lot of anguish, but I understand. You were protecting your dad, worried I might make things more difficult between your parents.'

She glanced at her father. 'Yeah, something like that.'

Simon smiled sadly at his daughter. 'I guess we need to have a serious conversation, hey?'

Keira nodded and then stepped out of view.

I looked up the footpath to see Shane wrestling with the throne chair. It seemed to have gotten caught in the police tape when he was dragging it out.

'Thanks for that, Simon. Gotta go, but I want to give you a heads-up and tell you that Faith is in town.'

'Faith?' His face came close to the screen. 'She's here in Shadow Creek?'

'She's staying with Donna for a bit and might want to contact you. Also, I think I know who Donna's father is.'

'You do? Who?'

Shane was now sitting on the chair, looking my way, and drumming his fingers on his knees.

'I really need to go, Simon. I'll just say, it's very likely not Leo. Talk again soon.'

I hung up and dashed off to give aid to my long-suffering husband.

54

Simon shut and locked his bedroom door. He knelt on the floor and reached under his bed, dragging out a small brown suitcase that once held his boyhood collection of Matchbox cars. A flick of the silver clasps and the suitcase yawned open. Like a marauder eyeing a casket brimming with jewels, he studied the jumble of trinkets hoarded from times past and selected a photo frame. Splayed behind the glass was a tiger dragonfly, its body striped yellow and black—an early attempt at preservation before taking up photography. He placed it on the bed.

Next, he removed a large envelope handed to him by Rev McKenny on the afternoon of Donna's christening with the request to pass it on to Faith. Yet Simon had found it days later, wedged between his bed and the wall. On discovering it contained a page of artwork, he'd kept it for himself.

As he'd done many times since, he fingered the pencilled drawing of a woman cradling a baby against her chest. Both naked, the mother had dark tresses and the face of Faith, while the small child had fair curls. He'd always known the infant depicted

Donna, but there were subsequent viewings when Faith's image transformed into his mum and he was the infant. At the time, he hadn't questioned the lifelike sketch. Though when he matured, he recognised it as a reproduction of Gustav Klimt's Mother and Child, with the woman's features altered to match Faith's. It was then he suspected Wes McKenny of knowing her more intimately. It riled him that his father's accusations of Faith being a flirt may have been true after all.

Simon replaced the sketch in the envelope and set it aside. He took a velvet drawstring pouch from the stash and lifted out a recent acquisition, admiring the rose gold teardrop glinting in the light. Had Abby realised she'd lost her earring during their picnic by the water hole? She'd not asked him about it, so maybe not. *Finders keepers*. He dropped it into the bag.

He leaned over and removed a small zip-lock bag from a drawer in his bedside table. Seen through the clear plastic was a dirt encrusted finger bone: one of the bigger ones, a metacarpal. Simon couldn't pass up the opportunity to snaffle a token from Mitch Shepherd's remains before reburying them deep in the ground. It might even serve a need if things turned sour. He added it to the velvet pouch and his eyes caught a sparkle of red beckoning from within. Hesitating, he plucked out his father's bloodstone ring and slipped it on his right middle finger, the simple act ushering forth the dreaded memory of his father's death.

Chances Crossing, 25 February 1979

His father is in a drunken stupor on the farm house front verandah while Faith naps in the bedroom. In a huff, Uncle Leo has gone walkabout. Seizing his chance, Simon lifts the baby from the bouncinette and slips her inside an old backpack. He feeds his arms through the straps and hoists the pack onto his shoulders before sneaking away, intending to hike the five kilometres into town to tell the cops about his father's harmful intentions.

In fear of being caught racing down the driveway to the front gate, he chooses a route through the forest edging the property. When he skids in mud, and Donna whimpers, he realises he's forgotten to collect the baby bottle of expressed milk stored in the fridge. If he is quick, he'll have time to nick back to the house and get out again unseen, but not with a bawling baby. Scanning the surrounds, he spies the Bunya pine pinpointing the site where his mother's wrecked car was dumped. He sprints over and places Donna inside, promising to be back soon.

On returning home, the sound of yelling has him faltering outside the rear door.

'Where is she, Carl?' he hears Faith scream from the lounge room. 'She can't have walked out on her own.'

'Bloody hell,' his father snaps. 'Don't get your knickers in a twist. She'll turn up.'

When Simon dashes into the kitchen to collect the baby bottle, he finds luck is not on his side. Faith enters as he opens the fridge, her eyes wide and wild, face as pale as milk.

'Simon!' She clasps him by the shoulders. 'Where's Donna? Have you been looking after her?'

He isn't game to speak the truth, not with his father swaying behind Faith and grinding the palm of his hand into his forehead. Get him angry while he is suffering from these tension headaches and out comes the worn strap used for punishment since his dad was a boy. Simon shudders as he imagines the sting of leather whipping the back of his legs, and tells Faith he's been playing by himself.

'Leo must still have her,' his dad says. 'Do you know where he's gone?'

Simon sights a bruise forming under his father's left eye. Has Faith slogged him? 'I think he went to the creek. I saw him go through the rear gate.'

Faith jerks her head to look out the window. 'Why would he go down there in this weather? My God, he wouldn't hurt her, would he?' Not waiting for an answer, she darts outside.

His father scowls and rakes his fingers through his hair. 'Christ Almighty, son, you must have noticed your uncle was in one of his foul moods. You should have stopped him.' He pokes Simon hard in the chest. 'Stay here in case Leo returns. And this time, numbskull, make sure he doesn't leave.'

Simon waits for his father to rush away before kicking a chair and sending it crashing against the wall. 'I hate you,' he hisses, and then jumps as loud knocking comes from the front door.

He scurries down the hall and turns the knob to find the annoying Rev McKenny standing on the coir door mat, looking sheepish as usual.

'Hello, young fella. Is Faith here?' The man peeks over Simon's shoulder, his nostrils flaring as if sniffing her out.

'No. Dad and Faith have gone off to ... to move the cattle to another paddock.'

'Oh.' The gangly man seems disappointed and turns to glance up at the sky. 'Yes, more rain coming. The creeks are up. Wasn't sure I'd make it out here.' He fidgets with an oversized envelope before holding it out. 'Can you please give this to Faith?'

Simon has to yank it from his hand. Eager for the man to leave, he goes to shut the door, but the Reverend's foot blocks it from closing.

'Tell Faith I ...' A blush darkens the man's cheeks. 'Ah ... never mind.' Then he moves away and plods down the stairs.

Simon shuts the door and runs to his bedroom. Tossing the envelope onto his bed, he pulls on a jacket and returns to the kitchen. He takes the bottle from the fridge and races outside to the yard.

Once again, he skirts the bushy ridge only to pull up when a cockatoo screech startles him. He searches the dripping branches above but cannot locate the raucous bird. The squawk is repeated more loudly, and he redirects his gaze downhill to where he now thinks it has come. The third cry is more discernible. 'Help me,' he hears.

Alarmed, Simon pushes through the scrub until his feet hit the path leading down to the creek. Peering between slender tree trunks, he catches movement near the water's edge. A few steps closer he sees an arm flailing from a hole in the dirt and recognises the voice shrieking for aid. His stomach grips.

Simon discovered fresh tracks in the long grass down here a few months ago, and realised this was the route the wild dogs used to get to the farm and kill the chooks. Information gleaned from his uncle enabled him to construct a deep pit lined with narrow wooden spikes. Some were fixed to rise from the base, while others pointed down at an angle from the sides to make it harder for the dogs to escape. Covered by a grassy trap door, he'd hoped to snare a few predators ... not capture his father.

He slinks over and peers into the trench to see his dad stuck on his right side and panting. Their eyes meet.

'Thank God you've turned up, son. My leg is impaled. Pull me out.'

Simon draws back, out of his father's view. Why should he help him? His dad doesn't care about him. Doesn't care about anyone. He should just leave him to suffer. He starts to turn when his name is shouted, and he hears the pain in his father's rasp.

Chewing his mouth, Simon leans in and seizes the outstretched hand. He tugs, but the skin is slimy with muck and he falls back clutching only his father's signet ring.

'Fool!' his father growls. 'You'll need to dig the spikes out first. Or break them, at least.'

Simon pockets the ring and gets on his knees to reach into the pit, though the damage caused by the wooden stalks he'd painstakingly sharpened with a hunting knife has him gagging. Some have speared through his father's right thigh. Others have torn flesh to shreds.

'Don't wimp out on me, boy,' his dad barks.

Simon first digs with his fingers into the earthen wall to dislodge angled wood not embedded in his father. Then he does the same to a spike stabbing into thigh muscle. A shriek sends him reeling back.

'You're bloody useless,' his dad groans, 'just like Leo. Why did the bastard build this death trap?' He sucks in a gulp of air. 'Give it another go.'

Simon cringes at the sight of blood oozing around the spikes, soaking into his father's clothing, mixing with the mud. 'I can't,' he whines, and shuffles back.

'Do it!' his father commands.

Simon feels water soaking his knees, sees it spilling into the trench. Leaves and sticks float and swirl around him.

The creek is overflowing.

His father notices it too. 'Get help. Quick!'

A puzzling sound distracts Simon as he scrambles uphill: a thundering noise, like a wave barrelling towards a beach. He twists around and sees the swollen creek below is littered with forest debris. Amid the flow, a broken tree branch pirouettes, pleading with twiggy fingers for assistance before being swept away. He glances back at his father, whose head and one arm are the only things visible in the flooded pit.

'What's that noise?' his dad bellows.

Terror seizes Simon's limbs when he sees a wall of water

surging from upstream. Even if he had the words to describe what is about to happen, there is no way he can get them out through his constricted throat.

'Simon? Simon!'

He covers his ears to stifle the cries and watches in horror as his father disappears beneath a rolling brown sea.

Seconds later, Simon's legs spring into action with a will of their own.

Pushing through the bush, noises unnerve him—the repetitive woop-woop of a pheasant coucal, the creak of branches bending in the wind, the tapping of raindrops on leaves—all as familiar to him as breathing. Yet now they are haunting, accusatory. He quickens his pace to arrive at the car wreck and save the baby before losing her, as well.

Could he have rescued his father on his own? Could he have gotten help in time? These questions have troubled Simon over the years, but not as much as the one that haunted his dreams. *Had he wanted his father to die?*

He wrenched the bloodstone ring from his finger and slid the suitcase back under the bed. The framed insect lying on the mattress has him pondering the belief of some cultures that dragonflies represented change and overcoming hardships. Was it time to take a leaf from Leo's book and cease casting stones at himself? Live free of self-recrimination? Not alone, though. He could never do it alone.

Simon found Keira in her bedroom listening to music on her iPhone. He removed the headphones from his daughter and asked, 'Want to head into the city with your old dad?'

She arched her eyebrows. 'Can we go to Southbank? There's a

cool Mexican restaurant Mum takes me to. They make the best paella.'

'Only if we visit the Gallery of Modern Art first. I want to show you there's more to graffiti art than vulgar words and cartoon penises.'

Keira glowered at Simon before following it up with a grin that warmed his heart.

55

Leo crossed the road to the Shadow Creek cemetery when a sickly odour compelled him to pull up with a start, his eyes searching. A brushtail possum lay at the foot of a power pole. Dead by electrocution, a large black crow was eviscerating the carcass. He told it to scoot, and the bird flapped skyward with a string of bloody guts dangling from its beak. A shiver coursed through him and he hurried through the wrought-iron gates.

The small cemetery was well kept, the mown grass marred only by the litter of vibrant red flowers dropped by a poinciana tree standing respectfully to one side. The gravel paths were weed free, and so were most of the gravesites, with not a vase of dead flowers in sight. Had a local group made it their duty to look after the resting places of the departed, or was there a diligent caretaker? Whoever it was, they'd helped make Leo's visit a less dismal experience.

He first paid his respects to his parents who shared the same site. 'Together again,' was the simple wording he and Carl had chosen for the epitaph scored in white on the dark granite headstone. After a few moments of reflection, he moved on.

A pure white headstone marked Eileen's grave. On the top edge rested a single long-stemmed rose, its pink petals dried by the sun. *Simon's doing?* He gave a sigh. Though Carl refrained from talking about her death, Leo was conscious his brother had carried guilt in tandem with grief knowing she was leaving him— leaving their marriage—when she'd driven away that fateful night.

'It's like I'd held onto her so tight out of fear, that I crushed her to death,' was what Carl had once told Leo in a fit of remorse after a few drinks at the pub.

Yet he'd done the same with Faith, even after Leo had warned him about repeating history. What would have happened if Carl hadn't died, yet struggled to love Donna as his own child?

Leo followed a path leading to the columbarium and scanned the name plates until he found his brother's niche. Carl Olof Sweetman. Named after their maternal grandfather, known as Charlie, whose Swedish ancestors stemmed from Vikings.

He smiled as he remembered playing a childhood game with Carl, pretending to ransack a village and sail away with their plunder. The ship they'd made from corrugated iron only got as far as the middle of the dam before it sank, taking some of their mother's good silverware with it. Leo's thoughts drifted to other fun times involving his brother before their dad, and the farm, and girls got in the way. A knot formed in his stomach. If only his last memory of Carl hadn't been so heart-wrenching.

Chances Crossing, 25 February 1979

With the aid of the kerosene lamp, Leo follows Faith's directions to where she'd last seen Carl on the bush track. Not finding any sign of him there, he walks down to the creek. The flood has subsided, but the water is still fast-flowing, the noise of its turbulence blocking out every other sound.

A spindly branch sticking up from a large puddle on the bank has him recoiling when he realises it is a human arm. Dropping to his knees, Leo delves into the sludge, grips the arm, and pulls. First a shoulder appears, and then a head that droops sideways. He wipes the face clean of mud and thrusts his fingers into the mouth to clear the airway, even though he suspects Carl is long past saving. More pulling with no result indicates the body is caught somehow. He has to get him out.

Letting go so he can use both hands to bail out water, the body once again dips below the surface. Eventually, Carl's left side comes into view. Further scooping reveals a set of wooden spikes fixed into the ground has skewered the right thigh. Hefty wrenching releases the leg, allowing Leo to haul Carl out and perform chest compressions for no one's benefit but his own—convincing himself he has done all he can to bring his brother back to life.

Exhausted, Leo slumps beside Carl's corpse and eyes the muddy three-foot-deep trench imbedded with spikes. He has seen traps like this before, but not here in Australia, not in a place well away from a war zone. Bile scorches his throat. There is one other person on this property with the knowledge to construct such a deadly trap, and only because Leo has instructed him. He was crazy to think advising the boy on how to build a punji-style pit to catch wild dogs wouldn't lead to disaster. Carl's death from being impaled and drowning in the flash flood is his fault as much as Simon's. He can't allow the kid to be blamed for this tragedy.

Dragging the body to the creek's edge, Leo pushes it into the swirling flow. By the light of the lamp, he watches Carl floating downstream before bobbing and sinking under the surge.

Leo turned at a crunch of gravel.

A woman walked down the path carrying a posy of flowers, her cornflower-blue cotton dress fluttering around her calves. He shielded his eyes from the sun and took in her slim figure and shoulder-length grey hair streaked fashionably with shades of brown. Recognisable features, now softened with age, caused his chest to tighten.

'Faith?' he rasped.

She pulled up a couple of metres away. 'Leo.' She stepped closer. 'You never left?'

He nodded. 'I came back to see Simon. He's set up a photographic gallery on the old property.'

Her half-smile showed dimples now linked to her mouth by fine lines. 'I had an inkling he'd do well.'

'And you?' Leo checked her left hand and noticed it lacked adornments. Relief and sadness melded together.

'Always on the move. I travel a fair bit,' Faith said, with a shrug. 'Arrived back last night from New Zealand for Donna's birthday. She lives here now.'

'Yeah, I heard.'

'Who'd have thought, hey, after ...' Her gaze dropped to the flowers in her hand. 'I did care for Carl, you know ... and Simon.'

Leo frowned. 'Why didn't you stay and make a go of it with him ... with us?'

'You'd have ended up despising me just as Carl did. Watching Donna like me, searching for clues every year, resemblances, fearing the worst.'

'No.' He scraped the toe of his jogger over gravel. 'I'd have loved her as my own, no matter what. Tests can be done to prove who her father is.'

She shook her head. 'I couldn't bear finding out.'

'But she could be mine. Wouldn't you want to know that?' Her glance away and the silence that followed disturbed him.

'I need to be honest with you, Leo. There was … another.'

'Another what?' A chill snaked up his spine. 'You mean your brother and I weren't the only ones?'

Her *yes* came out more like a hiss.

Leo swore under his breath. 'Who else did you screw, Faith?'

'Never mind. I'm only saying the matter is more complicated.'

'I think the horse has already bolted where your secrets are concerned,' he sneered. 'You've already told me what you did to Mitch. I even know where his body is buried.'

'But … how? I don't even know—'

'Don't worry,' he jumped in, 'I'm not going to dob. The bastard got what he deserved and his remains will remain hidden. Just tell me who the other guy was … or were there several?'

She stiffened. 'Only one other.'

'Was he some random pick up? A local?'

'It was Stoney.'

Leo couldn't have been more shocked. 'You're shitting me. Why that filthy—'

'No!' She clutched his arm. 'It wasn't like that. I'd gotten drunk at the pub after seeing Mitch at the Shadow Creek Show. You and Carl weren't around and I was scared, angry. Stoney gave me a lift home and tried to cheer me up. It's all rather hazy. We smoked a few joints and … well … one thing must have led to another and I woke up the next morning with barely a remembrance of what we'd done.'

'But you knew you'd had sex?'

'There was … physical evidence. No need to go into details.'

'Was that the only incident, or had you two been carrying on for a while?'

'The only time. It was just a lapse due to a combination of alcohol and weed.'

And what was the reason for her lapse with him that night of the storm? Pity? 'You never told Stoney there was a chance he was Donna's father?'

'No. We never spoke of it. It was probably a blur to him as well.'

'Did Carl find out?'

'Of course not. Like I didn't tell Carl about us. You did that. I thought Donna was Carl's baby up until he told me about his sterility, right before he died. And then I was afraid to discover the truth, because it might mean ...'

They shared a look of horror.

'Are there any other secrets you want to get off your chest, Faith?'

'From my time in Shadow Creek, or my entire life? I don't think there's enough time for that.' A blue fairy wren hopping across the lawn close by briefly drew her attention. 'One thing I should have admitted to you ... way back ... is that I loved you.'

Leo's breath caught in his throat.

'You and Carl were as different as chalk and cheese. Unlike him, you let your guard down and showed the real you, warts and all. We talked about anything, remember? Carl's love was bound by rules and expectations. With you, I was never on tenterhooks wondering if I was doing everything correctly.' She reached up and stroked his cheek. 'If I'd met you first, if you'd been the one to collect Simon at the museum that day, things may have turned out differently.'

Leo withdrew her hand. Was she speaking the truth or only placating him? He took a step back. 'How dare you not tell me. You knew darn well how I felt. You could have ditched Carl, run away with me.'

'I couldn't, because I still loved him. Carl had given me a new start in life. I couldn't just toss that aside.'

'And after ... you couldn't begin a new life with me?'

'I wasn't the same person. I didn't love myself, let alone expect someone to love me ... a murderer.'

'But who better to understand that than me? You should have trusted me, Faith.'

She rubbed the fold of skin between her eyebrows. 'Maybe.'

'And now?' Leo asked, deflated. 'Have you found happiness?'

'Happiness?' Faith laughed. 'My life's been a royal stuff up. Me and relationships don't make a good fit. I even battle with getting things right with my daughter. I realised on the flight back to Brisbane that my constant travelling has been a way of running away from myself. How sad is that?'

'You can never escape yourself, Faith. I know for a fact you need to make amends with your past, forgive yourself, and move on. That's what I've learned, and only recently, too.'

She seemed to consider this before tapping his shoulder with the posy. 'Hey, want to grab a drink at The Axe like old times?'

'Like old-timers, you mean.'

'Like people of a more mature age, thank you very much.'

'S'pose,' he shrugged. 'I've got nothing better to do for a few hours.'

'Just give me a minute, will you?'

Faith stepped in front of Carl's niche, and removing a single carnation from the bunch of flowers, placed it in the receptacle alongside. Leo watched with mixed emotions as she kissed her fingers and pressed them against his brother's name. When she turned around, he saw tears in her eyes.

'I see your hair is longer than mine,' Faith said, giving his ponytail a tug. 'I like it.'

The day before, Leo had viewed a wall plaque in Abby's

bookshop that stated: *You're never too old to live happily ever after.* He'd derided its sloppy sentiment. Yet now, he felt a heavy weight lift from his shoulders. Even the hum of a helicopter flying high overhead on a sightseeing tour did nothing to rob him of the glimmer of hope stirring within.

Maybe the tide was turning.

As they retraced their steps through the cemetery, Faith dropped the remaining flowers from her posy into empty vases attached to headstones. Rounding a statue of a weeping angel bowing over a stone altar, Leo's joggers slid on loose gravel. If it wasn't for Faith gripping his arm, he may have lost balance and tumbled into a gaping hole in the earth.

'Careful,' she said, nodding towards the newly dug grave waiting to be inhabited. 'You wouldn't want to fall into that pit and break hip or something. Couldn't have two of you meeting the same fate.'

The hair on Leo's arms stood on end. How did Faith know Carl had fallen into a pit? He and Simon were the only ones with that knowledge ... other than Abby Eaton who'd overheard their conversation only yesterday.

When Faith slipped her arm through his and steered him towards the gate, Leo searched his memory for what she'd told him years before, soon after the flash flood.

She and Carl fought in the bush after he demanded she give the baby away. *'Things got violent, but I pushed him away,'* she'd said, or words to that effect.

What if when she shoved Carl, she saw him fall into the trap? Had her own anger stopped her from helping him out or running for aid? Did she view the accident as payback for his evil demands? Maybe it was the catbird call sounding like a baby that drew her away—an easy decision, her child's safety coming first. Leo even suspected she'd given him wrong directions to hinder his search for Carl. When his body was discovered in the creek, had she believed he'd pulled himself free, only to be caught in the flood and rendering her blameless of his death?

Blindsided by Faith's possible act of desperation, Leo sought no retribution. How could he? He was no better.

Returning her smile, he placed an arm around her waist and walked her into town.

56

Afternoon shadows flickered over the backyard like hovering ghosts. Slumped in the throne chair on the paved spot where a gazebo would soon stand, I swilled the last of my Bloody Mary. Shane's measure of gin to alleviate my anguish had definitely been on the generous side for my head felt light, ready to float from my shoulders if the breeze picked up.

Chewing the drink's celery garnish, I glimpsed Shadow Creek below the mountain ridge and wondered how many villagers feared their secrets would be exposed.

I thought of Simon keeping quiet about finding his father drowned in the pit, of Leo covering up shocking evidence to shield his nephew, of Stoney's help in hiding a murder, of Faith's inability to name Donna's father due to multiple liaisons, and Natalie's lie regarding Lester's conception. Then there was Gemma and Benji, not game enough to come out about their budding romance because they were related—though being third cousins may not be problematic, I told myself. All truths hidden to protect someone they loved, even if that someone was themselves. I made a promise. Whatever else Shadow Creek residents were keeping under wraps wouldn't be revealed by me. I'd learned my lesson about meddling. Unlike that proverbial cat, I only had one life.

Shane, busy digging around the edges of the paving with a shovel, had me considering the pact I'd made in the forest. Was it possible to keep my lips sealed about the macabre discovery and Faith's part in it?

My phone vibrated from inside a pocket of my jeans and I lifted it out. It was my sister calling. She must have heard about the store burning down from my parents.

I pressed the phone to my ear. 'Hi, Paisley.'

'Oh, little sis, so sorry to hear the awful news,' she gushed. 'And you were on the verge of opening your bookshop. I'd be a wreck if it was me. How are you coping?'

Coping? I studied the empty glass resting in my lap and wished a second helping of alcohol would materialise to take its place. 'Well enough. *Que sera* and all that crap.'

'Have they found the culprit?'

'The cops have a lead. They may have even charged her by now.'

'Her? A woman?'

'Yep. An old lady with a grudge.'

'Against you?'

'Mostly ... and her dead husband ... and another woman. Anyway, I'd rather not go into it right now. How are you? How's business?'

Paisley and her husband, Fletcher, managed Grassington, an historic country estate on Queensland's Darling Downs inherited by his elderly aunt. The imposing two-storey brick house built in the 1880s had recently been restored to its former grandeur and set up as a guesthouse.

'Since you've asked,' she said, dropping her voice to a whisper, 'things have kind of come a cropper.'

I watched Shane measure the paving area's length and width with a retractable metal tape measure. He sure was keen. Next, he'd be building a frame over top of me. 'That doesn't sound good, Pais. What's happened?'

'Fletch has ... er ... had a slight mishap, and I'm left to prepare for our first lot of guests single-handed.'

'Bloody hell. The klutz hasn't fallen off a ladder again, has he?'

'No, not this time. Don't tell Mum and Dad. They'd only want to drop everything and rush out here. Dad means well but, as you know, he takes charge a little too boldly. I don't think Fletch would appreciate being bossed around at the moment.'

'Sure. I won't tell. I'm good at keeping secrets.' At least I hoped I was. 'How are you going to tackle things? Pay someone to help?'

'Well ...' She cleared her throat. 'Seeing you have free time on your hands, what with the shop going up in flames and no job lined up, I was wondering ...'

I sat bolt upright. 'You want me to come lend a hand?'

'Indeed, I do. The guests arrive next week and there's so much to get ready.'

'And I'm your best bet?'

'I'm desperate, Abby. I wouldn't be asking you if I wasn't.'

'What about Skye?'

'Not a chance. Can you see our big sister walking away from her podiatry clinic for even a day? No, it's you I need ASAP.'

I chewed the corner of my mouth. Could I do this? Could I just up and leave one mess to help out with another?

'Let me talk it over with Shane. I'll call you back.' Then I hung up.

Shane squatted nearby and extended the tape measure upwards to around two metres. Locking it in place, he stood and checked the height for the gazebo. 'Who was that, and what do we need to talk about?'

'Paisley. She needs assistance at Grassington. Wants to know if I could come out for a week or so.'

He frowned. 'Right now?'

'Soon. Will the police expect me to hang about? A statement shouldn't take long to give. But then I might be required to help clean up the damage.'

'How about we give the shop owners a call, and you can talk to Sgt Feather tomorrow when you visit the cop shop.' He bent to unlock the tape measure and it retracted with a sharp snap, narrowly missing his ear. 'Do you really want to head out to Grassington?'

I considered this. Maybe it was a godsend, an opportunity to take my mind off my predicament. 'Well, I won't need to stay long. And there'd be scant chance of me getting into mischief out there.'

Shane gave me a quizzical look. 'Are you sure about that? Your intrusive snooping will probably run rampant without me being your Jiminy Cricket, pulling you into line.'

I bristled at his words. But then the thought of being unfettered, free to follow my instincts, sent a buzz of excitement coursing through me. Having only one life to live, why waste it stifling a natural propensity for sleuthing? If another opportunity arose, and I erred on the side of caution, I could use my curiosity for the greater good.

'You'll just have to trust me,' I told Shane. 'Anyway, how much devilment could be afoot at an antiquated country guesthouse?'

Plenty, I would soon discover.

ACKNOWLEDGMENTS

Firstly, I wish to acknowledge my father, Ronald JH West, who proudly served two tours of duty in Vietnam with the Australian Army. His war diaries and tearful telling of pain and loss inspired me to create Leo's character, a war veteran haunted by the past. Visiting Vietnam recently with my sisters, Sheron West and Debbie Dodds, saw our relationship deepen as we walked where our father trod and gained a greater respect for his service.

Once again I am grateful for my husband, David, for being a patient sounding board and always believing in me; Jane Ireland for her friendship and feedback; Writers Rendezvous for their continual support; and Chermside library, a perfect space in which to write and drink amazing coffee.

My thanks also goes to Graham Toseland at Fading Street Publishing and Hilary O'Brien-Pratt whose keen eyes and welcome suggestions improved my story greatly.

And to those eagerly awaiting this second Abby Eaton Mystery, I offer my heartfelt gratitude, hoping you keep turning the pages and wanting more.

ABOUT THE AUTHOR

Vicki Stevens is an Australian mystery/thriller author living in the lush countryside on the rural outskirts of Brisbane. Her keen interest in genealogy motivates her to write compelling and evocative stories inspired by lives and events from the past. *Saving Dragonflies* is the second book in her Abby Eaton Mystery series.

If you enjoyed this story please leave a few words or a rating with your retailer or on a book review website.

For more info: www.vickistevens.com.au

facebook.com/VickiStevensAuthor
instagram.com/vickistevens.au

www.ingramcontent.com/pod-product-compliance
Lightning Source LLC
Chambersburg PA
CBHW030238120726
47903CB00005B/1531